SMALL TALK

"I like your hair that way. Tumbled."

"Oh, boy. Is this where I'm supposed to say, Dominic, please, we don't know each other that well?"

"Probably. But if you don't mind, I'd rather we skipped that part, to tell you the truth. You know I'm attracted to you, right?"

Molly smiled. "I'm sort of getting that idea, yes."

"Why? Because everyone is attracted to you? I guess you're relatively used to that."

"No, you jerk," she said, running her fingertips down his lean cheek. "Well, yes, all right, I am relatively used to that. But I'm not always attracted *back*."

He lowered his head toward hers. "But you are, this time?"

"Oh yeah," Molly breathed on a sigh, looking into his soulful brown eyes. "You could say that . . ."

Books by Kasey Michaels

CAN'T TAKE MY EYES OFF OF YOU

TOO GOOD TO BE TRUE

LOVE TO LOVE YOU BABY

BE MY BABY TONIGHT

THIS MUST BE LOVE

THIS CAN'T BE LOVE

MAGGIE NEEDS AN ALIBI

MAGGIE BY THE BOOK

MAGGIE WITHOUT A CLUE

Published by Kensington Publishing Corporation

THIS CAN'T BE LOVE

Kasey Michaels

ZEBRA BOOKS
KENSINGTON PUBLISHING CORP.
http://www.kensingtonbooks.com

ZEBRA BOOKS are published by

Kensington Publishing Corp.
850 Third Avenue
New York, NY 10022

All Kensington titles, imprints and distributed lines are available at special quantity discounts for bulk purchases for sales promotion, premiums, fund-raising, educational or institutional use.

Special book excerpts or customized printings can also be created to fit specific needs. For details, write or phone the office of the Kensington Special Sales Manager: Kensington Publishing Corp., 850 Third Avenue, New York, NY 10022. Attn. Special Sales Department. Phone: 1-800-221-2647.

Zebra and the Z logo Reg. U.S. Pat. & TM Off.

First Printing: March 2004
10 9 8 7 6 5 4 3 2 1

Printed in the United States of America

*To insure peace of mind
ignore the rules and regulations.*
—George Ade

Chapter 1

Dominic Longstreet didn't notice that the melody of the sure to be a show-stopper love song from *Marie,* his musical in progress, dipped and soared in his CD player. He was not aware of the powerful purr emanating from the engine of his black Lamborghini. The lush, impressive, almost over-the-top Virginia scenery flashed by unappreciated.

He didn't notice because Dominic Longstreet was a man on a mission. He had an aim, a definite destination, and a damn good reason.

He was going to kill someone.

Not just any someone; he wasn't indiscriminate. He had a particular someone in mind.

Molly Applegate.

Molly Applegate? What the hell kind of name was that? Sounded like the second lead: the girl next door, faintly pudgy, wise-cracking, never been kissed, but with at least one good song to raise her role above the ordinary.

This Molly Applegate was going to have a song of her own. Her swan song, just before he slid his hands around her neck right beneath her double chin and squeezed until . . .

No. No, he had to calm down. He couldn't go barreling in there and strangle the idiot woman. First he had to introduce himself, explain his problem one more time.

Then he'd strangle her.

He steered with one hand as he searched on the console for his roll of antacids, then popped two in his mouth.

Dominic pounded the side of his fist against the steering wheel as he had to slow down in the minivan congestion of the suburbs of Fairfax, which gave time for the telephone conversation with the woman to play in his head once more. He had a great memory for lines, and he remembered every one of them.

"Preston Kiddie Kare, Molly Applegate speaking, and how may we help you today?"

Nice voice. Rounded, almost sexy. And the tone sounded helpful.

Talk about your miscasting.

So he'd quickly introduced himself on the phone and explained his problem. Explained that he was the uncle of Little Tony and Lizzie Longstreet, currently enrolled at Preston Kiddie Kare.

"Oh, Tony. Such a sweet boy."

She hadn't mentioned Lizzie. At least the woman hadn't tried to lie to him. Because anyone who'd met her knew that Elizabeth Packer Longstreet was to sweet what General William Tecumseh Sherman had been to the Atlanta Architectural Preservation League.

Dominic had then gone on to explain that his brother, Anthony, and his wife had put him in charge of their children. He hadn't called them "kids," which he'd considered at the time to be truly a mark of his loving guardianship.

He could be loving for three weeks, damn it. Anybody could be loving for three lousy weeks. If there was a good day care program close by and a live-in housekeeper handy for the rest of the time.

Eyes still on the road, Dominic searched for another roll of antacids.

He'd explained that Little Tony and Lizzie had been enrolled at Preston Kiddie Kare for three weeks. He'd paid in advance. But now he'd found out that the damn place . . . er, the *facility* would be closed for the following two weeks.

"Oh, yes, sir, Mr. Longstreet," Molly Applegate had said, damn near sung, back to him. "Today is our last day until Monday, July twenty-second. We're all quite looking forward to the hiatus."

Hiatus. His ass, hiatus!

But he'd gritted his teeth. He'd kept his cool. He'd told Molly Applegate that *he* was not looking forward to the two-week hiatus. *He* was looking forward to Little Tony and Leaping Lizzie being safely stashed at Preston Kiddie Kare from eight to five every weekday for those same two weeks.

"I'll bet you were," the damn woman had shot back at him, and then laughed. She'd *laughed.* He'd been ready to crawl through the wires and strangle her then and there.

So he'd slammed down the phone and grabbed his car keys, preferring to strangle the woman in person.

Dominic chewed on the antacids, making a face at the taste of banana. Who the hell had thought up banana-flavored antacids, for crying out loud? Had to be a sadist. Had to be a woman, a woman like Molly Applegate.

He had *plans,* damn it. Plans that didn't include Little Tony asking him to take him horseback riding, just so that the kid could do his favorite thing: pee in the bushes along the trail. Plans that didn't include Lizzie sitting beside him in the small theater on his property, producing a megaphone from God only knew where and shouting out stage directions to his actors—when she wasn't begging him for an audition.

This was all Tony's fault, his brother's fault. It was Tony who'd fallen in love, married, and produced two kids, just to leave them for a three-week tour of some Greek islands.

Hey, you see one armless statue, you've seen them all. How could this take three weeks?

How could he have agreed to take the kids so Tony and Elizabeth could desert them? What kind of parents would leave their little darlings with a man like Dominic Longstreet? Were they nuts? He ought to report them somewhere.

Dominic carefully slid the Lamborghini into a spot just vacated by a dark green minivan with three car seats in the back. No wonder the world was overcrowded. Some people reproduced like rabbits. You'd think they'd have a little restraint.

He got out of the car just in time to see a harried-looking woman carrying one child and dragging a little redhead by one hand as the kid's other hand trailed across the rear bumper of the Lamborghini, leaving a trail of peanut butter.

Dominic's head pounded.

He looked around the parking lot, to see about a million kids of all sizes and shapes being herded to minivans. They had three things in common. They all were *loud*. They all were wearing red, white and blue scarves around their heads. And they were all eyeing the Lamborghini as if it were a new kind of kiddie ride. He fought the insane urge to throw himself spread-eagle across his "baby."

The mothers didn't even notice him, which just went to prove how warped a woman's priorities could get once she'd given birth. Women he knew, who had coveted the diamonds he'd given them, had gone on to marry some guy and produce kids like these and become *changed* women. Diamonds? They couldn't care less. "Just let me show you these forty pictures of Little Timothy. Isn't he cute? And you really should marry, Dom. Honestly, it will change your life."

He absently rubbed at his chest. Yeah, like he had a problem with his life.

Thirty-eight years old, rich beyond even his accountant's

wildest dreams. Four Tonys for his four Broadway musicals, all of them still running somewhere in the world, with the latest still in Manhattan.

He had his rural Fairfax complex, complete with mansion, horses, both an indoor and outdoor pool, and his own theater and guest house. He had his Manhattan apartment at the Dakota. The chalet in Switzerland, his ski lodge in Vail. The manor house he was negotiating purchase on in England. The ranch he already owned in California.

He worked, hard. And then he played, hard.

Yeah. He needed a wife and kids. He needed them the way television needed another reality show.

"Hey, nice wheels."

Dominic turned toward the voice, expecting to see yet another harassed mother dragging yet another sticky kid. Instead, he saw legs.

Oh, God. Did he ever see *legs*.

Legs as straight and long as nature could make them. Legs as curvy and smooth as his dreams could make them. Legs that started with slim bare feet stuck into strappy, cork-soled heels and ended at the hem of a pair of white shorts just lengthy enough not to catch the attention of the vice squad. Legs that would shame Betty Grable, Ann Margret, and the entire kick line of the Rockettes.

Legs connected to a body—clad in those white shorts and a red, white and blue striped shirt that had been tied in a knot halfway up a flat midriff—a body that would have a lesser man falling to his knees and raising his eyes to heaven as he cried, "Thank you, *thank you!*"

"I said, nice car. Nice butt, too, but you probably already know that."

Okay, so now he'd look higher. Get the whole picture.

Oh, man.

Dark copper hair that made sense of that milky white skin.

Baby blue eyes the size of quarters, except they weren't round; they were tilted up at the ends, almost witchy. Definitely bewitching. A mouth full enough, wide enough, to give a eunuch second thoughts.

Put it all together and . . . well, Dominic was having trouble remembering why he was here.

"Uncle Dom! Uncle Dom! Look! I was the drummer boy and I limped and walked next to the flag and Dylan Simmons was the flute guy and he had a bandage over his eye because it's lazy and he walked straight into the wall and they gave him the flute to keep and so I got to keep the drum. Hear it?"

What followed was . . . Okay, it was a lot of noise, as Little Tony came marching up to Dominic, beating on the small drum.

Wait. It was all coming back to him now. He was here to kill Molly Applegate.

"Excuse me, miss," he said, prying the drumsticks out of Little Tony's hands, "but do you know the whereabouts of Miss Applegate's office?"

"Nope," the redhead said with a smile.

"But . . . but she's the owner, right?"

"Strike two," she said, grinning now. Oh, God, the teeth were straight and white, too. "Janie Preston is the owner. That's why it's called Preston Kiddie Kare. You know, that would be kind of your first clue, don't you think?"

Dominic swallowed a smart remark, because he had the funny feeling that this woman could top anything he said, without even trying.

"All right, then," he said, still being reasonable, "do you know the way to Miss Preston's office?"

"Sure," the redhead said pleasantly. "But I don't know why you'd want to go there, because she's not there. She's off playing undercover reporter at a political retreat in Cape May. That's in New Jersey. And she's making a fine mess of things, too, by all accounts. The undercover reporting, not New Jersey. I'm here to tell you that if the entire federal government goes pear-shaped in the next few days, I just want everyone to remember that *I* had nothing to do with it."

Dominic's head was spinning. What was the woman talking about? Did she have a screw loose somewhere? Then again, with those legs, did it matter?

"Do . . . Do you work here?"

"Here? Are you kidding? I'd rather have bamboo shoots jammed under my fingernails," she said, reaching down to ease the strap off the heel of her left foot. Then she straightened up once more, trailing those blood red fingernails up her long, gorgeous leg as she did so, and Dominic's brain did that memory lapse thing again.

"You do so work here, Good Golly Miss Molly," Little Tony said, jumping up to reach his drumsticks. "She's my teacher, Uncle Dom. Yesterday she taught me how to spit without dribbling it all over my chin."

Dominic's mind backtracked past the spitting lesson to the part where his nephew's statements interested him. Okay, he was sort of interested in the spitting lesson, considering he'd told the kid to knock it off last night, when Little Tony had been drinking bottled water, then spitting all over the front porch while his uncle was trying to have a serious talk with Cynara, who kept saying, "Ick! Oh, *ick!*"

"Good Golly Miss *Molly?*" he repeated, glaring at the beautiful woman who had somehow morphed from bombshell to nuclear weapon in a split second. *"You're* Molly Applegate?"

"Technically, yes," Molly admitted, then flashed her wide smile. "But, you see, you're looking for Miss Applegate, temporarily in charge of Preston Kiddie Kare, a job that ended, oh, about ten minutes ago. She's not here. She, at least in her mind, is already halfway to Washington D.C. and a very long bubble bath. I'm just locking up for her."

Dominic stabbed his fingers through his hair. It was a subtle move meant to check to see if the top of his head was still in place. It was, but only barely. "Now look here, Miss Applegate—"

"Molly, remember," she corrected. "As of five-thirty, which was the aforementioned ten minutes ago, I'm Molly. Miss Applegate has left the building."

"Stop that," he commanded, banging the drumsticks against his thigh, then manfully withholding a wince of pain. "You're the person in charge, the person I talked to, and you're damn well the person who is going to straighten out this mess. I paid for three weeks, not one week. And I didn't even get the full week, considering one day was the Fourth and you were closed."

"I didn't make it a national holiday, you know," she said, grinning at him.

"Yeah? Well, Lizzie got into the sparklers when no one was looking and stuck them in the ground in the pasture to spell out S.O.S., then lit them after dark. Some jerk in a private plane reported seeing it, and we damn near had a rescue team show up, for crying out loud."

"Please don't swear in front of the c-h-i-l-d. And, well, Lizzie's very . . . advanced," Molly said, looking actually *proud* of the kid. "At the moment, she's still stuck to the computer in my cousin Jane's office. Maybe you could get the tire jack out of your car and pry her out of there."

"You let Lizzie near a computer? What's she doing? Hacking into the Pentagon?"

"Not today," Molly said calmly enough, and that sort of impressed Dominic, until he realized that anyone who could remain calm around Lizzie was either heroine material or brain dead, and Molly Applegate wasn't wearing a Supergirl cape.

The parking lot was deserted now, except for the Lamborghini and a brand-new Mercedes. "Yours?" he asked, still trying to figure out the redhead.

"Mine," she said. "Already packed to the gills and ready for the road. So, since now you understand that Preston Kiddie Kare really is closed for the next two weeks, we'll just go get Lizzie, and we can all be off. Or you can stay here, although that seems a little silly."

"I paid for three weeks," Dominic repeated, not giving a damn about the money.

"I'm sure Janie will cheerfully refund your money, Mr. . . . wait a minute. You're their uncle, right? I don't think I was paying attention earlier. The bubble bath, you understand. Is your name Longstreet, too?"

"Yes, but that has nothing to—"

"And Little Tony called you Uncle Dom, didn't he? Dom Longstreet. Dominic Longstreet, right?" She gave her cheek a small slap and rolled those witchy eyes. "Of course! Where was my head? You're Dominic Longstreet."

"No, I'm not," Dominic said, taking a leaf from her book. "I'm Uncle Dom. Now, back to who's going to take care of these kids."

"No, you're not. You're Dominic Longstreet, and you've had four major hits on Broadway. I've seen them all, at least twice. Are you working on something new? I thought I read somewhere that you're working on something new."

"I am . . . I *was*. I *am,* damn it."

"Little Tony, close your ears. Uncle Dom just said that naughty word again," Molly said, clapping her own hands over her ears.

"You mean like you said when Dylan walked into the wall and started to cry?"

"You weren't supposed to hear that. Now, hands, ears, okay?" Molly said, and Dominic watched a very becoming flush of pink creep into her cheeks. Not that it lasted. She dropped her arms to her sides again and grinned at him. "So, you're here working?"

Little Tony, hands clapped over his ears, began to hum while he danced in place.

"Yes!" Dominic felt as if he'd climbed through a maze, just to end up back where he'd started. "That's exactly it. I'm working. I can't watch these kids."

"What are you working on?"

"Getting my plumber's license. It's been a lifelong dream of mine," Dominic said, all but growling. "What the hel—heck do you think I'd be working on? I've got the nucleus of the cast, my songwriter. I can't have kids."

Molly held out her hands. "Let me think about this," she said. "I'll go get Lizzie, and then maybe we'll talk, work this out."

"All right, but—" Words failed him, because she'd already turned to walk away, and walking away on those three-inch heels set her backfield in motion in a slinky, sexy, model-on-the-runway rhythm that made him consider taking Little Tony's hands from his ears and repositioning them across the kid's eyes. Eight was much too young to see something like that; the kid could be ruined for life.

Five minutes later, after Dominic had found a rag in his trunk and wiped off the peanut butter, and by the time Little Tony was on the forty-sixth verse of some song about a purple dinosaur, Molly was back, Lizzie in tow.

"Hi, Uncle Dom," Lizzie said, her arms swinging at her sides, just like Molly's, her strides long and from the hip, just like Molly's, and her chin lifted high, just like Molly's. The kid was a natural born mimic, and by the time she was eighteen, Tony and Elizabeth were going to need a good rest home.

"We worked it out," Molly said, patting Lizzie's blond head. "I'm already packed and ready anyway, and there's really nothing for me to do in D.C. I mean, I can take a bubble bath anywhere, and I already know a hair stylist here."

"She just called the newspaper she works for and quit," Lizzie supplied helpfully. She snapped her fingers. "Just like that, 'I quit.' They were heartbroken, weren't they, Molly?"

"Oh, definitely," Molly said, rolling those magnificent blue eyes again. Suddenly she was a young, sexy Lucille Ball, her comic expression the sort that could be seen from the last row in the balcony. "They thought I quit last week."

"I love you, you love—"

"Little Tony, that's enough," Dominic said. Then he pulled the boy's hands away from his ears—the kid was the obedient sort, and he'd be holding his hands over his ears until he graduated from college if no one told him it was okay to remove them. "I said, that's enough singing. Go get in the car. You, too, Lizzie."

"In the car? Oh, I don't think so, not both of them. That's a two-seater."

Dominic rubbed at his burning chest, feeling that if he burped, he'd burp banana. The thought didn't appeal. Peel? Ha! Banana peel. That was bad, really bad. Maybe he was losing his mind.

"Your point, Miss Applegate? Molly?" It was Friday night. Where in hell was he going to find another day care service between now and Monday?

"My point, Dominic—may I call you Dominic?—is that children must each have their own seat belt. You can't have both of those children ride in that car. Goodness, you know what you need, Dominic? You need a professional child care person . . . er, provider. Yes, a well-qualified child care provider."

"No kidding," he said. His headache was back now, too. It wasn't as if he didn't know where this was going. She'd quit her job. Her car was packed. She was about to volunteer her services as nanny or baby-sitter or whatever.

And then she was going to tell him she'd had the lead in her high school presentation of *South Pacific,* and she could tap dance, too. Amateurs. They came out of the woodwork wherever he went. No thank you! Not even for those legs.

And he'd tell her that, just as soon as he figured out another solution.

"So, this is how we'll handle it. You take Little Tony, and Lizzie will ride with me. She already told me she knows the way."

"Isn't this neat, Uncle Dom?" Lizzie said, her right fist jammed onto her hip, because Molly's right fist was jammed onto *her* hip. It was almost like seeing double.

"Oh, look at that face, Lizzie. He's thrilled," Molly said, pulling a key ring from her pocket. "See, he's speechless. Come on, let's ride."

Dominic watched them head toward the Mercedes, sure he should have more arguments to offer, but damned if he could think of a single one. Lizzie still had some ways to go to get that walk down right. Maybe he'd just have to be a good uncle and study Molly Applegate's walk for the next two weeks, then report back to her.

Chapter 2

You should never pump the children for personal information about their parents, their families.

That had been number two million and something of the thick list of rules and regulations Janie had made up for Molly in the hope that she would actually read them. And she had read some of them, even tucked them into her luggage when she'd packed up this morning; that list was better than a sleeping pill.

It had been Molly's idea for her cousin Jane to take her place at the intellectual retreat, posing as a paid companion (the platonic kind, for all those geniuses who could split an atom but couldn't get their own date), in order for her to get Molly the inside scoop on Senator Aubrey Harrison's possible run for president.

Molly had planned to do the paid companion thing herself, but then found out that one of her old boyfriends—who now hated her for some obscure reason—was Harrison's nephew, and would be attending the retreat with him.

But Molly had to land that story. She was on probation at

her Washington D.C. newspaper, and getting the scoop would save her job.

That's what she'd told Janie, and she'd meant it, at the time. Of course, she'd just quit that job without a look back, but that was only a detail. Because this week was good for Janie, who had already broken out of her ho-hum shell a little, and Molly was pretty sure her cousin was having a good time. Pretty sure, because Molly had turned off her cell phone, figuring it was time her cousin took care of herself instead of reporting in to her every day.

Janie had told her about John Romanowski, her assigned "companion" for the week, a real Nerd City college professor, according to Janie. She'd told her about lots of the other attendees, which included a major Hollywood star. And she'd even wangled a television news spot with Harrison, for crying out loud. The kid was doing all right for herself.

Sun, sand, lots of interesting people, the new chunky highlights in her hair? How did you compare that with herding a bunch of three-year-olds? When you got right down to it, she'd been the one who had done Janie the favor.

It had been Molly who had dressed Janie up and sent her off, promising to run Preston Kiddie Kare for the few days leading up to the annual closing for summer vacation.

It had been Molly who had sort of deserted Janie once her cousin was in Cape May, but Janie wasn't a total wuss. She'd be all right. Besides, Molly had kept her promise; she'd run Preston Kiddie Kare. The fact that she hadn't run it straight into the ground should be enough to make Janie happy.

They'd only had the one problem. Well, on top of the lights going out the first day, and four-year-old Mason Furbish stripping down to show April Fedderman his "wizzer," twice. Still, other than that, it hadn't been so bad.

But the one big problem had been Jane's staff screwing up this Longstreet business, misunderstanding the dates he wanted to use Preston Kiddie Kare as a place to dump his niece and nephew. The beauty of it was that it hadn't been Molly's mistake. Even "prettier" she was going to bail Janie out, sacrifice herself, and play child care expert for the next two weeks.

What a gal!

The fact that everything Molly knew about child care could be wrapped up in a red ribbon, then balanced on a demitasse spoon, with room left over for the entire cast of *Les Miserables,* was just a minor point, hardly worth anyone's consideration. Most especially Dominic Longstreet's consideration.

And this baby-sitting thing qualified as a job, sort of, so Molly was okay there, too. Because Molly's trust fund, a fund that had more zeros than most hard rock groups had tattoos, depended on her holding a job for at least ten months a year. Either that, or she had to marry, which she certainly wasn't going to do; she was having too much fun.

The restrictions on her inheritance, placed there by optimistic parents who had neglected Molly all of her life, only to decide to "teach her a lesson" in their will, had turned into just another lark for Molly Applegate. Irresponsible, flighty, here-comes-trouble Molly Applegate.

The will said she had to work ten months a year. But it had said nothing about keeping *one* job for ten months a year. And, with that thought, the employment market had become Molly's new playground.

So far, she'd been averaging six to eight different jobs a year. In the past twelve months, she'd been a lingerie model, a television spokesperson for a tire company, companion to an old biddy writing her memoirs, a house sitter in Monaco, a singing-slash-roller-skating car hop, a cocktail waitress in a Las Vegas casino, a professional dog walker in Manhattan, and she had just flung away the newspaper job, where she had been more of a glorified gofer than a reporter.

Some would call this flighty, she supposed, but Molly liked to call it diversity. And fun.

Running the nursery school had been fun, for a few days. She'd taught the kids a neat tap dance; they'd finger painted their own renditions of the *Mona Lisa*—until they'd run out of brown finger paint. She'd taught them the Bunny Hop. They'd called her Good Golly Miss Molly.

There was probably a lot more involved with child care than just playing with the kids, but Molly had muddled through with the help of Janie's staff, and the Post-It notes her cousin had stuck on darn near every surface, right down to one over the light switch that said, "Before leaving for the night, make sure you haven't left one of the children in the bathroom."

Which brought Molly's mind back to Janie's Rules, and that one about not pumping any of the kids about parents and family. And what, the student at no less than twelve private schools she'd been asked to leave told herself, were rules made for, if not to be broken.

"So," Molly said, as the Mercedes idled at a red light, "tell me all about your uncle Dom. We're talking details here, kiddo."

"The nitty-gritty. The skinny. Got ya. Sure, Molly. What do you want to know?"

Molly grinned at Lizzie. What a kid. If she and Lizzie had grown up together, gone to the same schools, they'd probably own the world by now. Or be doing five-to-ten in some women's prison.

"Start with marital status. Married? Divorced? Confirmed bachelor?"

"He's never gotten married, ever," Lizzie told her. "I heard Mom tell Dad one night that it's because he's such a self-centered, selfish bas—"

"Okay, that's enough of that question," Molly interrupted, trying not to grin. "So, confirmed bachelor. No girlfriend?"

Lizzie snuggled deeper into her seat. "Tons of them. They come, they go. Mom says that's because he thinks he's God's gift to—"

"Let's make a deal here, Lizzie. Tell me the facts, and leave your mom's editorial comments out of it, okay? I'm pretty sure I can figure the rest out on my own and, hey, that's most of the fun. The figuring out part."

Lizzie shrugged. "Okay. I guess that means you don't want to hear about Cynara?"

"Cynara? The Broadway star? That Cynara? *Au contraire, ma cherie*. Go on, dish."

"Well, Mom says—sorry. Cynara is at the compound. We call it the compound, because our house is sort of there, too, on our own property, but right next to Uncle Dom's. We've got ten acres. He's got a zillion."

"Let me take a wild guess here. Your mom has something to say about that, too?"

"I thought we weren't going to say what my mom says."

"Rules, my sweet, as I've just reminded myself, were made to be broken. Even mine. Besides, you know you want to."

Lizzie rolled her mischievous green eyes. "She says he's compensating. I looked that one up once I'd figured out how to spell it. It means he's using one thing to take the place of another thing that he doesn't have. Poor Uncle Dom, he must not have a lot, because he owns houses and stuff all over the place. But I like this one best."

"All right, onward and upward. Tell me about the place. Does it have a name? And, yes, I want both the official name and your mom's name for it."

"Well, Dad calls it the compound. Uncle Dom mostly just calls it the Virginia property. He doesn't name things. Mom calls Uncle Dom's part of it the Playground. Do you want to know what she calls the Lamborghini?"

Molly grinned. "No, I think I've already worked that one

out. Tell me more about the property. You know, give me the lay of the land."

"Okay. House. Barns. Stables. Horses. Trails. Two pools, one in, one out. Big guest house. Theater. And the Don't You Dare."

Molly peeked over at Lizzie. "The what?"

"That's what Uncle Dom calls his private studio, office, whatever you want to call it. So I guess he does name some things, huh? He and Dad and Uncle Taylor have the only keys. For the rest of us, it's Don't You Dare come in here. He even put another sign below that one last year that says 'That Means You, Too, Lizzie.' Mom says next year she expects to see a moat, with alligators."

"I'm going to like your mom."

"You won't meet her, remember. She's sailing the Geek Isles, and you'll be gone when she gets back."

"That's Greek Isles, Lizzie. But you know that, right?"

"Right," Lizzie agreed sullenly. "They didn't have to go, you know. Little Tony and I aren't that bad."

Molly felt a pang, and a protective urge. Her parents had left her, rumor had it, straight from the hospital where her mother delivered her (while wearing a Chanel gown, because she'd stayed at some party too long), and continued leaving her, regularly, until the day they'd taken off in a private jet that had done a nosedive into some mountains in Argentina.

But, hey, they'd taken care of their baby. They'd shipped her to every private school in the world, then plopped her down with Janie's parents for her final years of high school when no other private school would take her. And they'd written that stupid will, hadn't they? Made provisions for their baby's future.

Molly had visions of the plane going down, her parental units reassuring each other, "At least we're leaving Molly nicely aggravated."

"Do they go away very often?" she asked.

"Yeah. Heaps. They went to my mom's uncle's funeral two years ago without us, in Kentucky, for three whole days. And they go to dinner a lot. They're always going out to dinner when we're in New York."

Molly relaxed. "Lizzie, when you can count the days you see your parents in a year on the fingers of one hand, then come to me and I'll help you lodge a complaint, okay? It sounds to me like your parents are pretty nice people. Your dad works with your uncle Dom, doesn't he?"

"Dad writes, and Uncle Dom produces."

"I should have paid more attention to my *Playbill* when I went to see the shows. Your dad writes the words and music?"

"Just the words. Uncle Taylor writes the music to go with them."

"Oh, yes, you mentioned him already. Another brother?"

"No, silly. Taylor Carlisle. He asked us to call him Uncle Taylor. He's at the compound now. Along with Cynara," Lizzie ended, waggling her eyebrows at Molly.

"Interesting. Anyone else?"

"Mr. Cambridge. That's Derek Cambridge. He's supposed to be the male lead, opposite Cynara, in the new show. They're all there, rehearsing behind my dad's back."

"Really," Molly said, turning left between two fieldstone gates as Lizzie pointed to them. They'd been driving along a narrow macadam road lined on either side with three-railed white fences. "Is this all your uncle's property?"

"Pretty near. Ten acres are ours, remember? But they're all inside the same fence. Oh, did I mention Bethany White?" Lizzie made a face. "What a dork. Just because she's thirteen. Just because she's getting boobs. Big deal."

"A real loser, huh?"

"She doesn't think so. Bethany's a star. Just like her mother keeps telling everybody. What a pair of creeps."

"Let me take a wild guess here. Bethany's a child star? Complete with stage mother?"

"She thinks she's so hot," Lizzie said, folding her arms over her seat belt. "Look at me, I'm wonderful. My mommy says so. Give me a break."

"You two aren't exactly exchanging friendship rings, huh?" Molly said, slowing the Mercedes as the small city that was the compound appeared over the crest of a rolling hill. "Holy sh—wow, would you look at that! I'll say this, Lizzie, your uncle Dom compensates *good.*"

The house was huge, just huge. All white brick, three stories high, with a porch that ran all along the front, pillars lining the porch. Another house, smaller, that looked just like it, stood about two hundred yards away. Garages, stables, all those other buildings half hidden by trees, and all were connected by flowing brick pathways. There were two golf carts parked in front of the main house.

From the size of the place, there probably should also have been a freestanding map board labeled, "You are here."

"Our house is prettier," Lizzie said, unbuckling her seat belt as Molly pulled up and parked behind the Lamborghini. "It's brick, too, but not painted white. I can show you the outside, but I'm not allowed to go in while Mom and Dad are gone. I've just got to stay here."

"Gee, bad break, having to rough it like this," Molly said, slinging her purse strap over her shoulder as she walked around the front of the car, looking up at the house. "I'll bet they keep you on bread and water, too. Okay, let's go find your uncle Dom before he has time to hide."

They were halfway up the five steps leading to the porch and a massive, fanlit front door, when Little Tony came running around the far corner of the house, yelling, "You're here, you're here, you're here!"

"He's a bit volatile," Lizzie said in a very grown up voice that belied her eleven years.

Molly, who knew a lot about pretending to be older than she was, merely nodded. "Another of your trials."

"You're not kidding. He *follows* me, everywhere I go. It's disgusting."

"He admires you. He looks up to you. You should be flattered."

"Nice try, Molly," Lizzie said, holding out her arms so that Little Tony wouldn't barrel straight into her and knock her down. "What he does is *tattle.* He tells Uncle Dom everything I do. Don't you, you rat?"

"I do not." Little Tony grinned at his sister with the innocence of an eight-year-old, which was akin to the innocence of a kid with a baseball bat looking at a broken window and the ball in the homeowner's hands and swearing he didn't know what happened.

"Tell Molly the truth, Little Tony," Lizzie demanded.

Little Tony grinned at Molly. "He gives me quarters."

Molly bit her bottom lip. "Oh, look, dogs. I used to walk dogs in Manhattan."

"Why?" Little Tony asked as a mismatched pair of canines came sniffing up to them, the smaller one barking like a mad thing.

"I got paid to walk them," Molly explained. "But I only did it for a week. Do you have any idea the sheer size of the poop bag needed to walk six dogs? Hello, sweethearts," she said, bending over to pat the largest dog.

She didn't have to bend far, because the dog was a Saint Bernard, still probably in the puppy stage, as he looked to weigh only about half a ton.

"That's Rufus. He's mine," Little Tony said. "I got him for Christmas. And that's Doofus. He's Lizzie's. She got him for Christmas, too."

"Hello, Doofus," Molly said to the black teacup French poodle, which had just gracefully jumped up to land on Rufus's strong back. "You two look like a circus act."

"At least Doofus knows some tricks, and he barks at strangers, which makes him a watch dog," Lizzie said, picking up her dog and snuggling him against her chin. "Rufus only knows how to eat, wag his tail, and drool all over everything. Uncle Dom won't let him in the house."

"But he lets Doofus in the house? That doesn't seem fair," Molly said, looking sympathetically at the large and, yes, drooling dog.

"Rufus likes to cuddle on laps," Dominic Longstreet said, seeming to have appeared out of nowhere. The man was gorgeous, in a go-to-hell sort of way. "You ever have a Saint Bernard sit on you, Miss Applegate?"

"Molly, and no, I haven't. But I have been pawed a time or two by big dumb animals. I've found that if you just step down hard on their back paws, they find something else to do. So, Dominic, where are you going to put my luggage? I like rooms that go all sunny in the mornings."

Chapter 3

Watching Molly Applegate walk away from him once had been educational. Twice had been sweet. But now he was beginning to feel as if she were playing the lead, and he'd somehow gotten cast in a small, supporting role.

"Where do you think you're going, Miss—Molly?" he asked as she climbed the steps to the porch.

"Why, inside, of course," she answered, looking down at him over her shoulder. "I mean, I don't know about you, but I'm famished. We will be eating dinner soon, won't we?"

"Yes, dinner will be served in about—wait a minute. We're not talking about dinner here; we're talking about luggage. Aren't you going to help?"

"Oh, don't worry. I already popped the trunk," she told him, holding up her key ring and showing him the remote control, then turned to continue into the house.

He would have told her what he thought she could do with her damn luggage, except she was already gone, leaving him alone with Rufus and Little Tony, neither probably worth much more than an overnight bag apiece. Yeah, well, how much luggage could the woman have?

Walking around to the rear of the Mercedes, Dominic looked into the trunk, and swore under his breath.

He'd probably think about the fact that it was a matched Gucci set later, once he'd found someone to lug the seven pieces into the house and up to the third floor, where the live-in staff resided.

Except that the kids were on the second floor. If the woman was going to ride herd on the kids, she might as well be close enough to grab the reins.

"Kevin," he called out as one of the kitchen helpers approached along the drive, his head down as he whistled some tune, his gaze on the stone he was kicking in front of him. "How about a little help over here?"

"Sure, Mr. Dominic," the college student (theater major, naturally) said, breaking into a trot. "Have more of the cast arrived?"

"At least four of them, you'd think," Dominic said, hauling the largest case out of the trunk. "No, not the cast. We're just working with the leads."

"And me," Kevin reminded him proudly, because Dominic had needed a reader for some of the smaller parts, and Kevin had volunteered. Hell, the boy had damn near broken his neck, racing toward the theater when Dominic had asked if he wanted to run some lines.

Had *he* ever been that pitiful? Yeah, he had.

"This luggage belongs to Miss Applegate, who will be keeping Lizzie and Little Tony out of our hair for the next two weeks. We'll put the bags in the guest room between the kids, all right?"

"Sure, Mr. Dominic," Kevin said, pulling out another suitcase. "Wow, what's she got in here, rocks?"

"No, she reserves those for her head," Dominic grumbled, moving off, with three suitcases weighing him down. "I'm surprised she found any, with all the rocks that have to be in *my* head."

By the time he and Kevin had hauled all the bags up the steps and put them in the middle guest room, the dinner gong was sounding downstairs.

He was hungry. Not hungry enough to look forward to yet another dinner spent listening to the kids fighting with each other, but Tony and Elizabeth had made him promise to at least share the dinner table with their children, in the hopes of keeping them civilized.

At least Mrs. Jonnie would be pleased, considering how the housekeeper had made it her business to complain to him every night that she was "past it," just too old to entertain two active children. From now on, Molly Applegate would have the kids, 24/7.

And she could start tonight, at the dinner table.

Okay, so maybe he had more of an appetite than he'd thought.

He found Molly and the children in the living room, where Molly was standing at the mantel, holding one of his Tonys. Hefting it, as if to gauge its weight.

"Put that back," he said from the doorway.

"See? I told you he gets all goofy about those things. Like they were made of gold, or something," Lizzie said from one of the wing chairs in front of the fireplace. She sat there like a queen, her hands clasping the ends of the armrests, her feet swinging about two inches off the floor.

"I do *not* get goofy, Miss Elizabeth," he told her, grabbing the Tony from Molly's hands and jamming it back down on the mantel, beside the other three.

"Yeah, right," Lizzie said, rolling her eyes. "And I still say it looked pretty darn good in that Barbie skirt."

Molly looked at Dominic, and he could see the amusement in her eyes. "Laugh, Molly Applegate," he said, "but laugh while remembering that she's officially out of my hair and all yours for the next two weeks."

Molly's smile faded. "You have no idea what you just said,

do you?" she asked as Lizzie ran from the room. "What a jerk," she added, and then ran off after the child.

Dominic watched her go—it was really beginning to bug him, watching her go—and then turned to Little Tony, who was sitting on the floor, petting Doofus. "What was that all about?" he asked the child. But it was a rhetorical question.

Not that Little Tony saw it that way. Without looking up, he said, "Lizzie thinks you hate her."

"Hate her? Why would she think I—I do not!"

"She says you think she's in the way, and that she's dumb and a pest and can't do anything right, and that you can't wait until Mom and Daddy come home so you can get rid of us."

And then damn if the kid didn't hold up his hand for a quarter.

Dominic fished in his pants pocket and came up with one. "I'll double this if you tell me if she said anything else."

"Nope, that was it." He got to his feet. "I'd better go wash my hands," he said as the gong rang a second time. "Mrs. Jonnie says I always look like I worked in a coal mine all day long."

"Yeah, sure, go ahead," Dominic said, subsiding into the wing chair his niece had just bolted from to run away from him. He absently rubbed at his chest.

She thinks I hate her?

Man.

This was all Tony and Elizabeth's fault, damn it. They knew he stank with kids, didn't know how to handle them. He really had to do more, try harder. He liked the kids. Hell, he *loved* those kids.

"Having some quiet time to reflect on your behavior?" Molly asked, walking into the room to sit down in the facing wing chair. He barely reacted when she crossed those long legs of hers. He'd noticed, he'd have to be dead not to notice, but he had more important things on his mind right now.

Wow. Did this mean he was getting "past it" himself?

"How is she?"

"Lizzie's fine. I suggested that some revenge is always good for the soul and left her washing her hands and thinking up suitable punishments for you. Do you mind if we short-sheet your bed tonight? I mean, we could sneak in after you're asleep and stick your hand in a cup of water, but I know you didn't mean to be so horrible."

Dominic narrowed his eyelids. "I know I'm leaving this way too late, but who the hell are you?"

"I told you. I'm Janie Preston's cousin. She's somewhere else, so I ran the business for her these past few days. It was only supposed to be two days, but then our early Fourth of July picnic got rained out on Wednesday, so I decided to open again today, one day after the holiday."

"That has the ring of truth to it," Dominic said, "but I get the feeling you're leaving something out."

"Nonsense. Every word I said is true."

"Good. Now add some more. Like, tell me about the Mercedes, and the Gucci luggage."

Molly sighed. "Very well. The Mercedes is, of course, a precision-built German luxury car, and Gucci is—"

"Cute," Dominic interrupted. "That's not what I meant. Your cousin let you run her day care place, right? So that means you're a child care expert, right again? A child care expert who drives a Mercedes and totes around enough Gucci luggage to hold six wardrobes?"

He waited for her to answer, but she didn't. She just sat there, until she lifted one hand to inspect her manicure.

"Well? Aren't you going to say anything?"

"No, I don't think so," she said, smiling at him. "Oh, wait, those were questions, weren't they? Silly me. What were they again?"

"Mr. Dominic, I did ring a second time," Mrs. Jonnie said from the doorway. "The children are already in the dining room, setting an extra place for some reason. They were laughing, which is never good." Then she frowned at Molly. "You didn't tell me you had a guest, Mr. Dominic."

"Yes, Mrs. Jonnie, this is Miss Applegate," Dominic said, getting to his feet. He held out a hand to help Molly to her feet, because she'd held out a hand to him as if she expected him to be polite, and with the housekeeper watching he didn't have much choice.

"Hello, Mrs. Jonnie," Molly said, walking across the room to shake the housekeeper's hand. "I'm Molly, fellow drudge, which is to say that I'm not really a guest. Mr. Dominic has retained me as nanny for the children. Isn't that delightful? And I'm sure you'll be happy to hear that I will be in charge of them at all times, as well as dependent on you to tell me anything I should know."

"Well . . . yes, thank you, Miss . . . Applegate, was it?"

Dominic watched, his upper lip curling, as Molly wrinkled her nose and said, "Oh, please, Mrs. Jonnie. Call me Molly."

"I think I'm going to be sick," Dominic said as Mrs. Jonnie beamed, then left the room, her steps lighter than he'd seen them since the kids had come to stay. "What was that all about?"

"Nothing," Molly said, looking way too innocent for what Dominic was thinking. "She seems extremely nice. I've had a lot of dealings with housekeepers over the years. Good people. Why, in some homes, they practically raise the children, did you know that? Besides, it's always smart to be polite. You never know when it's going to come in handy, now do you?"

"Let's go get dinner," Dominic said, gesturing for her to precede him into the hallway. "But, once the kids are in bed, we're going to talk, Good Golly Miss Molly. Bet on it."

"Wonderful," she said, her smile showing no trace of anything save agreement. "Shall we say on the front porch, about nine? And a wine cooler would be marvelous. A blackberry one would be perfect."

And there she went again, walking away from him, unerringly heading toward the dining room, damn her, and leaving him to either run to catch up or follow behind like some tongue-lolling Rufus or Doofus.

The dining room was one of Dominic's least favorite rooms in the house, considering the fact that he either dined here alone, or with investors, prospective investors, or—for the most part—people who wanted something from him.

It was like a well-appointed office, with three courses, and an antacid for dessert.

He walked in, not really seeing the fine cherry furniture, the highly polished silver plate, the crystal displayed in large, glass-fronted cabinets, the hand-painted stucco walls, deep wood moldings, carved ceiling, or the elegant brass chandeliers that hung over each end of the long table.

And then he stopped, stared.

He always sat at the head of the table, with the children on either side, but halfway down the length, far enough away that when Little Tony chewed with his mouth open, he didn't have to see it or hear it.

But not tonight. Tonight, somehow, the four place settings were all halfway down the table, two on one side, two on the other side. Bunched together. Up close. Way too personal.

The vacant chair was beside Little Tony, and directly across from Molly Applegate, who was already in the process of spreading her white linen napkin on her lap in a quite exaggerated series of movements obviously meant for the children to observe and emulate.

"It's the first thing a refined lady or gentleman does when she or he sits down at the table," she said, looking at Dominic, who really didn't want to sit down, and who was feeling far from refined. "Isn't it, Dominic? You always immediately unfold your napkin and arrange it in your lap, whether there is food served yet or not. Watch, children, your uncle will demonstrate the process again."

Teeth gritted, Dominic pulled out his chair and sat down, grabbing the napkin out of its silver ring and jamming it into his lap.

"Very good, Dominic," Molly said, smiling at him. "Now, Little Tony, your turn."

Okay, so it was probably Dominic's fault. He had sort of yanked the napkin out of the ring with a little too much emphasis on the yank part. So when Little Tony did the same thing, and the ring went flying to his left, clipping the already filled water glass at Dominic's place, tipping over that glass so that the water ran everywhere, there really wasn't a lot he could say.

At least not a lot he could say in mixed company, as he leapt to his feet to avoid the waterfall.

Little Tony's bottom lip began to quiver as Lizzie said, "Oh, boy, you're going to get it now."

But Molly had also gotten to her feet, more slowly than Dominic, her moves graceful rather than panicked, neatly righting the glass, and was already patting at the spill with her own napkin.

"There we are, no harm done. Accidents will happen, won't they, Dominic? Luckily, we've got a lot of table to work with here. All right, everyone, we'll be shifting thataway, three seats each. Ah, Mrs. Jonnie, how nice of you to help. Little Tony was just demonstrating the absorbant properties of fine Irish linen."

Great. Now Dominic was supposed to be playing musical chairs, and with plates and cutlery.

But he smiled—because Little Tony was looking up at

him as if he were some horrible ogre getting ready to bite off his head—and then said, "This is fun, isn't it? Did I ever tell you about the time I spilled a whole punch bowl at a party? I did. Backed into it, and bam, over it went. Gallons, Little Tony. We nearly drowned."

"Huh?" Little Tony asked, carefully sliding his linen place mat along the wooden tabletop, to a seat two down from where he'd been sitting.

"Never mind," Dominic said, rubbing the child's blond head. "I'm just saying it's okay. Everybody has accidents."

"Wow," he heard Lizzie whisper to Molly. "Who *is* that on the other side of the table?"

The first course arrived. Soup. Vichyssoise, as a matter of fact. Little Tony took one slurping spoonful and made a face.

"You don't like it?" Dominic asked, surprised at how suddenly attuned he was to his nephew's presence, his likes and dislikes. "It's just cold potato soup."

"I like chicken noodle," Little Tony said, pouting. "This is dumb."

Dominic looked at Molly, who nodded her head.

Lizzie wasn't so subtle. "You eat dumb food, Uncle Dom. I haven't had a hamburger all week."

Mrs. Jonnie was clearing away the wet place mat.

Dominic asked her, "What's the main course tonight, Mrs. Jonnie?"

"Braised calves' liver, Mr. Dominic, your favorite."

The chorus of "eeeuuuwww"s from Lizzie and Little Tony—and Molly Applegate—made Dominic flinch. "Not good, huh?" he asked Little Tony. "What would you like?"

The boy shrugged. "Peanut butter and jelly sandwiches?"

Molly lifted her napkin to her lips to, Dominic was sure, hide an unholy grin. He was giving these kids gourmet food in a magnificent setting—when he got around to thinking about it that way—and they wanted peanut butter and jelly sandwiches?

"Sounds like a plan," Molly said, looking to the housekeeper. "Mrs. Jonnie? Do you have the makings of peanut butter and jelly sandwiches?"

"Yes, I think so, Molly. Chunky peanut butter, of course, and some nice orange marmelade?"

"Oh, gross, lumpy peanut butter. And no grape jelly? What is this, a *prison?*" Lizzie was clearly appalled.

"I . . . I could put them on the list for tomorrow's shopping trip," Mrs. Jonnie suggested.

"That would be wonderful, thank you. Kids, wouldn't that be wonderful? And you know what?" Molly said, pushing back her chair. "I think it would be very nice of us to go shopping for Mrs. Jonnie. That way you can pick out all your favorites. But no cold potato soup, and no liver, right? Come on, kids. Say excuse me to your uncle and ask his permission to leave the table."

"Wait a minute. Where are you going?" Dominic asked, suddenly feeling deserted as his niece and nephew mumbled their requests to be excused, then pushed back their chairs and got to their feet.

Molly answered him. "Why, we're going to the kitchen with Mrs. Jonnie. She's going to show me the telephone book, and I'm going to call out for pizza."

"Pizza!" Little Tony yelled, already jumping around the room like a frog with a hotfoot. "Pizza! Pizza! Pizza!"

"And garlic bread sticks?" Lizzie asked, obviously not as easily convinced.

"Is there any other way?" Molly asked, winking at Dominic. "Now, go on you two, help Mrs. Jonnie carry these plates to the kitchen."

Once they'd gone, helpful little buggers whom Dominic could swear he had never seen before, Molly leaned across the table, her elbows just missing the crystal glasses, and said, "See? I'm an expert on children. Having been one myself. See you later. Enjoy chewing on your liver."

Strictly on principle, he told himself, Dominic refused to watch her go.

It didn't feel like a victory.

Chapter 4

Molly tucked in Little Tony, dropped a kiss on his fore-head, and then went down the hall to check on Lizzie.

She knocked at the door, and after a few moments (during which Molly heard a dresser drawer close), Lizzie answered it. "You knocked?" she asked, looking part pleased, part surprised.

"Of course I knocked," Molly said, walking into the rather grown-up looking room and plopping herself down on the end of the bed. "I had to give you time to hide the evidence."

"What evidence?" Lizzie asked, her green eyes shifting toward the large maple dresser against the far wall.

"I have no idea," Molly said, rolling over onto her stomach and crossing her legs in the air. "That's because I knocked first. A person should be allowed privacy, unless there's some reason you can think of why she shouldn't?"

"Nope," Lizzie said quickly. "Not me. No reasons here. It's not like I'm keeping some soppy diary or something." She hopped up on the queen-size bed next to Molly, rolled onto her stomach to carefully hide the pen that had been lying there, and crossed her legs in the air. After a few moments, she said, "So. What are we looking at?"

Molly grinned. "The closet door, I guess. I wasn't really looking. I was thinking."

"Me, too," Lizzie said, nodding her head. "You know what I was thinking?"

"That you'd kill to have boobs?" Molly asked, giving her a small push that knocked her elbows out from under her.

"Well, yeah, that too," Lizzie admitted, regaining her look-alike pose. "But what I was really thinking is that the next two weeks aren't going to be so bad, you know? I mean, you're . . . You're not horrible."

"Yes," Molly said, rolling over and getting off the bed, to take up the Lotus position on the floor. "I've heard that. I'm not horrible. Of course, I've been called everything else. Here. Come on down here with me—do you want to learn some neat exercises?"

"Not particularly, no," Lizzie said, wincing as Molly easily moved into a more intricate position. "I'd rather ask you some questions."

Molly effortlessly lifted her right leg high over her head. "I figured you would. Okay, shoot."

"Well . . ." Lizzie said, drawing out the word. "To start, I heard Miss Janice telling Miss Leslie that you didn't know your backside from first base about running a day care and nursery school."

Molly frowned comically. "And here I thought they liked me."

"Oh, they like you. Everybody *likes* you. But there were those Post-It notes all over the place, most of them with your name on them. And when you got stuck in the jungle gym—"

"Not one of my finest hours, I know," Molly agreed. "So, what you want to know is what your uncle wants to know— am I trained in child care."

"Oh, I don't care about that," Lizzie said, slipping off the bed to try one of Molly's exercises, one that had her all but putting one ankle behind her neck. "I"—she grunted between words, as she tried to lift her leg higher—"I just . . . want to know . . . if you're an actress."

Molly, her own right ankle now behind her head, tried to turn that head to look at the child. It didn't work. "An actress? No, of course not."

"Okay, because you'd be surprised what people will do to get close to Dad or Uncle Dom. Like, you could have planned this whole thing, right? Just to get into the compound?"

"I could have," Molly agreed. "I mean, it's clever and devious enough, isn't it? I could have done that. But I didn't. Honest. I was just helping out my cousin, and now I'm helping out your uncle. That's me, helpful Molly Applegate."

She succeeded in releasing her leg and sighed as she collapsed against the floor. "In fact, I'm thinking of putting in for a merit badge."

Lizzie laughed, collapsing next to her. "You don't look like a Girl Scout."

Molly turned her head to grin at the girl. "That's because they threw me out. I have been thrown out of some of the—well, I shouldn't tell you that, should I? Come on, bedtime."

"Are you kidding?" Lizzie asked, scrambling to her feet. "It's only eight-thirty. On a Friday. I don't have to go to bed yet. Get real."

"Not ready, huh?" Molly said, getting to her feet. "Okay, here's the thing. I promised your uncle I'd meet him on the porch tonight, to discuss my *qualifications*. That leaves us only a half hour to short-sheet his bed, hit up Mrs. Jonnie for a snack, get you a shower, and find a good DVD somewhere to slip into that television over there. Do you think we can do it?"

"He won't fire you, will he?" Lizzie asked five minutes

later, while they were performing their girls' school magic on Dominic's bed.

"No, he won't fire me. He's desperate. Now, a shower, a snack and a DVD, and we're all set."

It was only five minutes after nine when the opening credits of *Shrek* appeared on the large television screen, and only a minute later when Molly looked in on Little Tony, to see him fast asleep, clutching a stuffed Saint Bernard.

The natives no longer restless, she then slipped into her own room. She ran a comb through her thick, chin-length mop of dark copper hair, brushed her teeth to get rid of the smell of garlic breadsticks, slid some glosser on her lips, gave herself a quick spray of cologne, and headed downstairs, armed and ready for battle.

She found Dominic on the porch, leaning against the railing and looking as if he was wound up tight enough to take off to the moon. The man was about as laid back as a crouching tiger.

"Right on time," she said, holding out her left wrist, the one with the slim, fourteen-karat gold watch on it. "Well, almost on time. Oh, and there's my wine cooler. You didn't forget."

She sat down on one of the white wooden rockers, picked up her wine cooler, and gestured toward him with the bottle. Sometimes, she knew, the one in power was the one who sat down and looked comfortable. "Join me? Or are you really set on digging your hands into that railing until it squeals for help?"

He looked down at his hands, braced against the railing on either side of him, and let go. "I've looked you up," he said, advancing on her with what the fainthearted might call *menace*.

Molly was silent for a few seconds, then carefully put down the bottle. "Well, that's a new one, even for me. You looked up my *what?*"

"Not what, Molly Applegate, *where*. I looked you up on the Internet."

She kept her smile wide. "Really? I'm on there? Are there pictures? If there are, I assure you, I did *not* pose for them."

"Cute," Dominic said, sitting down beside her at last, just as she was beginning to get a crick in her neck. The man was definitely tall, which she liked, because she was tall, too. He was also *very* handsome, which she also liked. But that was all she liked. She was pretty ambivalent about the rest of him. "Very cute."

"I aim more for sleek and sophisticated, to tell you the truth. Now, if you want cute, you'll have to wait for my cousin to get back from Cape May. She's got cute all wrapped up, with a pretty pink bow on it," she said calmly.

Dominic rubbed at his forehead. People did that a lot around Molly, but she never understood why. She wasn't even *trying* to drive him over the edge.

"What I'm saying, Miss Applegate, is that I typed your name into a search engine and got over five hundred hits. Balls you've attended, dinners you've attended, your name in your parents' obituaries from ten years ago. You're Margaret Applegate."

"And this is a bad thing?" she asked, wishing the Internet had never been invented. After all, who'd want to shop on-line anyway, when it was so much more fun to go to the stores and touch things?

"No, not a *bad thing*. It's a confusing thing. Confusing as in what in hell is Margaret Applegate, heiress, doing here, taking care of my niece and nephew?"

"You know, that *is* a very good question," Molly said, picking up the wine cooler again and taking a swig. "But I told you that I was helping out my cousin, filling in at Preston Kiddie Kare, right? That's a whole story you don't want to hear, trust me. But then you had a problem, which gave Janie a problem, and since I wasn't really doing anything important anyway, I decided to help you out. It's that simple."

She sent him a level stare. "If you've been following along, Dominic, I think this is the part where you say *thank you very much, Molly.*"

Now he was doing that rubbing-his-temples bit. People usually graduated to that whenever Molly tried to be sensible, which was why she'd usually found it easier to lie. In fact, she'd had a whole fib already made up, but now he had to hear the truth. Which was his own fault.

"The Mercedes, the Gucci luggage . . ."

"The Lamborghini, the small city you've built here . . . your point?" she answered as his words trailed off.

"I worked for every penny I have," Dominic said, bristling.

"Oh? And you think I haven't? Try growing up as Margaret Applegate, Dominic, and see what a cake walk it wasn't." She stood up, holding the wine cooler with both hands. "I'm sorry, did I say that?"

She forced a grin, pretending not to be shocked by her own brief honesty that probably had something to do with the two kids upstairs, who had caused a short and never pleasant trip down her personal memory lane. "Look who's complaining, the little rich girl. Hey, and it worked, too. You look all sorry and embarrassed. I mean, you *believed* me? Growing up rich and pampered is a trial? Not hardly, Mr. Longstreet. Oh, look, we've got company."

Molly walked to the railing, to see two figures moving through the darkness that was broken by several strategically placed ground and pole lights.

She recognized them both the moment their faces came into the light. Derek Cambridge and Cynara. *The* Cynara.

Derek was handsome, but older than she'd thought, and shorter. Still, he was huge on the stage, and he had a great voice.

Cynara had a great voice, a great body, a magnificent face, and a reputation as a real bitch. That was probably just because nobody understood her. Molly could relate to that.

She turned to Dominic. "Oh, please introduce us. I'm so sorry I didn't bring my autograph book."

"You had dinner with Bill Gates last year, Margaret. I doubt you're all that impressed."

"You're probably right. Just, please, leave the Margaret part between the two of us, okay? I'm here for Lizzie and Little Tony, remember?"

"Sure," Dominic said, getting to his feet. "That way Derek will be chasing the nanny, rather than the heiress."

Molly opened her mouth to say something, then realized she had nothing to say. Dominic had sounded . . . upset. What *was* the man's problem? It wasn't as if he was baby-sitting *her.*

"Darling, there you are!" Cynara's voice was low, sultry, and dripping with emotion: a mix of delight, sorrow, accusation, apprehension. This woman was *good.*

Molly quietly mouthed those same words, trying for the same inflections, then ended in a whisper, "I did that well, didn't I?"

"Shut up," Dominic hissed as Cynara allowed Derek to help her up the stairs. "Hello, sweetheart, how was your afternoon?" he asked as Cynara lifted her cheek for his kiss.

"Dreadful," Cynara said, gracefully staggering past Molly, to sit in her recently vacated chair. "You have no idea what a taskmaster Taylor can be when you're not around. He's . . . He's positively *abusive.*"

"He made Cynara sing 'If This Is Love' four times," Derek Cambridge said, giving Dominic a pat on the shoulder as he brushed past him, to present himself to Molly. "Derek Cambridge, you lovely creature. It has been a dreadfully long day, as that dear lady over there just said, so if you could agree to simply imagining me prostrate at your feet?"

Molly extended her hand, palm down, wrist limp, and allowed Derek to bend over it. "I would forgive you anything, Mr. Cambridge, but that you ignore my presence."

Then she shot a quick glance at Dominic, who looked, oh, about a good three seconds away from exploding.

Still holding Molly's hand, Derek said, "Dom? Come, come, friend. Finish the introductions. I must know what name to give the woman I will dream about tonight."

Molly stiffened. Waited.

"Molly," Dominic said after a mind-shredding pause. "Her name is Molly, and she's going to be nanny to Tony's kids for the next two weeks."

Molly exhaled.

"The nanny?" Cynara looked Molly up and down, and then smiled. "How old is your nephew, Dom?"

"Oh, don't worry, ma'am," Molly said, with the emphasis on *ma'am*. "He's immune to feminine wiles for some time yet. Unless, of course, you feed him pizza."

Cynara smiled, and Molly noticed that the woman's lips were a little thin. Yes, definitely not a happy woman. "I'm quite sure you amuse yourself with remarks like that, my dear. And please, I give you permission to call me Cynara."

"Yes, thank you so much, Cynara," Molly said, and dropped into a quick bob of a curtsy. "And you can call me Molly."

Dominic coughed.

Molly stepped into the breech. "Could I possibly get you something to drink? Cynara? Derek?"

"A scotch on the rocks sounds good to me, Molly, thanks," Derek said. "Cynara?"

"My usual. Spring water, chilled. Three ice cubes. And a twist of lime."

"Watching the old weight, huh? Got-ya, " Molly said, then walked off before the actress could answer her, feeling

Derek's gaze on her legs as she headed for the door. It took so little to make some men happy.

Once inside, she crept into the dark living room, to stand next to the open window.

"I don't like her," Cynara was saying. "That red hair? Those ridiculously short shorts? She looks cheap. Common."

"You should look so cheap and common, darling," Derek said, then laughed. "Dom, did you see those legs?"

"I may have noticed," Dominic said. "Now, back to this afternoon. I'm sorry I had to leave, but I had to clear up something with the kids. What's wrong with the song?"

"What's wrong with the song is that Taylor keeps changing the tune."

"That's true enough, Dom. He wants her to find a note they both can live with. You were rather flat, Cynara, darling. Sorry."

"Flat? You mean as in unlike that gut you're carrying around, Derek? I heard you were mentioned for the role of the grandfather in Wildhorn's next effort. Or was that Santa Claus in the next Disney?"

Molly put a hand over her mouth to keep from laughing, then tiptoed from the room, heading for the kitchen. She rather liked these people; they were so fake they were real.

"Mrs. Jonnie? Hi. I need scotch and a glass of spring water."

"Three ice cubes, slice of fresh lime, I know," Mrs. Jonnie said, slowly pushing herself up from the table. "Same thing, every night. Scotch is in the glass-fronted cabinet over there. I'm guessing that Mr. Carlisle has gone to New York for the weekend?"

"He's not here," Molly said, motioning for Mrs. Jonnie to sit down again. "Do they all stay here, in the house?"

"No. There's a guest house. You probably saw it when you came in? It's just a little ways down the lane. Mr. Dominic hired a temporary full staff for it, so the others eat there, unless they're invited up here. The prima donna has her panties in a twist about that one, let me tell you. Glasses are in that cabinet behind you."

Molly lifted out two glasses, one short, one tall, and put them on the counter. "Cynara's after Mr. Dominic?" she asked the housekeeper.

"Honey, that one's after anything in pants. But she's not the prima donna. That would be little Miss Bethany. Thirteen years old and a real princess. I don't know if someone should slap her or her mother. They're not here tonight. Friday night is hair night, I understand. You know, the night when Mama puts all those *natural* curls in the kid's head?"

Molly smiled, remembering Lizzie's comments about the child star. "Sounds like a new play, *The Brat and the Stage Mother.* And they're also in the guest house? I didn't realize it was that large."

"That's because this place is so big. Everything else looks small around it, you know? Lime is already sliced and in the fridge, dear. Ah, now I can go to bed. They only have one drink each night, then take off again. Mr. Dominic keeps early hours when he's working."

"Does he often work here? I know he has his own theater on the grounds."

"He and Mr. Tony work here a lot, yes. But Mr. Tony made Mr. Dominic promise to take these three weeks off and just be with the kids. Mrs. Elizabeth confided in me, sort of, and said that they're hoping Mr. Dominic relaxes for a while, instead of working all the time. Something about being too stressed and heading for an early grave, that sort of thing."

"But he's working?"

"Oh, yes, he most certainly is, and Mr. Tony is going to be very unhappy if he finds out about it, let me tell you. There's a tray propped up against the side of the fridge, dear."

Molly retrieved the tray and placed the two drinks on it. "This is it? No pretzels, no nuts?"

"Only the ones on the front porch," Mrs. Jonnie said, winking at Molly. She slowly got to her feet. "Oh, you might want to take another can of cold soda from the fridge out there with you, in case Mr. Dominic wants a second one. He doesn't bother with a glass."

Once the can was on the tray, Molly headed back to the foyer, deliberately stepping out of her heels before she reached the end of the large carpet placed over the hardwood floor. On tiptoe, she headed for the open window once more.

Eavesdroppers seldom heard anything good about themselves, one of her former keepers had warned her. But that was all right; nobody ever had much of anything good to say about her anyway. Still, what she heard now was refreshing, because it wasn't about her.

Had she really expected actors to speak of anyone but themselves?

Chapter 5

"Flat. F-l-a-*bad*, darling. Trust me. Any flatter, and your voice would have to send out for implants."

"Very funny, Derek. You ought to go on the stage. Oh, wait, you *were* on the stage. How soon we forget."

"Speak for yourself, darling. I'm not the one still trying to remember the new lyrics."

"How wonderful for you, Derek, dear. You'll always have your memories."

Ego. Artistic temperament. Constant sniping and sarcasm, even between old friends, old lovers. They were Dominic's biggest headaches as a producer. Raising money? No problem, not after his first hit. He had investors lining up to back his shows.

It was always the personalities that took most of his effort, that kept tossing their monkey wrenches into his life. When he really thought about it, he was a baby-sitter, just like Molly, except that his "charges" were old enough to throw real darts.

Dominic lowered his head and concentrated on his now

empty soda can. The problem was, Derek was right. Cynara wasn't sounding her best with this new music. He knew she was always a little slow on the up-take when it came to new melodies, new lyrics, but this was more than that. Sometimes it seemed she couldn't *find* the melodies.

"I'll have the piano tuned," he said when his two stars continued to glare at each other. He could damn near see sparks flying between them in the near dark. "I think Taylor said something about a problem."

"*Au contraire,* my friend. That's not what he said this afternoon." Derek seemed very happy to repeat what the man had said. Dominic gave a moment's thought to handing Derek a quarter, except that wouldn't be necessary. Derek dished the dirt for free. "What he said then was that Cynara here was killing him. Just killing him. I thought I saw a tear in the big guy's eye, but I couldn't be sure."

"Musicians," Cynara said, sniffing. "What do they know?"

"Tell you what," Dominic said, pushing himself away from the porch railing. "Tomorrow's Saturday, and I know I promised everyone a free day, but why don't we all get together around one, just to go over 'If This Is Love,' and the second duet as well. Cynara, you were probably just having an off day."

"I was having a fine day," Cynara said, "until Taylor took it into his head to be such a bully. Besides, I'm having my nails done tomorrow morning. I can't possibly be back here until two, at the earliest."

"Ah, the weekly claw sharpening," Derek said, winking at Dominic. "Wonder who she's planning on scratching. Could it be the new nanny?"

"Who?"

"Nice try, Cynara," Derek said, clapping his hands. "She's young, she's gorgeous, she's *here.*"

"No, she's not. She's in the house somewhere while we're

out here, dying of thirst," Cynara pointed out. "Perhaps she's growing a lime tree?"

Dominic had been wondering much the same thing. Molly had been gone for at least ten minutes. "I'll go see what's keeping her," he said.

He had taken three steps toward the door before it pushed open and Molly appeared, barefoot, carrying a tray.

"Here we go! Would you believe I got lost? No, of course you wouldn't. I certainly wouldn't." She deposited the tray on the white wicker table, then stood up, wiping her hands together. "Actually, I was hiding out in the living room, eavesdropping."

"Very funny," Dominic said, motioning for her to come stand next to him. He might as well not have bothered, because she just sat herself down in the chair beside Cynara's, crossed those long legs again, and immediately became the center of the world. Damn it, how did she do that?

Cynara picked up her glass and took a long drink. "It's what I'd do," she said, looking at Molly. "Eavesdrop. Hear anything interesting?"

"Not a lot, no," Molly said, wrinkling her nose.

"Stick around and do it some more. You will," Cynara told her, lifting her water glass in some sort of toast Dominic knew a mere man would never understand. But it appeared that somehow, Molly and Cynara were bonding.

The thought chilled his blood.

Derek laughed, slapping Dominic on the shoulder. "I feel a sudden need for a codpiece, old sport. Have any lying around?"

"Sorry, no," Dominic said, distracted for a moment as Molly uncrossed her legs, then crossed them again, this time left leg over right. He actually believed he could hear the silken whisper of skin sliding over glorious skin.

"Yeah, me too," Derek said, close to Dominic's ear. "But

the great Cynara hasn't killed her yet, and, for Cynara, that's damn near a declaration of love. Amazing."

Molly looked up and smiled, obviously having heard Derek, but Cynara, always more involved with herself than anyone or anything else in the universe, was busy frowning at her nails.

"Look at this, will you? Two chipped. I look as if I've been gnawed on. This shouldn't happen in a week."

Molly dutifully leaned over and looked at the hand Cynara held out to her. "Pitiful. Who does them?"

Cynara sighed. "Here? Some little blonde who chews gum and tells me about her boyfriend Bluto, or something like that. What can I say? We've only been here for a week. I know positively no one."

"Oh, no. No, no, no, Cynara," Molly said, sitting back, shocked. Dominic knew she was faking all this concern. She had to be faking, didn't she? Women didn't like other women; everyone knew that. But, if she was putting on an act, damn she was good at it. "I've got just the salon for you. Really. And I'm sure I can arrange a trim while you're there. You'll adore Angel. Just let me call first thing tomorrow morning and set it up. How about a seaweed wrap as long as you're there?"

"You could do this? My dear, that would be *très magnifique!*"

"*Certainment!* Angel's a doll. They're all dolls, so very talented. And *très convenable.* You and your great fame are safe in his hands. Oh, and look at this," she said, sticking one leg out in front of her and wiggling her toes. "It's a new color. Have you ever seen a red like that?"

"Let me see," Cynara ordered, and Molly dutifully lifted her leg and set her foot down in the woman's lap. "Oh, my God! That's *gorgeous!*"

If Cynara started to drool, Dominic was going to make a

break for it. Then he looked around and noticed that Derek already had. He turned and followed him out onto the lawn.

He should have stayed where he was.

"Okay, Dom, come clean. Who's the classy dame?"

Dominic raised one expressive eyebrow. "Come clean? Dame? What is it, Derek? You're auditioning for a touring company of *Guys and Dolls?* Next thing I know, you'll be hitching up your pants with your forearms and rolling your shoulders."

"Don't try to change the subject, old friend. Your nanny speaks French. Worse, your nanny speaks Cynara. Quick, tell me the last time you saw Cynara that she wasn't sticking a knife in some other woman's back?"

"Oh, come on, Cynara's not that bad. It's just that she's getting a little old to play the best parts."

"Aren't we all? But back to the nanny. And, much as I hate to be redundant—those legs of hers. My God, if Helen of Troy launched a war with her face, imagine the damage that little lady could do with those legs. Now tell me again that she's the nanny and not Cynara's replacement. Then do even better than that, and make me believe it."

"She's the nanny, Derek," Dominic said, not as shocked as he might be that Derek had taken two and two and made five. Actors, the most paranoid creatures in the world, did this sort of math all the time. Come to think of it, so had he, until he'd learned the truth. "Ask the kids. She works at the day care I parked them at this week. The place is closing for the next two weeks, and Molly agreed to help me out."

"Good thing you're the producer, Dom. You can't write for crap. That's lousy fiction. Nobody—correction—no *body* that looks like that works at some small-time nursery school."

Dominic rubbed at his chest. He wasn't going to convince Derek, not unless he told him the truth. But he'd pretty much promised Molly he wouldn't do that. She didn't want to be

Margaret Applegate, for some reason. And he didn't want to lose her. Correction. He didn't want the kids to lose her, because they liked her.

Right. That was the only reason.

"Okay, okay, I give up," Dominic said, drawing Derek farther from the porch. If he couldn't go with all the truth, he'd go with half of it. "I am worried about Cynara. Taylor called me on my cell earlier, and you're right. He thinks Cynara isn't up to the role."

Derek nodded sagely. "So you brought in the legs. That's why you were gone so long, picking them up at the airport. The legs."

"Would you stop with the legs! I brought Molly home. That's all I'm going to say."

"And you want me to keep quiet, pretend I don't know? So that's it? Cynara's out?"

"No, she's not *out*. I'm just saying I'm aware that we might have a problem."

Derek nodded. "When do we get to hear her?"

"Hear who? I already said, Cynara's going to run through two of the songs again tomorrow. With you, remember?"

Was the evening getting warmer? Dominic slid a finger beneath his collar. He used to lie better than this.

"Not Cynara. Pay attention, Dom. You're a lousy conspirator. I'm talking about Molly. When do we hear her?"

Dominic shoved his hands into his pockets. Okay, he had a good lie now. He knew one would come to him; in this business lying *was* part of the business. *"We* don't. Tony and I do. We don't work by committee, Derek, and Tony's floating in some boat somewhere on his second honeymoon, so nothing happens until he gets back. *If* anything's going to happen. Cynara may still pull it together. Now, let's just keep this between ourselves, all right? Here comes Cynara."

"I don't want her hurt," Derek said quietly, and Dominic

looked at him, because, for Derek, that was one hell of an admission.

"Dom! Your nanny is a doll," she said, going up on tiptoe to kiss his cheek. "She remembered that she has this Angel person's cell number in her purse and called him. It's all set for tomorrow at nine. I can't believe how Molly has been in Virginia for only two weeks, and she already has the cell number of the top stylist in Fairfax. I may steal her from you, Dom, so be warned. Come on, Derek. You need your beauty rest. Good night, Dom."

"Yeah . . . good night, Cynara," Dominic said, watching as his female lead slipped her arm through Derek's and the two of them headed back to the guest house.

He gave a moment's thought to walking the length of the drive to the roadway, just to look for the rabbit hole he must have driven into on his way to Preston Kiddie Kare, but decided against it. Instead, he headed back up the steps to the porch, and Molly.

She had her back to him and was speaking into her cell phone.

"Yes, Angel, thank you. Your private work area would be best. And that other thing? About me? Wonderful! I knew I could trust you not to gossip. I'll see you next week. Oh, I know, I know. How on earth will I muddle through? I'll need the full treatment next week. Uh-huh. Yes. You're an angel, Angel. Toodles to you, too."

She snapped the phone shut, stuck it in her pocket, and turned to face him, her smile wide. "Oh. Hi, there. You eavesdrop, too?"

"If I do, I don't announce it like it's some kind of virtue," Dominic said, slipping into what, up until tonight, he had considered *his* chair. "What was that all about?"

"Oh, nothing. I just called Angel again to thank him for taking Cynara with no notice. And," she said, grinning, "making an appointment for myself, for next Saturday." She spread her arms to indicate her entire body. "You really don't think I do all this by myself, do you?"

"I . . . I hadn't really thought about it," Dominic said, considering covering his nose, which was going to begin growing any moment now. "Won't this Angel person tell Cynara who you are? Or doesn't he know?"

"Oh, he knows. I had my stylist in D.C. arrange things here with Angel before I came to help out Janie. But he's very discreet. He's promised not to give me away." She cocked her head to one side. "Or have you already done that?"

"Good night, Molly," Dominic said, getting to his feet.

Molly pushed him back down before he was halfway there. Just put her hands against his shoulders, and pushed. "I'm sorry," she said, and he wondered if she was sorry for the push, or for questioning him.

"So am I, that I didn't read the fine print on the agreement with Preston Kiddie Kare before today. Now you sit down, Molly."

"Hmm . . . That sounds ominous. And very familiar. Sit down, Molly, and hear the bad news. Sit down, Molly, and explain why you drew that anatomically correct male nude in art class. We were studying still lifes, you understand. Sit down, Molly, and wait here until the floor matron packs your bags and the limousine comes to get you out of our school before we lose our accreditation. Well, you get the drift. Sit down Molly is never good news."

"Sit down, Molly," he repeated.

She sat down, folded her hands in her lap, and instantly she was an awkward schoolgirl, her toes turned inward, her shoulders slumped. It was amazing.

It was acting.

The woman was a menace.

"Cut that out," Dominic said before he could stop himself.

She straightened. Crossed her legs. Picked up her wine cooler and gracefully lifted it to her lips. Threw him a look that would solidify mercury. The penitent schoolgirl was now the woman in charge. "Yes?" she said. "You seem to have a problem, Mr. Longstreet. Would you care to share it?"

It was acting.

The woman was a chameleon.

And she scared the bejezzus out of him.

He looked at her for long moments. "What the hell was my question?" he asked at last.

"I don't think you had one," Molly said, then swallowed down the last of her wine cooler, her long, white throat moving as she drank. He watched every swallow, mesmerized.

"I didn't?" Then he shook himself back to reality. "Yes, I did, damn it. Are you still going to tell me that you're happy playing Molly Applegate, baby-sitter?"

"Probably," she answered smoothly. "Why? What else do you want me to be?"

"Not what, Miss Applegate, but where. We could start with the South Pole."

"The children might take a chill, although they'd probably get a kick out of seeing the penguins."

If Dominic were a volatile man, instead of a calm, cool, collected sort of man, he would be screaming now.

"Look, Molly," he said, trying to gather up his sanity and stuff it back inside his head. "You've met Cynara."

"Ah, good, we're starting with the obvious. Go on."

Dominic rubbed at his burning chest. He had to stop drinking soda; too much carbonation. "Don't interrupt. You've met Cynara. If I were to believe that nonsense you were spouting earlier, you were eavesdropping, which means you heard Derek talking about a problem I'm having with Cynara."

"She's flat. Yes, I heard. But Derek was just being snarky. I mean, I've heard Cynara on the stage. She's marvelous."

"Yes, she is. But not yet, not with this new material. She's really struggling."

"That's too bad."

"Oh, it's more than that," Dominic said, getting to his feet, so he could pace the porch boards. "It took Derek all of ten minutes to decide that I've brought in a replacement."

"Me?"

"That didn't take *you* long. You're even faster than Derek," Dominic said, turning to look down at her. "Now tell me you didn't already think of it before I said anything, and I'll try to believe you."

"I didn't think of it. Lizzie did." Molly stood up, took three steps in his direction. "Let me guess here. You're still not buying that I'm the good samaritan here, are you? I don't know why. It's all so logical."

"No, it's not. If I'm supposed to swallow the idea that you were helping out your cousin—Janie, right?—then the first question my mind comes up with is, why didn't you just hire someone to take her place? You've got the money."

Molly nodded. "That would have been my first thought, too. But Janie had other ideas. I think she thought it would be character building for me, or something like that. Give me a little lesson in real life. I wouldn't go so far as to say that Janie thinks I get everything handed to me on a silver platter, and what isn't handed to me I can just buy. That I'm flighty and need grounding and that I'm a butterfly that flits from place to place as the winds take me, or that it's time I showed a little personal responsibility. But that would be pretty close."

She looked up at Dominic, pulling a face. "Actually, that would be more than pretty close."

"Okay," Dominic said, nodding. "Now, how do I justify having you here, taking care of Tony's kids? You've just about admitted that you don't know the first thing about child care."

Molly grinned. "I know how to dial out for pizza. You don't want me teaching them, Dominic. You want me watching them, keeping them out of your hair for the next two weeks. That, I can do. I'm very good at keeping out of the way of grown-ups who don't want kids around, cluttering up their lives."

"I never said they cluttered—oh, hell. All right, all right, it's settled. You're in charge of the kids. Back to Cynara."

"Yes, we did sort of leave her hanging out there in the ether, didn't we?"

"It won't take her long to start thinking that I've brought in a possible replacement and hidden her—you—here at the house."

"But I don't sing," Molly told him. "I can tap dance," she said, breaking into a quick two-step for a second. "And I've seen *Chicago* three times. In my dreams, I'm Catherine Zeta-Jones. I've even practiced in front of a mirror, and I took dance lessons for a million years. Of course, that was in about a dozen different schools. But I don't sing. Oh, all right, I do sing. But I've never *sung,* if you know what I mean."

"I can't tell you how uninterested I am in amateur song and dance. Just don't sing or dance around here, okay?"

Molly held up one hand. "Actually, I'm lying. I did sing professionally."

"And you *forgot?"*

"It was that month I was a singing, roller-skating carhop at a retro restaurant in California. But I kept getting hit on, so I had to quit."

"Hit on? I can't imagine why," Dominic said, trying to picture Molly in plunging neckline, short skirt, roller skates. The manager must have wept when she quit.

"Yes, well, maybe you can't. But that's my only professional singing or dancing experience. Or acting experience."

No acting experience? What I've been watching just comes

to her naturally? Damn. "All right, all right, subject closed. I just want to make sure you understand that Cynara's pretty fragile right now. And, right now, she sees you as a friend. From friend to enemy takes Cynara about two seconds."

"So stay away," Molly said. "I understand."

"And you're going to listen?"

"No," she said, grinning at him. "She's already asked me to sit in on the rehearsal tomorrow, so that I can tell her that Derek and this Taylor guy are all wet. Her words, not mine."

Dominic felt his fingers drawing into fists. "Why in hell would she do that?"

"Probably because I suggested it. She's so surrounded by judgmental men, you understand, and should have an ally. One with the proper hormones. Good night, Dominic. I have to be a good little nanny now and go check on my charges."

"Wait." He put his hands on her shoulders, acting before he could think.

She rolled those huge blue eyes. "Goodness, Dominic, you are the slave driver, aren't you? It's nearly eleven o'clock."

What was he doing? Why had he grabbed her? Was he really that afraid to watch her walk away from him again? Was his libido that shaky?

"I just wanted to thank you," he said at last. "These two weeks are extremely important to me, but without someone to watch the kids . . ."

"You're welcome. Besides, I'm having fun," Molly said, and stepped closer, to give him a kiss on the cheek.

The hell she would! Dominic turned his head at the last moment, so that her lips connected with his. He felt those lips move, reshape themselves into a smile.

"What?" he said, a breath away from her.

"Nothing." She kissed him again, lightly, her mouth just grazing his. "This is nice."

His eyes still open—he wanted to see her—he kissed her upper lip, then retreated slightly. "No, this is nuts."

She giggled against his mouth, then bit his bottom lip, just nipped it lightly. "As long as we both understand that."

Dominic slid his hands down the bare skin of her arms. "You should go check on the kids."

"Yes, I should," she agreed, then ran the tip of her tongue over his upper lip. "Good night . . . boss."

He dropped his arms to his sides, and she was gone.

Chapter 6

Molly felt . . . delicious.

She exited the bathroom, the steam from her tub wafting into her bedroom on the scent of jasmine, a large, fluffy white towel wrapped around her, the ends tucked over her breasts.

Picking up her silver-backed brush, she sat down at the antique cherry vanity table and smiled as she dragged the smaller white towel from her head to reveal the spikes of copper curls.

She made a cross-eyed face at her reflection, then brushed back her hair, so that it lay sleekly against her head; sophisticated, killer bitchy. And she waited. One . . . two . . . three . . . fo—*pop*. The first curl to break loose flopped down on her forehead, and she tried to blow it back into place.

Too late. Shown the way, more curls made a break for it.

"And don't we just *love* humidity," she said, picking up the brush again, while arming herself with the battery-operated blow-dryer.

As she dried her hair, taming its fullness into its usual thick, slightly swingy cap that hugged the back of her neck, fell in artful disarray over her forehead, and swept forward on the sides to accentuate her high cheekbones, she looked around the room assigned to her.

Definitely a woman's guest room, with the floral wall-paper, the ruffled curtains, the dressing table, plus the lovely variety of toiletries she'd discovered in the bathroom.

Someone had unpacked for her, hanging her dresses and such in a free-standing armoire, while the rest of her clothing had been carefully arranged inside paper-lined drawers. Her shoes were lined up in two rows at the bottom of the armoire (Molly believed only barbarians traveled with less than a dozen pair of shoes).

Her silver-framed photographs were distributed quite well around the room. Her vanity set and perfumes were in place on the vanity table. Even Janie's list of rules had been unpacked and was waiting for her on one of the tables beside the four-poster bed.

She was here. She was settled in. She was staying.

And she felt comfortable.

Molly felt comfortable wherever she was, partly because she was so accustomed to finding herself in the midst of strangers, and partly because, when she moved, she moved everything she loved right along with her. She'd learned to be her own anchor, her own center, because there had never been anything or anyone else she could cling to with any sense of certainty that it or they would be there tomorrow.

Except for Janie and her family. There had always been Janie, would always be Janie.

Molly spent a moment or two wondering if she should call her cousin again, but the news update she'd seen before heading off for her bath had given her most of the answers to questions she'd thought of while she listened to the lengthy, excited, and mostly confusing voice mail message her cousin had left for her on her cell phone.

Janie had done good on her little adventure, more than good. Janie had nailed the story, bless her. And that didn't look like all she'd nailed, Molly thought with a smile, recalling the tall, dark, and definitely not nerdy man standing next to her cousin on the television screen.

It was almost disconcerting. Janie wasn't the one who was supposed to have adventures. That was Molly's job, and she'd gotten really good at it over the years. She was supposed to be having one of those adventures right now.

But this time felt . . . different. She didn't know why.

Slipping into a navy satin sleeveless top and matching tap pants whose price met or exceeded a lot of women's wardrobe budgets for a month, Molly decided that kidding everyone else was fine, but kidding herself was just plain unproductive. She did so know why this time was different.

Dominic Longstreet. Yummy. Tall, blond, handsome, all those good things. Funny, adorably bemused, intelligent, talented. And rich.

Rich was good. Not always good, because some people believed they could never have enough money, so that rich or poor, Molly could never know who liked her for herself, and who chased her for her bank balance.

But Dominic didn't chase. He'd get rid of her if he could, as a matter of fact. Knowing who she was, he'd tell her to take a hike so that he could get on with his work.

This could be depressing, if he hadn't kissed her. If he didn't look at her the way he did.

She'd told Janie to go find herself a summer romance, that it would do her cousin good. And what was good for the cousin was good for the one giving advice.

Molly took the towels into the bathroom and hung them over a rack, so that no one else had to pick up after her. She'd spent enough years following the maids around her parents' many houses, helping them clean up for her parents' guests, most of whom treated their surroundings like their own personal pigpens and the servants as their own personal chattels. Her parents had been just as bad.

Whatever her parents did, Molly made sure not to do. Anything that upset them, she made sure to do.

At first, she'd done it to get their loving attention. Then just to get their attention. Then just to bug the hell out of them, or so she'd told herself.

She refused to be the poor little rich girl who spent decades on a psychiatrist's couch, or took to drugs and alcohol, or treated marriage as a sport, cutting almost yearly notches into her bedpost, to mark the change of husbands . . . or lovers.

When she admitted it, which was seldom, and only to herself, her parents had done her a very large favor, writing that will of theirs. Daring her to marry as an easy way to gain absolute control of her money was just what she'd needed to *not* go racing to the altar. And being forced to seek "gainful employment at least ten months per year" had set her off on a cross-country and even international adventure that had, so far, lasted nearly ten years.

Molly uncapped a bottle of her favorite lotion and rubbed some between her palms before bending to stroke the lotion onto her feet, her legs.

She loved the feel of lotion against her skin.

Loved the caress of silk and satin against her skin.

Loved walking, long-legged, swinging those legs from the hip, her head held high, her shoulders squared.

Loved feeling male and female eyes watching as she passed by—the former admiring, the latter sometimes envious, at least until they figured out that Molly Applegate was about as threatening as a marshmallow knife.

Loved laughter. Loved fun. Loved shocking people, even herself. Loved *life*.

But she hated the dark.

Molly finished applying lotion to her arms, chest, and throat, and replaced the cap on the bottle.

Now what? She wasn't tired, wasn't even close to tired.

She thought about sneaking into Lizzie's room and borrowing the *Shrek* DVD, but didn't want to take the chance of waking the child.

She thought about going down to the kitchens and getting herself some warm milk, but that never worked, and then she'd have to brush her teeth again.

She thought about Dominic Longstreet. Her "inner angel," Molly's name for her conscience or some other, more careful part of herself, or whatever it was, woke up and warned: *No, don't go there. You had your kiss, you had your fun. Now quit. This is not a man to play with and then walk away. This is the kind of man who does his own walking away.*

Then again . . .

"When you get right down to it, Molly, old girl, he's perfect," Molly told herself, slipping her arms into a matching navy blue satin robe that just skimmed her thighs as her "inner angel" slunk back to a corner, familiar with defeat. "We have a few laughs, a nice summer fling, and we both walk away. It's what I want. All I want."

Molly drifted over to the window, and saw her reflection in the glass. "Liar," she told herself while her "inner angel" wept in relief. "This one's dangerous. He could get in. And *nobody* gets in."

She turned away from the window and headed for the television remote control that lay on the night table. She waited until the large screen, revealed when she'd earlier opened the doors of a second, smaller armoire, came to life. Then she walked over to the door and pushed down the switch that turned off the lights, leaving the room lit by the flashing images, the air filled with the theme song of some crime drama series rerun.

She climbed into the bed and plumped up the pillows behind her, prepared to watch the tube until the infomercials came on, at the least . . . and awoke to an earthquake all but shaking her out of bed.

This earthquake, however, had pretty bizarre sound effects:

"Get up, get up, get up!"

"Little Tony, stop bouncing on the bed. She could barf."

"No she won't. Get up, get up, *get up!*"

Molly slowly turned onto her back, pulled the pillow off her head, and blinked. "Are we under attack? Quick, women and children under the wagons."

"Huh?" Little Tony said, no longer bouncing, which was just about the smartest thing he'd done in his young life, because Molly had been entertaining homicidal thoughts no nanny should ever have, unless she was playing lead in some teenage slasher movie.

"Molly? I tried to stop him."

Molly opened one eye, to glare at Lizzie. "Liar."

Lizzie tipped her head to one side. "Well, yeah, but you're not supposed to know that."

"Honey, there's nothing I don't know about being a pest. What time is it?"

"Seven o'clock," Little Tony said helpfully. "Real late."

"Not for someone who fell asleep at three, it isn't," Molly grumbled, throwing back the covers and aiming her legs toward the edge of the bed. "Want to know anything about hair replacements? Just ask me, I know it all."

"Molly, you're mumbling," Lizzie told her. "But, wow, those are neat pajamas. Mom has pajamas sort of like that, but she only wears them when Dad comes home after being away for a while. Do you wear pajamas like that all the time?"

"Only if I don't have silk sheets on the bed. Then I just sleep in the—" She caught herself in time and pushed at her hair, trying to wake up. "What time did you guys say it is?"

"Seven-o-three, now," Little Tony told her, peering at the digital clock on the night table. "I'm hungry."

"Bully for you. Go downstairs and get breakfast, why don't you?"

"Aren't you coming down? You *are* the nanny. Lizzie said so. We dressed ourselves, but now you have to take care of us."

Molly slowly turned her head to glare at Lizzie. "You're enjoying yourself, aren't you, you little monster?"

Lizzie smiled, her lips closed tight over her teeth, her eyebrows raised as she nodded.

"Okay. Okay, okay, okay. I'm the nanny. Little Tony? Go away, I have to get dressed. Lizzie? Stay right here."

"Where am I supposed to go?"

"Didn't you hear Molly? Go downstairs for breakfast, you bozo brain," Lizzie told him, putting her hands on the back of his shoulders and steering him toward the door. "Us women have to talk."

Molly hid a smile as she shuffled, barefoot, toward the bathroom. "Bozo brain? Nice."

"It's a term of affection," Lizzie said, following after Molly, just to have the bathroom door close in her face. "Well, that was rude!" she called through the wood. "It's going to be ninety-three today, in case you're interested. No, don't thank me. I'm just *nice.*"

"I really like that kid," Molly said as she looked at herself in the mirror over the hand-painted sink, running her tongue over her teeth as she idly wondered what had died in her mouth. She blinked, then scrubbed at her mussed hair until Angel's inspired cutting took over and the mop settled itself in its usual style.

She turned on the tap and splashed cold water on her face, the shock to her system not actually jolting her awake, but at least getting her running on more than one cylinder.

Ten minutes later she was washed, brushed, and wearing a moss green Donna Karan V-necked, sleeveless sweater that just nipped her waist and a pair of khaki short-shorts she'd picked up in a boutique in the Bahamas.

She sat down at the vanity table while Lizzie stood and watched, to stroke face lotion over her skin. She followed that with a light tracing of eye shadow and added her favorite mascara. She pulled a small brush from the drawer and used it to tidy her naturally dark eyebrows, brushing upward, just as she'd been taught. A little blusher, some lip gloss, another finger fluffing of her hair, a squirt of her favorite perfume, and she was done.

"That's it?" Lizzie asked, twisting off the top of one of the more than a dozen bottles and tubes arranged in the open drawer. "What about the rest of this stuff?"

"Oh, I don't use that unless I'm going somewhere special, or at night. This is all I need most of the time."

"Man, my mom is going to hate you. But, then, she's old."

"Really? How old?"

"I don't know. Thirty-seven, maybe? Ancient. How old are you?"

"Twenty-eight. I'm only half ancient," Molly said, patting Lizzie's cheek as she got to her feet. "Okay, let's find me some shoes, then go get breakfast, and then we can head out for the grocery store. Did you make a list?"

Lizzie was still reciting from that list as they entered the large kitchen, to see Little Tony already halfway through a stack of blueberry pancakes.

He looked up when he saw them and shifted a mouthful of pancake to his left cheek. "She's coming here for breakfast again. Hurry up and eat so we can get out of here."

"She?" Molly looked to Lizzie for an explanation.

"Bethany White," the girl told her, rolling her eyes. "It couldn't be anyone else. Her mother thinks Bethany should pretend to be friends with us to impress Uncle Dom. Hey, maybe we can poison her."

"Here, here, none of that," Mrs. Jonnie said, placing a fresh, steaming platter of blueberry pancakes in the center of the large wooden table. "I thought it would be nice to invite Miss Bethany up here to be with you children today, since nobody's working."

The housekeeper then shot a quick look at Molly and gave a slight shake of her head that pretty much said, "In a pig's eye I did."

"No way!" Lizzie screeched in protest. "She only comes up here to make trouble. Besides, we're going to the grocery store, and she's not invited."

"So there," Molly finished for her. "I guess you told her, didn't you?"

Lizzie folded her arms across her flat chest. "Darn right, I did."

"And now you can apologize," Molly told her, pulling out a chair and sitting down. "My, don't these pancakes look good."

"I'm not apologizing," Lizzie said, still standing there, being as mulish as any eleven-year-old girl could be. "I didn't say anything about Mrs. Jonnie. I was talking about Bad-breath Bethany."

"Ah, but you screeched at Mrs. Jonnie."

Molly waited. Mrs. Jonnie bit her bottom lip. Little Tony kept right on eating.

"I . . . I didn't mean to yell at Mrs. Jonnie, Molly. I was mad at Bethany for horning in on us."

"Good. Now tell Mrs. Jonnie."

"I'm sorry, Mrs. Jonnie," Lizzie said, looking straight at the housekeeper. "I didn't mean to yell at you."

"That's all right, poppet," Mrs. Jonnie said, easing two pancakes onto a plate and putting it at Lizzie's place. "Here, sit down and eat."

Lizzie said thank you, sat down, spread her napkin neatly in her lap. What a little lady. And then she grinned. "You're not going to take Bethany along with us, are you?"

"You got that in one," Molly said, grinning at her.

"You just wanted me to apologize to Mrs. Jonnie."

"Two in a row. You're good. This is, after all, your outing. Your plan. One of you two would have to invite Bethany in order for her to be included."

"We're not going to do that, right? Unless we should?" Little Tony asked, his green eyes wide; eyes the same color and shape as his sister's but without the spark of mischief Lizzie couldn't hide. Little Tony was a sweetheart, but a follower. And almost painfully fair and honest. *Ah, well,* Molly thought, *at least he won't grow up to be a lawyer.*

"No, Little Tony, we are *not* going to—oh, great, here she comes."

Molly turned her head toward the back door, the one Lizzie was glaring at, just as it opened with the sort of flourish that would normally be followed by the appearance of a Rayban-clad Secret Service agent preceding the president.

But this was no Secret Service agent, although the Raybans were in place.

Bethany White was small for thirteen, but definitely budding. Her ebony curls tumbled around a heart-shaped face and what looked to be violet eyes. Her lips were full and red, her skin flawless ivory. She was a young Elizabeth Taylor in *National Velvet,* Molly, the sleepless viewer of millions of late night movies, decided.

"Oh, the brats are here," Bethany announced in a baby-doll high voice that still had a purr to it.

"Miss Bethany," Mrs. Jonnie said quickly. "We're having blueberry pancakes this morning."

"They are. *I'll* have a poached egg on low-fat whole wheat toast," the child pronounced, smoothing her manicured

hands down her scoop-necked white knit shirt and over her short flowered skort as she walked completely around the table, moving her gaze from Little Tony, to Lizzie, and coming in for a landing on Molly. "Mama Billie told me *all* about you. You're the nanny. Yeah, *right.*"

The young Elizabeth Taylor was gone, replaced by Mata Hari.

"Good morning, Bethany," Molly said, turning her head to say hello. "I'm Molly Applegate. How delightful to meet you."

"You bet it is," Bethany said, throwing back her head. "Now get up, that's my chair."

Okay, goodbye Mata Hari, hello Patton in Italy.

"There's another chair over there," Molly said and then turned back to her pancakes, which were really quite good. "I'm willing to bet your cute little behind will fit there just fine."

Lizzie snickered into her orange juice.

"You can't talk to me that way!" Bethany protested, standing her ground.

"Really?" Molly said, still concentrating on her breakfast. "Who did, then?"

"What . . . What do you mean, who did? *You* did. And I'm going to tell Mama Billie, and she's going to have your job!"

Molly shrugged her shoulders. "Hey, if she wants to be a nanny, more power to her."

Lizzie lost it, snorting orange juice out her nose.

Molly calmly handed her a napkin.

"You'll all be sorry! I'm *telling!*" Bethany White stomped out of the kitchen, the screen door slamming behind her.

Mrs. Jonnie said, "Well, I never. Make her a poached egg, will I, just as if I'm a waitress in a diner and she can order whatever she likes? Nobody will do it at the guest house, and I'm not going to do it up here."

Little Tony asked if he could have Bethany's pancakes.

"That was *so* majorly cool," Lizzie said, dabbing at the orange juice on her shirt.

"No, that was *so* majorly a brat," Molly said, earning herself a heartfelt "You go, girl!" from Mrs. Jonnie. "But now she's gone, and we never talk about anyone behind her back when we can do it so well to her face, right? Little Tony, are you about done?"

Lizzie ran off to change into a clean T-shirt, and five minutes later, with Mrs. Jonnie's shopping list tucked into her purse, the Gang of Three piled into Molly's Mercedes.

"You know," Lizzie said, strapping herself into the front seat, "you're pretty smart, Molly."

"How so?" Molly asked, smoothly putting the car into Drive and heading around the large paved circle, to head for the highway.

"Because you didn't yell, or try to make Bethany sit down and eat breakfast, or even just ignore what a brat she is, which is what Uncle Dom said I should do. You just talked to her, your voice all sweet and gooey, and drove her nuts. I always yell, and then I'm the one who gets into trouble."

Molly grinned at her pupil. "Ah, grasshopper, how quickly you learn. Bethany White doesn't get herself into trouble; she's a carrier."

"Huh?"

"Have you studied Typhoid Mary in school yet? No, I suppose not. Maybe they don't even say Typhoid Mary anymore, but just give you the facts. Okay, I'll explain. Typhoid is a disease that before it could be controlled, spread to lots of people. You with me so far?"

"Hanging on your every word," Lizzie said, rolling her eyes. Clearly she wasn't in the mood for a health lesson this Saturday morning.

"I'll ignore that," Molly said, turning onto the highway.

"Anyway, lots of people got sick, but some didn't. I guess one of these people was named Mary—I'm sort of fuzzy on the specifics."

"That's a relief," Lizzie said, grinning. "Okay, okay, I'll be quiet now."

"Thank you. These people who didn't get sick turned out to be carriers of the disease, special cases who didn't get sick, but who carried around the bug or virus or whatever typhoid is, and *gave* it to everyone else. Carriers. Get it now?"

Lizzie chewed on her new information for the time it took them to reach the shopping center Molly remembered seeing on their way to the compound, then said, "Okay, I understand now. Bethany does her big Miss Here I Am, and I do something stupid, or yell, or something, and she gets away with it while everyone gets mad at me? She *carries* trouble around with her and gives it to everybody else. Is that it?"

"Exactly. So, unless you know how to handle her, she gets you into trouble, while she comes off smelling like a rose."

"Roses make me sneeze," Little Tony offered from the back seat, then went back to his hand-held computer game.

"But what if it doesn't work?" Lizzie asked. "What if she just sticks around and drives me crazy?"

"She won't. Oh, maybe at first she will, but when she figures out that she's not scoring points anymore, she'll either begin to behave, or go away and find someone else to drive crazy."

"Good. Maybe she'll pick Uncle Dom, and he'll fire her sorry ass . . . I mean, her cute little backside."

"There you go," Molly said, the lesson completed as she was slipping the Mercedes into a spot just vacated near the facade sporting the word *groceries*.

They got out of the car, and Lizzie grabbed a huge metal shopping cart from a long line of carts while Molly blithely walked straight past it and into the store.

She stopped, confused, and looked around at the sheer magnitude of the place. People, everywhere. Aisle after aisle of merchandise. And not a bit of food in sight. "Where are we?"

Lizzie told her, and then explained that superstores like this one carried almost anything, from clothing to school supplies, to pots and pans, to toys, to television sets and linens. "And food. The food's back there," she ended, pointing to her right to indicate an area a good football field's length away from where they stood.

But between the front doors and the grocery section of the store lay . . . paradise.

Molly looked into a cart being pushed past them by a young woman, a small child strapped into a special seat in the cart. She saw a package of diapers, a bag of dog food, a pair of sneakers, a roll of wrapping paper, a big, blue plastic ball, a pretty red candle. . . .

"I can't believe this place," she said, trying to take it all in.

Molly bought food (mostly prepared food) at corner grocery stores. When she shopped. Mostly, she ate out, and she would have to be given a couple of hints before she could locate the pantry in her own kitchen in the only house that had belonged to her parents that she hadn't ordered sold upon their deaths—so many places they'd been, to get away from her. She frequented boutiques or used a personal shopping service for everything else.

She hadn't even realized there *was* an "everything else." She'd always sort of assumed that "everything else" was just there. You didn't have to actually go out and buy it yourself.

Her childhood home, in Connecticut, was always fully staffed and ready for her. When she traveled, either to work or to play, she stayed in five-star hotels, working for close to minimum wage, then returning to her seven-hundred-dollar-a-night suite at the end of the work day. It was just one of the many things about Molly's life that drove Janie nuts. . . .

Molly sighed. She'd been so *deprived*. There was an entire world here that she didn't know existed. And the *prices!* You could buy a garden hose for five dollars? Who knew?

Molly grinned. "Little Tony," she said, rubbing her palms together, "go get us another cart, please. *This* is going to be fun!"

Chapter 7

Dominic stood at the window of his private study in the small building beside the theater, looking on as Molly and the kids carried bags into the kitchen of the main house.

They were also laughing, sort of skipping along, even under the weight of some very large plastic bags, and he was suddenly feeling like some lonely old man who watched from windows while life went on around him.

They tripped out of the kitchen, heading for the trunk of the Mercedes again, and he watched as they pulled out more bags. Even the backseat was filled with bags; Little Tony had been half buried beneath them. Mrs. Jonnie had told him earlier that the trio had gone grocery shopping.

Must have been one hell of a sale on peanut butter and grape jelly, he thought with a shake of his head, before turning back to answer the phone.

The call was on his private line, the one only a very few people knew. Too many, actually. It was time he changed the number again.

"Longstreet," he said, picking up the cordless phone as he dropped into the large leather chair behind his desk.

"Hey, Dom! You're in the office?"

Dominic winced. Busted. "Yeah. Hi, Tony. I was just catching up on a few things. How did you track me down?"

"Easily. Mrs. Jonnie is a lousy liar. You're not supposed to be in the office."

"And you're not supposed to be calling me. You're supposed to be smoothing suntan lotion on Elizabeth's back and whispering sweet obscenties into her ear. Wasn't that the plan?"

"It was, until she saw the shops on this island we're on now. I'd tell you the name of the place, but I don't know it. I just know that Elizabeth has learned to say 'Do you take American Express?' in Greek."

Dominic smiled. "Lucky you."

"I am, actually. And so are you, because I said no when Elizabeth tried to talk me into an extra week. Say thank you, Tony."

Dominic opened his mouth to say exactly that, and then stopped himself. Three weeks with Molly strutting around the place in those short shorts instead of two? Would she stay if he said he needed her? Did he need her?

"Was she upset when you turned her down?" he heard himself ask, hoping he wasn't hitting too hard on the brotherly concern. "I mean, I know you said three weeks, but if Elizabeth has her heart set on a month, then what can I tell you?"

"You can tell me the name of the tranquilizer you're on, if you're actually volunteering to be in charge of Lizzie and Little Tony for an extra week."

"Good point. But just so you know that it's all right with me. I mean," he hesitated, cleared his throat, "that is, if Elizabeth asks again."

There was a short silence before Tony said, "You've

buried them in the south pasture, haven't you? Sent them to some boot camp in Arizona? Super-glued them to their beds?"

Dominic planted his feet on the desk as he leaned back in his chair. "May I remind you that these are *your* children we're talking about?"

"My point exactly."

Dominic chuckled, and swung his legs down, stood up. "To tell you the truth, I did get some help with them," Dominic said, walking back over to the window, to see what Molly was up to now. "For Lizzie's sake, you know. I thought she might need a woman around."

There was a long silence, followed by, "You imported a bimbo, didn't you? Damn it, Dom, those are my *kids!*"

"Don't be a jerk, Tony. I did not import a bimbo. I don't even date bimbos. Taylor, now *he* dates bimbos."

"True. I overreacted. But you're supposed to be with the kids. Not throw them off on some hired help."

Molly dashed past on the lawn, being chased by Little Tony and Lizzie, all of them heading in the direction of the stables, and all of them carrying absolutely *huge* plastic bags. She was eating up the ground with those long legs, and her free and easy laughter carried up to his window.

"Molly's really good with them, Tony. More of a pal, you know? They . . . They play together."

"Oh, you hired some teenager? All right, that's okay, I guess. Even Elizabeth knows you can't be with them all day. I mean, they're ours, they're cute, but three weeks of them, full time? So everything's under control?"

"Sure," Dominic said, opening the window and sticking his head out, trying to see around the corner of the office, to the stables. "Couldn't be better."

"And you're not working?"

Dom pulled his head back into the office and returned to

his desk. "I'm not working. You were right, I did need a vacation."

"You did, Dom, you really did. I know you think you play hard, but that's the problem. You do everything *hard*. You don't know how to relax, do nothing, just go with the flow. Elizabeth bet me five bucks you'd talk Taylor into having rehearsals at the theater while we're gone."

"Did she really?" Dominic said, looking at his watch. Eleven o'clock. They weren't going to run through the songs until two. He could probably make a couple of calls, most especially to Taylor in New York, and maybe write down a few ideas he'd had about set design. "Tell her she owes you five bucks."

"Well, good, bro. You know, I am worried about you. I let Elizabeth do the overt nagging, but I'm still worried about you. You chew antacids like candy. You're heading for an early heart attack. You have to learn to slow down and enjoy what we've got. Remember Sid? Sid worked the way you do. Right up until the five bypasses before he was fifty. Now, granted, he was already on his fifth marriage, too, and snorting something up his nose, but . . ."

Dominic was no longer listening. Holding the phone with one hand, and grasping a sketch of the set design for the opening number, he stepped to the window yet again, following the sound of laughter.

Little Tony was running across the grass, looking behind him as he ran. What was that in his arms? It was big, it was Day-Glo yellow and blue and green, and it was plastic. He stopped, pumped at the thing, then turned and shot it. A *geyser* erupted from the front of the object.

A water gun? That was a water gun? Damn. It was the *biggest* water gun Dominic had ever seen.

Except for the pink and yellow one Lizzie carried as she rounded the corner, shooting a stream of water at Little Tony that had to be traveling at least thirty feet.

"You're it!" Lizzie called out in triumph. "Now go get Molly."

Molly?

Dominic murmured "uh-huh"s into the phone to his brother while looking for Molly.

And there she was, almost directly below his window, sneaking up on the kids.

She had a water gun—cannon—whatever. She had some sort of power pack strapped on her back, fat plastic tubes that he was pretty sure also held water. She had a sweatband around her head. It was Day-Glo pink. She had an unholy grin on her face that told him she was on the attack as she crept along in her bare feet.

Dominic stepped back from the window. "Tony?" he asked, interrupting his brother in the middle of describing some-body's debilitating stroke, suffered while holding one of his infamous twelve-hour rehearsals. "Do you remember our water pistols?"

"What? What did you say? I'm talking about Harvey Gooding's stroke at the unheard-of international calling cost of at least a zillion dollars a minute, and you're asking me about water pistols?"

"Yeah," Dominic said, dropping the set design sheet to the desktop and starting to loosen his tie. Why the hell had he worn a tie today? It was Saturday, for crying out loud. "We had those little guns with the plastic stoppers in them, remem-ber? Mine was orange. We'd squirt each other a couple of times and then have to call time out and stop and fill them again from the garden hose. We spent more damn time filling them and searching for those little plastic plugs than we did shoot-ing them."

"Okay, listen to me. Are you sitting down? Sit down, Dom. Maybe put your head between your knees."

Dominic pulled the phone from his ear and stared at it, then kicked off his loafers. "Tony?" he said, putting the phone on Speaker so he could strip off his socks and roll up his slacks. "Look, I've gotta go. Little Tony . . . Your kid wants to go horseback riding. Okay? Have a great time, kiss Elizabeth for me, do the rest for you, and I'll see you back here in a couple of weeks."

He pressed the button that disconnected him from his brother's voice and checked the scene outside the window once more as he grabbed his tie and tightened the Windsor knot around his forehead, so that the ends of the tie hung down over his left ear. Rambo, the Ralph Lauren Edition.

Lizzie was pressed against the tree to his left, a good two hundred feet away.

Where was Molly? He narrowed his eyelids and scanned the area. Okay, Molly at eleven o'clock, behind the Mercedes.

Now all he needed was Little Tony. He most definitely needed Little Tony.

Dominic exited the office, the door facing the theater, so that he was out of sight of Molly and the kids, and moved to his right, to the end of the building.

He stopped, then slowly leaned his head forward, around the corner. Sure enough, there was Little Tony, his water cannon pointed toward the lawn as he backed up, using his shoulder to feel the wall as he retreated.

"I'll take that," Dominic said, putting out a hand and grabbing the water cannon. "The women have you outnumbered, sport. Time to call in the reinforcements."

"Uncle Dom?" Little Tony looked up at his uncle, blinking.

"Just call me Rambo," Dominic corrected, ruffling the boy's hair. "Now, you stay here. And not a word, okay? But first, show me how to work this thing."

"You're going to squirt Lizzie?" Little Tony asked, clearly hopeful.

Dominic nodded, Little Tony showed him how to "pump for power," and he moved off. He'd squirt Lizzie. Sure. Once he'd gotten Molly.

Slowly, stealthily, bent nearly in half, the water cannon tucked into his gut, Dominic made his way along the side of the house.

The Mercedes was about thirty yards away, on the drive. Little Tony said this sucker could shoot fifty feet. How many feet were there in thirty yards? Thirty yards, divided by—no, *times* three feet in a yard, and you get—"Damn it!"

Dominic nearly dropped the water cannon to protect himself from the stream of ice-cold water that hit him square in the face as he rounded the corner of the building.

He blinked, shook his head, and saw Lizzie standing in front of him, pumping her water cannon for another shot.

"My turn, Sergeant! There'll be a medal in this for you once we're back at headquarters. Now fall back and take cover behind the lines."

Dominic turned at the sound of Molly's voice, and the next thing he knew he was spitting out water again.

His water cannon was fully pumped, but he was shooting blindly in the direction of the water coming at him in a steady stream. So he held his fire to conserve his "ammunition," but kept advancing, his body half turned away, his shoulders hunched.

Molly seemed to sense what he was doing and began to back up, still firing.

"You like getting a bath, huh?" she shouted, pumping the cannon again. "Come on, big boy, you don't scare me!"

After the shouts, the bravado, she then turned and ran, and Dominic took off after her, grinning so hard he was pretty sure he looked like a homicidal maniac.

"Go get her, Uncle Dom! Soak her!" Lizzie shouted, clearly

a woman who chose sides by aligning herself with whoever looked like the winner of the moment.

Watching Molly run, long-legged and barefoot, was all the impetus Dominic needed to stay to a pace that would keep her within range, but not overtake her too quickly.

Lizzie was running too, which meant that Little Tony was running, unarmed, but trying to remedy that by yanking on Lizzie's water cannon. Molly ran past the Mercedes and cut to her left, heading downhill across the grass, toward the guest house, never looking back, never slowing down.

"Uncle Dom! Don't let her get to the porch!" Little Tony yelled. "That's home base. You can't squirt her there!"

Dominic picked up his pace, leaving Lizzie and Little Tony to follow along as quickly as they could.

"Shoot her now, Uncle Dom, shoot her now!" Lizzie yelled. "You're close enough!"

Still running, and with Molly only yards from the safety of "home base," Dominic stopped, dropped (he watched a lot of war movies), and opened fire . . . just a moment too late to realize that Molly wasn't heading for the porch. She'd already cut to her left again, away from home base.

Which left a thirty-foot stream of cold hose water shooting directly at the porch just as Bethany White, probably disturbed by all the shouts, opened the front door and stepped out onto the boards.

"Oh, cripes," Dominic said, getting to his feet as Bethany stood there in her frilly white blouse and little skirt, dripping water from her suddenly straight hair to her pristine white sneakers. She couldn't be any wetter if he'd tossed an entire bucket of water at her.

Bethany just stood there for several moments, blinking rapidly and gulping air, her arms at her sides, before Dominic saw her take a deep breath and, in a voice that could carry to the last row of the cheap seats, scream, *"Mama Billie!"* as she sloshed back inside the guest house.

"Oh, boy, now you're in trouble, Uncle Dom," Little Tony said commiseratingly, coming up to stand beside Dominic. "She's telling on you."

"Yeah. I'm busted." Dominic felt eight years old again. And he liked the feeling.

"Nice shot, Uncle Dom," Lizzie said as she approached, her water cannon hoisted up to rest on her shoulder. "But you're a dead man."

Dominic looked down at his niece. Soaking wet, but with her eyes nearly dancing in her head, her grin wide and childish and free. "Well, if I'm dead anyway . . . ," he said, and picked up his water cannon, pumping it.

Lizzie reacted quickly, lowering her water cannon and pumping it furiously. But she wasn't quick enough. Dominic got her good as she squealed and laughed, and then he took off to find Molly, who'd disappeared, probably to reload at the hose at the stables.

Fools rush in, he told himself, moving surreptitiously from tree to tree, building corner to building corner, as he circled around toward the stables.

Finally, running out of cover, he stepped from behind the last tree trunk, then quickly dropped to his knees and dove for the ground behind a water trough just as a round, white missile flashed by his head.

"What the—" He turned himself around and belly crawled to the edge of the water trough in time to see another round, white missile shoot past, landing just beside him.

He picked it up. A plastic baseball?

He heard the "ping" of some mechanism, and another ball went whizzing past.

"I'm not afraid of no steenking plastic baseball," he yelled, standing up, exposing his body to the baseball that bounced harmlessly off his chest.

Molly squealed and abandoned the toy pitching machine, dropping back to what appeared to be her next line of defense: a large blue and yellow monstrosity that looked an awful lot like a cartoon version of an old-fashioned gattling gun John Wayne would have been ashamed to use.

Soft-tipped foam darts bounced off him as he held up his arms to protect himself.

"You're not playing fair!" Molly yelled, loosing the remainder of her ammunition at him. "That's cheating! You're dead. I've killed you ten times, at least. Come on, Dominic, I won. Lay down and die the way you're supposed to!"

"Nah, nah! You missed me!" he yelled at her as the last Styrofoam missile landed wide, and she squealed, picked up the water cannon again, and pumped it with all her might.

"So?" he said, still advancing. "What are you waiting for? Shoot me."

She stood there, feet only lightly planted, knees bent, as if ready to spring either right or left. "I don't have to. You're dead."

"And you're out of water, aren't you?"

She made a face at him and pumped again. He'd noticed that she was dry as a bone; nobody had squirted her yet.

That lapse could be remedied.

He reached up to adjust the tie, which had fallen over one eye, and said, "Gee. Maybe I'm out of water, too. Tell me, Molly, do you feel lucky?"

She chanced a quick look at his water cannon. Oh, yeah, she was out of water, all right. She'd dropped back to the stable, leading him on, because she had these other toys set up here. But she hadn't had time to unstrap those plastic tubes from her back and reload.

"You're out of water?" Molly asked, relaxing her body slightly, and dropping her arms to her sides. "Then it's a draw."

"Nope," Dominic said, and opened fire.

Molly squealed, holding up her hands as the water cannon did its job, soaking her from head to foot. She danced in a circle, and he kept firing. She crossed her arms over her chest, and he kept firing.

Molly squealed again. He held the cannon low against his hip and kept firing.

Sigmund Freud would have had a field day with the whole scene, Dominic thought, and kept firing.

At last the water stream grew shorter, weaker, and he lowered the toy. "All cooled off now?"

It wasn't the greatest line, but if he'd asked her if she wanted to share a cigarette, she'd have every reason in the world to leave and never look back.

Molly bent her head, then pushed her hands over her dripping hair, so that it all slicked back from her face as she looked at him.

As he looked at her.

Looked at the way her thin moss green and very wet sweater clung to her breasts. Defined her breasts . . . and showed him clearly that, yes, she was definitely cooled off now.

"Uncle Dom! Uncle Dom! Bethany's mom wants you at the guest house. Right now!"

Dominic quickly looked over his shoulder, to see Little Tony racing down the hill toward them, the happy bearer of bad news. He dropped the cannon and fumbled with the buttons of his wet shirt, finally just ripping them off so that he could toss the shirt to Molly. "Here. Put that on."

Molly caught the shirt, then looked down at herself. "Oh,

boy, he's too young for this," she said, bunching up the shirt and holding it in front of her.

"I'm not," Dominic heard himself say, only realizing that he hadn't said it quietly enough when Molly began to laugh.

Chapter 8

Molly stepped from the bathroom, still rubbing her wet head with a hand towel, to see Dominic sitting at his ease in the chair in front of the fireplace.

"I knocked, but you didn't answer," he told her. "Do you mind?"

"Not if you don't, no." This was moving fast. Maybe too fast? Especially the part where her heart lifted just at the sight of the man.

"No. I don't think I do."

She looked at him sitting there, his blond hair still darkly damp, his clothing much more casual now—khaki slacks and a black silk knit pullover—his brown eyes alive with mischief and, perhaps, appreciation. Molly, who had spent the first eighteen years of her life being pretty much invisible to her parents, liked being appreciated.

"And aren't we both lucky that I took a change of clothing with me into the bathroom?" she said, sitting down at the vanity table.

"Oh, I don't know, Molly. Depends on how you look at it," he said, grinning at her.

She pretended to ignore that remark, instead quickly holding up the pale yellow towel. "See this? Look—it's Martha Stewart."

"The woman should sue. It doesn't look a thing like her."

"Funny. I mean it's a Martha Stewart towel. I found it at the store today and bought it. I thought maybe she might need a little help after all those problems."

"One towel. That will probably make all the difference for her. You bought those toys, too, didn't you? I started reading out the kids for going to their house to get them after being told they have to stay away from the place with their parents gone, and they told me those are your toys."

Molly folded the towel several times and set it on the vanity top. "I'm going to give everything to them as gifts, before I leave. Except my soaker gun. I believe I've grown emotionally attached to it."

"The kids also said you bought almost everything in the entire store."

"Were you forced to use thumbscrews, or did they volunteer all this information? Never mind." She leaned closer to the mirror, wrinkled up her nose, which was a little shiny, then decided she didn't care if that shine could be used as a lighthouse beacon. "I didn't buy everything. Nobody could do that. But it was wonderful. You can buy *anything* in that store. Food, toys, clothing . . . garden hoses."

"You bought a garden hose?"

She sprayed herself with cologne, her chin lifted so the cool mist settled on her shoulders and chest. "No. But I could have if I wanted to. Isn't America great?"

"You're scaring me here, Molly. I thought Neiman Marcus would be more your stomping grounds."

"And you'd think right. But this was so much fun. And

you know we had a lot of packages. You saw us unloading the car, which we did without your help, as I recall," Molly said, pulling a comb through her hair.

"You saw me?"

Molly opened a drawer and pulled out a plastic diffuser, attaching it to the handheld hair dryer. "Saw you seeing us? Yes, I did. But you walked away for a while and missed us taking some of the bags down to the stables. I, however, did not miss seeing you wrapping your tie around your head and heading for the door. It's a big window, you know. Did you have fun?"

"Yes, I had fun," he said, shaking his head. "I'm paying for it, having to invite Bethany and Billie to Sunday dinner, but I did have fun."

He hesitated a moment, then said, with all the enthusiasm of a prepubescent boy, "Did you see her? Man, I got her good."

Molly grinned. "You're proud of that?"

"No, I'm not proud of that. Oh, okay, I'm proud of it. That's probably the first time that kid has been treated like a kid. I feel a little sorry for her."

"So do I," Molly said, picking up her hair dryer as she stood up, her back to him, her legs slightly spread. "That child would probably be a lot happier if she couldn't sing and dance, although I have a feeling her Mama Billie wouldn't be so thrilled. Now excuse me for a few moments, I'm going under," she ended before easily bending just about in half at the waist and turning on the hair dryer.

She could still see Dominic, looking at him from beneath the hem of her sundress. He was upside down, but she could still see him, and he was looking straight at her, his expression sort of puzzled, sort of intrigued, sort of amused.

He was really cute, when he wasn't looking so serious. And, with that tie around his head, and his slacks rolled up, he'd even looked a little silly. He had fun like a man who didn't have much fun anymore, but still remembered how to do it.

Because there was a huge difference between skiing in Vail or riding horseback in Virginia, or whatever else he did for "fun" these days, and just plain cutting loose and being a kid again. No one was freer than a kid, no one indulged themselves as completely as a kid, and no one let it all hang out better than a kid.

She switched off the hair dryer and lifted her head, shaking it so that her hair fell into its natural soft, corkscrew curls. She was in a natural curls, shiny nose mood, for some reason. "There," she said, applying some lip gloss before smoothing down her robin's egg blue sundress that just skimmed her breasts and hips, a deceptively simple dress that only a great designer could fashion. "What's next?"

"I have no idea," Dominic said, also getting to his feet. "You really don't care that I'm in here?"

Molly shook her head, and her curls bounced. She felt young and carefree. Maybe this was her waif mode, she wasn't sure. "Nope. Should I be worried or something?"

He closed the space between them and put his hands on her bare arms. "I think so, yes. I like your hair that way. Tumbled."

"Oh, boy. Is this where I'm supposed to say, Dominic, please, we don't know each other that well?"

"Probably. But if you don't mind, I'd rather we skipped that part, to tell you the truth. You know I'm attracted to you, right?"

Molly smiled. "I'm sort of getting that idea, yes."

"Why? Because everyone is attracted to you? I guess you're relatively used to that."

"No, you jerk," she said, running her fingertips down his lean cheek. "Well, yes, all right, I am relatively used to that. But I'm not always attracted *back*."

He lowered his head toward hers. "But you are, this time?"

"Oh, yeah," Molly breathed on a sigh, looking into his soulful brown eyes. "You could say that."

His grin was rather lopsided, and adorably insecure in a man who could raise millions of dollars with just a handshake. He pressed a kiss against her throat, just below her ear, then whispered, "So? What are we going to do about this?"

Molly eased her body against his, feeling the kick of arousal that had claimed her much too seldomly in her twenty-eight years. She was remarkably inexperienced, as a matter of fact, having thought herself in love only once, in high school, and in lust only twice since then. "Well . . . ," she said, as he nibbled at her ear, "I suppose we could *explore* that attraction, as long as we both know it won't go anywhere."

There, she'd said it. This was when he'd either look at her in disappointment, or grin at her in relief. Disappointment that, no, she wasn't the marrying kind, or relief that she recognized a fling when it was offered to her, wouldn't be clingy while it was running hot, and wouldn't be messy and weepy once it was over.

Dominic edged slightly away from her, once more looking down into her face. He didn't look disappointed. Then again, he didn't look relieved, either.

He looked . . . determined. Yes, that was it. Determined. But determined to do what?

She might have asked, but he was kissing her now, and Molly was too caught up in that kiss to play Twenty Questions. She cupped both hands against his cheeks as his hands ran down her sides, began moving up again, toward her breasts.

He tasted so good. His tongue teased hers, their mouths melding together.

Molly moved her hands, to press her palms against his chest, to feel his strong heartbeat beneath her fingers.

This was magic. This was romance. His heat, his hunger, her willingness to give as good as she got. Two equals, standing toe-to-toe, taking from each other. Giving back.

It didn't matter that she'd known him for less than twenty-four hours. She'd known of him, knew his reputation, his achievements, his genius.

But did any of that really matter? Molly didn't think it did. She'd been attracted since the first time he'd glared at her in anger and frustration. It was one of those chemical things, she supposed. An animal attraction thing. Whatever it was, he obviously felt it, too.

And that was enough.

Molly felt herself being backed toward the bed and didn't fight it, didn't try to play coy. She was too busy holding on to him, learning him. Too busy enjoying wave after wave of sensation as his hands learned her.

"Knock, knock, knock! See? You knocked, Molly, so now we're—whoa!"

Molly had somehow disengaged from Dominic's arms at the very first sound of Lizzie's voice, so that by the time the kid actually opened the door, she and Dominic were standing a good five feet apart, Dominic with his back to the door.

"What's up, kiddo?" Molly asked, pretending to rub at an itch just below her nose . . . because she had a feeling her mouth might be a little red, a little swollen. "Is it already time for lunch? I know I'm hungry."

She thought she heard a low, strangled moan from Dominic at that last statement, but she wasn't sure.

Little Tony ran into the room, slamming into Lizzie, who had stopped dead, her hand still on the doorknob. "What's the matter?" he asked, looking at his sister. "Doesn't Molly want peanut butter and jelly? Oh, hi, Uncle Dom. Are you going to eat with us, too?"

Molly waited for Dominic to turn around, but he didn't.

He walked to the window and looked out, as if he'd never seen the grounds from this particular vantage point before today.

"No, Little Tony, you just go ahead. I . . . I was just here asking Molly if she was still coming to rehearsal at two."

"Sure you were," Lizzie said, rolling her eyes. "Come on, Little Tony, let's go. I don't think Molly's going to be playing with us anymore."

"That's not true," Molly said, instantly understanding where Lizzie was heading, because she'd already been there herself, many times. Too many times. "I'll be downstairs in ten minutes, tops, and we'll have those sandwiches. And then you guys can introduce me to the horses, okay? We bought the carrots, remember?"

"Already washed baby carrots, I remember. Gourmet carrots." But Lizzie looked skeptical, which was a pretty good trick for an eleven-year-old. "And you'll skip rehearsal?"

Dominic finally turned away from the window (Molly hid a smile, thinking maybe she was even more potent than she thought she was if it had taken him that long to cool down). "No, Molly's still sitting in on the run-through. But if you want, you can come, too."

Molly bit her bottom lip as Lizzie's green eyes all but popped out of her head. "You're going to let me in? Last time, you said you'd boil me in oil if I ever tried to get into the theater again while you guys were working. Gee, Molly, whatever you're doing to Uncle Dom, keep on doing it."

Molly held her breath until the door closed behind the two children, then fell onto the bed, laughing, clutching her sides as she *howled*.

"That wasn't all that funny," Dominic said, flopping down next to her. "Do you think she knew what she meant when she said that?"

"God, I hope not," Molly said, sobering. She rolled onto

her stomach and propped her chin in her hands as she looked at Dominic. "What year do schools around here start sex-ed classes, anyway?"

"You really want to discuss that?"

"No, not really," Molly said, rolling over again and leaving the bed before her sundress wrinkled enough to clue in Mrs. Jonnie as to what had been happening—had almost happened—up in Molly's bedroom. "But we could discuss Little Tony for a minute. Poor kid."

"What do you mean, 'poor kid'?" Dominic asked, still lying stretched out on the bed, and looking more deliciously appealing than a triple fudge sundae. "He's a good kid."

"Which does *not* explain why you punish the child by calling him Little Tony," Molly said, bending over to peer into the vanity table mirror and fluff at her hair, check her lip gloss.

"It is lame, isn't it? But my brother is Tony to us and Anthony to anyone outside the family, so calling Little Tony either Anthony or Tony would be confusing, and Junior was out of the question. So, my brother ended up Big Tony, and the kid Little Tony."

"Why not Little Anthony?" Molly grimaced. "Oh, wait, you're a musical family. Little Anthony and the Imperials, right?"

"Right. You remember that group?"

"I love the oldies. 'Tears On My Pillow.' 'Hurt So Bad.' Oh, and 'Shimmy, Shimmy, Koko-Bop.' I love that one. Of course, mostly I hear just snippets, on late-night TV commercials."

"You watch late-night television? When do you find the time?"

"After midnight," Molly said, pasting a wide smile on her face. "So, clearly you couldn't call him Little Anthony, not without someone, somewhere breaking into song. But Little

Tony is really bad. What happens if he grows taller than his father? Then will they be Old Tony and Young Tony?"

"Good point, and I don't think Tony thought about that one. At least not the Old Tony part. Do you have any suggestions?"

"I do. Ask Little Tony."

"All right, fair enough," Dominic said, sliding off the bed. "Let's do that."

"Right now? We're having lunch now. Peanut butter and jelly sandwiches, remember?"

Dominic opened the door to the hallway and made a sweeping motion with his arm, indicating that Molly should precede him into the hallway.

She quickly slipped on her sandals and did just that, saying as they headed for the stairs, "You won't be able to keep this up, you know. I mean, it's fun for a while, but it isn't your life."

"What isn't my life?"

"Water battles, peanut butter and jelly sandwiches. They're fun, but you'd get bored if that's all you did. Play."

"Really? And what about you? Will you get bored before the two weeks are up?"

"No, not that quickly. But I will want to move on to something else sooner or later."

"Work. Another job."

"No, don't be silly. I play at those, too. I've played for the last ten years. Correction, I've never done anything but play. I have the attention span of a gnat. If you don't believe me, call Janie. She'll tell you. She can recite chapter and verse at the drop of a hat."

Dominic took her arm, stopping her in the foyer and turning her to him. "This is a warning, right? You're telling me that by the time I get used to having you around, you'll be gone."

Molly felt a small stab in the region of her heart. It surprised her. "Yes, that's what I'm telling you. I'd like to say I'm different than that, better than that, but I'm not. I don't . . . *do* entanglements. Not well."

"You mentioned Janie, your cousin. You haven't moved on from her."

Molly lowered her head. "No, I haven't. She's family. I'd probably kill for Janie, for any of her family." She lifted her head and grinned at him. "But, hey, don't spread that around, okay? It ruins the image."

Dominic slid his hands up and down her arms, then clasped her elbows. "You're a lot more complicated than I gave you credit for, Molly Applegate."

Molly felt her mouth going dry. Why did she keep having this insane urge to tell Dominic Longstreet the truth? Dump all her stupid woes and insecurities in his lap, and then push them to one side so she could sit on that lap, and wrap her arms around his strong neck? She was only building herself up for a fall, and this one would really hurt. "Man, I'm good," she said, her smile brilliant. "You fell for that?"

Dominic stepped back. "You . . . You were putting me on just now? Why?"

"It's what I do, Dominic. I am, by and large, the best actress you will ever meet. Face it, I'm a spoiled rich brat. A grasshopper, a gadfly, a shallow dilettante. Pick a failing and I have it. I may even have invented some of them. I'm an utterly worthless human being. Worse, I *like* myself the way I am. Now come on, I'm hungry."

"No, wait," he said, not letting go of her arms. "This started out with you telling me that I have more to my life than playing with my brother's kids. I agree. But I can balance that life. Work, play, family. I don't, I'll admit that, but I *can.* Are you saying that you *can't?* Or that you just never found a reason to do anything but run?"

"I don't run," Molly said, her heart pounding. "I have friends all over the country, all over the world. I just . . . I just *flit*, that's all."

She put her hands on his and stepped back. "Right now, I'm going to flit to the kitchen and eat a peanut butter and jelly sandwich, because, at this very moment, that sounds like a fun thing to do. Afterward, I'm going to go see the horses, because I like horses. Then I'm going to smile and cheer for Cynara because she needs somebody in her corner. And that, Dominic, is just about as far ahead as I like to plan my life. Now, if you'll excuse me?"

"You could have just told me you aren't interested, you know, that you've had second thoughts. So what was that about, upstairs? Some sort of test? If it was, I thought I was passing with a pretty good grade, until the kids showed up."

"Oh, you were, you do. I just want to be clear that you've got a life here, you've got your work, while I will probably be a thousand miles from here in a month, having myself another adventure." She made a face, shrugged her shoulders. "I . . . I just don't want to see anybody get hurt, that's all."

"You know, Molly, sexy as you are, suddenly you aren't quite so appealing. I think I'll be able to keep my hands off you, not drop to my knees and propose marriage, or hang on to your ankles pleading for you not to go when it's time for you to leave. So relax, you're safe."

He stepped back and let her pass, and Molly blinked rapidly as she headed for the kitchen. He didn't follow her, and that was a good thing.

And he didn't ask her who the "anybody" was who she didn't want to see getting hurt. That was probably also a good thing.

Chapter 9

The peanut butter and jelly sandwich sat in Molly's stomach like a rock for at least an hour. But, then, an egg-white omelet would have done the same thing; any food she ate had no choice but to lie atop the lump that had formed in her belly after having to chew and swallow her earlier words to Dominic.

Not that Molly thought she'd made a mistake. Or had she? Who knew? Maybe she'd missed the train, the boat, the flight, whatever avenue to Paradise anyone would wish to take, but it hadn't been a mistake to push Dominic Longstreet away. He was dangerous. He invaded her mind as if intending to take up permanent residency, both there and in her heart.

He had power, a power he didn't understand.

Janie understood, and her cousin never used the power. Nor did her family. They were careful, always, to keep everything light, keep it loose, not pressure Molly, so that when she moved closer, it was her decision, and when she drew back, they just waved her on her way, telling her to come visit again whenever she wished.

They *understood*. Dominic? No, men like Dominic didn't understand.

After feeding the horses all the carrots, and promising Lizzie and Al (Little Tony had decided on Al, at least for the moment) that they'd all go for a horseback ride tomorrow afternoon, Molly held onto their hands and walked back up the hill toward the theater.

"Are you sure you want Daisy, Molly?" Lizzie asked, skipping along, Doofus playfully nipping at her heels. Rufus was still at the stables, looking curiously at a Shetland pony that was only slightly larger than himself. "She's an awfully big horse."

Molly smiled at the thought of the palomino she'd just left. "Ah, but I'm betting she's a real lady."

"Not to Jonsey," Al said, mentioning one of the grooms. "She threw him off last week. Twice. But she's still not so bad as Sylvester. Uncle Dom's horse is just plain mean."

"Do you think Uncle Dom will go riding with us?" Lizzie asked as they climbed to the porch of the white brick building. "He's supposed to be interacting with us, you know."

Molly bit back a smile. "Your mother say that?"

Lizzie nodded. "We're supposed to be relaxing him."

Molly reached for the doorknob. "Really? And how do you think you're doing so far?"

"Not good, not good," Al said, shaking his head. "Uncle Dom doesn't relax all that good."

"That's because he doesn't like kids," Lizzie said, stepping back, away from the open door, as if reconsidering entering the theater.

"Oh, I think you're wrong there, Lizzie," Molly said, her heart hurting for the girl. "He had fun with the water cannons."

"Shooting *you*, sure."

"He shot us, too, Lizzie," Al said in his uncle's defense. "He just liked shooting Molly better."

Molly closed the door again and bent her head to rub at her forehead, the better to hide her expression. "I think you guys are giving your uncle Dom a raw deal here. He's an uncle, not a daddy. He doesn't quite know how to handle you guys. But that doesn't mean he doesn't love you."

Lizzie sort of tipped her head from side to side. "Okay. That's what Mom says. But he could try to get to know us. We're not babies anymore."

"Meaning?"

"He won't let her sing and dance for him," Al supplied, not even needing the usual quarter bribe.

"Oh, you shut up, Little Tony. You just shut up!"

"It's Al, not Little Tony. And *you* shut up," Al said, stepping closer to Lizzie, his hands drawn up into fists.

"Don't you tell me to shut up," Lizzie countered, going chin to chin with her brother.

"Oh, yeah?"

"Yes, yeah!"

"Ah, I see you've got everything under control out here," Dominic said, and Molly turned to see him standing with one hand on the doorknob, his head peeking out through the cracked-open door. "You certainly are a real wizard with kids, Molly. We, however, are rehearsing in here, so could you keep it down or move it somewhere else?"

Molly wanted to smack the man. Worse, she could tell that he *knew* she wanted to smack him. So she just smiled and said, "Sorry, we got sort of carried away. We were rehearsing a small skit, that's all. Weren't we, guys?"

Lizzie was quicker on the uptake and immediately agreed with Molly. Al, on the other hand, started to say something very much like "Huh?" before Molly drew him to her side and gave him a warning hug that had his face buried against her side.

"A skit," Dominic repeated. "Right. I'll pretend to believe

anything if it will shut you up. So you're not going to listen to the run-through?"

"Whyever not?" Molly said, lifting her chin. "Come, children. For our next exercise, we will practice being an audience."

And with that, she pulled the door open. Dominic had no choice but to stand back, and she led the children into the theater with the grand air of a duchess come to call.

"Yoo-hoo, Molly, over here!"

Molly waved to Cynara, then led the children down the short center aisle and motioned for them to precede her into the second row while she continued to the stage. She'd have been impressed with the theater if she hadn't been in private home theaters in New England, in Europe. Molly was like that; she just accepted what she saw, and rarely goggled, and had long ago learned to be happy wherever she might be at the time.

"Well, I can see you and Angel got along famously," she said to Cynara. "Your hair is fantastic."

Cynara pushed at her newly bouncy curls. "You like? Angel just snipped it here, snipped it there, and performed a miracle. I can't tell you how grateful I am that you found him for me. And look," she said, holding out her spread fingers, "a French manicure. Angel suggested it, saying it's the perfect thing for someone who gestures a lot. Like me, I guess. He said that otherwise, I'd be distracting eyes from my face, and we wouldn't want that, would we?"

As Cynara spoke, Derek Cambridge sauntered over to stand beside her. "Why don't you two have a slumber party tonight and talk all about nails and hair and whatever else it is women talk about," he said, rather snidely. "Lord knows, Cynara, you sleep alone anyway."

"By choice, my darling, by choice," Cynara purred, patting his cheek. "Not at all like you."

Derek glared at Cynara for a moment, then turned smartly on his heels and walked back across the stage, to pick up some sheet music from a plain wooden table and begin inspecting it.

"Poor, darling Derek," Cynara whispered, going down on her haunches to be eye-to-eye with Molly. "He was so certain I'd spend these three weeks rolling around in bed with him. As if I'd ever make *that* mistake again. Want to see Derek run? Just whisper the word *commitment* in his ear, and he'll be out of sight in a heartbeat."

Molly looked over at Derek, who had been sneaking looks at Cynara the whole time she'd been speaking. "You loved him?" she asked quietly.

"Ha! Past tense, yes, fortunately. Now we loathe each other. Isn't it obvious?"

Molly just shrugged and smiled. She initially had thought the two stars' animosity for each other was genuine, but she didn't think so now. Men and women, such complicated organisms. "What are you going to sing, Cynara?"

"Oh, the duet first," Cynara told her, standing up once more. "That way Derek can take a hike before I tackle the second act solo."

"I can't wait to hear you, Cynara," Molly said with sincerity. "I've never been to a rehearsal before. It's exciting."

"It's long, it's boring, it's hard work," Cynara said with a dramatic toss of her head. "But at least Taylor isn't here to stop me almost before I open my mouth and insist that I'm not grasping the melody. Perhaps if there *was* a melody, I could find it."

Dominic took a seat in the last row. "All right, Cynara, let's begin."

"It's like I told him," Cynara continued. "I need an orchestra, a *live* orchestra. Not a ridiculous boom box squawking at me. Where's the magic in that?"

"Cynara? Today, if you please," Dominic said, ruffling through papers he'd picked up from the seat beside him.

"And you watch Derek, Molly. Even here, just in rehearsal, he insists on trying to move me about in order to show his best side. He upstages me constantly, shamelessly. The man would upstage the corpse at a wake, I swear it. And another thing, if he ever—"

"Cynara?" Molly interrupted. "Dominic wants you to start."

The woman looked to the rear of the theater and shrugged. "Well, why didn't he just say so? Excuse me, darling, it's time to sing for my supper."

Molly watched Cynara walk across the stage, a small space that got smaller as the woman drew all eyes toward her, with her marvelous carriage, the way she held her head, the air of "I'm here, you can applaud now," that she seemed to suddenly exude from every pore. It was amazing.

More amazing was the way she smiled at Derek, warmly, affectionately, even lovingly. She stopped beside him, took the sheet music he offered her, and thanked him with a kiss on his cheek, a quick stroke of her fingertips patting that kiss into place. Only then did she walk back toward Molly, to stand on quite the opposite end of the stage, her gaze still lovingly directed to Derek.

Derek blew her a kiss, then bent to press a button on the boom box, and Molly took her seat beside Lizzie and prepared herself to be thrilled.

Music, canned yet beautiful, introduced the song that truly began when Derek's voice joined it. He faced the audience, his hands clasped together in front of him, and sang of love: love promised, love lost, love he longed to feel again.

And then he ruined the mood by stopping, saying, "Damn it, Cynara, you were supposed to come in there. You waiting for an invitation, darling?"

Molly looked up at Cynara, who was paging through her

sheet music, trying to find her place. "Where?" she asked then, waving the pages at Derek. "Did *you* hear the violins? I know I didn't. If I came in any sooner, I'd step on your note, you idiot."

Derek bent down, pushed the button that stopped the CD. "Dom?" he asked, almost pleaded, looking toward the rear of the theater.

"Try it again, Derek, okay?" was all Dominic said, but Molly heard the weariness in his voice, the resignation. He didn't expect Cynara to do well. Molly could sense it.

And Cynara didn't do well. They ran through the duet four times, never reaching the end of it without a problem. A problem with Cynara. At last, Derek threw down his music and stormed out of the theater, saying he had better things to do than watch Cynara crash and burn.

That left Cynara on stage alone, to practice her second act solo, except that she begged a five-minute break so that she could visit the bathroom. She took her purse with her.

By now Molly had commandeered a copy of the sheet music for that solo. She already had Cynara's part of the duet down pat—repetition would do that for someone with Molly's quick mind—and now she was learning the solo.

It was beautiful. Haunting. And those were just the words. Tony Longstreet was a genius. By the time Cynara hit that last, long note, then let it cut off, leaving the audience reeling with the sudden silence after so much emotion, there wouldn't be a dry eye in the house.

"I'm bored," Al said before Cynara began her solo. "Can I go see Mrs. Jonnie and maybe see if those freezer ices we bought this morning are frozen yet?"

"Save me a blue one. I mean it, Al," Lizzie said, waving her brother on his way before crossing her arms over her flat chest. "Boys," she said, rolling her eyes. "How can he say this is boring?"

"You're enjoying this?" Molly asked, already knowing that Lizzie hadn't moved, hadn't fidgeted, had barely breathed as a matter of fact, since the moment she'd sat down.

"Oh, yes," Lizzie told her, then sighed. "I take dance and voice, you know, but Daddy and Uncle Dom and Mom keep telling me it's a long, hard road between wanting to be on the stage and actually getting there. Mom was on Broadway, you know. She danced and sang in the chorus. That's where she met Daddy. It was all very romantic."

"No, I didn't know that. You have very talented parents, Lizzie."

"Maybe, but they don't seem to want me to do what they did, and I'm good. I really am. I don't know, Molly. Cynara sounds pretty bad. And we haven't even seen her dance yet. Oh, hi, Uncle Dom," she ended as Dominic sat down in the seat Al had just vacated.

"How goes it, pumpkin?" he asked, rubbing her hair, which earned him a grimace from his niece.

"You rub Al's head, Uncle Dom. You give me a kiss."

"Who's Al?" he asked, looking at Molly.

It was as if their argument had never happened. And if he was okay with that, she was okay with it, too.

"Your nephew. He says he wants to be called Al. For Anthony Longstreet. A. L. Get it?"

Dominic shook his head. "Elizabeth isn't going to go for that one."

"Oh, don't worry," Molly said with a small wave of her hand. "He's just trying it out. I'm sure he'll change his mind at least a dozen times before he lands on a name that suits him. But you have to admit, anything's better than Little Tony."

"I'm back!" Cynara announced unnecessarily, tossing her bag onto the table, then smoothing down the skirt of her dress. "Shall we begin?"

Dominic excused himself and went up on the stage, heading for the boom box, while Molly tilted her head and looked at the somehow less frenetic Cynara. She was even smiling, which was a pretty neat trick, after the abuse she'd taken at Derek's hands about her singing.

Five to one there's happy pills in that purse, Molly told herself, then sighed. *Maybe this air of confidence is just that— an air. Not the real thing.*

"No, thank you, Dom, darling, I don't need the sheet music. I know the song." She took her place center stage, folded her arms so that her fingers rested on the opposite shoulder, then tipped her head to the left, and down. A tragic heroine, where the smiling woman had stood only moments earlier.

Dominic depressed the button to start the CD, and once more music so haunting that Molly felt goose bumps rising on her arms filled the theater.

As did Cynara's voice. And, for the most part, she was wonderful. Fantastic. For the most part.

Unfortunately, that kept her performance far less than perfect. She came in late at one point, went flat at another, seemed to be searching for the correct note near the end.

"Man, she stinks," Lizzie whispered out of the corner of her mouth, sinking low on her seat. "Look at Uncle Dom. He doesn't know what to say."

Neither did Molly.

Bertha White, who called herself Billie and whom her own daughter addressed as Mama Billie, however, did not seem to have any trouble finding her voice, or her comments.

"Pitiful!" she called out, letting the door of the theater slam behind her as she advanced on the stage. "You expect my Bethany to appear with *her?* If her dancing is as bad as her voice, I'm pulling Bethany straight out of here, do you understand? We can't afford to appear in a clunker."

Molly took inventory of Mama Billie and was quickly unimpressed. The woman had the coal black hair of her daughter, although hers definitely came out of a bottle. She had the same ivory skin, but it was blotched with angry red spots at the moment, and remarkably unbecoming.

The woman was also rapidly running to fat and fighting it with too-tight clothes and overly snug belts mercilessly yanked around her middle. She was, all in all, that rare creature that Molly, who liked almost anyone, took an instant dislike to.

"Billie, this is a closed rehearsal," Dominic said, hopping down from the stage. "Kindly leave, and I'll speak with you later."

"Oh, you'll do more than that," Billie told him, pointing to Cynara. "You'll get rid of her, that's what you'll do. I don't care who you sleep with, Dominic, but you're not going to foist that has-been off on my Bethany."

Lizzie slunk lower in her seat, trying to pull Molly down with her. "I'm a kid. I shouldn't hear this stuff," she whispered, her eyes tightly closed.

"Why, Bertha," Cynara crooned from the stage, "I had no idea you were so jealous of me. I imagine throwing yourself at Dom this past week has met with the same sort of rebuff you've grown used to over the years. Pity. You could use a good—"

"Cynara! All right, that's enough!" Dominic stepped between the two women, Billie standing on the floor, Cynara looking ready to do a swan dive off the stage, to take the other woman down. "Cynara, we'll quit now and try again Monday, when Taylor's back, all right? And you," he ended, grabbing Billie's arm, "you come with me."

Molly exhaled in relief when the theater door closed, and looked up at Cynara, who seemed no worse for wear. "You okay, Cynara?" she asked, but the woman ignored her. She just put down the sheet music, picked up her purse, and did the proverbial Exit, Stage Right.

"I guess she's not okay," Lizzie said, getting to her feet.

"Man, did you see Uncle Dom? He had smoke coming out of his ears."

"He didn't look happy," Molly agreed, mounting the steps to the stage, knowing that was an understatement. He'd looked ready to blow, poor guy. "Wow, everything looks so different from up here. Come up, Lizzie. It's wonderful."

She'd hoped only to redirect Lizzie, take her mind off the ugly scene they'd just witnessed, but there was something about standing on this stage, this small stage in this small theater, that had Molly looking around in real excitement, her heart keeping time with the foot that had begun to beat against the boards.

"Do you want to see my *Good Ship Lollipop* tap rendition? It knocked 'em dead in second grade," she said, grinning at Lizzie. And then, without waiting for an answer, she began swinging her arms as she launched into a two-step, singing along as her own accompaniment.

"Oh, that's so lame," Lizzie said, rolling her eyes. "Nobody does Shirley Temple anymore, Molly. Not even creepy Bethany."

"You know about Shirley Temple?" Molly asked, still tapping.

"Doesn't everyone? Mom makes me watch her DVD of *Little Miss Marker* with her at least once a year. She has all those dumb movies. And she cries. Come on, Molly," she said, moving beside her, "try this instead. Watch, then try to follow me."

Molly stopped dancing and watched as Lizzie slowly lifted one hand to her head, as if holding on to the brim of a hat, and cocked the other hand on her hip.

"Hat on head, right?" Molly asked, mimicking the move. "We're doing something from *Chicago*?"

Lizzie held her pose. "I saw that movie four times. Three times with Mom and Dad, and once with my friends. It's great.

But my favorite is still the stage version. You know, the two of them, all in black . . . dancing . . ." Lizzie said, pointing one toe in front of her, then slowly dragging her leg back in a wide arc until her feet were together again. "You see it on stage?"

"I certainly did, with Bebe Neuwirth, as a matter of fact," Molly said, moving her leg in the same smooth motion. "Ever see the movie *All That Jazz?* Not the song, the movie."

Then she had a quick mental flash of one particular dance sequence in that film, one that had her, when she'd first seen it, fanning herself with the TV Guide. "No, scratch that, you're much too young for *All That Jazz.* But Bob Fosse's choreography, even if they didn't use all of it in the movie version of *Chicago?* He was a genius."

"I know. Mom never worked with him, but she worked with some of his choreography, when she was in touring companies, you know." Lizzie pinched thumb and forefinger together and drew them across the brim of her imaginary hat, then moved her shoulders to the beat of the music that was obviously playing in her head. "He worked with hats, lots of times. And long, smooth moves. Like this," she ended, then turned away from Molly to bend nearly in half and stride long-legged across the stage, her arms straight and swinging high.

"That's good, Lizzie."

"Yeah. Mom taught me this whole dance with hats and canes. She knows a lot of dances. Come on, Molly, do it with me."

Molly looked down at the skirt of her sundress. "Can we take shorter steps?"

"Sure. Okay, this is what you do. You keep your legs really straight, and bend over, sort of hunching up your back. Arms straight, too. Head turned to face the audience. Three long steps, then you come up halfway, close your eyes, one beat, open them, next beat, and shoot the audience the look."

"The look," Molly repeated, trying not to laugh. "What would you know about shooting somebody the look?"

"I told you, Mom taught me. Well, I watch her a lot, and ask questions, and then she teaches me."

"Okay, shoot me the look."

Bless the child, she did just that. Big green eyes closed, opening wide as her arms came up, as she snapped her fingers, shot Molly a look that was already good, but would be a real killer when this kid hit puberty.

"Oh, I've got to try this," Molly said, joining Lizzie in her trip around the stage.

"Great. Let's go." Lizzie continued that classic Fosse walk around the stage, and by the time she was halfway around, Molly was behind her, both of them pausing, rising, snapping their fingers, shooting their invisible audience the look, then dropping down again, continuing the dance. Molly's sundress hampered those long strides a little, but not enough to notice.

"Okay, enough, enough," Molly said, laughing as she straightened up again. "What show is that from, anyway?"

"I don't know. Mom knows lots of dances, and that's how she exercises. She says she has to keep her girlish figure. But it works really neat with *All That Jazz*. I mean, I can't do it like a big production number—Little Tony's such a lump, and he's too small to lift me up or anything. Wait, I'll show you."

Lizzie ducked into the wings for a second and returned with two bowler hats, two canes. "My secret stash," she said, tossing one hat and cane to Molly. "Sometimes I make Little Tony—Al—sneak in here and practice with me, but I mean it, Molly, he really stinks at it. You ready?"

Molly put the black bowler on her head at a jaunty angle, tapped it down, then twirled the black, white-tipped cane like a baton. "Ready. What are we doing? Your *All That Jazz* number, right?"

"Yup. You sing?"

Molly gave the bowler another tap. "Does Russell crow?"

"Huh? Does Russell Crowe what?"

"Never mind, lame pun. Yes, I can sing."

"All right, then. On three, Molly. One, two—'Come on, babe . . .' "

Chapter 10

Dominic wearily leaned against one of the porch posts, debating about chewing another antacid, and maybe chasing that down with some of the white chalky stuff he kept in his dresser drawer ever since Tony had seen it in the office and blown a fit all over the place.

Dominic still didn't know which was worse: Cynara's obvious difficulty with the work, or Billie White's obvious difficulty with being a human being.

It didn't used to be like this. It used to be fun, damn it. Excitement; always something different. Even the problems were fun, because then he could solve them.

He still enjoyed producing, most of the time. But sometimes being the producer meant being the big boss, the referee, the cheerleader, and all too often, the Simon Legree in the bunch.

When had it all become a job? When had it all become such a damn *chore?* When had the race become a rat race, with him stuck somewhere, always stuck somewhere, in the middle of some maze?

Tony wanted the two of them to relax, take a break, take a year off, at the least. But that wasn't possible. When you're on top of the ladder, there's nowhere else to go but down. That's what Dominic knew, what he believed. Being on the top didn't make everything easier; it made it harder. The only thing more difficult to produce than four successes was another success. Ask Lloyd Webber, for crying out loud.

No, he couldn't think about taking time off, delaying this new production. Sitting around and counting his money had never been Dominic's favorite sport.

So think about the work. That's what he had to do. Think about the work.

If Cynara didn't improve, and soon, he'd have to seriously consider releasing her. He didn't want to do that. Cynara's name was a sure box office boost. And she was talented, with a string of hits to her credit. So what the hell was wrong?

He knew about Derek. Anyone who hadn't been living on the moon for the past five years knew about Derek. He and Cynara had been lovers. Past tense. But actors fell in and out of love, and in and out of each other's beds, and then went on to be friends. No harm, no foul.

He'd thought that was the way Derek and Cynara had handled their breakup. But now he wasn't so sure. Baby-sitter, referee, cheerleader, sure. But the advice to the lovelorn expert? He didn't think so.

Dominic absently rubbed at his chest, where something inside burned like the very devil.

And then there was Billie White. What a pain in his backside. Bethany White had talent, granted, but the world was full of talent. Billie might not know it—although she'd have to be thick as a plank not to, after he'd dragged her into his office and yelled at her for damn near an hour—but she and her daughter could be very easily replaced.

Release Bethany. Release Cynara. And explain both firings to Tony, who thought his brother was doing nothing more in Virginia for three weeks but kicking back, drinking a few beers, and playing video games with his kids? How the hell was he going to pull off that one?

And then there was Molly Applegate. Most important of all, somehow, he didn't know how, she was the most important of all.

Now there was a piece of work. She was either the biggest tease he'd ever met, or she didn't have a clue how powerful she was, how she drew him, how his mouth watered whenever he looked at her.

Pull him in, push him back. She had him off balance, and he was still trying to figure out how he'd gotten that way.

She'd seemed amenable to a flirtation, hell, a lot more than a flirtation, and then—*bam!*—it was thanks but no thanks.

"No, that's not what she said," he said, pushing his shoulder away from the pillar. "It was a warning, not a turndown. I'm the one who got all bent out of shape. Damn."

"Huh?" Al asked from his seat on the top step of the porch. "You say something, Uncle Dom?"

"Hmmm?" Dominic looked down at his nephew, who was brushing Rufus. The Saint Bernard was lying on his back, paws in the air, showing off equipment Dominic's sister-in-law promised wouldn't be there much longer if she had anything to say about it. Only time he'd seen his brother walk with his legs almost crossed was the night Elizabeth dropped that bomb on him.

"I thought you said something," Al repeated, going slightly cross-eyed as he used thumb and forefinger to pinch some Rufus hair from his tongue. His blue tongue. "Oh, here come Lizzie and Molly."

Dominic redirected his gaze from the huge puffs of Rufus hair Al had combed out—and that were now blowing all over the porch like furry tumbleweeds—to see Molly and his niece walking across the grass, toward the house.

They were laughing, holding hands, bumping into each other like children sharing some delicious secret. At one point, they stopped, did a small dance step before continuing on their way. Lizzie broke away from Molly, turned in a circle, then took a bow, flourishing an imaginary hat, then tossed that "hat" to Molly, who pretended to catch it. Then she turned in a circle, and bowed.

He could hear them laughing, the sound young and vital and carefree, and he rubbed at his burning chest and decided that he was the loneliest man in the world . . . and how the hell had *that* happened?

"Hi, Uncle Dom!" Lizzie called out as they approached the porch. "Something wrong with your chest?"

Dominic looked down, saw his hand pressed against his chest, and quickly dropped his arm to his side. "Nope," he said, "just doing my Napoleon imitation."

"Huh?"

"Don't worry about it, Al. Keep brushing that mutt."

"Rufus isn't a mutt, Uncle Dom. Mom says he's a very expensive pedigree-ded-ded . . ."

"Pedigree," Molly corrected as she bounded up the steps and then bent to rub Al's head. "He certainly is. And your tongue is blue, young man. And your lips."

"You had better have saved a blue one for me," Lizzie said, already pulling open the screen door and heading inside, obviously on her way to the kitchen.

"Al?" Molly asked, bending to lift his chin, to stare straight into his eyes. "Now tell me you saved a blue one for her."

Al nodded, but redirected his gaze to the porch floor. "There's still one left."

"Well, that's being a good brother." Molly looked at Dominic, and winked. "Now for the big question, Al. Will she be able to *find* it?"

The boy scrambled to his feet, his cheeks rather pink. "I guess maybe I could go show her, huh? It's right behind the ice cream . . . sorta stuck there." He looked at Molly, hopefully. "I think it fell back there, don't you?"

"Absolutely," Molly agreed. "But no more for you, okay? Mrs. Jonnie said she wanted to serve an early supper, and it's almost five now."

Dominic watched as his nephew headed inside the house, just as Lizzie could be heard yelling, "Little Tony—you *jerk!*"

"How did you know he hid the last blue one?" he asked Molly, who was now sitting on the top step, gathering up puffs of Rufus hair.

"I told you. I was a kid once. Weren't you? And you're doing it again."

"Doing what again?"

"Rubbing at your chest. Does it hurt?"

Dominic dropped his arm to his side once more. "A little heartburn, that's all. I need another antacid."

"You need to stuff Billie White in a sack and mail her to Timbuktu," Molly said, getting to her feet, both hands full of Rufus hair. "And maybe everybody else, while you're at it. Lizzie told me you were supposed to be relaxing these three weeks, not working."

"Lizzie shouldn't tell tales out of school," Dominic said, reaching out to remove a small fuzzy Rufus tuff that had landed in Molly's hair. "And if Tony and Elizabeth wanted me to relax, they should have taken their kids with them, damn it."

"If you're going to treat them like a chore, yes, they should have," Molly said, stepping to her left, to get past him.

But he stopped her, placing a hand around her arm. "Hey, I got them you, didn't I?"

Molly rolled her eyes. "Sure. Take the easy way out. Hire somebody."

"You're calling hiring *you* the easy way out?" Dominic shook his head. "You're the worst of the bunch."

"If you think you've just insulted me, you haven't. I'm not leaving those children, Dominic, not until their parents come home to rescue them from you."

"Did I miss something here? Have I locked them in a closet, taken away their television privileges, what?"

"You make them feel they're in the way."

He could feel every nerve in his body tensing, rubbing raw against his skin. What was this? Anger? Guilt? "They *are* in the way, damn it. Weren't you there to hear Cynara? I'm up to my ears in problems."

"Which you wouldn't be if you hadn't gone behind your brother's back and invited everyone here to rehearse, when you were supposed to be interacting with the children."

"Interacting? And what the hell does *that* mean? More water battles?"

"For a start, yes." Then she sort of deflated, her shoulders slumping. "Oh, never mind. You can't force it, Dominic. Kids know these things, sense them. Either you want to be with them, or you don't."

Dominic let go of her arm and turned to walk to the end of the porch. And damn if she didn't follow him. He wanted her to go away. He had a headache. He had a dozen headaches.

"I'm sorry," she said, putting a hand on his back. "For some dumb reason I'm having a flashback mad-at-my-childhood moment, and taking it out on you. You're not the father; you're the uncle."

Dominic turned around, looked into Molly's curiously shining eyes. "Your parents pushed you off on hired help?"

"The moment the cord was cut," she said, and her smile was definitely too bright. "Lizzie and Al have great parents, I know that. But, for some unknown reason, they all seem to be worried about you." She caught his hand in hers as he lifted it toward his chest. "And if you don't stop rubbing your chest like that, I'm going to be worried, too. Are you sure you're all right?"

"I'm fine, just feeling a little out of it, that's all," Dominic said, but he didn't believe himself, and could tell Molly didn't, either. "I took two antacids already. Do you think I can take another?"

"I don't know," she said, leading him back down the porch, and indicating that he should sit down in one of the rockers. Okay, pushing him down into one of the rockers. "Maybe we should call your doctor. You're looking pretty pale."

"That's because you're scaring the hell out of me, looking at me like that," Dominic said, trying to smile, trying to talk himself out of how he felt. But, damn, there was this freight train sitting on his chest, and he was beginning to feel nauseous.

"You're sweating," Molly said, kneeling beside him.

"It's about ninety-six degrees out here. Of course I'm sweating," he said, to challenge her, to challenge the way he felt. And he felt bad. He felt really bad.

"Be quiet. I'm trying to remember symptoms. Is your left arm numb? Does your chin feel tight? Are you nauseous?"

"I'm not having a heart attack," he told her, attempting to get to his feet, even as his heart rate kicked into overdrive. He made it halfway before the dizziness hit him, and he sat back down. "Dammit!"

"Stay here. I mean it, don't move. I'll be right back," Molly said, and then she took off, the screen door banging shut behind her.

Dominic sat very still, trying not to remember that his father had died at fifty-six, from a massive coronary. But he was only thirty-eight. That was too young. Way too young. He concentrated on his breathing, taking in huge gulps of air.

The screen door slammed again, and Molly was back, the keys to her Mercedes in her hand. "Okay, Mrs. Jonnie's got the kids. She's going to have them bake some cookies or something, then have a late dinner because they ate so many of those ice things. There's no reason they have to know what's going on, so I told them we were going to take a drive to see if we can find a watermelon stand somewhere. Stay here, I'll go get the car."

"Watermelon?" Dominic looked at her in confusion.

"Or corn on the cob. Something. Hey, you wanted brilliance at a time like this?"

"I can walk to the car," he said, pushing himself to his feet, fighting the dizziness, the numbness that seemed to be invading his limbs. At least his chest didn't hurt anymore. He must have imagined the pain, that's all. Besides, he was too numb to feel pain. Wifty. Out of it. "See? I can walk."

And, with a true effort of will, he did just that, collapsing in the front seat and even allowing Molly to reach across him to fasten his seat belt.

"Where are we going?" she asked him once the Mercedes was on the highway.

"I thought you knew," he said, turning his head toward her as it lolled against the headrest. He wanted to say this was a bad idea; he didn't need a hospital. But his whole body felt so heavy, too heavy to move.

"Well, I don't," she said. "I'll just head toward town, okay?"

"There's a hospital about five miles from here," he told her, fighting the memory that it was in that hospital that he and Tony and their mother had watched his father die. "God, I'm so weak. Why am I so weak?"

"Men are always putty in my hands," Molly said, shooting him a smile and a wink. Then she put the gas pedal to the floor.

Five minutes later he asked, "You . . . You ever drive in the Indy Five Hundred?" Although speaking was an effort, he continued, "I think . . . we had liftoff over . . . that last bump."

"Complaints, complaints," she said, leaning forward over the steering wheel. "There it is. You're going to be fine, Dominic. I promise."

How he wanted to believe her. . . .

She pulled the Mercedes into the driveway in front of the Emergency Room, slammed the car into Park, and was gone before he could tell her he could manage to walk into the hospital on his own.

"He's perspiring, I think he's nauseous, he's pale, his chest hurts, and he's very weak," he heard Molly saying to someone, and then a pair of strong hands were all but lifting him out of the car and into a wheelchair.

He was angry. So very angry. And embarrassed, which he knew was irrational. "This is damn stupid," he said, but it was possible no one heard him, because he could barely lift his chin off his chest. He was like a marionette, but someone had cut all the strings.

Somebody did hear him, however. "Shut up," Molly ordered succinctly as she trotted alongside the wheelchair. "Nobody likes a difficult patient."

"I'm . . . I'm not a patient. I'm . . ." He managed to raise his head, to see himself being wheeled into a curtained cubicle holding a black leather litter a nurse was throwing a sheet over, and a bunch of equipment he really didn't want to recognize.

He was half helped, half lifted onto the litter. His clothing disappeared—but Molly didn't. She just stood there, watching him being stripped of what made him an independent man and turned into a helpless weakling.

Okay, he knew what was happening now. A nurse was slapping those sticky things on his chest. He was getting an electrocardiogram, an EKG. He got one of those once a year, from his internist in Manhattan. He could handle an EKG.

Then someone came at him with a needle.

"Is that really necessary?" he asked. Pleaded, damn it. His voice was pleading, like some sissy. But he hated needles.

"We have to draw blood and start a line, sir, just in case the doctor orders anything," the nurse told him. "It's procedure."

Dominic rolled his eyes, looked at Molly. God only knew why he looked at Molly, because the woman had the bedside manner of Darth Vader.

"Oh, don't be such a big baby," she said, approaching to stand on the other side of the litter, taking his hand in hers. "It's just a little stick, and if you're a good boy, maybe they'll give you a balloon."

"Go to hell," he told her, but he didn't mean it. He just wanted her to keep holding his hand. He just wanted not to be so damn scared.

A doctor showed up. At least his name tag proclaimed he was a doctor. He looked like he was still in junior high. He went straight to the EKG machine, read the tape the machine had spit out, and turned off the machine.

Why? Was he that bad? Was all hope gone? *Stop it, Dom, just stop it. Sit up, show them you're fine. Why the hell can't you sit up? Why have all your muscles turned to Molly's Silly Putty?*

"Mr. Longstreet? Hi, I'm Dr. O'Keefe. First thing—your heart's fine. I thought you'd want to know that."

Dominic shut his eyes as Molly leaned over him, gave him a hug. He felt a strange, embarrassing urge to let a sob escape him. He wasn't dying. But, if he wasn't dying, what the hell was going on?

"Now, I understand you had some chest discomfort, some nausea, and then an all-over weakness in your limbs?"

"That's right, Doctor, although we're sort of fuzzy on which came first," Molly said before Dominic could open his mouth. "And heartburn, he said, and he took some antacids. But then he just got very white and started scaring me."

"Mrs. Longstreet?" Dr. O'Keefe asked her.

"Yes, of course," Molly said quickly, extending her right hand. "I'm so sorry. Molly Longstreet. Wife, and not prone to hysteria, I promise. He'll be much calmer if I'm here. I can stay, can't I?"

"Certainly, you may stay. In fact, I think that's a good idea," Dr. O'Keefe said, and his expression clearly showed his appreciation of the woman standing in front of him, smiling at him as if he were some longed-for present she'd been handed on Christmas morning.

Dominic felt this insane urge to give a whistle and say, "Yo, Doc, down here. Remember me? Your patient?"

After a long moment, Dr. O'Keefe seemed to remember what he was supposed to be doing and lifted his stethoscope to his ears as he began his examination.

Molly stepped back, but didn't let go of Dominic's hand. He wanted to strangle her. He wanted to kiss her.

"Been under some stress lately, Mr. Longstreet?" the doctor asked at one point. "Perhaps you and Mrs. Longstreet here were having an argument today?"

"Oh, no," Molly said, lifting Dominic's hand to her lips to kiss it. "We never argue. We're newlyweds. But he has been under considerable stress with his work, poor darling. It was really bad today."

"No more than usual," Dominic said, realizing that he was actually beginning to feel a little better. But, if Molly was the cure, what the hell was the disease?

"He's lying, Doctor. Stress is Dominic's middle name. I heard the minister say so, at the altar," Molly said succinctly, and now Dominic wanted to gag her.

"I'm going to try something, Mr. Longstreet, okay?" the doctor said, nodding to the nurse, who opened a drawer behind her and came out with . . . a paper bag?

Dr. O'Keefe took the bag and shook it open, then held it

out to Dominic. "I want you to breathe in this bag, Mr. Longstreet. Seal it against your mouth and nose, and breathe in, breathe out. Nice, slow breaths, okay?"

"You're kidding, right?"

"Do it," Molly told him, taking the bag and holding it closed against his mouth while the doctor explained.

"I believe you have heartburn, Mr. Longstreet, and maybe worse than that, maybe acid reflux disease, and we can do a test for that next week, then prescribe the correct medication. But first things first."

Dominic pushed away the bag. "I blow in this thing for heartburn?"

Molly put the bag to his mouth again. "Do that again and I'll have to hurt you. *Breathe.*"

"No, Mr. Longstreet, you don't. You blow in the paper bag because you've been hyperventilating, and we're going to try to stop that."

Dominic didn't understand, but he *was* feeling better, some sensation returning to his weak, nearly numb limbs. So he listened, and he learned.

Hyperventilating wasn't always the fast gasps he thought it was. Sometimes it was just a few too many breaths a minute, over the course of hours, that had a cumulative effect and caused the weakness, the numbness. A person under stress might not even notice that he was taking those extra breaths, until the symptoms appeared. Then, once begun, ninety-nine percent of people panicked even more, breathed more quickly, and the next thing they knew, they thought they were dying.

"It's a normal reaction to panic. It's not fun, this feeling, is it? Employing a paper bag to breathe in is a good way of equaling the blood gases, as each breath alters the quantity of oxygen and carbon dioxide," Dr. O'Keefe said, "and you'll begin to feel better."

It was so logical. It was so embarrassing. But Dominic

kept breathing into the bag, and he kept feeling better. He wasn't dying. He was just nuts.

He said so. "I'm not dying. I'm just nuts."

"Idiot," Molly said, her Nurse Ratchett bedside manner this time extending to a quick backhanded hit on his shoulder. "You're not nuts. You're stressed. Overworked. But now that you know, you have to slow down, learn to relax, before something really bad happens to you. Eat right, exercise, get plenty of rest. Isn't that right, Doctor?"

"That would be my diagnosis, yes. My primary advice is to take a vacation, frankly," Dr. O'Keefe said, and an hour later Molly and Dominic were heading back to the compound, Dominic still muttering under his breath as he glared at the stress management pamphlets, the pill samples, an appointment for an upper G.I. test, the prescription for a stronger antacid . . . and another for some nerve pills.

"I'm not taking the nerve pills," he said, to himself, to Molly, to the world; he wasn't sure. It was sort of a general protest.

"Dr. O'Keefe said the one pill that he gave you is only temporary, and only when you start feeling anxious. The prescriptions are for that and something more long-term, but he did say you could see how you do on the Xanax, and then visit your family doctor before going on anything more long-term."

"I don't *get* anxious!"

"Yeah, right, tell it to the marines," Molly said, pulling the Mercedes to the shoulder of the road, just before the turn to the compound. "Look. Dominic. You just had a warning. Your brother said you were working too hard. Dr. O'Keefe said you were working too hard. There's an old adage, Dominic—when two people say you're sick, it's time to lie down."

"Before I fall down?"

"Exactly. Do you know how badly you frightened me?"

"Do you know how badly you treated me, *Mrs. Longstreet?* Did you really have to lie in order to stay in there with me? And what makes you think I wanted you there? I would have gotten more tender loving care from Rufus."

"You were being obnoxious," Molly told him flatly. "And somebody had to be with you to hear what the doctor said and you weren't going to tell the truth and you know it and you were scaring me and I was sure it was all my fault because we had that sort of argument after we kissed and before that I had you running all over with that water battle and I still don't know how I ever drove this car because my hands were shaking so badly and I kept trying to remember that CPR class I took and . . ."

Dominic pulled her close against him, and she buried her head in his chest as she burst into tears. She didn't cry politely. Molly was a very vocal crier, complete with hiccups and sniffles and a body that shook with the depth of her unleashed emotions.

And then she was done. Like turning off a faucet, she was done. She sat up, wiped at her face with the backs of her hands, and gave him a watery smile. "Well, that was dumb. You're the patient. I'm supposed to be comforting you."

"You were worried. I worried you. I'm sorry, Molly."

She nodded, reaching in her purse for a tissue to finish drying her tears. "You should be. And no more work, do you understand. You are officially on vacation, just like Dr. O'Keefe said. Look at those prescriptions again, Dominic. Dr. O'Keefe actually wrote one that says vacation, one a day for fourteen days—which I think was really cute. But he meant it, so, no more work!"

"And what am I supposed to do with Derek and Cynara and Bethany—and Taylor when he comes back on Monday? Hang them on a hook?"

"Works for me," Molly said, her chin determined as she put the Mercedes in gear once more. "Tonight, we watch videos with the kids. Tomorrow morning, we go to church if you're up to it. Tomorrow afternoon, we go riding. And you're going to relax if I have to tie you down and make you relax. You got that?"

"I'm not sure." Dominic smiled. "I'd have to figure out some way to explain all of this to Derek and Cynara and Taylor. And Billie White, God help me. In the meantime, tell me again about that tying down part, okay?"

"Jerk," Molly said, turning onto the lane. And then she grinned back at him.

Yes, he really was beginning to feel much better. He still felt stupid, but better. . . .

Chapter 11

Molly stood in her room and looked at the open suitcase on her bed. The open, empty suitcase on her bed.

She should be packing. She should be running. She should have been halfway to anywhere else but here an hour ago.

So why was she still here? Why had she spent an hour at the dinner table, talking with the kids about anything and everything, trying to keep them from realizing that their uncle looked just a little pale under his tan, that their uncle sort of picked at his food, and was very quiet?

Was it for the children? For Lizzie and Al? Of course it was. It certainly wasn't for Dominic Longstreet, who was a very nice man, actually; but she'd met hundreds of very nice men, and she'd never been tempted to stay around any of them and wonder if she should be taking his pulse or putting a cold cloth on his forehead . . . or carrying paper bags in her purse, for crying out loud.

She didn't like this, not at all. She didn't need anyone, and she certainly didn't need to be needed by anyone else.

"How would you know?" she asked herself, slamming the

suitcase closed and returning it to the closet. "Nobody else ever needed you before, remember?"

She walked over to the bed and flung herself across it, belly down, to lie with her chin propped in her hands as she looked at the wall. No answers there, so she flopped over onto her back and stared up at the cloth canopy.

She'd been so frightened. She'd never been that frightened in her life.

One minute she'd been laughing with Lizzie, and the next she was looking at Dominic as all the color drained out of his face and his brown eyes got all unfocused, as if he was trying to figure out something and hadn't a clue as to what that was, what was happening to him.

She'd asked him if his left arm hurt, if his jaw felt tight . . . and probably scared him into thinking that they did. Trying to help, making things worse. Pushing him toward panic.

But her first thoughts hadn't been for herself, which was an oddity all by itself, because Molly had taught herself to think of herself first (employing the theory, over the years, that "somebody should"). *How does this affect me? It isn't my problem, is it? Isn't there somewhere fun to be, so that I'm not here to feel anything even remotely considered* concerned *or, worse,* involved?

If not for herself, then her first thoughts could have been for the kids, which was where they should have been, shouldn't they? She was the nanny, not that she had any more experience with that job than she'd had with any of the other jobs she'd danced her way through in the past years.

Still, that's where her concern should have been, with the children. Yet she hadn't even thought of them until she'd skidded into the kitchen and stopped before she could yell to Mrs. Jonnie that she was rushing Dominic to the closest hospital. Seeing those two blue-lipped, blue-tongued kids grinning at her had kept her from panicking completely, though, so that had been a good thing.

She'd sucked it up. She'd been the adult. She'd been responsible. She'd smiled at the kids, then asked Mrs. Jonnie to help her find her car keys and told the woman what was happening only once the two of them were in the hallway, away from little kids with big ears.

She'd driven to the hospital without running the car into a tree, and she'd handled Dominic calmly but forcefully.

She'd been good. She'd been really good . . . until she'd amazed herself with that ridiculous meltdown on the way back to the compound.

Damn the man for scaring her like that.

And now she'd committed herself (*committed*, boy, there was an apt word!) to taking care of him so that he wouldn't turn blue as Lizzie's and Al's lips, or keel over or something.

Dominic had to relax, that's what Dr. O'Keefe had ordered, in no uncertain terms. And she had promised to make sure that he did.

The grasshopper was going to teach the ant how to relax and have fun. Really, when she got right down to it, where was the problem in this idea? How difficult could it be? She could do this, had darn near invented having fun.

Right after she locked Derek and Cynara and most especially Mama Billie in the root cellar, that was, if this place had a root cellar. If she knew what a root cellar looked like. . . .

"Cut it out," she told herself. "You told Dr. O'Keefe you aren't the hysterical type."

The grandfather clock in the foyer downstairs began to chime, and Molly looked at the bedside clock to see that she'd been in her room for over an hour. Somehow, it was eight o'clock, and it was time for Al's bath, a story, and bed.

Except that Mrs. Jonnie had volunteered to take care of that chore. Lizzie would also be getting her bath, changing into her pajamas, and then setting up a DVD in the great room, and Molly had already wangled a promise from Dominic that he'd be there at nine o'clock sharp, hungry for popcorn and ready to watch whatever movie Lizzie had chosen.

Of course, first she'd had to remind him that he could ignore her advice, not do what she told him to do, and end up overbreathing and going all numb and limp again, at which point she would hide all the paper bags and let him lie where he fell, helpless, until pigeons pooped on him.

Yes, he was being very obedient, when you got right down to it, but he was still feeling fragile, Molly was sure, and was probably still scared, as well. But that wouldn't last. By tomorrow, he'd be calling another rehearsal and making calls on his cell phone and pretending today had never happened.

Which brought Molly back to wondering what made her think she cared what he did, the dumb man.

"Well, I do, that's all," she told herself, and left the bedroom, marching off to the guest house to stick her nose in where she knew damn full well it did *not* belong.

She knocked on the screen door, then tried the inner door, which was unlocked, and stepped inside. "Yoo-hoo, anybody home?" she called out, casting her gaze around the large living room and dining room combination that seemed to take up most of the first floor of the building. Everything was green and white, and chintz, and very appealing, and Cynara was sitting on an overstuffed couch, her legs drawn up under her, leafing through a magazine.

"Cynara?" Molly said, advancing into the room, to stand in front of the couch.

"Oh, Molly, hello," the star said, smiling up at her. "I was reading and didn't hear you come in, I guess. Look," she said, holding up the open magazine and turning it toward Molly, "Is it just me being catty, or does it look like Brat Pitt needs some sleep? Those *bags* under his eyes." She turned the magazine around again, looked at the page, then dropped the closed magazine in her lap. "Oh, well, I wouldn't kick him out of my bed, would you?"

"I guess not," Molly said, sort of slapping her palms together in front of her as she tried to think of a way to make Cynara think that taking a few days off was her idea . . . because if Molly knew nothing else, she was certain that Dominic would murder her if she told anyone what had happened to him today.

"Um . . . Cynara? I've got a problem," Molly said, sitting down on the edge of one of the chairs facing the couch, pretty much assuming the role of nervous petitioner. After all, when asking for help, it's always a good thing to make the person asked feel as though she's being helpful, a part of the solution. That had always worked like a charm on her cousin, Janie. "You see, I'm taking care of the kids, um, the children. That is, Lizzie and Al. You've met them? Dominic's niece and nephew?"

"Tony's kids, sure. They're cute. All kids are cute. At a distance, which is where I wish Bethany White were at the moment. Are you sure there aren't any extra bedrooms in the house where you could stash them and get them out of my hair? Even a cellar would do. Preferably dark and dank, darling. That child screamed for an hour this morning, I swear it."

Molly's eyes went wide, just for a moment. Bethany White . . . the water cannon . . . Dominic having to invite Bethany and Mama Vulture to Sunday dinner. She'd forgotten. Just what she needed, another problem.

"Yes, well, Bethany to one side for the moment, it turns out that Tony and his wife, Elizabeth, made it very clear to Dominic that he was to spend these three weeks getting to know his niece and nephew better."

Cynara made a face. "I thought Tony liked Dominic."

"Oh, he does, I'm sure he does. Maybe it's just Elizabeth. Anyway, Dominic got a phone call from Tony a little while ago, and Tony read him out for not doing what he was supposed to do, so Dominic ended up promising to play Good Uncle for the next two weeks."

Cynara frowned. "Which leaves us where? I came here to work, remember? We all came here to work."

Molly shrugged. Here it was, time to go for the gold. "And now you're here for an all-expenses-paid two-week vacation, I guess, if you want one, until Tony gets back and rehearsals start again. Isn't that wonderful?"

She counted to seven, watching Cynara chew at her bottom lip, before the star slowly smiled. "Derek is going to be royally pissed."

Molly felt a lump in her stomach dissolving, and relaxed. "Oh, undoubtedly. And just think of how much fun it will be, parading around in your bikini, driving him nuts. I mean, I *have* seen him looking at you. You do have a bikini, don't you?"

Cynara tried to look indifferent, Molly supposed, but what the woman looked was interested. Very interesting. "You've seen him looking at me?"

"Definitely. He's always looking at you, and picking fights, just so you'll talk to him. Tell me if I'm wrong, but I think the man is in love with you. And who could blame him? You're fairly irresistible, right?"

Cynara nodded, accepting that praise as no more than her due. "I'll phone the salon on Monday, arrange a bikini wax," she said, getting to her feet. "We'll have picnics. I haven't been on a picnic in years. I'll make Derek feed me strawberries, and peel grapes for me. I'll drive him *crazy.* He deserves to be driven crazy, darling, trust me. And I'll sleep late, and see Angel at least twice a week. Get a massage, definitely a facial. Sleep again," she added, rolling her eyes.

"Do you know the last time I had a *real* vacation? Neither do I. And I get to break the news to Derek, all right? Ha, now we'll see how well he can suck in that gut in a bathing suit!"

"Two down, one to go," Molly said as Cynara all but ran out of the living room and up the stairs, undoubtedly to tell Derek that rehearsals had been canceled for the next two weeks. Would a huge Broadway star stoop to saying, "Neener, neener"? Probably.

Now to find Mama Billie and figure out a way to get her to pack up Bethany and leave for two weeks, sans Sunday dinner.

"Mrs. White?" Molly called out, stepping into the small room behind the kitchen, one that seemed to serve as a computer room.

"What? Can't you see I'm busy?" Billie White barked, never turning away from the computer screen.

"Yes, and a good evening to you, too," Molly said, reminding herself that more flies were caught with sugar, or whatever that old saying was. "I'm here with some good news. Dominic has decided to spring all of you for two weeks. You and Bethany can go home, relax, and come back in two weeks. Isn't that grand news?"

Apparently not. Billie White swiveled around in the desk chair and glared at Molly. "The hell with that bullshit. He's trying to get rid of us, isn't he? And all because of those damn kids of Tony's. All because I told him what brats they are, and how they envy my Bethany. That poor child was traumatized this morning. I may still sue, and he knows it, so don't you tell me he's giving us some sort of vacation, because I'm not buying it."

"Bethany's traumatized? It was a water gun, Mrs. White, not a real bazooka."

"Don't you sass me. You're no more than Dominic's whore, we all know that. God knows the man couldn't go more than a week without bringing in a bimbo." The woman's eyelids narrowed. "Unless you're Cynara's replacement?"

"I'm the nanny," Molly said, mentally picturing Billie White with a pig's snout—something she had done since she was a child—because she'd learned that striking back at idiots (at least while they were around, and bound to see you) only made you an idiot, too. "And Cynara and Derek will be staying here, vacationing."

"They're staying? Then why would Bethany and I go anywhere? He might think he can get rid of us, but he can't. We're not leaving, do you hear me?"

Molly was pretty sure Billie White could be heard in Williamsburg. "He did say you could stay," she offered, although it took all her resolve to smile as she made the offer. Someday, before these two weeks were up, she told herself, she'd probably be forced to cut this woman off at the knees. But not today, not with Dominic only hours away from his hospital stay.

"I'll just bet he did," Billie said. "And you keep those unruly brats away from my Bethany."

"I don't think that will be a problem, especially as Sunday dinner has been cancelled," Molly said, then turned on her heels and left the guest cottage, already trying to figure out how she was going to tell Dominic that she'd just tossed away two weeks of rehearsals.

But when she got back to the main house, the problem didn't arise, because when she found Dominic, he was sound asleep on one of the couches in the living room.

"Poor baby, you've had quite a day, haven't you," she crooned quietly as she snatched up a handmade afghan and spread it over him, because he was lying almost directly beneath an air-conditioning vent in the ceiling.

And then, resisting the urge to bend and kiss his forehead, Molly tiptoed out of the living room, to stop in the foyer. She pressed her back against the wall and gazed at her reflection in the mirror on the opposite wall.

"So tell me, Margaret. How did an irresponsible girl like you end up in charge like this?" she asked that reflection, before heading down the hall to the great room, following the smell of freshly popped popcorn.

Chapter 12

"Dominic?"

He turned onto his side. Molly had whispered his name in his dream. He liked the way she whispered his name.

"Dominic?"

He smiled and hugged the pillow. *Try* Dominic darling *now*, he thought inside his head. *Project. That's it. Once more, Molly, with feeling.*

"Mr. Longstreet, curtain up in one minute."

Dominic's eyelids flew open, and he sat up, all at once. "What? What?"

"Sorry," Molly said, sitting down beside him. "I was calling your name for five minutes, I swear it. But I didn't realize I'd get quite the reaction I did with that last try. Man, you are tense, aren't you?"

He took a deep breath, pushed his fingers through his hair. "Maybe. No. Yes." He slapped his hand against his knee. "Damn it, what was in that pill?"

"So you took it?"

He shot her an exasperated look. "Yes, I took it. Before

dinner. Half of it. I took half of it. But I'm not taking it again. Anxiety? I can't have anxiety, damn it. You got that?"

"Whatever you say. But you needed the rest, and still do. Now, come on, it's eleven o'clock. Time for bed."

He stayed where he was, still trying to get his bearings. "Why did you wake me up? I could have stayed here."

"Yes, and then I could have shown off all I learned at my massage therapy class, because your neck would be stiff."

Okay, he was waking up now. "You took a massage therapy class?"

She glared at him. "Why do men always make that face when I tell them about the class?"

"You don't know?" he countered quickly. Oh, yes, definitely. Definitely some waking up going on here.

She put an arm around his shoulders. "Come on, time to go upstairs. Unless you want something to eat. You barely touched your dinner."

Then she took her arm away and stood up, putting half the length of the room between them. "God! Do you hear me? I mean, do you *hear* me? I'm turning into Janie. And it scares me, Dominic, it really scares me. So, eat, sleep, get a crick in your neck, go back to work until you keel over—I don't care. You understand that?"

"Good," he said, getting to his feet. "I don't want a keeper, you know. I don't need a keeper."

"Now, that last part's debatable."

"You want this job or not? Make up your mind."

He watched as several emotions played across her beautiful, expressive face, then smiled when she settled on perplexed.

"Well, I am here," she said, then sighed. "And you do need help."

"With the kids. I need help with the kids. We've established that."

"And with yourself," Molly added, coming toward him once more. "Whatever train wreck you had this afternoon has been coming on for a long time. Your brother saw it, right? Well, now I see it. The question is, what do I do about it?"

"We could start with this," Dominic said, stepping forward and putting his hands on her shoulders, pulling her close, until their bodies touched. "And maybe this," he added, lowering his mouth to hers.

God bless the girl, she didn't play games. She not only accepted his kiss, but she gave back. In spades.

Their tongues tangled; their bodies melded. She had her arms around him, pulling him even closer before he could shift his hands to her waist.

He stumbled backward, toward the couch, already mentally undressing her, already seeing her lying beneath him, those long legs wrapped around his waist. . . .

She had her hands between them now. *Good. Good. Unbutton the shirt. No. Don't worry about the buttons. I have more shirts. Dozens of shirts. Wait. No, don't stop. Don't push me away. Don't end this . . . I don't want to end this. . . .*

"Dominic," Molly breathed into his neck. "I . . . I think I'm hyperventilating."

"Good. That makes two of us. We're a matched set. Can I blow in your paper bag?"

"Cut that out! No, really. Be serious, Dominic. We're in the living room. Anybody could walk in. Mrs. Jonnie . . . the kids. So let go."

"You first," he said, nibbling on her earlobe.

"Well, now we've got a problem," she said, arching her neck, allowing him greater access to her soft, sweet-smelling skin. "I don't want to let go."

"Can we make it upstairs like this?"

"I don't think so, no."

He slid his hands low, cupped her buttocks. "If I let you go, are you going to change your mind?"

"Are you nuts?" she asked as he slid one hand around her body, pressed his palm low against her belly.

"The jury's still out, remember?" he told her, moving his hand lower, to the hem of the hot pink shorts she'd changed into before dinner. To the hem, and then beneath it, to the silk of her panties, to the silk of her skin. The sweet, hot wetness of her.

"Up . . . upstairs," Molly gasped as her body sort of collapsed against his, her knees bending slightly, as if she might be having trouble keeping herself upright.

"Yeah . . . good thought," Dominic agreed, picking her up, holding her high against him as he headed for the stairs. "Your place or mine?" he asked, grinning down at her.

She lifted her head and licked his chin.

"Right. My place. It's closer."

He kicked his bedroom door closed, not bothering with the lights, as a full moon had sent a spill of light across his king-size bed. Sort of like runway lights at an airport for the horny.

They came in for a landing, tumbling onto the bed amid the half dozen decorative pillows he'd never seen the purpose of before now. Before Molly lay against them, grinning up at him, reaching up for him, pulling him down to her.

"Clothes," he mumbled into the cleft between her breasts. "Rid of the clothes . . ."

And, poof, their clothing was gone. The woman was a witch, a magician. The woman was . . . God! She was glorious!

"You're glorious," he told her, his chest rising and falling rapidly as she knelt chest-to-chest with him on the bed, her thumbs rubbing in small circles across his nipples.

He returned the favor.

She threw back her head, arched her back as she pressed her hands against the mattress, and he leaned forward, to kiss her breasts, to kiss her belly, to lave her navel with his tongue.

To hold her. To lift her. To bring her legs around him as he knelt there, leaning back on his heels. Pulling her closer. Closer. Pulling her in. . . .

Condom. His brain was saying *condom.* His passion was telling his brain to take the night off.

"Hold . . . hold on," he said, balancing himself with a hand pressed against her thigh as he leaned toward the night table, found the drawer pull, pulled open the damn drawer, and fumbled inside for a packet. *Please, please let there be a packet.* There! He'd found one.

Hurry. Hurry.

More fumbling. When had he gotten so clumsy? He looked at Molly, lying there on the bed, propped on her elbows, her long legs wrapping ever more tightly around his hips. Her smile was devilish.

He ripped open the packet with his teeth.

She laughed, a full, throaty sound that had him grinning along with her . . . and then he was sliding her closer, and she was rising up, reaching for him, taking him deep, deeper.

She pushed herself up, slid her arms around his neck, kissed his mouth, and he took her breasts into his hands as he began to move, as she moved with him.

So deep. So intimate. So . . . so different. This was sex, yes. But it was more. But what? More honest? More free? More . . . more . . . more. . . .

Now she was on her back, and he was kneeling again, still deep inside her, even as she did the impossible—she gracefully lifted her legs up and over his shoulders. He grabbed her hips, a surge of power going through him, rippling along every muscle, teasing every nerve ending, and drove into her. Again and again and again.

He wanted to open his eyes, look at her, but he couldn't. He was lost. Lost in sensations so powerful they were nearly frightening in their intensity.

Tumbling. He was tumbling toward her now, his hands braced against the mattress on either side of her, her bent knees somehow beside his head as she said his name, called his name, and he moaned, "Molly . . . Molly . . .

" . . . Molly?" he murmured sleepily, turning onto his side, reaching out his arm across the bed, only to find it empty. "Molly?"

He sat up, blinking at the sunlight that all but blinded him. "Molly?"

But it was morning, and she was gone.

Pressing his hands to his head, he collapsed against the pillows once more. "God. Molly . . ."

Every muscle in his body ached. But pleasantly.

Molly had told him she was on the pill, and eventually they'd forgone the condoms. Still, what the hell had happened here last night? Everything was sort of a blur, a tangle of arms and legs and. . . .

On the bed. They'd made love on the bed. Twice. He remembered that. Then again on the floor, when they'd fallen out of bed. In the shower, where he'd revived enough to make love again on the chaise lounge, because the bed was too far away.

With their hands, with their mouths . . . They'd made love this way, that way. Every way. Hell, around four in the morning, he was pretty sure they'd invented a way that hadn't been written up in any how-to books yet. Damn good thing he didn't have a chandelier in his bedroom, or they'd have figured out a way to do it there, too.

And now she was gone, and he didn't know what the hell came next.

When he saw her, did he take her in his arms, kiss her? Would they play it cool during the day, then spend the next two weeks of nights going at each other like bunnies before Molly made good on her warning to walk away, no regrets?

Is that what he wanted?

Sure. Sure, that's what he wanted. That's what he always wanted. That marriage and babies and domestic bliss stuff was what Tony wanted, but the whole thing left Dominic cold, and he was smart enough to know it.

He was thirty-eight, almost thirty-nine. He had his career, his shows, and they were his children, all he wanted out of life.

He was happy, fulfilled.

So why the hell did he also have a starter packet of Xanax on his nightstand?

Dominic crawled out of bed, heading for the shower, turning back to look at the ruins of his room. The pillows were everywhere. The bedspread was on the floor, along with some damp bath towels. His clothes were scattered. He felt something on the bottom of his foot, and when he looked, he found a shirt button stuck to his heel.

He'd have to clean up this mess before Mrs. Jonnie saw it and handed in her notice. Mrs. Jonnie had been with him for more than ten years, and he'd hate to lose her.

Although last night would have been worth it.

"Stop that," he told himself, retreating to pick up the bedspread. "Oh, and stop talking to yourself, or they really will be after you with a net. Rubber room time." He flipped the bedspread onto the mattress before heading to the shower once more. "Man, the things we could do in a rubber room . . ."

By the time Dominic was shaved and dressed, his imagination back under control, the bedside clock read five minutes after eleven, and he went downstairs to an empty house and a yellow sticky note on the front door.

We've gone to church, Uncle Dom. It was signed by Lizzie, and beneath her round handwriting was printed in very small letters, *Have you ever considered vitamins, Lazybones? Molly.*

He crumpled the note in his hand. Vitamins. Very funny. He had ten years on the woman, damn it. So she could play all night and still wake early, probably eat a huge breakfast, and go to church, for crying out loud.

The second note was in the kitchen, next to a full pot of coffee: *Horseback riding after lunch. Be there or be square.* He recognized the small, neat printing; Molly again.

Maybe the vitamins weren't such a bad idea.

Coffee dribbled onto his shirt when the slamming of the back door startled him, and he turned around just in time to see Billie White advancing on him with murder in her eyes.

"There you are!" she shouted as he ripped off a paper towel and began dabbing at the front of his shirt. "I want to talk to you!"

"It's Sunday, Billie. We'll talk tomorrow."

"We'll talk *now*," the woman said, pulling out a chair and sitting herself down.

How am I breathing? Dominic asked himself, his hand still to his chest. *Okay, breathing's good. Don't explode, don't get nuts. You're in charge, remember?*

"Billie, I said tomorrow. Be in my office at nine. I want to go over Bethany's contract with you."

Her eyelids narrowed. "Why?"

He had no idea. It just seemed like the right thing to say, so he ran with it. "There are a few matters. Those having to do with your presence, for one. I want to satisfy myself that there couldn't be some other arrangement made. Perhaps her father?"

"Richard? Richard is *not* a part of our lives."

Smart man, Richard, Dominic decided. "Nevertheless, Billie, something will have to be done. You and I? We aren't hitting it off, are we?"

Billie's cheeks colored. "We're not here to make friends."

"Hey, that's one thing that's working, right?" Dominic said, taking another sip of coffee. This was much better. No yelling, no screaming. Just polite conversation, some coffee, some watching Billie White's face turn red, then drain to white.

"All right, all right, no more talk about suing you," Billie said, getting to her feet. "Not that Bethany wasn't highly upset, the poor child, but I'll convince her that it was an accident."

"That's good, because it was an accident."

"Yes. Yes, of course. And we're your guests. We shouldn't be ungrateful. After all, this is a lovely place. Bethany and I will enjoy relaxing for the next two weeks at your expense."

Dominic frowned. "I beg your pardon? A two-week vacation at my expense? What the hell are you talking about, Billie?"

"I'm talking about our vacation. Derek, Cynara, Bethany. Me. Your girlfriend told us last night. No work for two weeks, until your brother gets back."

Molly. Billie had to be talking about Molly. "She told you that, did she? Last night?"

"She was lying?"

"No," Dominic said, turning away from the woman, figuring he could just kill Molly later . . . if he didn't thank her instead. "No, she wasn't lying, Billie. Where would you get an idea like that?"

"Because Cynara and Derek were invited to stay, but Bethany and I were invited to leave for two weeks. You could have been trying to trick Bethany and me so that we left, and then you could say we were in breach of contract."

He turned to look at her again, in some admiration. "Now, why didn't I think of that one? Go away, Billie. I am on vacation."

"We still have that appointment, tomorrow at nine? Something *has* to be done about Cynara, Dominic. She's pulling Bethany down. She's pulling down the entire show."

"As of now, no. No appointments, not for two more weeks," Dominic said, pouring the remainder of his coffee in the sink, because his chest was burning again. He wouldn't take the nerve pills, refused to take the nerve pills, but the wonder drug antacid the doctor prescribed could be a plan.

"But I—"

"You just don't know when to quit, do you, Billie?"

"Ask Cynara that question, Dominic," Billie said, folding her arms across her stomach. "She's the one who doesn't know when to quit. Her voice is gone, just gone."

"Again, my problem, not yours." He heard car doors slamming outside and put down his coffee cup. "Here's the deal, Billie. Stay out of my way, behave yourself for these two weeks, and we'll talk again."

"So you *are* thinking of making changes?"

"I could be."

"Cynara."

"Could be. Could be somebody else. Like I said, stay out of my way. Remember, I'm the big bad guy here. You want to keep me happy."

And then he left Billie White where she stood sputtering and headed toward the front porch, toward the voices he heard, his step suddenly light.

Chapter 13

"And I don't see what's wrong with Big Al," Al said as he climbed out of the car, continuing an argument with his sister that had gone on long enough for Mrs. Jonnie to begin whimpering in the front seat as she fanned herself with the weekly church bulletin.

"You're not big, that's why," Lizzie countered, tumbling out behind him, her long, coltish legs getting tangled up so that Molly quickly grabbed her elbow. "Thanks, Molly. Tell him. He can't be Big Al, can he?"

"I don't have to. You did. One thousand four hundred and six—no, seven times."

Lizzie goggled up at her. "You counted?"

"I estimated," Molly told her, glancing up toward the porch, to see Dominic standing there, looking at three large boxes. Her heart did a small flip, which made her rather angry, for reasons she didn't want to investigate. "Now, go get changed while Mrs. Jonnie fixes lunch, and then we'll take that horseback ride, remember?"

"I won't call him Big Al," Lizzie warned tightly. "Al was dorky enough."

"You don't have to call him anything you don't want to call him. Then again, he doesn't have to answer if you don't call him Big Al. It's one of life's dilemmas. Now, go on. I have to talk to your uncle."

"Just sandwiches, Miss Molly? We usually have our main meal at noon on Sunday, but I hadn't planned to go to church, ashamed as I am to admit that, and didn't have time to start the beef roast."

It did not occur to Molly that the housekeeper had begun calling her "Miss Molly," and was treating her as if she were the lady of the house . . . or that she was reacting as the lady of the house.

"That's fine, Mrs. Jonnie, thank you," Molly said, watching Dominic pick up one of the boxes, then shake it. "Excuse me, I think someone is being nosey."

Dominic looked good enough to eat. And she realized she was suddenly very hungry.

She bounded up the stairs and took the box from him, held it against her as a sort of barrier—or to keep herself from jumping him; one or the other. "Mine, I believe," she said. "Mine, mine, and again mine."

"The return address is in Connecticut," he told her, bending down to pick up another box.

If she reached out, just a little, she could slip her fingers through the hair on his bent head. So blond, so warm in the sunlight. "True. And unless Rufus and Doofus took lessons as bomb-sniffing dogs, I think we're done here. Unless you want to help carry these upstairs?"

He straightened, holding the two remaining boxes. "I have a choice?"

He was looking at her intensely. She'd have to be imagining things to believe she could see actual sparks flying back and forth between them.

"People always have choices," she told him. "They might not always have options, but they do have choices."

"Is that profound, or just muddled?"

"I don't know. Took your mind off the boxes, didn't it?"

"Among other things, yes. But now it's back on them. What's in here?"

"Clothing, of course. I had them overnighted to me. I couldn't possibly get by on what I brought with me."

He sort of snorted. A cute snort. "You brought seven suitcases with you."

She balanced the box she was holding on her knee and held open the screen door for him. "Yes, of nursery school clothing. Now I need vacation clothing."

"This one is too heavy to just be clothing."

"Shoes, I suppose," she said, following him into the foyer and heading for the stairs. "And my riding boots and hat."

"Next you'll be telling me you sent for jodhpurs."

"Not if you don't want me to, no. But I did. All well-bred young ladies of means learn how to ride, you know. A select few of us, who wander off the assigned trail, even get to muck out stables."

They made it to the second floor with the boxes, and he wasn't huffing and puffing, which she privately considered a good thing. Then again, after last night, why would she even consider worrying about his stamina?

"You're a good rider?"

"I manage," she said, putting down the box she'd carried, which made her realize that now she had nothing to do with her hands. She crossed her arms, watching as he dumped the remaining boxes on the floor, then dropped her arms to her sides. Then laced her fingers together. Then bit her bottom lip.

"You all right, Molly? How are you managing last night?"

God, how she hated postmortems! "What about last night?"

"It happened, for one thing," Dominic said, touching a finger to her mouth, running the tip of it along her moist bottom lip.

She backed up a pace, headed for one of the windows. The scenery was safer outside. *"It* happened a lot, as I remember the thing."

"True. And you're okay with that?"

She kept her back to him. "You're not?"

He was behind her. Close behind her. She could feel his warm breath on her nape. "I don't know. I'm still trying to figure out what happened."

Games! Molly didn't like playing games. Not this sort, anyway. She turned to face him, nearly went chest to chest with him. "Oh, come on. You know what happened."

He put his hands on her shoulders. "Yes, all right, I know what happened."

"Several times," she repeated, using all of her willpower to look into his eyes as she spoke.

"Several times, yes. Stop interrupting, Molly. I'm trying to say something here."

"Do you have to?" she asked him, lowering her eyelids, because looking into his eyes was doing strange things to her insides. "I don't think so."

"Yes, I have to, Molly. It was . . . Hell, it was wonderful. But it probably shouldn't have happened. I'd had a rough day. I'd taken that pill . . . You were feeling sorry for me . . ."

And she was off again, leaving him standing there with his arms still out as she made for the bed, braced herself against a bedpost. "Oh, please don't ruin it, Dominic. Please don't be a jerk. I wasn't exactly the martyr, you know. And I never do anything I don't want to do. Ever."

He nodded, and stayed where he was. "Okay, Molly. You wanted it, I wanted it. You know, I never realized that *wanted* is such a weak word. The question now is—what comes next?"

"Something has to come next? Why? Why can't we just . . . just . . . oh, damn it!"

"Just keep doing what we did last night? Is that it, Molly?"

She glared at him. "What? You want to hear me beg? That's quite an ego you've got there, Dominic Longstreet."

He closed the space between them in a few quick strides. "You're picking a fight? You are, Molly, you're picking a fight. I wanted to talk about last night, and you want to fight. Why?"

She crossed her arms and rubbed at her forearms, looked at the floor. "We . . . We already had this discussion. I'm here, you're here. In less than two weeks you'll still be here, but I'll be gone. I . . . I don't want anybody to get any other ideas. I don't want anybody to be . . . hurt."

She dropped her hands to her sides and sidled away, to head for the door. "So, last night happened. Who knows what will happen tonight, or any other night. We don't have to dissect it, do we? Why can't we just . . . just *enjoy* it?"

She opened the door, but he reached beyond her and laid his palm against the wood, pushing it shut once more, his arm trapping her. "What are you afraid of, Molly? What the hell are you afraid of? Commitment?"

She lifted her chin. "You're keeping me from leaving the room. Kindly step back."

He did. His expression suddenly cold, he did just that, and Molly fled down the hallway. She ran down the back staircase and nearly wept with relief when she entered the kitchen to see both children there, Mrs. Jonnie there. Protection. Just what she needed.

"Molly, we have to—oh, hi, kids, Mrs. Jonnie." Dominic stopped just inside the kitchen doorway and smiled at everyone. "Is it lunchtime? I could eat a horse."

"Uncle Dom!" Big Al exclaimed, eyes wide. "You shouldn't say that."

"Yes," Lizzie said, picking up a sandwich thick with sliced country ham, tomato, and Bibb lettuce. "We ride horses, Uncle Dom. We don't eat them."

Molly quickly made herself busy, helping Mrs. Jonnie pour drinks for everyone, determinedly pretending Dominic wasn't standing there, staring at her, wondering how to get her alone again.

"I'm Big Al now, Uncle Dom," Big Al announced with some pride. "Al was too short. I was going to be Al the Great, but Lizzie hit me, so I changed it to Big Al. Do you like it?"

Dominic pulled out a chair at the large round table and sat down. "Big Al. I guess it's okay. It might be a little too gangsterish. You know, Big Al sentenced to life in the Big House."

"Huh?"

"He says Big Al sounds like you're in the mob, you dweeb," Lizzie said, and Molly, just then sitting down across the table, shook her head at the child. "Oh, okay, okay. You can be Al the Great. See if I care."

Great Big Al (whatever) pushed out his bottom lip, which had begun to tremble a little. "I just want a neat nickname. You don't have to go poking fun at me, Lizzie." Then he pushed back his chair and ran from the room.

"Nice going, Lizzie," Molly said. "Got any idea what to do next?"

"You want me to go after him and apologize."

"That sounds like a plan," Dominic agreed, picking up his sandwich. "Then both of you come back here and finish your lunch."

"Do I *have* to?"

"No, you don't," Molly told her. "You do have a choice."

"And options," Dominic chimed in, grinning at Molly in a way that made her want to brain him. He was still angry, that was certain, but he still liked her. She was pretty sure of that one, because she still liked him, too. Even if she wanted to brain him, as Lizzie would say.

"Boys! Honestly!" Lizzie said theatrically, throwing down

her napkin. "All right, all right, I'm going. I hope you're both happy now."

"Are you happy, Molly?" Dominic asked as Lizzie stomped out of the room.

She grabbed the pickle spear from his hand and bit off a piece, grinned as he winced. "Delirious. You?"

"Ouch. I'm pretty happy, yes. And thank you. I refereed a couple of arguments this past week, and let me tell you, that one was a walk in the park. Everything I said was just more oil poured on the fire. You are good with children."

"Ah, I love praise. I think the trick might be to not treat them like kids. They're people, right? Although, if you handed me a kid still in diapers, I'd be running for the door before you got within ten feet of me." There. That ought to give the man a clue; she wasn't the settling-down type.

"You don't like babies, Miss Molly?" Mrs. Jonnie asked, setting a bowl of freshly washed green grapes on the table. "I just love infants, the smaller the better. They're so sweet and helpless."

Molly shivered. "Thank you, no. I prefer kids already walking, talking, and blowing their own noses."

Mrs. Jonnie chuckled. "They don't come that way, you know. If you want to have children, you pretty much start with babies. But, don't worry. You might not want babies now, but the minute you meet the right man, you'll want to have *his* babies. I've seen it a dozen times."

Don't help, Mrs. Jonnie. Please, don't help. Molly smiled weakly, and went back to her sandwich, her appetite gone.

But Mrs. Jonnie wasn't done. "Meet the right person, and it's only natural to want to have a child, children, with that person. It's the whole purpose of marriage."

"Can I peel you a grape, Dominic?" Molly asked quickly, to divert him. It might have worked on him, too, but Mrs. Jonnie wasn't playing along.

"Isn't that right, Mr. Dom?"

Molly kept her head down, her last bite of sandwich still in her mouth, as she was afraid to swallow for fear she might choke, waiting for Dominic to speak.

"Yes, I'm sure you're right, Mrs. Jonnie. Meet the right woman, get married, have babies. Lots of babies. It's a logical conclusion. Molly? What time are we going riding?"

She struggled to swallow, then said, "Um . . . half an hour? We can meet down at the stables?"

"Good enough," he said, getting to his feet, the other half of his sandwich in his hand. "I'll see you there. And I wouldn't mind if you brought the grapes," he ended with a wink.

"Too late, you had your chance," she called after him, then sighed. "He wants children, Mrs. Jonnie," she said before she could stop herself.

"Uh-huh, all men do. They want sons, but then they go absolutely nutty over daughters. And Mr. Dom is going to be forty in a few years. About time he settles down. I know Mrs. Elizabeth and Mr. Tony believe having a wife and a few children of his own will be the best thing for him."

Molly looked at her half-eaten sandwich. She was going to lose a lot of weight if she stayed here for the entire two weeks. Every time she turned around, something happened that made her lose her appetite. "I should introduce him to my cousin Janie. She loves kids."

"And you don't, Miss Molly?"

She looked up at Mrs. Jonnie, smiled brightly. "Oh, I adore kids."

"But you don't want any of your own?"

She just shook her head. "You know what? I really should call my cousin Janie. She should be home now, and I want to hear all about her week in Cape May. If you'll excuse me?"

"Certainly. But you didn't finish your lunch."

"I'll take it with me," Molly said, picking up her plate,

wondering if horses liked ham sandwiches, because otherwise she was going to have to choke down the rest of this one herself.

Once back upstairs, she dug in her purse for the number of the cell phone she'd given Janie and sat down on the bed, to call her.

The phone rang several times, long enough for Molly to learn two things: Janie wasn't answering the phone, and Janie had yet to figure out the voicemail feature on that phone.

She disconnected and tried Janie's home number. No answer. Then she remembered: Janie's parents had gone on vacation, to some cabin, to bird watch. Janie had been slated to go with them, until Molly had talked her into going to Cape May in her place.

Now Janie was nowhere, just when Molly needed her. She was going to have to wing this one without Janie's always astute advice.

She retrieved a letter opener from the desk between the windows and slit the tape holding the three boxes closed, searching inside them until she found the riding clothes Mrs. Beeme, housekeeper of the Connecticut house, had packed in tissue and shipped to her.

She located her riding boots and reinforced riding hat in another box. Her bikinis with matching wraps, one of them a black number with an ankle-length, sheer black sarong-type skirt definitely designed to drive men out of their tiny minds. A few nightgowns, all of them silk or satin. And a huge, floppy-brimmed black straw hat—to go with the black bikini, of course.

Everything was here, as requested . . . and suddenly she wondered why she owned nothing flannel, or terry cloth. Nothing inconspicuous.

As she dressed, Molly hummed the love song from Dominic's new musical under her breath, because the melody haunted her, just as she knew it would haunt millions after they'd heard it for the first time. Dominic had another Broadway hit on his hands if she was any judge. She could understand why he wouldn't want to wait, postpone his plans.

She could also understand why he was so uptight. Sneaking behind his brother's back was bad enough, but now he had Cynara singing off-key, and Mama Billie being a royal pain in his posterior. It couldn't be easy, putting a major show together.

"And a lot harder doing it from a hospital bed," she told herself, checking her reflection in the mirror. "That's where you come in, Mollyanna. You are his recreation, his safety valve when he needs to blow off some steam. That's the choice you made, and now, for as long as you're here, you're out of options. So *stop* arguing with the man, for crying out loud. Besides, you know you want to."

Then she pulled a face at herself and left the room.

Chapter 14

Dominic sat on the edge of the chaise lounge in his bedroom and struggled to pull the hem of his jeans down over his riding boot. One down, one to go.

He'd been having a conversation with himself for the past twenty minutes, one that had a lot to do with trying to figure out one Molly Applegate.

She was an heiress. Okay, he could live with that. He had grown up in a comfortably well off family, and he was now rich. Very rich. Sinfully rich.

But he'd worked for what he had, every last penny of it.

Molly had inherited her millions, but she'd told him she'd worked for them as well. She'd been sarcastic about it, with an undercurrent of sadness he'd not been too deaf to hear. Poor little rich girl.

Helping out her cousin, taking over the day care for a lark.

He'd bought it all, once he'd decided that she had a way of handling Lizzie and Big Al that would leave him free to concentrate on the rehearsals.

Boy, had that been a joke. The rehearsals? He couldn't concentrate on anything . . . except Molly.

He'd kept her identity a secret, because she'd asked, and because he believed she might need protection from Derek, who he was sure would make a dead set at her if he knew she was rich. Hell, Derek should have made a dead set at her anyway. But he hadn't.

Bringing Dominic back to Cynara. She and Derek had been an item, and now they weren't. Or were they? And did he care? Would the sparks flying between his two stars help or hurt the production? And what happened if he ditched Cynara? Would Derek walk?

It was almost easier to think about Molly, much as she drove him nuts.

She was maddening. She was beautiful, sensual, quixotic, funny, wildly unpredictable, and he couldn't keep his hands off her. He'd be nuts to *want* to keep his hands off her.

And she was sad.

He could sense it, at odd moments. Frenetically active, flitting from here to here to over there. Why? What kept her moving?

He pulled down his other jean leg and stood up, stamping his feet firmly into the boots.

She'd granted him every intimacy, and yet she held a part of herself at arm's length. Push, pull. Advance, retreat. Yet not a tease.

And, eventually, with full warning, she'd run. She'd laugh and play here . . . then go flitting off to laugh and play somewhere else. No roots, no ties, no commitments.

Was that it? A fear of commitment? Was it all that how-to, psychobabble best-selling book easy?

The phone rang on his nightstand, and Dominic answered it, figuring the call was for him anyway. "Hello, Dominic Longstreet here."

"Mr. Longstreet, good afternoon," a male voice said into his ear. "This is Attorney Gerard Hopkins, of Hopkins, Goldblum, and Smythe, calling for Ms. Applegate. If you could kindly summon her to the telephone?"

The voice was cool, contained, and with the unmistakable sound of the Northeast in each clipped word. Along with something else. A small slice of distaste?

Dominic grabbed a pen and wrote the lawyer's name and firm name on the notepad he kept beside the bed.

"I'm sorry, Attorney Hopkins," Dominic said, just because he wanted to. If this Hopkins character could be a prick, so could he. "Ms. Applegate is indisposed at the moment. May I inquire as to the nature of your call?"

"You may not, Mr. Longstreet. Indisposed, you said. I trust Ms. Applegate is well?"

"You could trust that, yes," Dominic answered, wondering why he was getting angry. "Would there be a reason to suppose that she's not?"

There was a pause on the other end of the line, followed by what could only be a long-suffering sigh. "Ms. Applegate has been known to . . . She's a suitable nanny, Mr. Longstreet?"

"Oh, yes, definitely. I'm thinking of giving her a raise. Kid could probably use a few bucks."

"Very amusing, Mr. Longstreet. I think we both know that Ms. Applegate is in no need of funds."

"No, and neither am I," Dominic said sharply. "You understand what *I'm* saying?"

"Yes, Mr. Longstreet. I assure you, I have thoroughly researched your background. Please, don't be insulted. It's part of my job."

"And what would that job be, Attorney Hopkins?"

"I am the family attorney, of course, and manage Ms. Applegate's affairs."

"Affairs? How nice for you." Dominic wanted to bop this guy, high society accent and all.

"Don't be crude, Mr. Longstreet. Molly is a very special person, with very specialized needs. I'm sure you've noticed."

Hell, yes, he'd noticed. "No, I haven't noticed. What are you talking about?"

"Again, Mr. Longstreet, this conversation is veering off in a direction I do not care to take. Suffice it to say that Molly is highly strung, rather capricious. A friendly word of warning, Mr. Longstreet. Don't get attached. She doesn't like feeling attached."

Go to hell, Hopkins. "She's the nanny, Hopkins."

Dominic was pretty sure the attorney smothered a snicker. "This week, yes, I imagine she is. Next week? Who knows what, and where, she will be next week. Yes, well, you're a grown man, so I'll dispense with any further warnings. Now, if you'd please just supply me with your fax number? There are some papers I need her to see."

"You worked for her parents?"

"Mr. Longstreet—"

"Answer the question. You worked for Molly's parents?"

"I did, yes. The number, Mr. Longstreet?"

"What were they like?"

"I can sense that you wish to be difficult. All right. They were . . . They were *distant,* Mr. Longstreet, rather self-absorbed. And, before you ask, yes, they neglected Molly shamelessly. Now, that number?"

Dominic gave it to him, then hung up, ripping the page from the notepad and sticking it in the drawer of the nightstand.

Hopkins had a poker up his ass, but Molly seemed to have found some small soft spot in the guy, because he'd sounded a little sad, even a little angry, speaking about her parents.

Was that it? Was that the reason? She hadn't been loved as a child, and now she was afraid of the emotion?

Could be.

Maybe the "game" she played, constantly moving, taking silly jobs, playing at life, wasn't a game at all. Maybe it was some form of self-defense.

Dominic rubbed at his chest, feeling the heartburn the new pill hadn't entirely banished.

He didn't need this. He didn't need a beautiful, mixed-up Molly Applegate with her come-get-me-now-go-away problems, her poor-little-rich-girl problems.

Yeah, sure, and she needed his problems?

Yet she'd taken them on, taken him on, and taken him to bed. Several times, as she seemed determined to remind him.

He unzipped his jeans and tucked in his shirt. The way he saw it, he could either spend the next two weeks trying to figure out Molly, or he could enjoy her, as she'd pretty much suggested.

"Not suggested. *Warned,*" he told himself, heading for the stables.

Big Al was waiting for him on the porch, dressed in jeans and riding boots and a large yellow straw hat that was kept from falling down over his eyes only by the width of his ears. His head still had some growing to do, to grow into those ears.

"Like my hat, Uncle Dom? Molly bought it for me at the store yesterday. It's a real cowboy hat, she said, but I don't think so, do you? I think it's a kid hat, but I like it."

"It's a good hat, Big Al," Dominic said as they walked toward the stables. "But you can't wear it to ride. You need to have a reenforced helmet, remember?"

"My bike helmet, I know. I'm just wearing this for now."

"Okay. Where's your sister?"

"Oh, she and Molly are already at the stables. Jonsey is saddling the horses. Molly's going to ride Daisy."

Dominic raised one eyebrow. "You told her Daisy is a jumper?"

Big Al shrugged.

"Maybe we'll start off riding around in the stable yard, then head for the trails, okay?"

"Okay," Big Al, ever the cooperative one, said. "But then we'll go on the trails?"

Dominic rolled his eyes. "You will, I'm sure," he said, then waved as Lizzie came out of the stable, leading a small brown pony. She was already wearing her bicycle helmet, and Dominic made a mental note to take them to a nearby shop and have them fitted for proper riding helmets . . . like the black one Molly wore.

Damn, she did have jodhpurs. Tan ones. And knee-high shiny brown boots. And a deeper brown riding jacket worn over a snow white blouse with lace at the neck. She was tall, slim, and those long legs moved in free, lengthy strides as she led Daisy from the stable.

"Hi! Jonsey is saddling Sylvester for you now," she said, then steadied Daisy next to a mounting block and lithely vaulted herself up and into the English saddle.

Five minutes later, they were off, Dominic's idea of staying in the stable yard not even mentioned, because after a quick, "I think she needs to burn off some excitement," Molly and Daisy were racing together across the unfenced meadow to the line of trees five hundred yards in the distance.

"Wow, look at her go," Lizzie said from atop her small pony. "I wish I could ride like that."

"You just concentrate on keeping your feet in the stirrups and the bit between Brownie's teeth, okay?" Dominic told her, watching Molly fly across the ground, Daisy's hooves throwing up clumps of grass and dirt. "Come on, let's get started."

He had to fight to control Sylvester, who obviously also wanted to run, keep the gelding's pace slow enough that Lizzie and Big Al could keep up, and Molly was walking the palomino in slow circles by the time they caught up with her.

"She's a beauty, Dominic," Molly said, patting the mare's neck. "Jonsey says she's a great jumper, and I'll bet she is."

Her huge eyes were dancing, pink tinged her cheeks, and her smile was wide and happy. Carefree. Mercurial? Yes, she was. But she enjoyed the good times. She jumped into everything she did with both feet, even if she never intended to stay.

"How about you watch the kids while I let Sylvester burn off some of his energy?" he suggested, then gave the gelding a quick tap with his boot heels.

"Woo-hoo, Uncle Dom! Ride him!"

With Big Al's shout in his ears, Dominic held the reins loosely yet with control, squeezed his knees against Sylvester's sides, and the two of them took off across the meadow.

Both he and the horse loved a good gallop, cutting through the breeze, the sound of Sylvester's hooves pounding against the earth, the sun in his face; the amazing satisfaction found in the glory of a clean, fast, hard ride.

Molly.

Dominic shook his head. Did everything he did have to remind him of Molly?

When Sylvester finally slackened a little, Dom used the reins and his legs to slow him more, then turned him, to canter back to the edge of the meadow.

"Fun?" Molly asked.

"Fun," he agreed. "Lizzie? You want to lead the way?"

Lizzie urged Brownie forward. "I'll show you my favorite spot, Molly. There's a little stream and a log to sit on and everything. You'll like it."

"I'm sure I will," Molly said, directing Daisy to follow Brownie, which left Big Al and Dominic to bring up the rear . . . and Dominic some time to enjoy watching Molly from the rear as she sat Daisy with her own special style and grace.

Would he ever go riding again without thinking of Molly? He doubted it.

Halfway to Lizzie's favorite spot in the woods, Big Al turned around on his pony and said, "Uncle Dom?"

"*Now*, Big Al? Can't it wait?"

"Uh-uh. Right now. I saved up."

"You would. We're taking a break, Lizzie," Dominic called to his niece.

Dominic edged Sylvester beside the pony on the trail and leaned down to hold the animal's bridle as Big Al dismounted.

"What's up?" Molly asked, looking back at Dominic.

"You don't want to know," Lizzie said in some disgust as Dominic dismounted, tying Sylvester's reins to a nearby bush.

"Bathroom break," Dominic muttered, giving Big Al's shoulder a small push, to guide him into the trees.

"He likes to pee in the woods," Lizzie said. "If Mom found out, she'd kill him."

"Mom isn't going to find out, though, right?" Dominic called back over his shoulder . . . which wasn't a smart move, because Big Al had kept walking, and the branch he'd pushed forward swung back, clipping Dominic in the nose. "Damn it! Big Al—that's far enough. I'll meet you back at the horses."

"Is this some sort of ritual?" Molly asked as Dominic returned to the trail, rubbing at his sore nose.

"I think he thinks it is," Dominic said.

"You're a good uncle," Molly told him, smiling down at him.

"Yeah, I am, aren't I?" he agreed, knowing his own smile was sheepish.

It wasn't until they were back at the stables that Dominic even remembered his problems—other than his problems with Molly, which weren't all that bad if he'd just relax and stop thinking so damn much.

His reminder came in the shape of Billie White, who was waiting for them in the stable yard, arms crossed over her chest, one foot beating against the dirt like a wife about to virtually take the head off her husband who had come tripping home at three in the morning. "You could have invited Bethany to go riding with you, you know," she said as soon as Dominic was within earshot.

"Bethany rides?" Dominic asked, dismounting to go help Lizzie.

"No, she doesn't. But she's a very bright child, and I see no reason why you can't teach her."

Dominic recognized this for what it was—a blatant attempt to keep Bethany in the forefront of his mind, keep the kid visible, give the little darling a chance to worm her way into his good graces or whatever. "I don't think that's a good idea, Billie. I'm not a very patient teacher."

"I could give her a few lessons."

Dominic turned to glare at Molly, who was pointedly ignoring him.

"Really," Molly said, helping Lizzie (she'd be the one wearing the disgusted expression) dismount. "I'd be happy to give Bethany riding lessons."

Billie looked at Dominic in disgust. "I wouldn't think of such a thing," she said, then added quietly, through clenched teeth "How your sister-in-law sleeps nights knowing you're subjecting her children to your live-in lover is difficult enough."

"What did she say?" Molly asked, coming up to Dominic as he watched Billie storm back up the hill toward the guest house.

"She said thanks, but no thanks," he told her. "She doesn't really want Bethany to ride. She just wants to make sure I don't forget the kid's here."

"Oh," Molly said, taking off her riding helmet and shaking her head, the burnished curls she hadn't bothered to tame again today turning to liquid fire in the sunlight. "Too bad. I really do feel sort of sorry for that kid. Anyway, thanks for the loan of Daisy. I enjoyed our ride."

"We can go out again, just the two of us?" he suggested, watching as Jonsey led the ponies into the stable, followed by Lizzie and Big Al, who were learning responsibility by grooming their own mounts.

"Now?"

"The horses aren't tired."

She smiled. "I would enjoy another ride."

"Yeah. That's what I was thinking, too."

She looked at him quizzically, then shook her head. "Shame on you, Mr. Longstreet."

"I know, Ms. Applegate. I'm a terrible man." Terrible, yes, and his heart was pounding, he wanted her so badly. She was like a drug, a drug he needed at least once a day. If somebody could bottle whatever the hell Molly had, they'd make a fortune. "So, what do you say?"

She was already leading Daisy to the mounting block. "I say, last one to Lizzie's stream in the woods gets to groom both horses when we get back."

"We're coming back? Damn," he said, putting his foot into the stirrup.

What the hell. He'd take what she gave him and think about tomorrow when tomorrow got here. . . .

Chapter 15

Introspection was not Molly's strongest suit, as the lone psychologist her parents had sicced on her had declared in his written report before the man unexpectedly took an extended leave from his practice for "personal reasons." Molly knew this because she had found the report after picking the lock on her father's desk and reading it for herself.

She'd been thirteen, but she'd known the definition of introspection, because she had always been an exemplary student. Well, nearly always. There was that one semester she decided to be an underachiever, to see if her parents would sit up and pay attention. They didn't, Molly didn't like playing dumb—it was too much work—so she went back to being her intelligent, if misbehaving, self.

And she'd stayed away from introspection. She simply *did*. Thinking about what she'd done and why she'd done it seemed a waste, as what was done was done, and thinking about it wouldn't change that.

No, examining her emotions, her thoughts and feelings, had never been a good idea. Too painful, for one thing. She concentrated on the now, the moment, the feeling at that moment.

It had always worked before. . . .

"Molly?"

She turned in the saddle, for they were on a length of trail where they couldn't ride side by side, and looked back at Dominic. "Yes? I'm going the right way, aren't I?"

"Who knows," Dominic said, shaking his head at her. "Yes, okay, you're going the right way. The stream is around the next bend in the trail. I was just calling your name. You've been . . . quiet."

"I could sing a song?" she suggested, grinning at him. "Recite poetry? Do Mark Antony's speech from *Julius Caesar?* You know, 'Friends, Romans, countrymen, lend me your ears; I come to bury Caesar, not to praise him.' "

"God, no, please. Why do you know that speech?"

"Speech class, of course. I was told it was unladylike to pretend I was Mark Antony, but I still got an A for the speech. I wasn't allowed to pick my speeches after that, but I was kicked out of that school a month later anyway, so it didn't matter." She eased Daisy to a stop as the small clearing opened before them. "Although, thinking back on it, maybe it wasn't all because I dared to do what the teacher called a *man's* speech. It might have been the sword. What do you think?"

He'd dismounted before her, tying Sylvester's reins to a tree branch, and helped her down from Daisy's back. "You brought a sword to class?"

"Borrowed it from the History Department. It wasn't a really *big* sword."

"But you brandished it, didn't you?" he asked, tying Daisy's reins on another branch. "Right about where Antony says, 'For Brutus is an honorable man; So are they all, all honorable men'?"

"Brutus was a brute. Hey, I wonder if that's where the

word brute came from. Brute, from the Roman, Brutus. What do you think?" Molly asked, sitting down on the log they'd all sat on an hour earlier, her face toward the stream. And then she was on to the next *moment.* "Oh, Lizzie's right. It is pretty here."

"You're pretty here," Dominic said, sitting down on the log beside her, his back to the stream—the better to see her face when he leaned close, stroked the lace at her throat. "You're pretty everywhere."

She pulled up one leg, clasping her hands around her bent knee as she leaned against him. He smelled of leather and horse and, faintly, of minty mouthwash. "Flattery will get you everywhere, Mr. Longstreet."

"I was hoping," he said, grinning at her, cupping a hand around her chin. "Come here."

Molly was happy to oblige. His mouth was warm against hers, warm, and insistent, and everything she'd remembered from their night together. She twisted slightly on the log and put a hand against his chest, hard beneath the soft, sun-warmed cotton of his shirt.

She let him be the aggressor, knowing she'd all but jumped him last night. When he slanted his mouth, his tongue scraping the roof of her mouth, she contented herself with stroking the underside of his tongue with her own.

It was Dominic who began the duel, teasing her until she pushed her tongue forward, and he bit it, lightly, then sucked it into his mouth as he held on to her shoulders and fell back, the two of them sliding off the log, her body on top of his.

He put his hands on either side of her head, moving her this way and that as he did mind-shattering things to her mouth, as he sent her pulses racing, as she tried to rise up, just enough to unbutton his shirt.

She adored the soft blond fuzz on his chest, the way it tickled her palms.

She broke their kiss and straddled him on her knees, pushing herself up to where he could open her jacket, her blouse. She'd worn a white satin, front-closure bra, and she sighed when he undid the snap and she felt her breasts, already aching for his touch, tumble into his hands.

Her head lifted, she concentrated on the sensation as he pinched her nipples between thumb and finger, rubbed at the aroused peaks. Touched the tip of his tongue first to one, then the other; pressed a kiss to the center of her chest, against her wildly beating heart.

She moved against him, straining to be closer, the ache between her legs urging her on, spurred even higher when Dominic inserted a hand between them, pressing his fingers against her as she moved.

Her riding jacket pulled at her arms as she reached for him, but taking time to remove it was time lost forever, and if Molly had ever lived in the moment, this was the moment.

She sat back slightly, tickled his palm as he moved his fingers against her, then began her assault on his belt, his zipper.

There was something so sensual, so forbidden, about making love while fully clothed, as if they were afraid they could be discovered at any moment, yet were too far gone to stop, and the hell with the consequences.

Consequences. Introspection. Totally unnecessary to the moment.

Dominic seemed to think so, too, because Molly could feel his desire even through the heavy jeans, and when she finally was able to lower his zipper, his sigh of relief was almost comical.

Still bracing her knees on the ground on either side of him, she undid the waistband of her jodhpurs, then rose up enough to slide them, and her satin panties, down to her thighs . . . which was a pretty tight fit . . . a move that had her tumbling forward, entirely off balance, onto Dominic's chest.

"Having some trouble?" he asked, his tongue in her ear.

"It's not as easy and graceful as it is when I've read about this in books," she admitted, knowing the only way out of her jodhpurs would be to call a temporary halt and yank off her riding boots. "It's a lot more work."

He laughed, low and deeply, against her ear, and Molly realized that she was in about the most awkward position she'd ever found herself, and she didn't care. She wasn't embarrassed; she wasn't frustrated. She was enjoying herself. Open, free, easy.

Trusting? *That* was a new feeling.

"Molly, unless you want me to burst, please stop trying to pull your clothing down any farther, okay?"

All right, so maybe she was a little bit embarrassed. "Sorry," she mumbled into his chest. "Don't stop . . . touching me. Please?"

"Not on my life," he said, slipping his free arm around her back and then rolling them to his right, so that he was on top of her. Her legs no longer spread quite so wide, he was then able to push down her clothing, all the way to her knees, to the top of her boots.

"Man, I'm good," he said, straddling her now, his hand once more between her legs. "So are you," he told her, supporting himself so that his weight wasn't entirely on her as he moved his other hand between her legs, spreading her, caressing her before he slid two fingers into her. "Do you like this? Tell me you like this."

"Oh . . ." Molly swallowed hard, looking at him, seeing him kneeling in the sunlight as he lowered his head, watched her, watched himself touching her, learning her.

"So beautiful . . ."

Molly closed her eyes, gave herself up to the sensations

rippling through her. She was safe with this man. She was going crazy with this man. This man was all . . . everything. . . .

He found her center with the soft pad of his thumb, and she arched against him, frantic that he might leave her, stop, not keep touching her, as the need built, as the heat built, as stars began circling behind her now tightly closed eyes.

She grabbed at her hair with both hands, her every muscle taut, her every nerve on edge, her body tightening against his fingers as they thrust in and out of her, as his thumb ground against her, as her teeth clenched in her need. Such a deep, deep need . . . for him . . . for his touch. . . .

"Oh, no," Molly said, her eyes popping open all at once. "Oh, no, that's too much," she said, frightened as what she had moments earlier believed to be the crest of her passion climbed again, rose higher, threatened to explode through her every pore.

And then, with the inevitability of a wave crashing against the shore, the nearly unbearable pressure became unbelievable pleasure. Her body, taut, arched like a bowstring, went still, as the center of her exploded, melted, pulsed against him, with him. On and on and on. . . .

She held up her arms in sudden need, eyes still tightly closed, and he came to her, slid inside her, moved inside her as he held her, as she roved his back with her hands, dug her fingernails into him, tried to take all of him inside her, hold all of him at once.

When he thrust into her one last time, and she felt his muscles tighten beneath her hands, she lifted herself up while he filled her, touching her womb with his firmness, with his release.

Molly finally opened her eyes.

Well, the birds were still in the tree branches overhead. They hadn't scared them away. The sun still filtered down through the leaves, dappling everything in the small clearing. Water still bubbled over rocks in the stream. One of the horses was noisily chewing on something.

Obviously, she hadn't died.

"Oh . . . wow . . ." Molly said when she could at last get her breath.

"Yeah. Good golly, Miss Molly," Dominic said, still not moving, his breathing rather labored. "You wouldn't happen to have a paper bag I could blow in?"

"You're hyperventilating?"

"I was doing something there," he said, turning his head slightly, to press a kiss against the side of her neck. "Tell me, what just happened?"

"You don't know?"

He kissed her again. "It was a rhetorical question. I think. Am I crushing you?"

"It's a nice weight."

"Nevertheless," he said, easing himself up onto his knees once more, then moving one leg so that she could scoot out from beneath him.

They straightened their clothes quickly, quietly, and then Molly leaned back against the log, stretched her legs out in front of her. "You wouldn't want to be starting back any time soon, right?"

"No. Not for a few minutes. A century," he said, also reclining against the log. "I have a feeling you're not much for postmortems, Molly, but . . . Well, I don't know about you, but I'm still shaking."

"Oh, you want compliments now?"

"No. But something happened . . ."

Molly nodded her head. "I know. It was . . . it was . . . different. I've never felt . . ."

"Right," he said when her words died away. "Me, neither. God, listen to me. I'm being about as articulate as a three-year-old."

To start your membership, simply complete and return the Free Book Certificate. You'll receive your Introductory Shipment of 3 FREE Zebra Contemporary Romances, you only pay $1.99 for shipping and handling. Then, each month you will receive the 3 newest Zebra Contemporary Romances. Each shipment will be yours to examine FREE for 10 days. If you decide to keep the books, you'll pay the preferred subscriber price (a savings of up to 20% off the cover price), plus shipping and handling. If you want us to stop sending books, just say the word… it's that simple.

FREE BOOK CERTIFICATE

Yes! Please send me 3 FREE Zebra Contemporary romance novels. I only pay $1.99 for shipping and handling. I understand that each month thereafter I will be able to preview 3 brand-new Contemporary Romances FREE for 10 days. Then, if I should decide to keep them, I will pay the money-saving preferred subscriber's price (that's a savings of up to 20% off the retail price), plus shipping and handling. I understand I am under no obligation to purchase any books, as explained on this card.

Name _____

Address _____ Apt. _____

City _____ State _____ Zip _____

Telephone (____) _____

Signature _____

(If under 18, parent or guardian must sign)

CN034A

Thank You!

Offer limited to one per household and not to current subscribers. Terms, offer and prices subject to change. Orders subject to acceptance by Zebra Contemporary Book Club. Offer Valid in the U.S. only.

lll.u.l..lll....llt.l.l.l.l..l.l..ll.l.l..lll.l..lll..l

Zebra Contemporary Romance Book Club
Zebra Home Subscription Service, Inc.
P.O. Box 5214
Clifton , NJ 07015-5214

PLACE
STAMP
HERE

"We do get along," Molly said hopefully. Hopeful that they could end this conversation, and soon. She wasn't into introspection—hadn't she just told herself that?

One of the horses snorted, and Molly grabbed on to that, asking a question that had bothered her earlier, but that honestly, she couldn't care less about at the moment. Still, it was a way out of a conversation that might find her being too honest for her own good.

"Why did you geld Sylvester? He's such a great horse."

She felt Dominic's eyes on her and kept her expression tuned to mildly inquisitive as she turned to look at him. "Really. Why?"

"You ask the damnedest questions. I didn't geld him, as a matter of fact. I bought him that way. His owner told me that there had been . . . a development problem."

"Oh," Molly said, sitting up, putting the flat of her hand on Dominic's stomach in order to help herself to a sitting position on what was, after all, the sloping bank into the stream. "You mean like Funny Cide, that Kentucky Derby winner?"

"I don't remember. What was the reason Funny Cide was gelded?"

"Oh, something about an undescended testicle," she said, moving her hand lower, knowing she was making him uncomfortable, but right now, uncomfortable was better than romantic. "You know, like the package was all there, but there wasn't anything in one of them."

Dominic shifted slightly against the ground. "That would be a problem."

"Oh, yes. That's why they had to geld Funny Cide, so that he could perform correctly on the race track, something like that." She moved her hand even lower, cupping him through his jeans. "I don't quite know how they do it. I guess it's just a quick snip, snip . . ."

Dominic's hand covered hers. "Cut that out. Wait, scratch

that. Don't cut anything. Damn it, Molly, can we change the subject?"

"Sure." She pulled her hand free and sat up straighter. "Pick one."

"I did, but you redirected me nicely, or not so nicely, depending on how I look at it. But I'm guessing you don't want to talk about what just happened here."

She picked up a small twig with three leaves still on it and began twirling it between her fingers. "We had sex. Good sex. *Very* good sex."

"And that's it?"

"Since the beginning of time, yes, that's it. Sex."

"Just sex."

"All right. Therapeutic sex?"

"For you or me?"

"I wasn't the one in the emergency room."

"Keep this up, Molly, and it could be arranged. Are you trying to tell me we're having sex to relax me or something?"

"I don't know. Are you relaxed?"

"No, damn it, I'm not. I'm not relaxed. I'm also not stupid enough to believe you didn't enjoy what we did."

"I didn't say I didn't."

"Okay. Okay, I get it. It's the no strings bit again, right? You're afraid I'm going to cling. Or, worse, that you might be beginning to feel something for me that goes way beyond two adults enjoying each other."

"Don't be ridiculous," Molly said, getting to her feet, to glare down at him. "You know, if you're going to insist on rehashing everything every time we make—every time we have sex—then we're not going to do it anymore."

He leaned back against the log, crossed his arms and his legs, sighed, and said, "Isn't that just like a woman. Withholding sex to prove her point."

"Ooooh, don't you push me, Dominic Longstreet."

"Me? Push you? Hey, nobody pushes Molly Applegate. She runs away all on her own."

He was right. She had already stepped over the log and was actually in the process of heading toward the horses and taking Daisy and herself out of here when he'd all but dared her to run.

"Why are you doing this to me, Dominic?"

He got to his feet. "I could ask you the same question. And don't frown, like you don't understand what I mean. You're driving me crazy. I hold you, knowing you'll soon be gone. I feel you come alive in my arms, knowing you're already planning for the day you leave. And you know what else? I'm standing here, right now, wanting you again so badly that I—"

He was so cute. Wasn't he cute? Oh, yes. He was *so cute!*

Molly didn't know she was moving until she was in his arms, her mouth wildly pressing against his, her fingernails dragging down his back, her riding boots a good four inches off the ground.

She felt him try to grab her, to steady the both of them, but he couldn't do it. She had launched herself with some abandon, and that force carried them both backward, down the bank, and into the stream . . . where they fell, full length, into the water.

They broke apart and came up sputtering—not that the stream was more than two feet deep.

Dominic shook his head, like a dog after a bath, sending water everywhere. "What did you do that for?"

"I don't know. Purely impulse, I guess. I didn't mean to do it," Molly said, holding up her arms, looking at her ruined riding jacket. "We're pretty wet, huh?"

"The Atlantic Ocean is pretty wet. We're drenched. How in the hell are we going to explain this when we get back to the stables?"

"A sudden shower?" Molly suggested, and she grinned as Dominic's shoulders began to shake.

"Isolated storm," he said, then laughed out loud as he splashed her.

"Fast-moving front passing through the area," she countered, splashing him back.

And the battle was on.

They splashed and laughed, and generally behaved like lunatics unexpectedly put in charge of the asylum, and then they reluctantly left the stream and rode back to the stables, nothing settled between them . . . to be greeted by Billie White, who kept showing up like a bad penny.

"You're all wet!"

"Observant, isn't she?" Dominic said to Molly, winking at her.

"There was a sudden, freak, passing front shower," Molly told the woman as she maneuvered Daisy straight at her, so that Billie had no choice but to step back. "Happens here in Virginia all the time."

"But . . . But you're both all muddy."

"Billie, if we'd both grown two heads and ridden in here singing opera, how does this become your concern?" Dominic asked, and Molly kept Daisy moving. He was more relaxed, definitely, but he wasn't comatose, and if Billie White knew what was good for her, she'd back off. Now.

That was what Molly was going to do . . . and for the same reason. Self-preservation.

But maybe not just yet. . . .

Chapter 16

Molly had always needed time to herself, time alone. She could be the life and soul of every party . . . and then feel the sudden need to go away, step back, be by herself.

Once she and Dominic had gone back to the main house to shower and change, once the children had been settled in the kitchen with Mrs. Jonnie, with the rubber stamp set she'd gotten for them on their trip to the store, Molly slipped out and commandeered one of the golf carts, setting off down a macadam path she'd yet to explore.

This path also ended alongside a stream, undoubtedly another stretch of the bubbling water she and Dominic had played in earlier. She set the brake, leaned her forearms on the steering wheel, her chin on her forearms, and stared at the sun dancing on the water, at the tall trees on the other side of the bank. And she shifted her mind.

Ah, peace.

Ah, quiet.

Ah, just her.

She could stay here all day, letting her mind relax, letting her body relax, not being on display, on show, or even on her good behavior. She could stay here for hours, for entire days, always complete within herself, content with herself.

"Okay," she said aloud after about ten minutes. "That's enough of that."

Alone was good. A long bubble bath was good.

But the kids might need her. Dominic might want her.

Is it still running away if you leave knowing you want to come back?

But she wouldn't go back. Not yet. She had something to prove to herself first.

She had to prove that she didn't *need* to go back.

Molly climbed out of the golf cart and set off to her right, following a dirt path that led along the stream.

Maybe she'd find wildflowers to pick and tuck behind her ear. Maybe she'd find enough to take back to Mrs. Jonnie, who could put them in a vase on the dining room table.

Maybe she'd find another small clearing like the one along the riding path and call it her Secret Place. Maybe she'd show the kids, and they'd have a picnic there. They'd think up a name for the place and build a pretend campfire and dance around it and. . . .

"Stop that!" she ordered herself, and a few birds in the tree branches above her angrily squawked in protest. "Oops, sorry about that," she told the birds, and kept moving.

The path came very close to a small overhang that ended in the stream. Molly kept her head down, concentrating on her footing as she came to a fairly sharp right turn, so she heard the voices in time to stop, remain hidden.

". . . and I don't see why we can't just take up where we left off. We had a good thing together, and you know it."

"Good for whom? What are you so afraid of anyway? That I'd *cling* too much?"

Molly stepped back. Derek and Cynara. Arguing.

She really should keep backing up, backtrack, and never let them know she'd discovered them. That would be the polite thing to do.

She stayed where she was and sort of leaned her head closer, the better to hear them.

"I tried marriage once, remember? It didn't work."

"Oh, come on, we've all tried marriage at least once. What were we—twelve? You and that chorus girl, me and Clive the bloodsucking fortune hunter."

"Her name was Maryjane."

"Was? What? She's dead?"

"Only to me," Derek said. "All right, all right. I was twenty-three. What did I know?"

"What did either of us know, darling," Cynara said, and the edge had left her voice, to be replaced by a near purr. "But we're no longer ignorant babies, are we?" Her voice hardened again as she ended, "Unless you're afraid?"

"Oh, don't try that crap on me, Cynara. Prove you're not a coward, marry me? Besides, who do you think we are? Lunt and Fontaine? Cronyn and Tandy? Everyone will expect us to work together all the time. All right, it worked for them. But there was also Liz Taylor and Richard Burton, remember? Working together didn't exactly do great things for them. It didn't for dozens. And it wouldn't for us. We'd kill each other within a month if we had to work together all the time, then go home with each other every night."

"So you went home with my understudy one night instead," Cynara said, and Molly winced. That had to have hurt.

"It was a mistake."

"No, Derek, *you* were the mistake. I mentioned marriage, barely mentioned it, and the next thing I knew you were running as fast as you could in another direction. Straight at Louise. And then Jane. And then Brenda, Nancy, Kathleen.

Determined to show me that you weren't ready to be married, to be *tied down.* It was a small company, Derek, so I guess you should be glad I kicked you out before you got to Jason."

"That's not funny."

"No, you're right. It's not funny. It's pathetic. Why didn't you just have the guts to tell me no? No, you had to embarrass me, make a fool of me, and I had to smile and say we'd mutually agreed to part and we're still the best of friends. Best of friends? I could have killed you."

"You did, when you threw me out," Derek said, so quietly that Molly had to step closer to hear him. "I haven't been the same since, Cynara. And neither have you. Look at this production, for crying out loud. You're about to get bounced, darling."

"Bounced? Don't be ridiculous. It's Taylor's music, if you can call it that. It doesn't fit Tony's lyrics, the breaks are badly timed . . ."

"Don't *you* be ridiculous. The music is fine, Cynara. You're just not getting it. And, damn it, Cynara, if you don't get it soon, you're gone."

There was a short, uncomfortable silence, before Derek added, "Unless you're doing this on purpose? Is that it, Cynara? You signed before I did, and now that you know I'm in, you want out? Do you hate me that much?"

"I'm trying to fail? Now who's being ridiculous. Not to mention having an ego the size of Manhattan. If I wanted you gone, you'd be gone, Derek, with just a snap of my fingers. As you said, I was signed first."

"All right, so if that isn't it, why did you bring me out here on this stupid picnic?"

"Not for the reason you thought, obviously. Or did you seriously believe I'm the roll-in-the-weeds type?"

"It was a pretty good roll, darling, until you wanted to start talking."

Molly put a hand to her mouth to stifle a giggle that was fast rising to her lips, and stepped back, stepped on some loose twigs. She winced at the sound the breaking twigs made.

"What was that?"

Molly turned into a statue.

"What was what, Derek? I didn't hear anything. Oh, wait, now you think I've hidden a photographer in the trees? Is that it? Something juicy for the tabloids? I know, Derek, I'll be Fergie. Quick, suck my bare toes."

"Cut that out, Cynara. But now that you mention it . . ."

"It's not a photographer, Derek. It's a bear. A big, bad, wooly bear, and it's going to bite your head clean off! Ooooo—aren't you scared?"

"God, you can drive a man mad," Derek said, but his tone had changed, become lower, almost seductive. "Come here."

"Make me, big boy. Look, I'm all afraid. I'm even cringing. Oh, not the buttons on my blouse. Please, sir. You can't open them. My bra? No, not my bra, good sir. Stop, stop . . . um, darling, I always said your best talent lay in your tongue."

It got very quiet, and Molly knew it was time for her to go. She backed up two paces, then turned and tiptoed another ten feet before breaking into a run.

"Whew!" she said to the air as she reached the golf cart. "I'm much too young and innocent to hear stuff like that."

Then she grinned, turned the golf cart, and headed back toward the house. She'd just passed the theater when Lizzie and Big Al spied her and began running down the hill from the main house, each of them carrying a large sheet of paper.

And arguing.

"It is not a trachodon, you dork. Yours is just a plain old rhinoceros. I've got the trachodon. Molly, look!" Lizzie said, waving the paper in her face as Molly got out of the golf cart. "Isn't this a trachodon?"

Molly grabbed the paper in self-defense. It was covered

in different-colored stamped outlines of about a dozen animals. "Which one?"

"The green one, on the top. That's a trachodon, right?"

Molly looked at the outline. Fat, dragging tail, a sort of huge ruff on top of its head, one short horn on its snout, two long horns jutting forward from its forehead.

She handed the paper back. "Personally, I think it's my home economics teacher from my junior year. Mrs. Haggerty. See? The same small, beady eyes?"

"Oh, come on, Molly. Tell him. His is only a stupid rhinoceros."

"She doesn't know," Big Al said. "Told you so. Girls don't know nothing about dinosaurs."

"Girls don't know *anything* about dinosaurs," Molly corrected, longing to draw them both close for a group hug. They were so darn cute.

"See?" Big Al crowed. "I told you girls don't know nothing—anything."

"I know they aren't really *purple* and sing stupid songs," Lizzie countered hotly.

"Big know-it-all jerk."

"Runty know-nothing dork."

"Gee, and there I was," Molly said, "wondering what made me think I wanted to be by myself for a while. And miss this sweet interaction between siblings? What was I thinking?"

Lizzie, mouth open, surely ready to say something else insulting to her brother, shook her head and said, "Sorry, Molly. But he doesn't know anything about dinosaurs."

"Neither do I," Molly admitted. "But I have an idea. I'm betting there's a set of encyclopedias somewhere in the house. After dinner, we can read all about them."

"Encyclopedias? Can't we just go on-line?"

Molly smiled sheepishly. "Sorry. I keep forgetting who I'm talking to here, don't I? Okay, Miss Worldwide Web queen, we'll go on-line. Now, if you two promise not to declare war once I'm gone, I'd like to make a phone call."

"Only if he stops changing his name," Lizzie said, pointing at Big Al, who was turning his paper sideways and squinting at the pictures he'd stamped on it.

Molly raised her eyebrows. "He's not Big Al anymore?"

Big Al smiled up at her. "Nope. I'm Butch."

Lizzie groaned.

"Butch, huh? Where did you get that one?" Molly asked, biting the insides of her cheeks.

Butch shrugged. "I dunno. It's good, isn't it?"

"We'll try it out," Molly said, looking meaningfully at Lizzie. "I think this is good, Butch, that you're trying different names, getting the feel of them."

"See? I told you it was all right. I'm Butch!"

"I don't know why you can't just stick with Dork. It fits," Lizzie said. "Come on, *Butch*, let's go show these to Mrs. Jonnie. She said we could make dinosaur cookies with some molds she has somewhere."

"Bless Mrs. Jonnie," Molly said, watching as the two children ran to the corner of the house, on their way to the back door of the kitchen. Then she headed for the steps to the porch, and inside, climbed to her room to retrieve her cell phone.

She punched in Janie's cell phone number, prepared for it to ring and ring.

"Hello? Molly, is that you?"

"Janie?" Molly said, sitting down at the dressing table and pushing off her sneakers. "You finally figured out how to answer your cell phone. Congratulations."

"Very funny," her cousin's voice shot back at her. "And you finally learned to turn yours *on*. Where are you? Are you back in Washington?"

"Not exactly. But you will be happy to know that Preston Kiddie Kare still will live to serve another day."

"Oh, that, yes, I should have asked, shouldn't I? I forgot."

Molly frowned at the cell phone. "Who are you and what have you done to Jane Preston?"

Janie laughed, and it was a free and easy laugh.

"I repeat. Where's my cousin? You sound like her, but you can't be her."

"I can and I am. Listen, I don't want to tell you everything on the phone, but I did leave you a message about some of it. Did you see the newspapers?"

"Not really, no. I've been . . . sort of out-of-touch."

"Oh, well, you should. Or just turn on any news program. There have been some very interesting developments to Senator Harrison's campaign for President."

Molly, who two weeks ago had lived for getting the dirt on Senator Aubrey Harrison, yawned as she turned to the dressing table mirror and pushed at her hair. "I'll have to check that out. Listen, Janie, I just called to . . . um, to make sure you're all right, that I didn't put you in over your head."

"Why? Because you knew you were putting me in over my head when you first suggested the plan? Isn't it a little late for you to worry about me now?"

"Oh, don't go all schoolteacher on me, Janie. The week's over, and you're obviously still alive. Just tell me you're all right."

"All right? Molly, if I didn't know that you had nothing to do with it, I'd say you should be taking bows about now. I mean, I've never been—what? Oh, hang on a sec, Molly."

"Janie, no, I've got to—oh, hell," she said, allowing her shoulders to slump as she waited for her cousin to get back on the line. And who was her cousin talking to, anyway?

"Ohmigod, Molly, are you near a television? CNN, Molly. We were there, as witnesses. I think I just saw myself! It was all so beautiful. And we just adore Henry. Look, I've got to go watch this. Call me later?"

"But I wanted to—" Molly said, before realizing that her cousin had disconnected. She dropped her forehead into her hands. "I just wanted to ask you if you thought I was capable of ever being in love. That's all. Nothing important."

Molly put down the cell phone and stood up, looking for the remote control for the television set, then turned it to CNN, in time to hear the tail end of the entertainment news:

". . . surprise elopement, and her spokesperson reports that Miss Hythe and publisher Henry Brewster will honeymoon at an undisclosed location before Miss Hythe begins filming on her next movie. This is the first marriage for both. Back to you, Jim."

Molly stared at the photo until it was replaced by a picture of a derailed train, then clicked off the set and sat down at the dressing table once more.

The reporter had said Henry. Janie had said Henry. Janie had said she was there. There, meaning at the ceremony, obviously. Just as obviously, Janie knew Henry.

"*Obviously,* I'm missing something. And drop-dead gorgeous Brandy Hythe? God, he's almost a half-head shorter than she is. And pudgy. Cute, but pudgy. And she looked so damn happy. Is love really blind, or does it just leapfrog over any obstacle if it's real, true?"

Then, at last, the penny dropped. They had all been together at the intellectual retreat. That's how Janie met them. But who's the *we* she mentioned? Did Janie meet someone, too? She may have hinted about her escort . . . but Janie wasn't the spontaneous sort, never had been. Still, she certainly did sound happy.

Happy, and out of reach. Just as her aunt and uncle were out of reach, not that she'd ever confided in them. But it would be nice to be able to talk to somebody.

She was so confused! One moment she wanted to run,

and the next she wanted to jump Dominic's bones, and then go bake a cake, or dust something.

It was hormonal. It had to be. A temporary aberration, brought on by spending time with too many kids. It was a domestic urge that would pass, if she just gave it time.

It was being needed, possibly—definitely—for the first time in her life.

Oh, Janie needed her, but that wasn't the same. Janie also had her parents.

What did she, Molly, have? What had she ever had?

A trust fund.

A million acquaintances, but only one real friend, Janie.

A house, but never a home. No one to come home to. No one waiting, or worrying, or greeting her with a kiss, even with a "Where the hell have you been?"

"And let's all have a pity party for Margaret," Molly said, getting to her feet. "I'm *happy,* damn it!"

Then she wiped at her damp cheeks with the back of her hand and called out, "Come in!" to whoever had knocked on her bedroom door.

Cynara opened the door a crack and poked her head in. "Molly?" She entered the rest of the way. "Okay, you're alone. Good. I guess you didn't hear my knock. Can we talk? Girl talk?"

Molly nodded, then sniffled. Then sighed, pulled herself together. "Sure. What do you want to talk about?"

Cynara hopped up on the bed and sat there like a queen on her throne. "Men, of course. Is there any other subject?"

"Not lately, no," Molly agreed, and pulled up a bit of mattress to call her own. "Shoot."

"It's Derek," Cynara said with a theatrical sigh. Since she was a star, it was a pretty convincing sigh. "He's driving me insane."

"Typical of the species," Molly agreed, nodding. "What's he doing?"

Cynara began playing with her manicure, chipping at the bright red polish with a thumbnail. "He loves me. I know he loves me. He knows he loves me. But he pretends that it's all just sex."

Molly shifted uncomfortably on her portion of the mattress. "Gee. That's tough."

"It's *stupid*. Why won't he just admit that he loves me? He keeps putting up roadblocks, you know? We'd lose interest and fight if we had to work together all the time, and everyone would expect us to want to work together all the time. He chases me, but the moment I give in, he takes off again. Like this afternoon."

Molly lowered her eyelids and looked at her crossed legs as she swung them off the edge of the bed. "What . . . What happened this afternoon?"

"We made love, of course. Or, if Derek was telling this story, we had sex. Fabulous sex. I'd talked him into a picnic, you understand. We ate some chicken and salad, and then we made love. And then he picked a fight. He *always* picks a fight." She shrugged eloquently. "So then we made love again, we fought again, and now he's driven off all in a huff and I want to kill him."

"He's confused?" Molly offered hopefully. "I mean, maybe being in love scares him? The . . . I don't know . . . the loss of independence? Worrying that someone else is dependent on you and you're not as great as he—I mean, as *you* think? That maybe what you think you see isn't really there? It's all fake, just for show? I mean, inside, she—he could be really insecure? Running scared?"

Cynara turned her head and looked at Molly. "Okay, I give up. Was that really deep, or don't you know what you're talking about either?"

Molly tried to laugh, but that laugh sounded hollow to her own ears. Not that Cynara seemed to notice. "I don't know. I was just thinking out loud, I suppose. Love is scary, you know? And what you think you want one day might not be what you want the next day, right? Maybe some people just don't have it in them—anything *real,* anything worth anything. So . . . So they just keep moving, before anyone notices?"

"Oh, he's fickle, all right. He'd be trying to get in your pants if Dom hadn't warned him away. But he always comes back to me. Always. Isn't it time he just gave up and admitted the inevitable? We love each other. How can that be scary?"

"I don't know," Molly said, ready to weep in relief as the dinner bell gonged. She hopped off the bed and went to retrieve her sneakers. "It just is, I suppose. Are you hungry? I know I'm starved."

Chapter 17

Dominic looked up from the last page of the fax he was reading and frowned. "Taylor. You're back a day early."

Taylor Carlisle, a broad-shouldered man with bright red hair and freckled skin, pulled up a chair, straddling it. He wrote music; he looked like a linebacker.

"Tony called me, tracked me down in New York," he said without preamble, his low voice a pleasant rumble. "He said you're still working. Do you want to tell me how the hell he knew you're still working?"

"He caught me. He called me on the private line here in the office," Dominic told him. "But he's wrong. I'm not working."

"Excuse me? I thought we were working. I'm back here because we're working, and because instead of killing myself I should just be slitting Cynara's throat. I'm not much for self-sacrifice."

"I know, I heard her. Yesterday. Her timing's all off."

"And she goes flat, Dom. She's ruining the best song Tony and I ever wrote."

"We'll give her another two weeks, all right? I canceled rehearsals, but everyone is staying here until Tony gets back, so I'm hoping she'll try to improve on her own before we have to make a decision."

"Tonight, two weeks from now. Take all the time you need, Dom. I've already made mine. She's gone."

Dominic shrugged. "We'll see. But Tony has to be in on any decision like that. So, are you going to stay, or head back to New York? I was going to call you later tonight, to tell you rehearsals are canceled."

Taylor rubbed at the red, fuzzy soul patch beneath his lower lip. "No, I'll stay. Tony threatened—I'll stay."

"Tony told you to watch me," Dominic said, getting up from his chair to look out the window. His back to his friend, he said, "I'm all right, Taylor. I admit it, I had a bit of a scare while you were gone, medically, but I'm fine. It was nothing serious."

"A medical scare? I leave for one lousy weekend and you go medical on me? Cripes, Dom, what happened?"

Dominic put his back to the window. "Let's just say that all work and no play make Dom blow in a paper bag."

"Oh. All right, smartass, if you don't want to talk about it, just say so."

"Maybe later, Taylor, okay? For now, I have something else to tell you." He picked up the fax, the one Gerard Hopkins, Esquire, had sent to Molly. "We've acquired another guest."

Taylor crossed one long leg over the other. "You've imported some recreation? Is that what the doctor ordered? I want this guy's name, now. I mean, I've been feeling a little medical myself lately."

"Would you shut up," Dominic said, putting down the fax. "I had a problem on Friday. The damn day care place I dumped the kids in closed down for the next two weeks."

Taylor put up a hand. "May I be excused? Either that, or

you lay down bear traps around the theater for Lizzie. She's a cute kid, but I don't need her telling me what's wrong with the work."

"She was right about the opening," Dominic said, hiding a grin. "It was too abrupt."

"We would have figured that out. I mean it, Dom, she's cute and all, but she keeps asking for an audition. Why me? Why is she picking on me?"

"You're here? You're not related to her? Maybe you'd listen?"

"But I'm not here. I'm leaving, remember? Wait. Tell me about this other *guest.*"

Dominic sat down. This one was going to take a while. So he began at the beginning and ended fifteen minutes and several interruptions later with, "But I promised that nobody would know she's really Margaret Applegate."

"But you told me?"

"I had to tell somebody. And you get around. You might even recognize her. I mean, by rights, I should be watching out for her. She's . . . Well, she's different. Instead, she's watching out for me. Although if she tries to check my pulse, I might take another look at the arrangement."

"So nobody else knows who she is? Yeah, well, that figures. The kids wouldn't know, and the rest of them are all too wrapped up in themselves to take notice of anything that isn't orbiting them. Now tell me the parts you left out."

"You've got all you're going to get," Dominic said with a wry smile. "Just be nice to the lady, don't chase her, and don't let on that you know who she is."

"Don't touch, that's what you're saying. Good looking, right?"

"Gorgeous," Dominic admitted, shaking his head. "Gorgeous, nuts, mercurial, sweet, sexy as all hell. I mean, her legs could—never mind. Just hands off."

"Oh-ho. Oh-ho, oh-ho, oh-ho. Don't tell me. The Dominic is smitten." Taylor stood up and put the chair back against the wall. "Where is this creature, because *this* I've got to see."

"You'll meet her at dinner, which is now, I suppose," Dominic said, gathering up the pages of the fax and inserting them in a manilla envelope. "Come on, let's go."

Dominic had just locked the door to the office (a move he thought had a thirty percent chance of keeping Lizzie out), when Big Al came running down the hill, calling his name.

"Dinner, Uncle Dom! Hey, hi, Uncle Taylor, you're back! It's me, Butch."

Dominic looked at Taylor as both of them mouthed, "Butch?"

Butch (nee: Big Al, Al, and Little Tony) skidded to a halt and beamed up at Dominic. "How'ya like it? Butch, I mean. I just picked it. It's my new nickname."

"Why Butch?" Taylor asked as the three of them headed toward the main house.

"I don't know. Al was too short, and Big Al was kind of stupid, but not as stupid as Little Tony. So I'm Butch."

"Ah, the age-old nickname problem. I hear you, buddy. There isn't a lot you can do with Taylor, either."

"Hey, we tried Stinky, but you threatened to break Tony's nose," Dominic reminded him, as he, his brother, and Taylor had known each other since grade school. "Butch is okay."

"You don't like it," Butch said, hanging his head. "Lizzie says I should be a dog, to be called Butch." Then he brightened. "What about Killer?"

"Stick with Butch," Dominic said as Taylor coughed into his fist. "Is Molly downstairs yet?"

"Yeah. Her and—I mean, she and Lizzie are setting the table. We're having fried chicken."

"Ah, Mrs. Jonnie's famous fried chicken. I knew there was a reason I came back a day early. Lead on, Butchie-boy."

Butch ran ahead.

Dominic tried to impress Taylor with the gravity of his request one more time. "When I introduce you to Molly, behave. No barking or drooling, get it?"

"What? How gorgeous can she be?"

"She might be wearing shorts," Dominic said quietly.

"Really." Taylor turned to look at his friend. "You could always throw a blanket around her."

"Or a bucket of cold water on you. I mean it, Taylor. She's not what you think."

"How would you know what I'm thinking?"

"I know you, that's how. Beautiful, rich. To you, that means, 'Hey, baby, let's play.' And she's not like that."

"How about I slit my palm and write it in blood? I, Taylor Carlisle, will not chase Margaret Applegate."

"Molly. Call her Molly."

"Cripes. Let's get this over with, all right? And I wish you hadn't told me. Now I'll be sure to spill the beans."

"You'd better not—okay, there she is."

Dominic stopped walking, because Taylor had, and watched Taylor, rather than Molly, who was shaking out a tablecloth on the small service porch outside the kitchen.

"Oh . . . my . . . *God*. Darling, where have you been all my life?"

"Exactly," Dominic said, not without pride. "Now do you understand my warning?"

"Oh, I understand your warning. What I don't understand is why you haven't already built a barbwire fence around her and posted No Trespassing signs."

"We're friends."

"Sure, you are. This medical problem? The doctor didn't suggest you try those little blue *up-boy* pills?"

"No, damn it. I told you. I'm under stress."

"You're telling me? You've got *that* prancing around here

playing nanny to Tony's kids? Under stress? I'd have imploded by now."

"That's enough," Dominic said, feeling a sharp, quick anger.

"Whoa. I wondered how long it would take. You are involved, aren't you? Your heart, I mean. I won't ask about the rest of you because I can tell this one's off limits for locker room talk. Is it the real thing, Dom? Has the mighty finally fallen?"

"I don't know. It's all happening pretty fast. I just know that the closer I try to get, the more she backs away. She's driving me crazy."

"There's a ride I wouldn't mind taking. Okay, okay!" he added quickly, holding up his hands in surrender when Dominic growled at him. "No more jokes. I can see this is serious stuff here. Tell you what. I'll take care of Cynara and Derek and Dracula's wife and spawn, and you and Molly try to figure out what's going on, okay? But don't let her go, Dom. That's not one you'd get over easily."

"Tell me about it," Dominic said, returning Molly's wave. She still stood on the porch, wearing a black tank top and beige short-shorts, her feet slipped into low-heeled sandals. Her hair glinted in the sunlight, her smile was open and welcoming, and no one would ever know they'd both made love and fought just a few hours ago.

"Dinner's ready," she called out, then smiled at Taylor. "Hello. Butch says you're Taylor Carlisle. I'm Molly Applegate." She held out her hand, and Dominic bit his bottom lip as Taylor said, "Happy to . . . good to . . . that's me, Taylor."

"He's only articulate with notes," Dominic said, slapping Taylor on the back to urge him into the house, then hung back to smile at Molly. "Hi," he said, looking into her soft brown eyes.

"Hi, yourself," she said, standing up on tiptoe, to kiss his cheek. "Tell me that's not work in your hand, because then I'll have to hurt you."

He looked down at the envelope. He'd totally forgotten. He forgot everything when Molly smiled at him. "This? No, this is for you. Your attorney called, then sent it to my fax."

"Gerry?"

"You call him Gerry?"

"Oh, he sounds like a snotty, bad-tempered grizzly, but he's just an old teddy bear. I hope you didn't mind that I gave him your number. He has this thing about knowing where I am at all times and won't settle for cell phones, because I once made him believe I was in Connecticut when I was really in San Francisco. He doesn't trust me, but he's okay."

"The fatherly sort?"

"Hardly. The fiscally responsible sort." She motioned to the envelope he still held. "I suppose you read that?"

"If I said no, would you believe me?"

"Nope. Hand it over."

"It's a report on your proposed charity disbursements for the quarter. He wants to be sure you approve. You're into a lot of different charities, aren't you?"

"Giving something back," Molly said, slapping the envelope against her bare thigh. "Gerry calls it a great tax deduction. I call it how can one woman spend all that money? It seems only fair to spread some of it around."

"Don't do that, Molly."

"Do what?" she asked, smiling at him.

"Pretend it doesn't matter. Pretend you don't really care. I saw the list of charities. Specifically named women's shelters, child abuse hotlines, food banks, homeless shelters, orphanages, spread out all across the country. You could have just written a check to one of the big funds if all you wanted was the deduction. You picked out the charities yourself, didn't you? On your . . . *travels*."

"You forgot the zoos, and the environmental stuff," she said quietly. "I like animals and trees. Animals like trees, too. Especially dogs, huh? Can we change the subject?"

He lifted her chin with his index finger. "You know, I'm starting to get really crazy about you, Good Golly Miss Molly."

She bit her lips together, nodded.

"You're not going to say anything?"

Mouth still firmly shut, she shook her head.

"So I should back off a little? Cool it a while?"

"Okay," she said so quietly he had to bend close to hear her. "I promised the kids I'd do something with them tonight anyway."

"Tomorrow?"

She dipped her head a moment, then looked up at him, smiling. "Tomorrow is another day. I heard that somewhere."

"Hey, are you guys coming in for dinner or what?" Lizzie asked from the doorway. "Uncle Taylor is teasing Mrs. Jonnie about marrying her for her fried chicken, and it's really getting dumb in there."

Dominic held out his arm. "Shall we, Miss Applegate?"

Molly tucked her arm through his. "I would be delighted, Mr. Longstreet."

"Dorks," Lizzie said, rolling her eyes as she led the way to the dining room.

During the course of the meal, Taylor entertained them with stories about a new restaurant in Manhattan he'd visited on Saturday night, one dedicated to the theme, said Taylor, of celebrating the highest prices for the least food on the plate.

That led to a discussion of restaurants, with Molly waxing poetic over Emeril's in New Orleans, which led to her telling the kids what Mardi Gras was all about—the G-rated version—which led to Taylor recounting stories of his trip to France last year, which led to, at last, dinosaur cookies for dessert.

"We're going to look up dinosaurs on the computer, Uncle

Dom," Butch said, biting off the head of a badly misshapen something-or-other. "You want to see, too? How about you, Uncle Taylor?"

"Not me," Taylor said, holding out his hands. "I never could get real excited about anything with horns or tails."

"Which certainly doesn't explain Lettice Carruthers," Dominic said under his breath. Boy, he was feeling better. Better every minute. Better every time he looked at Molly. Younger. Definitely happier. Almost giddy.

"I heard that, Dom," Taylor said, getting to his feet. "Okay, off to the guest house, to see if I can get to my room without disturbing Mama Billie in her bat cave."

The kids giggled at that, then picked up their plates without being asked, and carried them to the kitchen.

"So that's your big night? Looking at dinosaurs on the Internet?"

"I'm the nanny, remember? Besides, I've always wondered if a bronto sauruses. Haven't you?"

"Okay, you sold me. Let's go."

Ten minutes later they were all in the living room, and Lizzie was in charge of her laptop with the wireless Internet feature, gizmo, whatever she called it, and they were visiting the wonderful world of dinosaurs.

Butch sat on Dominic's lap, so that Dominic could rub his chin against the kid's hair, and Molly sat beside Lizzie, who definitely enjoyed her moment on the stage as she found a site that actually showed a minimovie of animated dinosaurs.

Butch began to flag about an hour later, and Molly took his hand and led him off for his bath, leaving Dominic with Lizzie, and feeling pretty good about himself.

It was nice, spending an evening with the kids. As the saying went, he wouldn't want to do it for a living, but he was enjoying his niece and nephew more than he thought possible.

"How did you find all those sites, Lizzie?" he asked when he believed he'd seen enough dinosaurs to last him the next decade.

"A search engine, of course. Here, look, I just go to one of them, like this one, and then I type in what I want to find out about. Like, Mardi Gras. Spell it, please, Uncle Dom?"

They explored Mardi Gras sites for a while. Then Lizzie typed in her father's name, surprising Dominic with the number of hits.

"I can do it with any name. Watch," she told him, and promptly typed in Molly Applegate.

"Hey, no, that's okay. Do me instead," Dominic said quickly.

Did you mean Margaret Applegate? the damn search engine shot back at her. Just as the search engine he'd used had shot back at him. Modern technology could be a real pain.

"No, that can't be right. She's Molly, not Margaret. Never mind," Dominic said quickly. "Try Uncle Taylor."

"No, let me try Margaret Applegate first," Lizzie said, already clicking on something on the screen.

And there she was. Margaret "Molly" Applegate. From A to Z and Here to There . . . The screen was full of photographs of Molly. Each click brought another page, another story, another revelation.

He'd already seen a lot of these. Margaret Applegate at a Black and White Charity Ball, making a comically sexy face at the camera as she posed in her long black gown and even longer white feather boa. Margaret Applegate in diamonds, at the opera. Margaret Applegate sheltered by a huge straw hat at the Kentucky Derby. He hadn't seen that one. No wonder she knew about that horse, Funny Cide. She'd been there.

"Wow," Lizzie said almost reverently. "They're all our Molly."

Denial would be more than stupid; it would be useless. "She doesn't want anyone to know," Dominic said, motioning for Lizzie to turn off the computer—not that the kid wouldn't go back to it the moment his back was turned.

"Why not?"

"She's on vacation," Dominic said hopefully. "I mean, first she was helping out her cousin, who owns the place I stuck—that is, the place you guys were last week—and now she's on vacation and helping me out."

"So it's a secret?"

"A secret, yes."

"And Little Tony can't know?"

"Butch. And no, for God's sake, don't tell him."

"Can I tell Mrs. Jonnie?"

Dominic sighed. "You're not getting the hang of this, are you, Lizzie? A secret means you don't tell *anybody*."

"I'll bet you told Uncle Taylor," Lizzie said as she sat back against the couch cushions and folded her arms across her childish chest.

"I did not!"

"Did so. I can tell. You look guilty."

"I beg your pardon? What does that mean?"

Lizzie shrugged. "I don't know. Mom always says that to Dad. It works for her."

"I don't think I want to go there right now, Lizzie. Look, just don't tell anyone, okay?"

"Okay, but it's a pretty big secret. I don't think I've ever had such a big secret to keep. I mean, *wow*. Big, *big* secret. I might need a little help keeping it."

"How about this—don't blab, and I'll buy you a new bike? Ten speeds."

She looked just like her father when she grinned like that, and Dominic knew he was in for trouble. "No, but keep going, you'll think of something."

Dominic cocked his head as he looked at her. "Money? How much?"

"Not money, Uncle Dom. You'll go swimming with us to-morrow."

Dominic sat back, surprised. "That's it? That's all you want?"

"No, I'm just getting started," Lizzie said, smoothing her hands over the lid of the laptop. "After swimming, then you'll maybe take us for another horseback ride another day, and maybe to the movies another day?"

"Deal."

"Not yet, Uncle Dom. One more thing. *Then* you'll let me sing and dance for you, after I've had more time to practice."

He reached out and scrubbed at her hair. "Everybody wants to be in show business," he said, then dropped a kiss on her head.

"Is it a deal, Uncle Dom?"

He held out his hand, and she took it. "Deal. And you know something, Lizzie? You may look like your dad, but you've got a lot of your mother in you."

"Yes, I know," she said, looking very happy indeed.

Chapter 18

"Hello, Billie, beautiful day, isn't it?" Molly said as she rounded the corner of the office Monday morning, after knocking to see if Dominic was there—he wasn't.

"That's Ms. White to you, missy," Billie said, lifting her chin. The woman was eating well, that was for certain. In fact, with the violet eyes and bouffant hair, she was looking more and more like Elizabeth Taylor during the Senator John Warner years. "I assume Dom isn't in his office?"

"You assume a lot more than that, I think, Ms. White," Molly answered pleasantly, then added, "No, he's not there. When I find him, shall I tell him you're looking for him?"

"I deliver my own messages," Billie said shortly, then turned to walk away. She'd taken only a few steps before she stopped, turned to face Molly once more. "Wait a minute, let's get this over with, shall we?"

"I beg your pardon?" Molly thought, *Sure, I beg your pardon—for wanting to drop-kick you to the moon.*

"I have a child here, *Ms.* Applegate. A young, vulnerable, impressionable child. Not to mention Tony's children, such as they are. They do not need to be exposed to licentious behavior. Have I made myself clear?"

Maybe the moon isn't far enough. "No. I don't think so. Please, tell me more."

Billie rolled her eyes. "Oh, come on. I saw you, remember? Coming back from your *ride.* All muddy and messy and with your mouth all swollen, both of you with your clothes all crooked. It was disgusting. You're screwing the boss."

Since saying "I am not!" would be both a lie and dignifying Billie's crude statement, Molly said nothing.

"Ha! You didn't think anyone would say so, did you? Not out loud. Well, I won't have it, I'm telling you now. Not with my Bethany here to see your sluttish behavior. It's bad enough Derek and that floozy tiptoe into each other's rooms every other night after my baby's asleep. I won't have you *flaunting* such filth right out in the open. It's obvious and disgusting."

"Dirty minds often find a lot to look at while they're in the gutter," Molly said, shrugging.

"Oh, and what does *that* mean?" Billie said, sniffing. Okay, snorting. Molly wanted to think of it as snorting. Like a piggy.

"It means, Ms. White, that you have a filthy little mind," Molly said, smiling at the woman. "I would have thought that was obvious. Oh, and disgusting. Let's add disgusting, shall we? And it's one thing more, Ms. White. It's really none of your business."

"I've *made* it my business, young lady, and I use that term loosely. Running around here in those indecent shorts, stealing away to screw Dom, talking him into canceling rehearsals so you can dig your claws deeper into him, make him look the total fool. I know what you are."

"You know, *Billie,*" Molly said, her tone soft and measured, "I do believe that one day you and I *are* going to have a reckoning. But first I'll have to get over my reluctance to dirtying my hands on you."

She turned away, but turned back when Billie called out, "And I know you're here to replace that cow, Cynara. That's the only good thing, that she'll be gone."

"Okay, this one we'll correct now, and forever, okay? I am not here to replace Cynara. I'm not even slightly interested in replacing her."

"That's not what Derek says. He's sure that's why you're here."

"You don't stop, do you?" Dominic had warned her that this could happen, but she hadn't actually believed it. She definitely didn't believe that Derek was confiding in Billie. "He said that? To *you?*"

Billie looked away for a second. "He may not have said that, exactly, or said it to me, but I heard him last night, talking to Cynara."

"Wow. Tell me, Billie. Does an ear against a bedroom door work, or did you have to use a glass?" Molly asked, more angry than she'd been in years.

"He said he knew who you are," Billie said, pointing a finger at Molly. "He wouldn't say anything else to Cynara, because he still wants the cow in his bed, but he *knows*. Oh, yes, he knows. And so do I."

"Right. Well, it's been fun, Billie. See you," Molly said, and this time when she turned her back she kept it turned and kept walking, all the way to the theater.

She lucked out, and Derek was there, sitting in the second row, going over some sheet music.

"Derek? May I speak to you for a moment?" she asked, walking down the short aisle, then boosting herself up so that she sat on the stage, facing him. He looked tired.

"Sure, Molly," he said, putting down the sheet music. "What's up?"

Molly lifted her gaze to the high ceiling, trying to gather her thoughts, then decided forthright was the way to go with this one. "You think Dominic brought me here to replace Cynara?"

"Well, you don't do the beat-around-the-bush act real well, do you, darling? Okay. Yes, I thought it, at first. I mean, look at you, for God's sake. You're perfect for the stage. Tall, gorgeous. And those legs? I don't know how he'd work showing off your legs in period costume, but he'd be nuts if he didn't try."

"Thank you, Derek, that's really very sweet," Molly said, swinging those bare legs, which she'd crossed at the ankle.

"You're welcome," he said, saluting her. "But then I figured out who you are, so now I know you're not here to take Cynara's place."

Molly kept her smile bright. "Is that so?"

"You *are* Margaret Applegate, aren't you?"

Molly nodded.

"I thought so! It took me a while, and you had that glorious hair of yours hanging halfway down your back when I saw you, but I knew it was you. About five years ago? A charity performance of *The Gazebo*? Do you remember?"

Molly nodded again, and smiled. "Five years ago. Chicago. I remember."

"So you and Dom are an item, right? I mean, that's what all this nanny to Tony's kids thing is about, keeping yourselves private until you're ready to go public. He's a lucky man, Dom."

"I . . . we . . ." Molly found herself lost for words. It all sounded so logical when Derek said it. Even if he was wrong.

"I mean, I should have realized it immediately, but Dom introduced you as the nanny, and we see what we're told, right? Not that I blame you two for the deception. Billie White would have been all over you, kissing up, if she knew who you really were—are. What happened? You showed up unexpectedly, didn't you? That's why Dom canceled the rehearsals for two weeks, so he could be with you. Not that I blame him."

Again, it all sounded so logical. Derek should be writing for the tabloids.

"Would you believe me if I told you the truth, Derek?" she asked at last.

He scratched at the back of his head. "I don't know. You mean I'm guessing wrong here?"

"You could say that."

"Damn. Don't tell me you've decided to back the show and want a role for your money. Don't tell me that, Molly."

Molly held up her hands. "Please, no more guessing. I'm getting dizzy here. Look, my cousin owns a day care that's closed for these two weeks, and I took her place for a few days before it closed. I was handy, Dom needed a nanny, and I volunteered. He didn't even know who I was at first. *And,* although I do admit to loving the theater, and yes, I can dance a little, sing a little, I have absolutely *no* ambition to be on the stage, so I'm not here to replace Cynara. I mean, I roller-skate, too, and I can whistle better than most men, but I'm not about to take those talents on the road, either. Understand?"

Derek visibly relaxed. "But you and Dom *are* an item, right? I can't be wrong about that one."

"Shame on you, Derek," Molly said, grinning at him.

He laughed, but sobered quickly. "I won't tell anyone, Molly. God knows I know the feeling of having everyone prying into my private life. I couldn't be within ten feet of Cynara if we weren't safe here, without our names being linked again, without the whole thing being blown up in the press somewhere. You see, theater is a circle, a small circle of people, who very often circle like sharks. It would be way too intense. Man, she'd run so fast I wouldn't see her go."

Molly wet her lips, trying to decide what she should say. If she should say anything. If she should be a good girl and mind her own business.

But what fun was that?

"You and Cynara? Gosh, you two seem to get along like cats and dogs," she said, then waited.

Derek got up from his seat and boosted himself up onto the stage, to sit beside Molly. "We used to be an item, you know. A couple of years ago. Until I fu—until I screwed it up." He looked at her, smiling wryly. "That would be in the literal sense of the word, darling."

"You cheated on her," Molly said, not bothering to try to make it sound like a question.

"Left, right, and center, I cheated on her. Publicly cheated on her. I was a jackass. She mentioned marriage, and I ran for the nearest exit. Hell, I think I left skid marks. And worse, in our world, that exit sign usually has a bimbo standing under it."

"You didn't love Cynara?"

"Love her?" He sighed (theatrical people seemed to be very much into heartfelt sighs). "I don't know," he admitted flatly. "I honest to God don't know. We had a lot in common. The same hopes, the same dreams. And the sex? Ha, the sex was terrific. But did I love her? If I'd loved her, could I have walked away? Hurt her like that?"

Molly gazed at her own folded hands. "Maybe you were afraid. It's a big commitment, marriage. And kids. Most people want kids."

"I wouldn't mind kids, although I think we're both a little old for the babies thing," Derek said thoughtfully. "Either way, I wouldn't mind. But you know, it isn't really that. I live for the stage, always have, but it's the same thing, night after night after night. I love it, and it's always different, a little, each night, but after a year of doing the same show, the same part? I get bored. I need to move on, try my hand at something new."

"I understand, Derek. What is fun one day, may not be fun the next."

"Fun. Is that it? Fun? Damn it, darling, you didn't have to point that one out to me. It makes me sound so shallow."

"Sorry. But you were afraid that if you and Cynara got married, then maybe a year later you'd decide it wasn't fun anymore?"

"God, don't help. That's even worse." He hopped down from the stage. "But you know what, darling? You're right. That was how I was thinking. Stupidly. I mean, Cynara isn't a part in a play. I'm not a role. Much as I like make-believe, there comes a time when real life comes knocking, you know?"

"And real life has come knocking, Derek?"

"More like running at me with a battering ram," he said, shaking his head. "Ever since Cynara kicked me out, as a matter of fact. Oh, I tried to tell myself I'd be all right soon, but she's it. I mean, she's it." He shrugged his shoulders. "I don't know if I loved her then. But I love her now."

"But she doesn't want anything to do with you?" Molly knew that wasn't true, but she really wanted to keep Derek talking, not so much to hear what he had to say, but so that *he* heard what he had to say.

She wouldn't think about how familiar his words seemed to her. That was better left for another time, when she was alone, and maybe feeling faintly masochistic.

"I don't know. She's going through a tough time, Molly. Her voice? Something's wrong there. She really needs to be concentrating on her voice. And I can't help thinking she's getting some of her own back on me now. You know, leading me on, getting me to propose, just so this time she can be the one who takes a hike. She can be mean. I love her, but she can turn bitch into an art form."

Molly hopped down from the stage. "Okay. You goofed, not knowing you loved her, afraid of commitment. Now she's in trouble professionally, you do love her, and you're afraid of commitment. What hasn't changed here?"

"I'm still a coward?" he asked her, his smile, his soulful eyes, showing Molly why, even as he edged toward fifty, Derek Cambridge was still a great leading man.

"There's a lot of that going around, Derek," Molly said, kissing his cheek. "But, now that you know, maybe you can figure out a way to deal with it. Thank you, Derek."

"Thank me? For what?" Derek called after her. But Molly was already on her way to the door and only waved to him on her way out.

"*There* you are," Lizzie shouted, running down the hill toward her, and Molly waved even while she sighed. She couldn't seem to take more than three steps in any direction this morning without bumping into someone. There had to be less foot traffic in Times Square.

"What's up, Lizzie?" she asked her, slinging an arm around the girl's shoulder as she tried to steer her back toward the house and Lizzie tried to continue toward the theater. "I thought you and Butch were watching a movie."

"It's over. Disney movies are short. You know, to hold the limited attention span of kids like Butch," Lizzie told her, once more heading for the theater. "Hi, Mr. Cambridge," she said as Derek exited the building. "Is my uncle Dom in there?"

"No, sorry, sweetie. Molly?" he said, lifting his chin toward her. "Thanks again. I've got a lot to think about."

"Don't we all," Molly called after him.

"What was that all about?" Lizzie asked as Derek headed back to the guest house.

"You writing a book?" Molly asked, playfully nudging the child with her hip.

"Naw. Come on, Molly, you've got to help me," she said, grabbing Molly's hand and dragging her toward the theater.

"Help you what?" Molly asked, holding open the door so that Lizzie could enter ahead of her.

Lizzie didn't stop pulling her until they both stood on the stage. "My audition," she said, turning to grin at Molly, her eyebrows waggling. "My *aud-dition*. Can you believe it? Uncle Dom is giving me an audition."

Molly narrowed her eyelids. "Lizzie Longstreet, what did you do? And stop trying to look innocent, because I'm not buying it."

"I didn't do anything, honest. It's *because* I'm not doing anything, Uncle Dom says. So see? He's just rewarding me for being good. Now, I've been thinking, Molly. I could do something on my own, but I'd much rather do it with you. You know, what we were fooling around with the other day? You'd do that for me, wouldn't you? So I wouldn't have to do it alone?"

Ordinarily, this idea would have hit Molly as a lot of fun, something she'd adore doing. Ordinarily.

"We'd do it in front of your uncle Dom?"

Lizzie nodded happily. "And I'll bet Uncle Taylor, too. It is an audition."

"I don't know, Lizzie. I mean, I could help you rehearse, but I'm not that good. I could ruin it for you."

"Not that good? You're terrific! Come on, Molly, please?" She pressed her palms together and dropped to one knee. "Pleasepleaseprettyplease?"

Molly rolled her eyes. "Okay, get the hats and canes and let's do this. But I'm warning you—oh, forget it," she ended, because Lizzie was already gone, running into the wings for the props.

"We'll lock the doors," Lizzie said when she returned to center stage. "I've made up a note," she said, opening one button of her blouse and reaching inside to pull out a folded piece of typing paper, holding it up to Molly.

"'Keep Out: Rehearsal In Progress.' So I guess we're not hiding, right? Just being private?"

"Right," Lizzie said, skipping down the short flight of steps and heading for the doors.

Molly stood there, holding her hat and cane, shaking her head. When Lizzie came back, Molly tapped her hat onto her head and pressed an index finger beneath her nose to serve as a mustache. " 'And this is another fine mess you've gotten me into, Stanley.' "

"Huh?"

Molly shook her head. "Never mind. Let's get started, okay?"

"Shouldn't we talk about our costumes?"

"I thought this was an audition, not a show," Molly reminded her.

"I know, but it's important to get it right. I already talked to Mrs. Jonnie, and she said she can sew up costumes for us. We just have to go shopping. Black tap pants, white shirts, and tuxedo jackets with tails. Oh, and those neat fish-netty stockings? Anything we can't find, Mrs. Jonnie will make. Except the stockings, she can't make those. Did you know she used to be a seamstress in the theater, before she retired and Uncle Dom hired her as his housekeeper? She did, honest. Oh, and the right shoes. We need the right shoes. Sequins on the tap pants, of course."

"Of course," Molly said, her stomach dropping to her toes. "When is this audition?"

"I don't know. When we're ready? I was down here earlier, and I've got an instrumental all set in the CD player. It's not a live orchestra, but this is only an audition, right?"

"Hooboy," Molly said, giving in to the inevitable. This was a long way from *Good Ship Lollipop*.

An hour later, Molly knew they wouldn't be ready for that audition soon, not with Lizzie changing the steps every time they ran through the number. She was sitting on the edge of the stage, holding her aching side, when Lizzie danced off up the aisle, reminding Molly to be ready to rehearse again after dinner that night.

"Only if you can find me," Molly whispered quietly, lying back on the stage and staring up at the bars of lights hanging from the ceiling. "I think I need vitamins."

What a morning! Billie White, Derek Cambridge, some personal revelations just licking at the corners of her mind for whenever she decided she was strong enough to examine them, the next Broadway Sensation. And it wasn't even noon.

A person could sure stay busy, doing nothing. . . .

Chapter 19

Dominic levered himself out of the Lamborghini and headed for the house, still sort of rubbing at his gut and, all right, maybe wincing a bit in memory. He didn't know if he was hungry, or if he never wanted to eat again. He definitely knew he wasn't in any hurry to drink anything handed to him with the advice, "Drink it fast; it doesn't taste so bad when it's cold."

"Hi, Uncle Dom," Butch said from his seat on the porch steps. "You still sick?"

Dominic looked at his nephew curiously, then dropped his hand and sat down beside him. "Who said I was sick?"

"Oh, nobody," Butch said, scrubbing at his face, almost as if he thought the move might make him disappear.

"Here you go," Dominic said, pulling a quarter out of his pocket. "Now, spill your guts. Wait, I'll rephrase that. Just tell me what you know."

"Okay." Butch nervously passed the quarter from hand to hand. "Lizzie went looking for you this morning and saw the note in your room where you wrote down that you had to be at the hospital this morning for an army test. Lizzie says that means you're sick."

Dominic chewed on this for a few moments. "Oh. All right, I've got it now. You mean a G.I. test, Butch. And it is a medical test. You drink this liquid chalk stuff and then they take X rays of you, even while you're swallowing."

"See? I told you you were sick."

"I'm not sick, Butch," Dominic assured him. "I've got a little problem with reflux and—"

"Huh?"

"Pills fix it right up, okay?" Dominic said, realizing he should keep his explanation simple.

"Okay. That's good. Because I wouldn't like it if you were really sick or anything. That kind of stuff scares kids, you know?"

Dominic slid his arm around the boy and pulled him close. "So that's why you've been sitting here? Waiting for me?"

"Uh-huh." Butch nodded against Dominic's chest. "I was worried."

Dominic felt . . . damn, he felt wanted. Loved. Where had his head been all these years that he'd barely registered Tony's kids until now? They were great kids.

"Well, I'm sorry, buddy. I'm sorry I worried you, and I'm sorry Lizzie saw the note. Mostly, I guess I'm sorry I just didn't tell you guys what was going on."

"Lizzie says Mom says you work too hard."

"Tell Lizzie to tell her mom—" He took a breath. "She can tell your mom that she's right. But, hey, I'm learning. We're on vacation now, aren't we? Two whole weeks of swimming and horseback rides and water battles until your mom and dad get back. Which reminds me. Where's Lizzie?"

"She's in the kitchen, talking to Mrs. Jonnie." Butch looked up at Dominic with those big, blue eyes. "They have *secrets.*"

"Wouldn't let you in, huh?"

Butch shook his head. "It's okay, I went around to the back stairs and crept down them and heard everything. They're talking girlie stuff, clothes, so I don't care if it's secret. Can we play catch after lunch, Uncle Dom?"

Dominic got to his feet. "Sure we can. But I don't have a mitt anymore, kiddo."

"Oh, that's okay. Mom has all the team stuff at our house because she's our coach. She just keeps it all now that the season is over. You gotta clean everything, you know. Men don't do that, so last year all the team got head lice from the batting helmets."

Dominic cocked his head to one side, doing his best to dismiss the part about head lice. "Elizabeth—I mean, your mom coaches your baseball team?"

"Well, yeah. Dad can't be home enough, so Mom does it. They wanted her to help at the refreshment stand and make cakes, but she told them no, thank you, she'd rather coach the team. And they let her."

"There isn't much anyone won't let your mother do, when she decides she's going to do it," Dominic said, feeling rather proud of his sister-in-law. Molly would like her. Elizabeth would like Molly. Together, they could make him and Tony give serious thought to digging a hole somewhere and crawling in it to hide. "Okay, here's the deal. Right after lunch we'll drive over to your house and get the gear."

"Maybe Lizzie and Molly will play with us, too? And Uncle Taylor? We could play a real game. Have teams?"

Dominic had a quick mental vision of Taylor who, irregardless of his size and build, had never played football, or baseball, or indulged in anything more athletic than hanging upside down from the rafters at a frat party, to chug beer from a long tube. "Sure, we can ask Uncle Taylor. And Kevin, too, since we won't be running lines today, and anyone else you can think of, okay?"

"Okay. Right after lunch. You go tell Molly. She's still down at the theater."

"What's she doing down there?"

Butch just shrugged. "Practicing?"

Practicing, Dominic repeated inside his head as he made his way down to the theater. Where the hell did that answer come from? He scratched at his head, which itched, for some reason.

Oh, right. Head lice. Head lice, and the power of suggestion.

He stopped when he saw the sheet of paper taped to the door. "Rehearsals, is it?" he said, pulling the paper down, folding it, and slipping it into his pocket. "I'll give her rehearsals."

He put his hand on the knob, then remembered that Lizzie wasn't here. So, if Lizzie wasn't rehearsing for that audition she'd roped him into, and if Molly wasn't here watching her rehearse—what was Molly doing here?

"Only one way you're going to find out, Einstein," he told himself and opened the door, slipping inside quickly, trying to be quiet.

He needn't have bothered. The portable CD player was on, and he recognized the overture for the second act coming to a close. Next up would be Cynara's supposedly show-stopping love song. As he stood there in the near dark and listened, he heard the opening bars . . . and then he heard a voice.

She was sitting sideways in the center seat in the front row, her head against a sweater she'd rolled up and placed on the arm rest, her long bare legs stretched out across the seats.

She was sitting there, and she had begun to sing. Softly, not at all hesitantly. Not a voice that would rock the rafters, not unless it was highly amplified, but a voice that could move a rock to tears.

The words Tony had written suddenly held a whole new meaning for Dominic. The music wept.

When the melody built, where her voice should have soared, Molly still sang softly, slightly below the notes, the sheer lack of flamboyant passion making the words so much more real, so damn affecting.

She sang of love, of wanting to know, needing to know what it was. Her heart aching . . . was this love? His face in her dreams . . . was this love? And, if this is love . . . what now? What now . . . ?

Dominic slipped outside once more, softly closed the door. And then he just stood there, staring at nothing.

They'd been wrong. Tony had been wrong. Taylor had been wrong. They'd all been wrong.

This wasn't a soaring, powerful, take-it-to-the-cheap-seats defiant shout of frustrations, questions.

This was a sad inquiry, a baring of pain, a woman asking questions of her own heart . . . and finding no answers.

"Cats," Dominic said out loud, blinking. *"Cats.* 'Memory.' Not once, but twice. Once plaintive. Then again, at the end, as the whole damn thing. The whole damn show wrapped up in the force of that song. Why didn't we see it? We do it *twice."*

He was already on the move, heading toward his office. "We do it twice. Tony changes the lyric just enough for it to show love found, not just love looked for. And *then* Cynara can go for the rafters, and the people will be on their feet, cheering her. Of course, of course, it's perfect, it's—"

He stopped. Took a breath.

He wasn't going to work, damn it. He wasn't even going to write himself a note—as if he'd forget this one. He wasn't going to find Taylor and grab him by the shoulders and make him listen, make him understand. He wasn't going to be the producer, the one who drove everyone nuts with his thoughts, his suggestions that they'd all damn well listen to or he'd know the reason why.

He was going to play catch.

He stood there, nodding his head. He could do this. He could put the show on hold for two lousy weeks. He didn't want to be popping pills the rest of his life. First something for the stupid reflux. Something for the anxiety. What would the next *something* be for?

No. No, he'd put this on the back burner. Good ideas could wait. He wouldn't think about it, wouldn't think about how Molly's pure and incredibly sad voice had taken all the bits and pieces of the show and put them all in the right place.

He wouldn't think about how Cynara could screw it all up anyway, even now that everything was so close to perfect.

So what would he do?

Tossing Molly to the floor and making wild, insane love to her seemed like a good place to start.

His step light, a smile playing at the corners of his mouth, he headed back into the theater, to see her on the stage now, practicing a dance step.

"Hey," he called out as he walked down the aisle. "I hope you've got your union card."

"Oops," she said, leaning on the slim black cane she was holding and looking at him from beneath the brim of her black bowler hat. "Where do I sign up?"

"Why? Are you contemplating a life in show business?"

"God, no. When it comes to performing, I make a great audience. I was looking for you earlier. You didn't tell me your test was today. How did it go?"

"You mean Lizzie doesn't have the results yet?" he asked, walking up onto the stage.

She lifted the hat from her head and placed it on his, not that it fit. "I think it's nice of you to give Lizzie an audition. Sweet. Magnanimous, even. So, what's she holding over your head?"

Dominic took off the hat and put it on her head once more. "I'm insulted. Why can't I just be a terrific uncle, giving the kid a chance?"

"Because," Molly said, dancing away from him as she held the cane in both hands, doing a neat little shuffle and ending by slapping down one end of the cane as a sort of accent to the punchline, "nobody over the age of six would believe you, *ba-bump.*"

"Funny," Dominic said. "Am I supposed to be your straight man here?"

"That depends." She two-stepped back to him, banged down the other end of the cane. "A woman can always use a straight . . . man. *Ba-bump.*"

"Margaret Applegate!" Dominic said in mock shock. "Please, my innocent ears."

"Nice to know some part of you is innocent," she said, tipping her hat forward over one eye, then dancing away again.

Mercurial. That's what she was, and he was fascinated. One moment singing a sad song, the next trying her hand at vaudeville and bad jokes. And always giving her all.

She stopped halfway across the stage, the brim of the hat nearly hiding her eyes, and planted those gorgeous bare legs a good two feet apart as she leaned both hands on one end of the cane. "Your turn, big boy. Your props are over there."

He looked around, saw a matching hat and cane lying on the side of the stage. He held up one finger as if to say "be right back" and gathered them up.

She was facing the seats by the time he joined her, and he tapped the too-small hat as far down on his forehead as he could, planted his feet apart, knees locked, then pressed both hands against one end of the cane.

"What now?"

"Now we push up on our toes and come down again. On

two—one, two . . . that's it. Repeat. No, Dominic. Keep your legs straight, don't move your shoulders. Just lift from your heels, and down, so your shoulders stay where they are and your backside goes out."

"I like my backside where it is, thank you."

"I like it, too, Mr. Tight Buns. But work with me here, okay?"

"All right, all right. What do I do again?"

"Lift from your heels, and down. Give the audience your what-the-hell-is-your-problem look. That's the technical dancing term, you understand. And one, and two . . ."

"Do that again. Please," he said, leering at her backside. "I'll give you a quarter."

"Cut that out. This is serious business here. We're dancing."

"I don't dance, you know," Dominic said, trying to keep a straight face.

"Thanks for the information. I wouldn't have had a clue. Okay, now the knees."

"I thought we weren't supposed to bend our knees."

"Consider it progress," Molly said, not looking at him. "One two, up on your heels. Three four, flat on the floor. Five six, everything stays still except you bend your knees—outward. Seven eight, bring them back. Start again."

"Piece of cake," Dominic said, concentrating with all of his might. Raise the heels, down, bend the knees, up. Glare at the audience. Raise the heels, down, bend the knees, raise the heels—*no,* not up until the knees are straight!

He could do this. A reasonably bright rhesus monkey could do this. He tried again. Up, down, up, down, up, up higher—"Damn it!"

"Don't give up your day job, kiddo," Molly said as Dominic took an involuntary step forward, the too-small hat falling onto the stage.

"Funny—not," Dominic said, scooping up the hat and putting it and the cane back where he'd found them. "I guess I also make a great audience. And now, a more sympathetic one."

"Good, because we're going to need one of those," Molly said, putting her hat and cane with Lizzie's.

"Meaning?"

"Meaning, Mr. Producer, sir, that Lizzie has somehow conned me into joining her in the audition. I wanted you to know how hard this is, so you'll have pity on me . . . us. Although I have to tell you, I don't think we could be *that* bad if we worked at it."

"You were good at it," Dominic said, stepping closer to her. "You're good at a lot of things."

"Yes, that's me. What's that old saying? Jack of all trades, master of none? Ever wonder who Jack was? Poor guy. Anyway, the strange thing is that I like it that way. I always have."

Dominic felt her stepping back, even though she hadn't moved a muscle. "Your resume must be two feet long," he said, trying to sound only mildly interested, when all he wanted to do was grab her by the shoulders and ask her why. *Why? Why do you feel this need to keep moving?*

"Oh, go ahead, Dominic," she said, with a shake of her head. "Ask me. You want to know why I go from job to job to job. From thing to thing, whatever. Admit it. You're dying to know."

Did she also read minds, or was he that transparent? Was this a trap? Would he be showing too much interest if he did ask? Not enough if he didn't?

When had women gotten so complicated? No, scratch that. It was Molly who was so complicated. Maybe because she was the first one he'd ever tried to understand, ever wanted to understand.

"All right, I'll bite. Why?"

She slipped her arms around his shoulders. "I haven't the faintest idea," she said, purred, into his ear. "Wanna neck?"

He had to admit it. It was easier just to give in. Not ask the questions. Not push the wrong buttons.

"Oh, what the hell. I didn't want to talk anyway."

He pulled her close, captured her mouth as she giggled up at him.

At least for some of Molly Applegate, he knew what buttons to push. . . .

Chapter 20

And here he is, ladies and gentlemen, the hottest producer on Broadway today. Class, all the way. Suave. Debonair. Well dressed. In charge. Mature.

Dominic glared at Molly. "Out? What do you mean, I'm out? You need glasses?" he said, taking off his ball cap and throwing it to the ground. "I was safe by a mile."

"You were out, Mr. Longstreet," Kevin said, then sort of gulped. "Maybe you were out? I could be wrong? You were probably safe?"

"That's some really great kissing up, Kevin, but I'll handle this one." Molly stepped closer to Dominic even as Kevin retreated, went up on her tiptoes, went chin-to-chin and chest-to-chest with him. "You were so out you were in the next state and had to *phone in* how bad you were out. Now stop being a baby."

He blinked. "What the hell do you have in your mouth?"

"Bubble gum." Molly grinned as she tongued the lump of the gum between teeth and cheek. "Strawberry flavored."

"The whole pack?"

"It's called a wad of chew. All baseball players do it."

"Not with strawberry bubble gum, they don't."

"Yes, they do. Sugarless, too," Molly told him. "Want some?"

"Come up to my bedroom and ask that," Dominic said, but quietly.

"You wish," Molly responded. "And you're out, so stop being such a baby." She turned away and waved her glove above her head. "Batter up!"

Dominic picked up his hat and slapped it against his thigh, admiring Molly's walk back to the mound. Well, it would have been a mound if they'd taken time to build one.

As it was, there had been bases in the equipment bags he and Butch had found in Tony's garage, and a rubber for the pitcher to stand on, and a chalk line marker they'd used to measure out the diamond.

It was no field of dreams, but it would do . . . especially when Molly was getting ready to pitch again.

She'd leapt heart and soul into the idea of a baseball game. Hell, she leapt heart and soul into anything she did, right down to the ball cap sitting almost sideways on her head, and the wad of gum in her cheek.

He looked at her and felt like a kid. A kid with a crush on the most fantastic girl in town.

She grinned at him, then took off her ball cap and flourished it as she bowed in his direction. "Any time it's convenient, Mr. Longstreet," she yelled to him, and he realized he had to go back out into the field because they'd agreed that everyone would play outfield, or else they'd be chasing balls all day. He caught the mitt Mrs. Jonnie tossed to him and took Taylor's place in center.

They'd actually made up teams.

Dominic, Lizzie, Jonsey, and Taylor on one side.

On the other side, Molly, Butch, Kevin. And Carl, the gardener, who had a pretty darn good swing. Carl had hit home runs both times he'd been at bat, and Dominic was beginning to wonder if Molly had already known he was good and brought him in as a ringer. He wouldn't put it past her.

Mrs. Jonnie had volunteered to keep score and hand out fruit and cold drinks.

Taylor patted Dominic on the shoulder as they passed by each other. "You'll like it out here, Dom. Best view in the house, when Molly's pitching."

"Hey, I warned you—"

"Looking, Dom," Taylor said, holding up his hands in mock defense. "Not touching, not even thinking too hard. Just looking."

"Oh, go bat, would you?" Dominic said, grinning at his friend.

The deal was that they'd throw underhand to the kids, overhand to the adults, and Molly was pretty good at both. Not great, but good. Besides, she had a windup and follow-through that sort of took your mind off the idea of swinging anyway.

Taylor took one swing and missed. Then Molly threw the next one about three feet over his head.

"Oops! That one sort of slipped. Sorry," Molly said, and went into her windup again.

Taylor swung, connected, and Carl—clearly the man had potential never before fully tapped—dove in front of Dominic and caught the ball.

"Nice catch, Carl," Dominic said, taking the ball before trotting in to the mound, because Taylor had been the third out, and now he would pitch to Molly's team.

Butch came up to the plate, his plastic batting helmet nearly covering his eyes, and stood there, feet together, looking scared out of his mind. Dominic's heart ached for the kid.

"Time!" Molly called, and ran in from left field, to help Butch with his stance. She sort of nudged his feet apart, positioned the bat higher on his shoulder, whispered in his ear, then gave him a kiss on the cheek and a pat on the behind—which would make her a damn popular manager if she took her coaching act to the Major Leagues.

"Be kind," she said then, walking close to Dominic, holding her mitt up in front of her mouth.

"Hey, I'm doing the best I can. I'm aiming the damn ball at his bat."

"Cover your mouth with your glove when you talk." She took his arm, looked toward the plate, then turned the two of them toward the outfield.

"What's with the mitts? Why are we turning around?" he asked, looking toward Taylor, who just shrugged.

"I don't want anyone to know what we're saying."

"Butch reads lips? I never knew."

"Cut it out. This is what conferences are like on the pitcher's mound. Don't you know anything? And I'm not kidding, Dominic. Give him a slow, easy one. He hasn't had a hit yet, poor kid."

"I told you, I've been trying," Dominic said out of the corner of his mouth. "I throw this thing any slower and it'll go backwards."

"Yeah, yeah, just maybe move closer, huh?" Then she dropped the mitt to her side, turned and waved encouragingly at Butch, and went back to her place in the outfield.

Dominic shook his head. And then he moved closer. "Okay, Butch, you ready?"

"Uh-huh," Butch said, nodding, then had to step out of the box and pick up the batting helmet that had fallen off. He stepped back in. "Okay. Ready."

He looked about as nervous as a turkey the day before Thanksgiving.

Dominic stepped closer.

Closer.

He threw the ball.

Butch swung from his heels.

Butch *hit* the ball.

The ball *hit* Dominic.

"Cripes!" he said, sort of *strangled,* and clasped mitt and hand to his crotch as he dropped to his knees.

Butch ran to first base and was rounding second by the time Molly reached Dominic. She bent in half and looked into his face. "Are you all right?"

"Rrummpff-rrummpff," Dominic said, or words to that effect.

She moved closer. Whispered, "Ah, poor baby. You want I should kiss it better?"

Hormones that didn't seem to understand the pain he was in came to life. "Don't . . . help," he said, still trying to catch his breath.

Butch had passed third, sort of skipping as he ran. Stopped, picked up his helmet, hitched up his shorts, and began running again.

"Don't . . . Don't you want to make the play?" Dominic asked Molly.

"Oh, right." Molly picked up the ball, which hadn't bounced that far away, and tossed it over her shoulder. "Whoops."

Butch scored. Butch jumped up and down on home plate, arms in the air, and cheered himself. Mrs. Jonnie came over to hug him.

Dominic tried to get to his feet, just as Taylor strolled in from the field. "Hey, Dom, what's up? My guess would be nothing, and not for some time."

Dominic said some words that had Molly plunking herself down on the ground, holding her stomach, and laughing as she beat her heels against the grass.

"You let him score. You guys are all nuts," Lizzie said in disdain, stomping past them on her way to get one of the apples Mrs. Jonnie was now offering everyone to celebrate Butch's "home run."

Dominic manfully got to his feet, refusing Molly's offer that he lean on her, walked over to Mrs. Jonnie, and sat down in a folding chair.

"I have an ice bag if you want it, Mr. Dom," she said, then bit her bottom lip.

"Women always think this is so funny," Dominic complained, giving some serious consideration to her offer. "I guess the game is over?"

"Postponed due to injury," Molly said, holding an icy can of soda against her forehead. "We can play again tomorrow."

Dominic was pretty sure his smile was sickly. "Good. Are we done having fun now, or do I have to have more fun?"

"I don't know. It's only three o'clock. We could go swimming?"

"Or take a nap," Taylor said, lowering his big frame to the ground, his forearms on his bent knees. "When did we get so old, Dom?"

Old? He wasn't old! Dominic stood up. "Swimming. Good idea. In an hour?"

"Right," Molly said. "That will give you time to clean up here. Losers clean up, remember? Carl scored the winning run. I've decided we'll start over from scratch tomorrow."

"Man," Taylor said, shaking his head. "That's really adding insult to injury, isn't it, Dom?"

"Here you go, *losers*." Lizzie tossed two large canvas equipment bags in front of Dominic and followed Molly and Mrs. Jonnie back toward the house.

"I really like her," Taylor said, watching Molly walk away. "I think she's good for you."

Dominic lifted the brim of his ball cap and scratched at

his head. "If I survive her. You're right, Taylor, we're old. I mean, what am I trying to prove here? Oh, cripes, here comes Mama Billie. What the hell could she want?"

Taylor scrambled to his feet, picking up one of the equipment bags. "I'll go get the bases in, okay?"

"Chicken," Dominic called after him. "Rat deserting the sinking ship."

"Right. Cluck-cluck and snick-snick, or whatever rats say," Taylor shot back at him, trotting toward home plate just as Mama Billie's shadow covered Dominic's face.

"I can't believe the cruelty," she said, her fists jammed on her hips. "What sort of monster are you?"

Dominic leaned sideways in the chair and reached into the cooler, to pull out a can of beer. "Let me take a wild guess here, Billie. Bethany wouldn't play baseball on a bet, but we should have asked so that she could say no?"

"What? Play baseball? Are you out of your mind? What if she got hurt? I won't jeopardize her career like that. How could you think such idiocy? That's not what I'm talking about."

Dominic popped the top, took a swig. "Then I give up. What's up your—what's your problem now, Billie?"

"As if you didn't know."

"I *don't*—no, I'm not going to do this, Billie. Go away." He pushed himself to his feet and headed toward the pile of bats and balls.

She followed him. "It's your niece," she said, bending down when he bent down to pick up two bats, standing up when he stood up. "Bethany was up at the kitchen this morning, and she heard her. Heard them both. Your niece and your housekeeper. Your niece is going to *audition* for you. Audition? Ha! That's just a ploy, isn't it? You've already decided to replace my Bethany with that . . . that *amateur*. Just because she's your niece. That's why you said rehearsals were canceled. *That's* why you wanted Bethany to leave."

Dominic dropped the bats and said wonderingly, "You know something, Billie? You're insane."

"My Bethany's crying on her bed. Devastated! I knew something was up. I always knew something was up. I just thought it was that Applegate woman. I was close, but not close enough. Well, let me tell you, Mr. Longstreet, Bethany isn't going *anywhere*. We have a contract."

"Trouble, Dom?" Taylor asked, dumping the bag of bases on the ground. "Hi, Billie. Man, your face is red. Too much sun, or are you getting ready to pop something?"

Dominic pinched the bridge of his nose with thumb and index finger. "You're not helping here, Taylor."

"Oh, don't play dumb, Taylor, even if you are good at it," Billie spat. "You know what's happening. He's trying to get rid of my Bethany."

"He is?" Taylor looked at Dominic. "Billie, yeah, I'd understand. Have Carl stash her body under the roses or something. But Bethany's only a kid."

"Shut up, Taylor." Dominic tried not to laugh, tried to be the big, bad producer. Tried to be angry. It wasn't working. His smile broke through. "Look, Billie, why don't you go get Bethany, bring her to my office, and I'll tell her she's still got the part, okay?"

"I should be calling our agent."

"No, Billie, you should be going to get Bethany so she can stop crying. That is your concern, isn't it? Bethany?"

Billie gave a toss of her head, then turned and marched back toward the guest house.

"Are you really thinking about getting rid of Bethany?" Taylor asked, once the woman was out of earshot.

"No, but the stashing-Mama-Billie-under-the-roses idea might have been inspired, Taylor," Dominic said. "Come on, let's pick up this stuff. Butch! Finish that apple, and let's clean up around here."

"It *was* a home run, wasn't it, Uncle Dom?" Butch asked as they loaded mitts and balls into a large bag. "Lizzie says it was an error, but it was a home run. I got all the way around, right?"

"Right, buddy," Dominic said, motioning to Kevin to take care of the bagged equipment. "You touched them all. Now, we're going to go swimming in a while, but you probably should take a shower first. You're wearing an awful lot of the ball field."

Butch brushed at the chalk on his legs. "Swimming, huh? And Mrs. Jonnie said we're going to cook outside tonight. Hamburgers and hot dogs and everything. This is like a real vacation, isn't it?"

"It sure is. Taylor? You'll join us?"

"For hot dogs and hamburgers? Wouldn't miss it." He put his arm around Butch's shoulder. "Come on, kiddo, let's help Kevin. Dom? You going to be all right?"

"Why? Am I still walking funny?"

"Okay, that too. I mean with Billie? You know? Stress?"

"I'll be fine," he said, and as he walked over to the office, he realized that he was going to be fine. And, when the throbbing stopped, he might even be great. . . .

"Boo!" Molly said, stepping out from behind a tree as he neared the office. "Are you okay?"

Dominic looked at her, shook his head. "You know, if one more person asks me if I'm okay, I might not be. What are you doing?"

"Waiting for you, of course." She looked around, then pulled him behind the tree. Pressed a hand against him. "Tell me where it hurts."

He moved her hand. "Molly, flattered as I am, there's something a woman might not understand here. Happy as I might be to . . . to *see* you, I'm not quite ready for prime time yet, understand? You know that old saying? It feels so good it hurts? Trust me. It hurts."

"Oh," she said, and she blushed. She actually blushed. "I had no idea."

"Yes, well, now that you have, don't start thinking about curling up with a good book tonight, because I'm feeling better every minute."

"Mr. Longstreet, is that a proposition?"

"If I made it an order, you'd just ignore it. File it under wishful thinking, all right?"

She ran a finger down his chest, stopping at about his waist. "Your place or mine? Yours, I think. Now, why aren't you going back to the house?"

"Mama Billie. Every time I think she's not going to be any more trouble, she comes up with something new. The latest is that she thinks I'm training Lizzie to replace Bethany."

Molly frowned. "Why would she think that?"

"Bethany eavesdropped on Lizzie and Mrs. Jonnie, and she knows about the audition, as Lizzie insists on calling it."

"Oh, boy. That's not good. And wait until she finds out I'm in this audition with her. And I just convinced her that I'm not here to take Cynara's place. You know, Dominic, it would be a lot easier if you just told Billie White to go home for two weeks."

She held up her hands. "No, scratch that. One, I shouldn't be interfering, and two, none of this is Bethany's fault, poor kid. You know what? I'm going to invite her to go swimming with us. And to the cookout."

"And that's not interfering?"

She held out a hand, sort of wiggled it. "It's close. But we can't just ignore that she's here. That's mean."

Chapter 21

Molly sat cross-legged on Lizzie's bed and watched as the girl glared into the full-length mirror in her room.

Lizzie's expression was a cross between disgust and threatening tears, and Molly's heart went out to her. Not yet a young woman, no longer just a kid, the poor thing was caught in prepubescent limbo, and that, Molly remembered from her own youth, was just about the worst, the most frustrating feeling in the world.

"Look at this, Molly. I'm *flat*. I look like a hot dog with two strips of material tied around it. It's embarrassing. I look like a kid. A kid hot dog! I'm *not* going out there. Not with Bethany Boobs out there, *sticking* herself out all over the place. You can't *make* me. Why'd you have to go and invite her, anyway?"

Poor sweetheart. She did look sort of like a slender hot dog—still cylinder shaped from neck to hip, with not a curve in sight except for the gentle sweep of her spine, and a cute little bubble-butt that had real possibilities, especially if she kept dancing.

"Your legs are good," Molly said, trying for a compliment.

Lizzie blew raspberries through her lips. "Big deal. They're long, that's all."

Molly tried again. "I'll bet your mother looked just like you when she was eleven."

"I'll be *twelve* in two months." She slapped her hands to her chest. "And *nothing.*"

Okay, she'd take one more shot. "It could be because you're going to be tall."

Lizzie rolled her eyes. "Now that's just plain dumb." Then she frowned. "Isn't it?"

Molly had no idea. "No, I think it's possible. Your body is too busy getting . . . getting *long,* to think about getting . . . *pouffy.* Is your mother tall?"

"She was a dancer. Of course she's tall. But *she's* got boobs. You're tall, and *you've* got boobs."

"I didn't, not until about ninth grade, I think. There I'd be, in gym class. Everyone else was reaching behind their backs to unhook their bras, and I was still pulling an undershirt up over my head. But I had nice long legs, like yours. So I wore short shorts."

"You still wear short shorts."

"Hey, what's already good gets better, and the rest eventually catches up. Now, come on, you're not going to hide in here while everyone else is outside at the pool, having a good time."

"No, I suppose not. But Bethany better not be a screamer. You know, get a drop of water on her, go screaming like some baby. I still don't see why she has to be here."

Ah, crisis averted. "Because she *is* here," Molly said, getting off the bed. "You know, it's her mother who causes so much trouble. And, if Bethany only has her mother as a role model, she's just going to grow up to be like her. Maybe, if you show her what being a kid is really about, she'll start to have some fun."

"Right. Sure. Do you believe that?"

Molly shrugged. "I'm trying. At least give her the benefit of the doubt."

"Okay, okay," Lizzie said, taking one last look in the mirror, tipping her head to one side. "The legs *are* pretty good, aren't they? And the hair. It's not everybody who has naturally blond hair, you know. I get that from my dad and Uncle Dom." She picked up a beach towel with a badly faded depiction of Ozzy Osbourne on it and draped it around her shoulders. "Okay, I'm ready."

"Good for you. I'm not. You go check on Butch, and I'll meet you guys down at the pool. And no going in the water unless your uncle Dom or some other adult is there."

Lizzie rolled her eyes. "I know. But we both can swim really well. Mom made sure of that."

They left Lizzie's bedroom, Lizzie heading for Butch's room and Molly slipping into her own bedroom. She closed the door, then leaned against it, sighed.

Alone at last.

How did parents do it? Keeping them occupied. Keeping them safe. Keeping them entertained. Worrying about them. Averting tantrums. Hoping for them, dreaming for them, then worrying about them some more. All that love, all that responsibility. All that opportunity for heartbreak. . . .

"Thank you, but no thank you," Molly said, pushing herself away from the door. She adored Lizzie and Butch, she really did, but when she left them, she'd leave them with a smile. Call them, write to them, hopefully see them again. Enjoy them, always. But be responsible for them?

"Drugs, gangs, smoking, trying to get into the best college. Who are their friends? Will they drink and drive? Have unsafe sex? And then they get married, have babies of their own, and it starts all over again, with the chicken pox and the skinned knees and the crying because they don't fit in and they don't have boobs yet and anything else they can think of to be unhappy and break your heart. Being a parent never stops."

Or never starts, in the case of her own parents. They might as well have laid her like an egg on some beach and been blissfully swimming a hundred miles away when she'd hatched.

"I won't do that to some innocent child," Molly said as she stripped off her shorts and tank top and headed for the bathroom. "If you don't have it in you, you shouldn't pretend you do."

As she held her head under the marvelous waterfall shower, Molly fought feelings of guilt that washed over her with the water.

She was selfish. She was shallow. She was a good-time girl who ran from responsibility. There was some place, some *place* deep inside her, that should be filled with something . . . but was empty. Whatever should have been there had never been nourished, fed, encouraged to grow.

Maybe if she knew what was supposed to be there, what was missing, she could fix it, fill it. God knew she'd been looking for that nebulous *something* all of her life.

She reached for the bath puff and the liquid body wash and began soaping her body.

Her outside was good. She worked at keeping it looking good.

That way, nobody could see through to the empty spot inside.

"Stop that," she told herself, vigorously scrubbing at her arms. "Save it for tonight, the way you always do. At least then you've got commercial breaks."

She hung the shower puff back on a hook on the chrome shelf and began soaping her hair. Began to sing.

". . . gonna wash that man right outta—hey!"

"Hey, yourself. Did you hear the news, Molly? We're supposed to conserve water," Dominic said, slipping into the shower stall.

She tried to glare at him, which was pretty hard, when all she wanted to do was melt against him.

"You idiot. It's the middle of the day. What if one of the kids—"

"Taylor has them down at the pool. He's showing off for them, doing cannonballs into the deep end. Thus the aforementioned water shortage," Dominic said, rubbing against her. "Here, let me do that."

She dropped her hands to her sides and tipped back her head as Dominic's long fingers pushed into her sudsy hair, began to massage.

"Ah, Dominic, you're good at this. Have much practice? Don't answer that."

His soap-slippery hands slid down to her shoulders as she turned to face him, as the large round head of the waterfall shower rained water down on her, sending white mounds of shampoo running down her face, down over her breasts. Down over his hands on her breasts.

She looked into his face, at the way the water darkened his blond hair, stuck his long eyelashes together into spiky clumps. His smile made him somehow boyish. His flashing eyes hinted of the devil in a mischievous mood.

And his hands, his fingers, his mouth, took her to paradise.

"My . . . my turn," Molly said at last, clinging to him, nearly breathless as her climax slowly faded.

He kissed her sopping hair just above her ear. "Promises, promises . . ."

"Oh, no," she said, reaching for the bath puff and body wash, "I always keep my promises."

She began soaping his chest, running the bath puff across his shoulders, making soapy designs in the intriguing blond fuzz on his chest.

"In . . . er, in-teresting texture that thing has," Dominic said as she lightly rubbed the mesh against his nipples. "I never . . . uh, Molly? You don't have to . . . oh, *damn* . . ."

She had gone to her knees, the bath puff busy, busy. "Poor baby," she said, not even bothering to wonder where her inhibitions had gone, because they'd pretty much packed up and left the building the first moment she'd seen Dominic Longstreet. "Oh, look, all better now . . ."

"Molly . . ."

She didn't hear him. She dropped the bath puff, watched as the sheeting water chased away the soap bubbles, chased them all the way down his straight, golden-haired legs.

Everything she did next seemed so natural, so right. Instinctive.

And Molly was a person who always gave her entire concentration to the moment at hand. . . .

She felt his hands on her shoulders, under her arms, lifting her up, sliding her along his body until she was looking into his eyes, and he was looking back at her, their bodies wet and slick and melded together. The water hitting them should be sizzling when it touched their heated skin.

"You . . . you are the . . . ah, hell," Dominic said, pulling her even closer, clasping her buttocks and lifting her against him as he backed out from under the shower and leaned against the tile wall, her legs wrapped around his waist.

She held on for dear life, maybe for her own life, nipping the skin of his shoulder with her teeth, swallowing down hard as he moved her against him, as he moved inside her, as he exploded inside her, as she exploded with him. . . .

And then he washed her again, and she washed him, and he left her again, not saying a word, without even the hint of a postmortem.

He just kissed her forehead and left her standing there . . . standing there until the water heater finally gave up and cold water brought her back to her senses.

"Wow . . . ," she said at last, blinking against the water running down her face, and finally shut off the stream and stepped out onto the carpet.

She pulled a large bath towel from the heated rail, wrapped it around her, and sat down on the edge of the tub. Tried to control her breathing. Attempted to gather her wits. Considered having her head examined. . . .

Six months ago, she'd been in Las Vegas, playing at life as a cocktail waitress. And going home alone every night. Well, not home. Going upstairs at the Bellagio, to her four-room suite, to count her tips.

Five months ago she'd been in Manhattan, slogging through slush and shivering while five dogs did their business in the gutters, and the Beagle did his on her boots.

Four months ago? Four months ago she'd been in San Diego, visiting an old friend—acquaintance, let's be honest about this—from college.

Three months ago. Still California, roller-skating at Danny's Drive-Up.

Two months ago.

Molly frowned, tried to concentrate. Nope, she couldn't remember. Oh, wait. Connecticut. She'd gone back to Connecticut, to recharge her batteries. She'd stuck it out a full three weeks, too. Hanging out in the kitchen, getting in Mrs. Beeme's way, then wandering through all those large, empty rooms, walking around those large, lovely, lonely grounds.

One month ago? That one was easy. Gerry had finagled her a job at the newspaper in D.C., as apprentice reporter. The job she'd quit without a look back.

So, that's where she'd been. The question was, where was she now? And where did she go from here?

She stood up, wrapped a smaller towel around her head, and wandered into the bedroom.

That was the question, wasn't it? Where would she be next month?

"I'm so tired," she said, sitting down at the dressing table and looking at her reflection in the mirror. "I'm so damn tired, but I don't know what else to *do.*"

She bit her bottom lip, kept looking at her reflection, watched as her eyes began to sting, as the tears welled up.

"Yes, you do," she told herself. "You could stop running. You could take a chance." And just like that, *bam,* the old fear sliced through her, a very real pain, and she covered her mouth with her hands, as she whimpered, *"Oh, God.* I don't know if I can."

"Molly?"

Molly pulled the towel off her head and rubbed her face with it, keeping her back to Cynara, who was standing just inside the doorway. She took two deep breaths, let them out slowly. "Hi, Cynara. What's up?" she asked, mentally slapping herself back into shape. One of her many and varied talents. . . .

"This, of course," the woman said, tottering into the room in ridiculous metallic gold platform shoes, her head high, her arms out at her sides as if she was trodding the runway at a fashion show. "I walked past the pool, and I think Taylor is giving Derek mouth-to-mouth right about now, to revive him. Like it?"

Molly watched as Cynara twirled in a circle. She had a marvelous body, and that was without the caveat of "for a woman nearing forty," and the bright yellow bikini showed off every bit of it, especially when Cynara dropped the short, billowing jacket that had only barely covered her backside anyway.

She wore a matching yellow hat with a flat brim, about a dozen slim gold bangle bracelets on one arm, and a huge orange, frankly fake plastic bracelet on the other. The necklace, made up of Day-Glo orange plastic balls the size of ping pong balls, matched the bracelet and the slash of orange across her full lips, the Day-Glo orange on her finger- and toenails.

"Cynara, I've never seen anything like it. Where did you find it?"

She prodded at the orange bracelet. "Oh, Angel put me on to this *fabulous* boutique, then met me there at lunchtime today. He picked out everything. Between you and me, he told me *he* shops there, too. It seems he's in shows on the weekends. Isn't that wonderful? I thought that was only in New York. But, really, do you like it? It's not too much?"

The outfit did have a bit of a Drag Queen look to it. . . .

Molly reached for her bottle of sun screen and began applying it to her bare legs. "That depends. What were you going for?" To herself, she thought, *If she's looking for work guiding jets onto aircraft carriers in the fog, she's definitely dressed for the job.*

"Derek's jugular, of course," Cynara answered, slipping her arms back into the short jacket with the stand-up collar. "Anyway, I've been sent up here to fetch you, darling, so chop-chop. I'm the only one who's still dry, you understand. Except for Bethany. Mama Billie has her wrapped in blankets and stuck under an umbrella, poor little twit."

"I'll be down shortly." Molly poured lotion into her palm and began applying it to her arms and shoulders. "How are you and Derek doing?"

Cynara sat down on the slipper chair, rubbing at her left heel. "I need to break these in," she said, then smiled at Molly. "We're doing very well, actually. He wants to help me rehearse some more, while we've got the time. I think he's worried about me."

"He is," Molly said, not believing saying so betrayed any confidences. "You know, I'd like to be there, too, if you don't mind? I'm beginning to get an idea about—"

Cynara stood up, held out her hands to silence Molly. "Thank you, darling, but no thank you. I don't mean to be cruel, but I think I can take it from here."

Molly blinked. "Oh. Okay," she said, watching Cynara hobble toward the doorway. "So much for playing Girl Scout." Then she called after the woman, wanting to at least tell her about her idea. "Cynara?" she called, still able to hear the click-slap, click-slap of those platform heels in the hallway. *"Cynara?"*

She got up, still holding her bath towel around her, and closed the bedroom door, locking it. "Either I just got the famous Cynara Brush Off, or I'm right," she said to herself as she pulled her bathing suit from the closet.

"Not that it's any of my business," she reminded herself as she slipped into the bottom half of her black bikini. "Not that I don't have enough problems of my own."

She clipped the bikini top around her stomach, then turned it so that she could lean forward, fit her breasts into the built-in cups. She shook out the black, nearly transparent sarong-type skirt and wrapped it around her, arranging it so it sat at an angle on her hips, skimmed just above her ankles, then unearthed three-inch heels that were little more than soles and a thin, braided-leather strap above her toes.

Bless Cynara, she was beautiful. Flashy, bigger-than-life beautiful. Theatrical.

Sexy was good. But Molly also strove for understated,

classy, and, Lord knew, expensive. Like the soft, finely woven black straw hat Mrs. Beeme had sent along, the one with the enormous rolled-up front brim that framed her hair and face, while the rest of it flowed back and down over her shoulders, the back of the brim actually large enough to nearly reach her waist. She adored this hat, and knew she was tall enough to carry off the look.

Her only jewelry was the delicate gold chain she clasped around her left ankle, and a huge black onyx ring she slipped onto the index finger of her right hand.

Some lip glosser, a bit of pinkish eye shadow, and she was ready. Defenses all in place.

Like Lizzie, she checked herself in the full-length mirror. Yes, everything in place. Everything the same as when she'd first worn this ensemble in Monaco last summer.

She looked good in black, with her white, never tanned skin, with her red hair.

Molly almost turned away from the mirror, then turned back, frowned. Something was different.

She patted her stomach. No, she hadn't gained weight. She turned this way, that way. No, she hadn't lost weight. It wasn't her body that was different.

Yes it was.

Molly lifted her hands to her breasts, stroked the skin above her suit with her fingertips. Her skin . . . tingled.

She put her hands to her cheeks. Closed her eyes. Could feel Dominic's hands on her, his mouth on her.

Her every nerve, her every muscle, every drop of blood that raced through her beating heart was different. More alive. More *lush*.

She dropped her arms to her sides and walked across the room, turned, and walked back to the mirror, watching herself as she walked.

Her walk was different. Even her *walk!*

She'd always been confident. But this was a new confidence. She'd always been aware of her body. But this was a new awareness.

"What has he done?" she asked herself. "What am I letting him do?"

Chapter 22

"Thanks for wearing them out for me," Dominic said to Taylor, as the two of them lay on chaises in the shade. Lizzie and Butch were sitting on towels on the grass, playing with some hand-held computer game. "I owe you one."

"Ah, my friend, you owe me a whole lot more than you think. While you were playing absent host, I went a round with Mama Billie for you."

"Taylor, don't do that," Dominic said, sighing. "I've got her under control."

"Oh? So you're okay with Bethany getting another solo?"

Dominic sat up so quickly, a few stars appeared in front of his eyes. "That's *not* happening. The show is running long as it is."

"That was pretty much my response." Taylor tipped his beer can to his mouth, then swallowed and said, "She'd prefer something soulful."

"Bethany plays the kid. The *funny,* pain-in-the ass kid."

"I thought so, too. But Mama Billie wants to showcase all of Bethany's talents. And she said you agreed."

"Like hell, I did. Where is she? I'm going to settle this right now."

"No need. I took care of it."

Dominic leaned back against the cushions. "Does this have anything to do with Carl and a shovel? Because I'm really warming up to that idea."

"That did border on the brilliant, didn't it? No, I just redirected her. I told her we were also thinking about doing something different with Bethany's role. Like, maybe eliminating it. I told her Cynara's a little *mature* to have such a young sister, and we were thinking about making the Melanie character older. After all, what we're doing is still a work in progress, right?"

"Funny. I didn't hear the atomic blast. What did she do?"

"She's off reading Bethany's contract again, calling her agent, sticking pins in a Dominic doll? Who knows? She's not here, and I can live with that."

"Great," Dominic said, feeling another Mama Billie headache coming on. "I think you just made everything worse."

"How so? I figure she's going to be up all night, stretching Bethany to make her taller, make her look older."

"Or she's twisted her ideas about casting again. First she thought I brought Molly here to replace Cynara. Then it was Lizzie replacing Bethany. Now? Now you've given her ammunition to think that Molly's replacing Bethany."

"Damn," Taylor said, then drained his beer. "That, my friend, never occurred to me. Sorry, I really thought I was being a help. Guess I'll go back to playing the piano and scribbling notes on a page, which is how Mama Billie describes my function around here."

"Do that," Dominic said. "Okay, next subject. I see Bethany, still sitting over there wrapped up like a mummy. Where's Derek and Cynara?"

"Doing the dirty behind the pool house? I don't know.

Last I saw them, Cynara was prancing around with a come-hither grin, and Derek was trailing after her with a dumb-shit look on his face. I think we can safely say that the two of them are an item again. That should make rehearsals easier."

Dominic was feeling his day going downhill even more. He'd had a lousy beginning, at the hospital, a pretty good middle—except for taking that ball in the *middle*—and a damn fine interlude with Molly. Now here he was, heading back into trouble.

"It should, shouldn't it, Taylor. Unless and until we cut Cynara loose."

Taylor was quiet for a few moments. "You know what? I quit. I'm back playing the piano and scribbling notes on a page. Dom, I wouldn't do your job if you paid me in Julia Roberts lookalikes. Hey, look at that. Here comes Molly. I'll bet you're wishing your equipment was back in working order. Damn. That's some real class over there."

"None of it is hanging out over here, that's for sure, not when you make comments like that."

"Gosh golly, Dominic, sir, you're no fun no more," Taylor said, getting to his feet and saluting him. "Look how nice I am. I'm going away."

"Yeah, yeah, just go," Dominic said, watching Molly's progress around the perimeter of the pool.

Those long legs. That ridiculous hat. The carriage of a queen. Huge round sunglasses that he knew were her private joke. The swing of her hips. Was she really the most beautiful woman in the world, or was he just so crazy about her that he thought so? And did it matter?

"Over here, Molly," he said, spreading a clean towel on the chaise beside him. "You're looking . . . Oh, hell, you know how you're looking."

She laughed at him and sat down on the chaise, the filmy skirt she had on splitting as she stretched her long legs out in front of her. "Will dinner be ready soon? I seem to have worked up an . . . appetite."

He leaned back on his chaise and looked at her, raked her up and down with his gaze. "You are *so* lucky those kids are over there." He reached out a hand, traced the small, colorful butterfly tattoo on her hip. "I noticed this before. Why a butterfly?"

"You know the story, Dominic. A butterfly flaps its wings in the Amazon, and the next thing you know, we're having a hurricane here. The butterfly is sort of my version of a storm warning." She took off her ridiculous hat and shook her head, so that her natural curls bounced. "Do you think the kids are ready for another swim?"

"You get that thing wet?"

"Of course I get it wet. What's the sense of having a bathing suit if you can't get it wet?"

"I don't know. I think we'd have to ask Cynara. What did you think of that outfit?"

"It doesn't matter what I think. She's happy, and since I don't see either her or Derek out here, I imagine he's pretty happy, too? Now, you stay here and rest, and I'll go see the kids, play nanny."

He watched as she stood up, slipped out of her heels, untied the sarong, and he gave a moment's thought to picking up that damn hat and laying it over his swim trunks. "I'm not tired," he said, with the halfhearted idea of joining her in the pool.

"Of course you are. You've had a long day. Just close your eyes, and we'll wake you when dinner's ready."

"I should act as lifeguard," he said, even as his muscles began to relax, as his entire body sort of *melted* into the cushions. "You do swim?"

Molly dropped her sunglasses on the chaise. "Are you kidding? I'll have you know I took the blue ribbon on the high dive at Miss Paulson's School For Young Ladies." She grinned. "That was just before I was asked to leave after the incident with the rum in the Kool-Aid punch during the tenth grade formal with Briarhurst School For Young Gentlemen. I don't know why they suspected me."

"Did you do it?" Dominic asked, trying not to laugh at her injured-innocent tone.

"Of course I did it. I just don't know where I slipped up, that's all."

"So it was off to another boarding school?"

She shook her head. "No, that was my limit. Word gets around in those schools. That's when I was shipped off to Janie and her family, to finish high school with her."

He looked at her, not smiling anymore. "I'm glad you had at least a few years with your cousin. Living with a real family."

"Uh-huh," Molly said, just a little too brightly. "At least that part worked out. Now rest. Resting is part of a vacation."

"Who says?" he called after her.

"I read it in a book," she said, then clapped her hands and said, "Lizzie? Butch? How about a swim before we eat?"

The kids scrambled to their feet and got to the edge of the pool just in time to see Molly dive in, springing from a great push-off, her body arching before she slipped gracefully into the water, her entry barely producing a ripple.

"Wow! I want to learn how to do that," Butch said as Molly surfaced, blowing bubbles from her nose, her hair water-slicked straight back from her face.

Dominic watched for a while as Molly gave the kids lessons, laughing when Butch hit the water belly first, sighing just like a proud parent when Lizzie damn near did a perfect dive on her fifth try.

Mrs. Jonnie appeared beside him with a paper plate holding two hot dogs and some potato salad. "Here you go, Mr.

Dom. Mr. Taylor's up there, helping me he says, and I'll feed everyone else when they get out of the water."

"Thanks, Mrs. Jonnie," Dominic said, taking the plate. "I could have come up and gotten this myself; you didn't have to bring the food down here."

"It was Mr. Taylor's idea. He said you probably didn't want to change views."

"Good point," Dominic said, as Molly, her back to him, bent down to adjust the position of Butch's feet at the edge of the pool.

So he ate, and then he took another sip of beer, and then he sort of *faded* for a while . . . not realizing he'd fallen asleep until Butch was shaking him, calling his name.

"What's up, Butch?" he asked, blinking a few times as he sat up.

"We can't find Molly," Lizzie told him, stepping out from behind the chaise.

Both kids, hair still damp, were dressed in shorts and shirts. Dominic looked at the sky, realizing that the sun had dropped fairly low on the horizon. "What time is it?"

"Seven o'clock," Lizzie told him. "We were swimming, and then we ate, and then Molly said we all should go shower and get dressed and meet her out here to play badminton. But she's not here."

Dominic ran his hands through his hair, still trying to orient himself. Man, he'd gone out like a light. "Why didn't anybody wake me?"

"Molly said you needed your rest," Butch told him. "You were snoring, Uncle Dom. Just like Dad."

"Marvelous. I really needed to know that," Dominic said, getting to his feet. "Okay, let's think. Where did you look for Molly?"

Lizzie started counting off on her fingers. "Her room, the kitchen, the living room, the theater, your office, the stables.

We were going to check the shed where Carl said you keep the badminton set, except the net is all set up already, because Carl did it."

"Maybe she took a walk," Dominic suggested, gathering up his sneakers and the towels that were on the chaises and heading for the house. "Give me a minute, okay? I'll get dressed and be right back."

"Do you think she was kidnapped, Uncle Dom?" Butch asked, clearly worried . . . and slightly excited by the idea.

"Dork," Lizzie said, then looked up at Dominic. "Uncle Dom? Remember, she *is* Mar—"

"I'll find her," Dominic said, cutting Lizzie off before she could finish her thought. He sat down again, slipped into his sneakers, the laces hanging open. "Look, I'll do it now. Here you go, take these towels and plates and cans back up to the house, then go play badminton. We'll meet you there."

Butch, ever obedient, began gathering plates and cans, but Lizzie was still looking at him curiously. "She didn't run away, did she?" she asked quietly, once Butch was on his way up the hill to the house.

"No," Dominic said. Quickly. Maybe too quickly. "She wouldn't do that. She said she'd play badminton with you guys, and that's what she'll do. I'm telling you, she took a walk. Now you take a hike, and let me go find her."

Lizzie bit her lips together, nodded, and picked up the towels as Dominic set off for a quick search of the grounds.

He started with the guest house, only to have Cynara, wearing a dreamy expression and some sort of caftan that nearly blinded him with its bright colors, tell him that, no, Molly wasn't there. "Now, excuse me, darling. Derek's . . . waiting."

"Wait," he said, holding the door open. "Where's Taylor? Where are Mama Billie and Bethany?"

"Out. They didn't leave notes, you know. We're all grown-ups here; we can come and go as we please. Now go away, Dom. I'm on vacation."

Dominic left the porch, stopped, looked around. The kids had already checked most of the buildings. Maybe Molly took one of the golf carts and went for a ride.

No. Both were sitting out in the driveway.

She could be anywhere.

And so what? They were all grown-ups here, as Cynara had just reminded him. Molly didn't have to report to him. She didn't owe him anything. He didn't owe her anything.

"Right," Dominic said, starting off again, this time at a trot instead of a walk. "Keep telling yourself that."

The shed, as the kids called it, was a windowless building, tucked out of the way behind the theater. Inside, Carl kept some garden tools, the riding mower. And badminton nets, obviously.

He called Molly's name as he rounded the theater and approached the shed.

What the hell?

"Like I can't afford a lock on these doors?" he said aloud as he slid the rake out from the two handles that held the doors closed.

He opened one of the doors. "Molly?" *This is stupid.* "Molly? Are you in here?"

Nothing.

He was about to close the door when he saw her. She was sitting on the floor, her back against the wall, her legs drawn up, her arms wrapped around her knees. Staring. Staring at nothing.

"Jesus," he said, throwing open the other door and letting light spill into the dark building. "Molly, are you all right?"

She didn't move.

Dominic went to his knees beside her, looked into her face. She was a million miles away.

"Molly, it's all right," he said, dragging her against him, rocking her until, after an eternity, her arms slipped around his waist and she drew in her breath on a sob.

"Oh, God," he said, his heart breaking. "Let's get you out of here. Come on, I'll help you up."

She went with him, unresisting, allowing him to sit her down beneath a tree. He held her hands in his, watching her closely. "Okay now?"

"Sure," she said, and he relaxed, just a little, to hear her voice. She was back with him. Part way, at least.

She pulled her hands free, laced her fingers behind her neck, and sighed. "Wow, anybody would think I was afraid of the dark, or something," she said, lifting her face to smile at him.

"Somebody locked you in there," he told her, immediately wishing he hadn't.

"No, don't be silly. I went in looking for the badminton set, and the door closed, that's all."

He decided to let it go. She was trying, trying hard, but he could tell she was still walking a fine edge.

"Molly, Carl already set up the badminton set."

"He did? Where?"

"Down near the stables, I imagine. It's the only really flat ground."

"Oh, that explains it. I came out the front door and walked around the other way." She picked up his arm and looked at his watch. "Oh, gosh, that was almost an hour ago. The kids must be worried about me."

She tried to get up, but he wouldn't let her. "Just stay here, Molly. I'll go tell the kids you've been found, and then I'll be right back." He tried for some humor. "You want I should bring a paper bag with me?"

She blinked, shook her head. "Just go . . . I'll stay here."

Dominic was pretty sure he'd broken at least one land

speed record, getting back to the house, asking Mrs. Jonnie to go tell the kids Molly was all right, heading back to the shed once more.

"Here you go," he said, sitting down beside her and handing her a cold soda. Her color was better. That was good. "Mrs. Jonnie says take your time. Taylor's back, and he's playing badminton with the kids. Now, tell me about it, Molly. You don't like the dark, do you?"

"I'm not its biggest fan, no," she said, popping the top on the soda can. "Anybody would think the poor little rich girl got locked in closets by the big bad matrons at the girls' schools or something, and now she can't stand the dark or confined places, and all that nonsense."

Dominic's stomach dropped. "Did somebody do that to you?"

She patted his cheek. "No, silly. That only happens in sad little foreign films."

"So you were never . . . locked up in the dark?"

Molly put down the can and hugged herself, rocking a little. "Not by anyone else, no," she said, avoiding his gaze.

Dominic pushed himself up beside her, slid an arm around her shoulders, pulled her close. "Tell me about it."

"There's nothing to tell," she said, trying to pull away . . . always pulling away, damn it.

"Tell me anyway," he said, kissing her hair. Tonight it smelled of lemons.

"All right, but I think you're mean to catch me in a weak moment. And it's silly. It was just a stupid idea, that's all."

"Tell me anyway."

"Stop pushing, I'm telling. In . . . In the summer, the parental units shipped me places. That's how I met Janie, when they shipped me to Virginia. To say I wasn't happy to be there is an understatement. So, one day when we were at Hartzell's Meats, my aunt buying hamburger or something, I locked myself in the meat room. The very ancient meat locker. It didn't have a window. Boy, was it dark in there."

"So it was a joke?" Dominic didn't think Molly had done it as a joke, but he needed to keep her talking, because she was drifting away on him again, and that scared him.

"It sure was. On me. They could hear me through the door, but they couldn't get in because the locker had this huge key, and I'd taken it in there with me. I told them I'd come out, I really would. Just as soon as they got my parents back from this place called Bali and they took me home with them. *Then* I'd come out."

She looked up at him, smiled tightly. "It was right after that I started paying attention to geography. Bali is a long way from Virginia."

"Then what?"

"Then? Well, the first thing everyone figured out was that there was no keyhole on my side of the door," Molly said, sighing. "After that, Mr. Hartzell called the fire department and the police, and my aunt cried, and five hours later they were able to break down the door because the old lock defeated the locksmith they'd called, and Mr. Hartzell got a new meat locker courtesy of Gerry . . . and I spent the rest of the summer at Janie's."

"Your parents didn't come for you?"

"Of course not," she said, smiling up at him, her bravado maybe able to fool everybody else—maybe even him a few days ago. "But aren't you lucky? Janie and her family are the only ones who ever had to know about that story until now."

"I think I can handle it," Dominic said, knowing that inside, he was longing for someone to beat into a pulp. "You said that was when you first met Janie. How old were you, Molly, that summer?"

Her face sort of crumpled as he watched. She'd been smiling, toughing it out, but it seemed that he'd finally asked the right question. She swiped at her nose with the back of her hand, buried her face against him, so that he barely heard her whisper, "I was seven."

"Ah, baby," Dominic said, folding her against him, rocking her as she cried.

An hour later, Molly taken up the back stairs and put to bed, Mrs. Jonnie helping her, clucking like a mother hen, Dominic was on his way back to the guest house.

He hadn't pushed Molly about the rake, the fact that she'd been deliberately locked in the shed. She had enough problems, God love her.

But that didn't mean *he* was going to let this one go.

Mama Billie and Bethany were just heading up the steps to the porch when he called her name. Her real name: "Bertha!"

"Go inside, sweetheart," Mama Billie said, pushing Bethany ahead of her. "Dom? You seem upset. What's wrong?"

He could say the obvious, a line he'd heard in a million movies, a million shows: "Don't play dumb with me, bitch." But he didn't. "You were out, Bertha? You and Bethany? When did you leave? Where did you go?"

"What?" she countered. Good move; answer a question with a question. "We went for ice cream. Why? Were we supposed to ask your permission first?"

"You locked Molly in the shed behind the theater, then set up your alibi. Didn't you? Taylor handed you a line of crap about replacing Bethany with someone older, and you finally snapped, thinking you'd figured out why Molly's here."

Mama Billie rolled her eyes. "So I locked her in a *shed?* Kill her, that I'd understand. That even makes sense. But what good would locking her in a shed do me? Dom, you really have been working too hard. Besides, my agent says you have to pay us whether Bethany is in the show or not. And, let me tell you something, the way this fiasco is going, we'd be better off that way."

Then she pulled open the door to the guest house and let it slam closed behind her.

Dominic just stood there. She was right. What good did locking Molly in the shed do for Mama Billie, for Bethany? *Spite?* Yes, that made sense. But how did he prove it? And how did he prove it without telling Molly that someone had locked her in that shed on purpose?

His hands drawn up into impotent fists, Dominic headed back up the hill, planning to sit beside Molly's bed until he satisfied himself that she'd be all right.

Chapter 23

Molly woke slowly, reluctantly, and opened her eyes. Dark. It was still dark.

And warm.

She moved her hand, realized that it rested on a warm body. *Dominic*. She snuggled against him, snuggled closer into his embrace, the dark not quite as frightening as it had been just a moment earlier.

Still, she wanted light. The curtains were drawn tight, the television wasn't on, there was no light burning in the bathroom. But if she just closed her eyes, stayed where she was, she'd be all right.

No, she wouldn't. She needed some light.

Moving slowly, Molly tried to edge out of Dominic's arms. He mumbled something and drew her closer.

"Dominic," she whispered. She tried to stay calm. Otherwise she'd panic, turn into an idiot. "Let go. Dominic?"

"Hmmm?"

"Dominic, let go."

"Molly?"

She let out her breath, tried to smile. Keep it together. "I'm not even going to ask whom you were expecting. Yes, Molly. Molly who wants to get up, turn on a light."

He lifted an arm to cover his eyes. "Oh, hell. Go ahead, I'm ready."

She rolled her eyes, then moved to the edge of the bed, found the nightstand, found the switch built into it. Both bedside lamps went on. "There," she said, mostly to convince herself everything was all right now. "Better?"

"We're taking a vote? If so, I vote *no.*"

"I'm sorry, Dominic. I didn't mean to wake you," she said, realizing that he was still in his clothes, and he was lying on top of the bedspread. "Wait a minute. Why am I apologizing? You're in *my* bed."

"Technically, yes, but I'm only here to keep you company. This is strictly a G-rated being together," he said, still shielding his eyes with his hand, chancing glances at her, blinking as he became accustomed to the light. "How are you doing?"

She looked at the bedside clock. Three o'clock. "How long have I been sleeping?"

Dominic sat up on the bed. "I don't know. Since nine?"

"Wow, I don't remember the last time I did that." Which wasn't exactly true. She did remember the last time she'd done that, and woke in darkness. She'd lain down to take a nap and had awakened in the dark because the lightbulb had burnt out, and flown into an immediate panic. "Excuse me."

She padded to the bathroom and afterward splashed cold water on her face, trying to shake the last of whatever nightmares might be lingering on the fringes, getting ready for an encore. Except she didn't remember having a nightmare. She just remembered Dominic holding her, and then waking in his arms.

Returning to the bed, Molly hopped up on it and leaned

over to give Dominic a kiss on the cheek. "My hero," she said. "Thank you for finding me."

She expected him to put his arms around her, to draw her in for a kiss, for more than a kiss. But he didn't. He simply pulled her against his shoulder. "And you're sure you're all right now?"

"Sure," she said brightly. "It had to be one of those post-traumatic shock things, I suppose. The door closed, it got dark, and I was seven again. Stupid."

"Not stupid. Totally reasonable. I'm just glad I found you."

She nodded. "You know what? You know what I should have done? I should have hopped on that big-ass lawn mower in the shed and rammed it straight through those doors. I don't know why I didn't think of it until now."

He rubbed her arm. "Those are steel doors, Molly. I'm glad you didn't think of it."

"Metal doors." She shivered. "Just like Mr. Hartzell's meat locker. He'd built it himself. We heard that story every time we went in there after that day. Built it with his own two hands, welded it and everything. He had a brand-new meat locker, big and shiny and perfect, and all he talked about was that hunk of junk. And I never got another free slice of cheese, let me tell you. But that was all right, because Janie always ripped her slice and gave me half."

"I like Janie. I haven't met her, but I like her. Molly, do we really need all this light?"

She sat up again. "No, I suppose not. Not this much. Mostly, I just keep the television on. You'd be amazed at the light TVs throw into a dark room."

He sat forward, sitting behind her, and put his hands on her shoulders. "But I'm here now."

"Yes, you are."

"So we can turn off the lights?"

She rubbed her fingertips against her forehead. "No. I'm sorry. No."

He was silent for a few moments, and she was sure she'd ruined something that might have been wonderful. Then he said, "Okay, lights on. And now we can talk."

Molly turned to look at him. God, he was wonderful, his blond hair all mussed, a shadow of beard on his cheeks and chin. "Talk? I don't want to talk about this anymore, Dominic."

"So we won't," he said, pushing himself away from her and off the side of the bed. He picked up one of the silver picture frames. "Let's talk about the photographs. This one's Janie?"

Molly nodded. "That's her, at high school graduation. She was valedictorian. She beat me out by two-tenths of a point."

"Pretty girl. Little, but cute. And this one—wait, I know. This one is you and Janie. What were you, twelve?"

"About that, yes. Right about the age Lizzie is now," Molly said as he held the photograph up so she could see it. "I should show that to her, to prove that flat-chested isn't forever."

"My niece is worried about the size of her chest? Gee, thanks for that mental image."

"Sorry. Back to the photograph. We were bird watching with my aunt and uncle. We went bird watching every summer, around the Fourth of July, and by then I was spending all my summers with Janie. Hence the binoculars around our necks. I can name almost every bird found naturally in Virginia. Do you want to hear the list?"

Dominic put down the photograph and picked up another. "Moving right along," he said, winking at her. "Are these the aunt and uncle?"

"Dancing at their thirtieth wedding anniversary party. It was quite the bash," Molly said, remembering how thrilled they'd been when Molly had surprised them with the party. Janie had done the hard work, the invitations, all the planning and grunt work, but it had been Molly's idea to have the whole thing held at a restaurant, and then present them with tickets for a cruise. "You have to reward that kind of longevity, don't you think?"

Dominic walked over to the dressing table. "I saw this one the other day. Who is she?"

"Mrs. Clauser," Molly said, then sighed. "She was the housekeeper in Connecticut until she died about twelve years ago. I used to think she was my mother. A mother I called Mrs. Clauser? I mean, I was three at the time, what did I know?"

Dominic was still working his way around the bedroom.

"The dog? Big ugly mutt. He's probably very special. What's his name?"

"Blackie. I found him and brought him home. The parental units never even knew I had him. He . . . He was run over by a delivery truck while I was away at boarding school." She coughed, just a little cough. "I kept Blackie on the grounds, but he ran free there."

That was the official story, the one for public consumption. The real one, Molly had found out later, was that her mother threw a fit when she saw Blackie. He'd gotten into her closet and chewed some shoes. So her parents had Blackie put down, had called him a "dangerous stray." Molly told nobody that story.

Dominic—such a wise and wonderful man—replaced the frame and picked up another. "I like this one a lot. Toga party, huh?"

Molly smiled. "In college, yes. Can you pick me out of the crowd?"

"I could pick you out of any crowd," Dominic said quietly, looking at her across the room. "Let's leave the others for another time," he said, rejoining her on the bed, picking up Janie's List of Rules as he sat down. "Tell me about this."

"That's a primer on how to run a nursery school and day care, written by a worried Janie for a seriously imbecilic cousin."

Dominic turned to the last page. There were ten pages, total, single-spaced. "She doesn't trust you?"

"She trusts me. And then she adds another rule. I particularly like number thirty-two, I think it is."

Dominic found it: *Do not, repeat, do NOT, under any circumstances, teach them the Wiggle Walk. It isn't funny.*

"What's the Wiggle Walk?"

Molly smiled. "Just something I tried one day. See, you sit on the floor, then bring your right foot up on top of your left thigh, then your left foot up on top of your right thigh."

"Okay, I've seen that."

"And then you push yourself up onto your knees and walk across the floor. The Wiggle Walk."

"You can do that?"

"I may not have invented it, but, yes, I can do that."

His grin was positively evil. "Do it."

"Not for ten million dollars. The Wiggle Walk makes you look idiotic. And only three of them could do it . . ."

"You showed them how?"

"Of course I showed them how. Janie dared me." Molly looked at the clock. "Only three-fifteen. Are you sure you want to stay up with me? I can turn on the TV, that's what I usually do. There's no better company in the middle of the night than minor Hollywood stars trying to make me believe they sleep on affordable adjustable beds."

"I don't want to leave you alone. You had a scare."

"I'm over it," Molly said, and that had to be the biggest whopper she'd told in a lifetime of whoppers.

She'd spent most of her life convincing herself that she just didn't like the dark; no big deal. Now, again, she had to face the fact that the dark terrified her, that being in close, dark spaces terrified her . . . and remember, yet again, how her parents had reacted to her fright in Mr. Hartzell's meat locker.

They'd ignored it. They'd ignored her. They'd made a career out of ignoring her. Call Gerry to have him find another school, tell him to write a check, go watch the bulls run in Pamplona.

Dominic took her hand in his. "I'll stay here."

She shook her head, smiled as she reached for the top button of her pajamas. "Okay. Whatever will we do, Mr. Dominic, sir? Oh, wait, I think I know."

"No, you don't. Not tonight, Molly, although I'm pretty sure I'll shoot myself in the morning. I think it's time we get to know one another."

Don't do this, Dominic. I can't do this. "Oh," she said, reaching for him, "I think we already know each other pretty well."

"Really? What's my favorite food?"

She sat back, frowned. "Your favorite food? That's getting to know each other?"

"It's a start, one I think we should make. And it's not calves liver."

She wanted desperately to play along. "Really? Darn, and that would have been my first choice."

"It's mashed potatoes. I *live* for mashed potatoes. Smooth, creamy, loaded down with butter or swimming with gravy. You know, dent the top of a big mound of them with a spoon and fill it with gravy? When we were kids, I'd eat my potatoes from the outside in, taking plain potatoes and dipping them into the well in the middle, trying not to break the dam."

"You're kidding, right?"

"No, no. It's very important, not breaking the dam. Obviously you're not a mashed potato dam connoisseur."

"Oh, *damn*. One of my many failings, yes."

"Shut up. And then, just as I was getting to the best part—where you're actually eating the dam?—Tony would reach over with his fork and break it."

"Oh, you poor baby. A definite drawback to not being an only child," Molly said, hugging herself. "Who's older, you or Tony?"

"Me, by eighteen months, which made me the big brother, the one who should know better, show some sympathy, and please stop running so fast so that Anthony can catch up. He was a real pain in my ass, especially when I hit my teenage years first, but we're good now. What's your favorite food?"

Molly shrugged. "I have dozens."

"If you were marooned on a desert island for six months and could eat only that one food?"

She didn't hesitate. "Pizza. It has almost all the food groups in it somewhere."

"Do you like it with lots of toppings?"

"Oh, please. I'm a pizza purist. I'll tolerate some pepperoni if I have to, but just give me dough and tomato sauce and cheese. Thin crust. Are you taking notes here?"

"I'll remember. Let's see, what else should we talk about? Movies? Books?"

"I feel like we're on our first date."

He stroked the back of her hand. "We are. I want to get to know you, Molly Applegate. I want to get to know all of you."

He didn't give up. And Molly decided that maybe she might dare to know all of him, too.

Except that was dangerous.

"You know I'm going to leave when your brother and his wife get back?"

"I've heard that rumor, yes."

"I am. I am going to leave. I'm cute and all, fun and

games Molly, but I tend to get on people's nerves if I hang around too long."

"They're a bunch of cowards, these people you're talking about."

"And I get bored."

"Are you bored yet?"

"No." She said the word quietly, not looking at him.

"Am I boring you?"

"No," she said, a little louder.

"The kids? They're boring?"

"I love those kids."

"Virginia. You're bored with Virginia."

"Would you stop it! I'm not bored. I'm simply telling you the facts. I'm not the solid, dependable type."

"Would you stay if I asked you to? If two weeks passed and you still weren't bored and I still wasn't ready to give you the boot? Would you stay then? See how long it takes for one of us to crack?"

Molly blinked back sudden tears. "You know, Dominic, sometimes I get the feeling you feel sorry for me. And I don't want you to feel sorry for me. I don't want *anybody* to feel sorry for me. I'm fine. I've always been . . . fine."

"Independent."

"Yes. Independent."

"Relying only on yourself."

"Yes."

"Not caring too much for anyone, because you know you're going to go flying off soon. Or is that just leaving before they can leave you? The way your parents were always leaving you?"

"No!" Molly nearly leapt off the bed, to sit down at her dressing table. "I'm not a child anymore. I don't think that way. It's not like that."

He was standing behind her now, his hands on her shoulders, not heavily, not trying to keep her still, but just to let her know he was there. "I think it is, Molly. I think that's exactly what it's like."

"I don't want to talk anymore," she said, shrugging off his hands and standing up to face him. To slip her arms around his shoulders. "Can't we do something else?"

She stood on tiptoe, to press her lips to his, but he didn't take her in his arms, didn't kiss her back. She ground her body against him. He didn't move.

"Okay, forget it," she said, dropping her arms to her sides. "I've got a deck of cards in my nightstand. You won't leave, you won't have sex . . . so we'll play poker, all right? Five-card draw, deuces and one-eyed Jacks wild."

She'd opened the nightstand drawer when he pulled her with him onto the bed. "Stop that, Molly. Stop running. We won't talk. We won't play games—any games. Let's just be together." His breath was warm against her ear. "Please."

He kissed her then, a sweet, soft kiss that brought tears to her eyes.

He kissed her mouth, her hair, her eyes, her chin.

His hands caressed her, not with passion, but with tenderness, a tenderness that made her feel fragile, made her want to weep.

She lay very still, soaking up every last bit of his tenderness, taking it into her, praying it might fill that empty space, that lonely place.

He opened her pajama top and kissed the skin between her breasts. "You're so beautiful, Molly. So beautiful . . ."

Molly closed her eyes, trying not to hear the words. *Not my outside. Don't talk about my outside, Dominic. Please let there be something* inside. *Something you can see.*

He kissed her breasts, her belly.

"So very beautiful."

Molly bit her bottom lip so that she wouldn't cry out. He

was saying only what he thought she wanted to hear. It wasn't his fault.

Dominic turned onto his back and pulled her against his side, tipping up her head with his hand, looking deeply into her eyes. "Pay attention, Molly," he said, his tone dead serious, more serious than she'd ever heard it. "We're not going to have sex, Molly. Not tonight."

Molly blinked, opened her mouth, found she had nothing to say.

"We're going to do one of two things right now, Molly. We're going to play poker, and I'll be damned if one-eyed Jacks are wild . . . or we're going to make love. Make love, not have sex. There's a difference, Molly, and you know it."

"Do I?" she asked, taking a deep breath.

He smiled, just slightly. "No, you probably don't. I like that. I want to be the first."

"You're scaring me, Dominic," she said, putting a hand on his chest, feeling his heartbeat, slow and steady. Funny. Hers was fluttering like that of a trapped bird.

"No, Molly, I'm loving you. I'm making love to you. Now, Molly."

And, with those words, he kissed her. Just kissed her, and went on kissing her, and kissing her, until her arms were around his neck and his hands were splayed against the small of her back. He sucked her bottom lip into his mouth, teased it gently with the tip of his tongue. Slanted his kiss again, their mouths open against each other, his tongue lightly scraping the roof of her mouth. . . .

His hands moved slowly, stroking her hip, cupping her buttocks.

He insinuated one leg between them, raised it so that the center of her rested on his thigh as he pushed, pushed ever so gently against her.

She held him, not to spur him on, but just to hold him,

just to feel the warmth of his skin, the muscles just below that skin, to feel his heartbeat, now growing stronger, faster. Beating for her.

His concentration moved to her breasts at last, and stayed there, stayed there until her throat felt thick, until her chest felt heavy with something, some emotion she couldn't define.

He kissed her stomach, her hip bones, brushed his face against the soft juncture of her thighs . . . and moved on.

He kissed the soles of her feet, the hollows behind her knees, the insides of her thighs.

But when he moved a little higher, Molly felt panic. She tensed her thighs, and he moved away, kissed her belly again, started over. . . .

She was floating, not overwhelmed with the need for an orgasm, but simply . . . *floating.*

When he came to her again, when his fingers carefully spread her, when his mouth and tongue claimed her, it wasn't an invasion. It wasn't frightening. It wasn't even blinding passion . . . not yet.

She lifted her arms and laced her fingers behind her head, arching her neck; her mouth open, her eyes tightly shut. Her legs fell completely open as she went boneless, her limbs turned to water.

The feeling in her chest intensified, making it difficult to breathe. Yet it was pleasurable, welcome. A filling up.

And then his tongue. . . .

He did things, impossible things, finding her in a way she had never known. Suckling on her, warm and moist and strong against her.

She'd never . . . no one had ever. . . .

He held her hips steady as her body convulsed, his mouth sealed against her, prolonging the pulsing sensations until she cried out, cried out his name. Over and over and over again.

For the rest of the night he held her, until her breathing became regular, and she felt an enormous weariness she couldn't fight . . . and when she woke the drapes were open to the morning sun, and Dominic was gone . . .

. . . and Molly turned her face into the pillow, and cried.

Chapter 24

Dominic, his hair still damp from his shower, wandered out onto the grounds with his coffee cup, just to see the sun disappearing behind a cloud.

It figured. They'd had some pretty good days; it was time for some rain.

They'd be housebound, the kids with Molly and him, everyone else stuck in the guest house. He liked that arrangement.

He took a sip of coffee, winced as its heat hit his tongue.

Molly. How was she doing this morning? Still hanging on, still claiming her independence, this supposed invulnerability? Didn't she trust him? Or was it that she didn't trust herself?

"She's so damn stubborn," he told Rufus, who had lumbered up to him, looking his usual friendly, pathetic self. "You're a man," Dominic said, looking at the Saint Bernard. "Well, for a little while yet, you're a man, until Elizabeth comes back and hauls you off to the vet. So tell me, man to man, do you understand women?"

Rufus stuck out a tongue the size and color of a slice of smoked ham and ran it around his muzzle. Then he drooled.

Dominic smiled. "Right. Same here. So, what are you doing today, Rufus? Got any big plans?"

"Yes, I'm thinking about writing a book on how to avoid loonies who think I should talk to them."

Dominic turned around, to see Taylor standing behind him, shaking his head. "Morning, Taylor. You do a great Rufus impersonation."

"I do a great song-writer impersonation, too, or I could, if I weren't on *vacation*. Tell me, does it get more scintillating than this, or is dog ventriloquism going to be the highlight of my day? Reminding you that it's only nine o'clock in the morning."

"You're bored?"

"Hey," Taylor said, taking the coffee cup from Dominic's hand and putting it on the porch. "You've got Molly. Derek's got Cynara. What have I got? And if you're about to say Billie White, I'll remind you that I outweigh you by forty pounds."

"Sixty."

"Whatever. I'll also remind you that I'm a city boy. Yesterday was fun, but I'm heading for the bright lights until you're ready to go back to work. Unless you've changed your mind? I really want to get this Cynara thing settled first. Derek's down at the theater with her now, rehearsing, and I can't stay here and listen to her keep murdering the best music Tony and I have ever written."

"You've been listening?"

Taylor nodded. "I admit that it's a difficult piece. But she's just not getting it."

"Molly got it," Dominic said, then wished he hadn't.

"Molly got it," Taylor repeated, stepping closer to Dominic. "You want to explain that one to me? Because, damn it, Dom, if you've been lying to me, if you're so cockeyed about her that you'd give her anything and she's here to—"

Dominic took hold of Taylor's arm, turned him toward the office. "Not here. Come on."

Ten minutes later, while Dominic sat behind his desk, watching, Taylor was scribbling all over a copy of their hopeful showstopper, their "million-dollar song."

"Yes . . . yes . . . That could work. Take it down. I can take it down. Like a throwaway, but then we bring it back, we bring it back hard. But we'll have to lose another song somewhere, or run too long. Damn. We need Tony, because the lyrics definitely have to change for this last bit—I'm not sure where." He threw down the pencil. "This doesn't work without all of us. Damn Greek Islands."

"The man's on his second honeymoon," Dominic reminded Taylor. "It's also our first totally nonworking vacation in ten years. We've all earned it."

"Right. But where is it written that I deserve it *here?* And now how do I leave, with this idea perking? I'd be useless to a woman."

"I've heard that about you," Dominic said, grinning as Taylor picked up the pencil and tossed it at him.

"Okay, look, Dom. Let me hear Molly sing the song. She doesn't know what she was doing, *you* don't know what she was doing, but if I heard her, I'd know, right? She sings, I listen, I get the hell out of Dodge and come back when Tony's here, and we're . . ."

"No."

". . . all set to . . . What do you mean, no? Why not?"

"Because she doesn't know I heard her, that's why not. It . . . It would be an intrusion on her privacy."

Taylor leaned back in his chair and scratched at his hair. "Cripes. You're in love with the girl, aren't you? Damn it, Dom, don't do this. Tony was one thing. He's the marrying kind, whatever the hell that is. But us? We don't fall in love with them. We damn sure don't marry them. It's distracting."

"I don't know about that, Taylor. I haven't taken a nerve pill or blown in a paper bag since Molly and I first—look, she's not a performer. I told you how she sang the song. You're a professional. Write it that way."

"Listen to what I say, write it that way," Taylor grumbled, getting to his feet. "Once, just once, I'd like you and Tony to consider me the freaking miracle I am, okay? I'm outta here."

"Taylor, don't do this," Dominic said as his friend headed for the door. "You don't even have to change the song if you don't want to. Maybe it was a bad idea."

Taylor turned around. "Are you nuts? It's a *fabulous* idea." He pointed a finger at Dominic. "And, by the time Tony shows up here, it'll be *my* idea, right?"

"What? You mean it wasn't?"

"Right. Good man. God, it feels good to be temperamental."

"Sure it does. Just the way it feels good to know that I might pretend to kiss your artistic ass, but we both know I was right."

Taylor sat down again. "So tell me about Molly. You're really in love?"

Dominic picked up the pencil and held it between his hands. "I think so, yes. Maybe. We're . . . We're getting to know each other better."

"Mrs. Jonnie told me you stayed with Molly all last night, after she got locked in the shed. I thought she'd be disapproving, but she was all smiles when she told me, so I guess she likes Molly. I like her, too. She's nice. She seems like a good sport. And there's those legs."

Dominic smiled. "I'm not asking for your approval, Taylor, you do know that?"

Taylor shrugged. "Still, I guess you've got it, as long as you take it slow, don't go nuts on me. *Now* can I please go to New York?"

"Sure. Just as soon as the audition's over."

"You bum. You *are* bringing in someone new. Who is she? Have I heard her? What are you going to tell Cynara?"

"Down boy, down," Dominic told him. "I'm talking about Lizzie's audition. I promised her one, and I want you there for moral support."

"To quote someone who said the same thing very recently—*no*. I will not get involved with family stuff. It's dangerous. Especially if Tony and Elizabeth find out."

"Molly's going to be in the audition with her. Some Bob Fosse choreography Elizabeth taught Lizzie and the kid adapted for *All That Jazz*. Mrs. Jonnie told me all about it. They've even got her making up costumes for them. Fishnet stockings were mentioned."

"Shit," Taylor said, then sighed. "You tell me not to talk about her legs, and then you go and talk about her legs. Okay, okay, you've got me. When is this audition?"

"I don't know. The end of the week?"

Taylor eyed him. "You never used to be a bastard, Dom. I'm supposed to live in that guest house with the lovebirds and Mama Billie until the end of the week?"

"I'll give you a guest room in the house, all right?"

"Ah, I knew I'd get what I wanted! Wait a minute. That's not what I wanted. I wanted to leave."

"But, since you're staying . . . ," Dominic said, picking up the sheet of music Taylor had been scribbling on and waving it in the air. "And, in return, I'll break my oath to be on vacation and go over to the theater to listen to Cynara. You want to come along?"

"Like I want a tetanus shot," Taylor said, following Dominic out of the office. "What the—hey, Butchie-boy, is that you?"

Dominic looked to his left, to see a pair of skinny legs in falling-down socks and the back of one very large black hat. The Hat That Ate Fairfax. The hat that covered everything from the knobby knees up of one Butch Longstreet. Molly's black straw hat. "Butch, what the—"

Butch turned around, holding onto the hat that otherwise would have covered his grinning face. "Hi, Uncle Dom, Uncle Taylor. Look—I'm a turtle!"

Dominic lifted the hat. "Does Molly know you have this?"

"No, sir," Butch said, dipping his chin. "Am I in trouble? Lizzie's with Mrs. Jonnie doing more secret stuff and Molly's still sleeping or something and there's nothing for me to do so I found this hat and . . . and now I'm a turtle?"

"Turtle soup," Taylor said, then laughed. "Oh, Dom, he's cute. Look at him. Don't you just get all warm and fuzzy and domestic looking at him? Bet you want five or six of your own running around here, right?"

Dominic dropped the hat back on Butch's head (neck, torso, and thighs) and said, "You go play, Butch, and I'll just take care of a few things in the theater with Cynara and Derek, and then see you up at the house in about an hour, okay? We'll . . . We'll do something."

Dominic watched Butch run off, nearly losing the hat in the breeze that had begun to kick up, then turned to Taylor. "You're a real pain in my backside, you know that?"

"What?" Taylor asked, looking as innocent as a three-dollar bill. "Did I say something upsetting? I mean, hey, you think you're in love, right? Love, marriage, here comes Dom with a baby carriage? Let's see here. You're almost thirty-nine. Have the first kid when you're forty, forty-one? By the time he graduates from college, you'll just about be collecting Social Security. Gee, sounds like great fun. Really. And there's bound to be more than one kid. Look at Elizabeth. What do you think this Greek Islands thing is all about, huh? Or didn't Tony tell you they're trying for another one?"

Dominic made a face, then headed for the theater once more, Taylor on his heels.

"What's the matter, Dom? Have I hit a nerve here? Maybe given you a dose of reality? You're not the marry and settle down with the little woman type. Okay, you were a little strung out, I'll grant you that. Too much work, maybe even playing too hard when you played, which wasn't often enough if you ask me."

Dominic stopped, turned. "Nobody asked you anything, Taylor."

"True. I agree, true. But I'm saying it anyway. Molly Applegate is *hot*. She's gorgeous, even rich. She's a lot of fun, and you need some fun. But the rest of it? God, Dom, *think*. And think with something besides your glands, for crying out loud."

Dominic felt his hands drawing up into fists. He wanted to hit Taylor. He wanted to clock him one, take him down. Shut him up!

Instead, he held up his hands and backed up two paces. "Go away, Taylor. Go to New York, go to Atlantic City and gamble, go to hell, but get out of here, okay? And don't come back until Tony's home. I don't need you, and frankly, I don't want to see your face for a while."

"Aw, cripes, come on. Dom? Come on, don't do this. Tony told me to watch you, remember? And I am, I'm watching you. I'm watching you make a damn fool of yourself over this girl. Sex isn't a cure-all, Dom, take it from one who knows. You had a scare. That doesn't mean you—"

"All right, Taylor, I get it. I understand what you're saying, all right? For God's sake, we've known each other for a couple of days. What do you think we're going to do? Elope to Vegas, or something?"

"I don't know what you're going to do. I just know you're not thinking on all cylinders. It's like you're playing house here, you know? And that's fine, for a while. But for the rest of your life? You really want to do this for the rest of your life?"

Dominic opened his mouth to answer Taylor and then shut it again. Because he didn't know. He just didn't know.

"She's . . . She's special, Taylor," he said at last, knowing he sounded lame, stupid. "I've never felt this way about a woman before. But, just so you don't have a breakdown or call Tony, I'll tell you one thing. She's made it very clear she's out of here when Tony and Elizabeth come home."

Taylor looked at him for a few moments, blinked. "Oh, brother. She said that?"

"Yes, she said that. More than once."

"And you wonder why you're so mixed up? Dom, there's nothing like a woman telling you she's leaving to make you want her to stay. Especially someone like you. You're so damn competitive. Well, I'll relax now, a little. This is going to end up as one of those hot and heavy things that cools off just as fast. I shouldn't have worried, or butted in on your business. Sorry, pal."

"Yeah," Dominic said, stuffing his hands into his pockets. "It's okay, just forget it. I mean, you're probably right. We'll just have to see how it goes. Now come on, let's hear how Cynara's doing so I can keep my promise to Butch."

His mind full of questions he damn well didn't have answers for, Dominic opened the door to the theater just in time to hear Derek saying, "No! For God's sake, Cynara, that's not it. Look, why don't we try it again, without the music. I want to hear you without the music getting in the way."

"Well, that's nice," Taylor said, standing close beside Dominic. "First I'm in your way. Now my music gets in the way. I'm telling you, Dom, this hasn't been one of my best mornings."

"Shhh," Dominic warned. "Let's just stay back here and listen."

They slipped into two rear row seats and watched Derek and Cynara on the stage.

Derek was looking hassled. Normally his hair was almost too perfect, but this morning it was a mess, as if he'd been repeatedly stabbing his fingers through it. He wore loafers with no socks, a pair of slacks he must have hung up on the floor the previous night, and his shirt was loose and hung open to his waist.

In short, Dominic's leading man looked to be rapidly falling apart. He pitied him, was beginning to identify with him, and that was a scary thought.

Cynara, however, had never looked better. Dressed in a bright pink blouse and a navy blue pair of those slacks that were either too short or too long—Dominic could never figure that one out—she appeared composed, in charge, and not at all upset that Derek was unhappy with her.

"You look so cute," she said, raising a hand to Derek's cheek. "I love it when you're flustered. My little bear. And how you love your honey. Don't you, little bear?"

"Got one of those barf bags handy, Dom?" Taylor whispered.

Derek kissed Cynara's palm, then stepped back. "Come on, darling, I mean it. One more time, without the music. You can do this. I know you can do this."

"And what would be the point, Derek?" Cynara asked, throwing down the sheaf of music. "I won't be performing without music, will I? It's the music that isn't right, not me. There are four octave changes in the first third, for God's sake. Any more, and I'd be *yodeling.*"

"Okay, that's it," Taylor said, slapping his hands down on the armrests. "This time I kill her and solve all our headaches."

"Good morning, Taylor," Molly said from behind them. "Is there a problem? I'm only asking because your ears are red."

Dominic took a steadying breath and turned to look at her. She looked . . . She looked wonderful.

"Hi," Molly said, looking at him, but not quite looking at him. "I saw Butch on the porch, and he told me where to find you."

"Are you okay about the hat?" Dumb question, but the only thing he could think to say. Because she was here, she was smiling, she looked as if there wasn't a problem in her life. Happy, uncomplicated. While he was tied up in increasingly small knots. How many years did a person have to practice before she could pull off a trick like this? Was it some "laugh, clown, laugh" thing? "Laughing on the outside, crying on the inside"? How did she shut it off, shut it out?

And, after years of it, when did she know what she felt was real, or just the real she wanted others to see?

Last night, she'd been real. She'd cried in his arms, then come alive in his arms. Gave herself to him. Gave her body, completely and utterly. For a while, all the defenses had been down; the façade had crumbled.

Or had it? Did he really know Molly? Or only parts of her?

"Dominic? Yoo-hoo. I said I'm fine about the hat. I mean, it's only a hat. Is something wrong? You looked a thousand miles away."

"No, nothing's wrong," he said quickly. "It's just more of the same. Cynara's still having trouble."

"I was afraid of that. But, you know, I've got an idea. Do you think she'd mind a small test? I have, well, I have this theory."

"I don't know. What kind of test?"

"Who cares?" Taylor said, getting to his feet. "All suggestions are gratefully appreciated. What do you have in mind?"

"Nothing earthshaking, I promise. Excuse me."

Dominic watched her walk down the short aisle, to where Derek and Cynara were standing on the stage, watching them.

"Hi, Derek, Cynara," Molly said, reaching into a large

purse Dominic hadn't noticed until now. "I've had this idea, for a couple of days now, and I was hoping you'd let me try it."

Derek threw Dominic a decidedly nasty look. "The role is filled, Molly," he said tightly. "I don't care what Dom told you."

"Dominic didn't tell me anything, Derek," Molly said, climbing up onto the stage. "I thought this up all by myself. I could be wrong, but I don't think I am. Cynara? Could you do something for me? I think I know your problem with the music."

Cynara rolled her eyes. "Look, Molly, you're a good kid, you really are. Even sweet. But no thanks. We're doing just fine."

"No you're not," Molly said, pulling something from her purse.

Dominic leaned forward in his seat. Headphones. Molly had pulled out a set of headphones. What the hell?

"But, I am, aren't I? A good kid, that is," Molly said, going over to the portable CD player that Derek had lifted onto the small table. "And I mind my own business, too. Usually. But when I see what I think I see? Look, just give it a try, Cynara, that's all I'm asking."

Cynara looked to the back of the theater. "Dom? What the hell is going on here?"

"You have an answer for her?" Taylor asked, as both of them walked up to the stage.

"Not a clue." Dominic motioned for Molly to lean down, so he could talk to her. "What are you doing?"

"I thought it would be obvious. It isn't obvious?"

"Stop that," Dominic ordered, barely moving his lips. "Are you all right? You were sleeping when I—"

"I'm fine," she said quickly, her smile bright. He could see no shadows in her eyes, not a single one. "I'm simply trying to return favor for favor."

"By making sure Cynara pitches a fit?"

"No," she said reasonably. "By helping Cynara. Helping you, helping Taylor, helping Derek. I'm just one great big bundle of helpfulness this morning. Now go away, and let me be helpful."

She turned her back on him and lifted the CD player, hunting for the plug-in for the earphones. "Ah, here it is. Derek? Would you please set the tape or CD or whatever to Cynara's solo? Cynara? If you'd come over here?"

Dominic sat down in the front row, right beside Taylor.

"What's she doing?" Taylor asked. "Cynara looks ready to blow."

"She says she's being helpful," Dominic said. Maybe this was a test for *him*. Would he be reaching for a paper bag in five minutes? One of those nerve pills the doctor had given him? Or would he just have to toss Molly over his shoulder and get her out of the line of fire when Cynara went ballistic?

"Darling, I don't see—"

Molly handed Derek the CD player. "You will, Derek, if I'm right. And if I'm wrong? Well then, no harm, no foul, isn't that what they say?"

"If that's sports talk, I really wouldn't know," Derek said tightly. "Oh, what the hell. Come on, Cynara. Humor the girl."

"Then she'll go away?" Cynara glared at the earphones as Molly held them out to her, then shrugged and slipped them over her head. "Now what?"

"Now, I go sit in the audience, and Derek starts the music. You sing."

"And *then* you'll go away?" Cynara asked, her smile dripping sarcasm.

"Absolutely," Molly said, then skipped down the stairs to sit next to Dominic. "This is going to work. I'm sure of it. Pretty sure of it. Really. I hope."

"That's what I like to hear, confidence," Taylor said as he sat back, folded his arms across his chest.

On stage, Cynara was adjusting the earphones, waiting for a signal from Derek.

She was the only one who could hear the music, of course, but when she began to sing, that didn't seem to matter. Her voice was strong, pure, and perfect.

"My God," Taylor whispered at one point, sitting front, his jaw dropped. "My God, that's it, that's it."

Dominic remained silent, but took Molly's hand as Cynara took the music higher, as the words his brother had written came alive, truly alive, for the first time.

Molly's voice had been pretty enough, but not strong. Her tone plaintive, while Cynara's soared.

Everything was so pure, so perfect. Everything he'd hoped, everything he could wish for, and more.

"Wow," Molly said as the song ended, as Cynara continued to stand there, looking at Derek, her expression puzzled.

"What?" she said at last, when nobody said anything. "What's the matter with you people? I've sung this song a million times."

"Not like that, you haven't. Damn it, not like that," Derek said, and he left the stage. Moments later, everyone could hear the side door slam shut.

"I'll go," Molly said, grabbing her purse and quickly getting to her feet. "He loves her, you know. I'm sorry. I think I just realized what Derek's realized. I'd been so wrapped up in believing this would be good news, and maybe it isn't. But she can be fixed? I'm sure she can be fixed. Dominic?"

He hadn't seen it, hadn't figured it out. Why hadn't he seen it? Molly called herself superficial, a butterfly who flitted from place to place. Passed herself off as shallow, selfish. And yet she had seen what nobody else had seen.

"Now where is she going? What's *wrong* with all of you?" Cynara asked from the stage, throwing down the sheet music.

"She wasn't really hearing all of the music until now. Not the upper registers. That's it, isn't it?" Taylor said quietly. "Cripes, Dom, Cynara's going deaf. What in *hell* are we going to do now?"

Chapter 25

"Derek. Derek, wait up, please," Molly called as she trotted after the man. "It's not terrible. This could be a good thing."

He whirled about to face her, his posture aggressive. "Do you know what you just did? *Do you?* You just killed Cynara's career. Take a bow, little lady, you destroyed one of the greatest ladies in the theater, all by yourself. Are you happy now?"

Molly took a step back. "No. No, that isn't it. She's got a small hearing problem, that's all. I'm sure it can be fixed. We don't know it can't be fixed."

Derek looked around, then grabbed Molly's arm and pulled her behind the theater. "With what? Hearing aids? Oh, yeah, that'd go over big. Okay, she's got hearing aids, we can hire her. But what if she gets worse during the production? What if the hearing aids don't work for her anymore? Can we take a chance? Build an entire show around a star who might not be able to perform? There's insurance issues, things you don't understand. Nobody will touch her. *Nobody.*"

"Dominic—"

"You didn't see their faces in there? They're already planning how to get rid of her. And they can do it. Buy her off, kick her out. It's in her contract. Damn it! Why didn't you come to me, talk to *me?*"

Molly didn't know what to say. "I . . . I didn't think—"

"Damn right you didn't." He raised his hands to his head, yanked at his hair. "This is going to kill her. She's done, she's just done. Everything's gone."

Molly tipped her head to one side, looked at the man. He was in obvious pain. He obviously loved Cynara. And he was obviously overreacting.

"Okay, that's enough," she said, folding her arms and tapping her foot against the ground. "You'd think her ears just fell off. She has a little problem, and you've already got her stone deaf and living in an attic somewhere, eating cat food."

Derek lowered his hands to his sides. "Why don't you just get the—"

"I'll go away, Derek, get out of your face. But first, I do have a question. Where are *you* going?"

"Me?" He blinked at her. "What do you mean, where am *I* going?"

Molly's heart was pounding. "I don't know, Derek. I'm just wondering. Wondering if you're going to desert Cynara now, the way you're saying everyone else will desert her? Is that why you're so sure? Because that's what you want to do?"

"I *love* that crazy woman in there," he shot back, pointing a shaking hand at the theater, and Molly could see tears in the man's eyes now. "I'm not going anywhere."

"Which explains why you're out here, when Cynara's in there, being told she's got a problem with her hearing. She needs you, Derek."

"And I don't know that?" He began to pace. "I . . . I couldn't face her. She sounded so wonderful. I mean, God!

Did you hear her? She's so damn talented. Gifted. How could this happen to her?"

Molly put her arm around him. "I don't know, Derek. Life isn't perfect, is it? But she has you, and I know how much she loves you. Together, the two of you should be able to face anything."

He set his jaw. "We couldn't last time. I left her. Marriage? Commitment? I ran like a rabbit."

"I know," Molly said quietly. "And if you're going to leave her again, do it now, Derek. She doesn't want or deserve anything less than your honesty. And your love, if you really mean it."

He drew himself up straight. "We'll get the best. Go to New York today, find the best."

"I can help you with that," Molly said, watching as Derek pulled a handkerchief from his back pocket and wiped at his forehead . . . then swiped at his moist eyes. "Stay here at least overnight and let me make a few calls. I know some people."

He grabbed her arm. "You do, don't you? Hell, you're Margaret Applegate. I already told Cynara about who you are. You've got to know some people. Specialists. The best."

Molly smiled, sighing inwardly. Was there anyone here who *didn't* know who she was? "I'll phone my lawyer, and he can get things in motion. He's good at that. Why don't you go check on Cynara?"

Derek pulled her close, kissed her cheek. "You know, this could be all right. It wasn't as if Dom wasn't going to give her the boot anyway. At least now we know what's wrong."

"She hasn't been fired yet, Derek," Molly reminded him, but he was already gone, heading back into the theater. "Oh, boy," she said, leaning against the side of the building. "No wonder I stay on the move. This standing still and getting involved isn't all it's cracked up to be."

She closed her eyes a moment, and when she opened them, she realized that she was looking at the shed she'd been locked in the night before. Pushing herself away from the wall, she walked over to look at the doors, the lock.

The doors had been unlocked last night, when she'd gone in looking for the badminton set, and they were unlocked now. A dead bolt. One that needed a key.

"Dead bolts don't lock themselves," she said quietly. Her skin went cold. Dominic had been right; someone *had* locked her in the shed. "Mama Billie," she told herself. "That miserable woman."

"I know," Dominic said from behind her. "She denies it, but you're right."

Molly turned to look at him. "She didn't know. She couldn't know how I'd react. To her it had to be some spur-of-the-moment bad joke. She's petty, and it was a petty thing to do."

"It doesn't matter why she did it. She did it. And right now I've got to deal with Cynara. But I'm going to get rid of Bertha, count on that, Molly."

"No, don't do that. You'd only be hurting Bethany."

"Who the hell cares?" Dominic said with some heat.

"I do, I suppose." She rolled her eyes. "God, I hate this. All these people, all these problems. How do you stand it?"

He looked at her, a white line around his mouth. "Lacing up your running shoes, Molly?"

She looked at the ground, then up at him. "It crossed my mind, yes. I won't lie to you and say it hasn't. But I'm here until your brother comes home. I said I would be, and I meant it."

She watched as his jaw tightened. "Don't do me any favors, Molly. If you want to go, go, if you want to stay, stay. I've never been really big into begging," he said, then turned away, headed back into the theater to solve another problem.

The skies opened as Molly walked back to the house,

drenching her to the skin in moments, but that was all right, because the kids didn't see her tears when she climbed the steps to the porch.

"You're all wet," said Butch, the master of pointing out the obvious.

Lizzie was sitting on one of the chairs, swinging her legs. "Can we go rehearse?"

Molly shook her head. "No, not yet, honey. They're pretty busy down there right now. Maybe tonight?"

Lizzie's bottom lip came out. "But what are we supposed to do all day? It's raining."

"I don't know. We'll think of—oops, hang on a moment." Molly reached into her purse, pulled out her cell phone. "Hello?"

When she heard Jane's voice she nearly lost it, nearly sank to the porch boards to weep in relief.

"Where are you? You are? Look, can we come over? The kids and me. In about an hour? Thanks, Janie."

She closed the phone, smiled at the kids. "That was my cousin, the one who owns the day care. How would you like to go meet her there?"

Butch clapped his hands. "Are other kids there?"

"No, I'm sorry, honey, the place is still closed. But all the toys are there."

"And the computer? Can I go on the computer? She's got a great game on there, with these black and white things," Lizzie said.

"Sure. Just let me go change into some dry clothes and tell Mrs. Jonnie where we're going. We can have lunch somewhere, as long as we're out."

And Dominic won't think I've run away, damn the man.

They were on their way within twenty minutes, and when Molly pulled into the parking lot there was Janie, waiting at the door with two large umbrellas. She opened one and headed for the Mercedes. That was Janie. Prepared for anything.

"Oh, it's so good to see you!" Molly said once they were inside, grabbing her cousin in a bear hug. "Where the hell have you been and what were you doing on CNN?"

"It's a long story," Jane said, looking meaningfully at Lizzie and Butch. "How about we get you two settled somewhere, so Molly and I can have a cousin-to-cousin talk?"

"Lizzie wants to go on the computer in your office," Molly said, trying hard not to wince. "She's good with it, promise."

Jane raised one eyebrow. "And you'd know this how?"

"I don't know. I let her go on it already?" Molly suggested.

"You're hopeless," Jane said, then smiled at Lizzie. "I'll bet you want to play Othello. Go ahead, honey."

Butch was already in the main playroom, just standing there, surrounded by a million toys and with no competition to keep him from playing with whichever one he fancied. The decision was too much for him.

Janie went to a closet and pulled out a large canvas bag. "Here, sweetheart, I keep these for the older children. How about you start here?"

Butch's eyes widened. "Legos, cool!"

"I'll say this for you, Janie," Molly said as they closed the door of the nursery behind them, "you're good at what you do. And it's a lot more than baby-sitting. The children need so much more than that."

"They do," Jane said, pulling out two of the rockers and sitting down in one of them. "They're nice children. You were being very generous, agreeing to take care of them. Do you want to tell me why you're doing it?"

Molly couldn't sit. She paced. "Hey, you know me. Anything for a lark. I was tired of that newspaper job anyway. Besides, their uncle's cute. Now tell me what you've been up to. You had yourself a busy week last week. I saw the CNN thing, and a story on the senator, so we can skip those. But what else? What happened with the professor? There's something going on between you, isn't there?"

"More than I'll tell you right now," Jane said, smiling. "John lives right here, you know, just outside of Fairfax. I'd tell you all about him, possibly for hours on end, except that you'll meet him soon enough, and because you look ready to burst. What's wrong, Molly? And don't tell me nothing's wrong, because I know you."

Molly bent over one of the cribs and picked up a pink teddy bear and held it protectively against her, took a deep breath, then let it out slowly. "Janie, am I nuts?"

"Are you *what?*"

"Nuts. Crazy. Three crayons shy of a full box. Not different. Not eccentric. Nuts."

"No, sweetheart, you are *not* nuts," Jane said, getting to her feet. "Why would you think that?"

Molly dropped her chin onto the bear's head. "Because I've just met the most wonderful, sweet, terrific man, and I think he thinks he's in love with me and I think I think I'm in love with him, and all I want to do is run. Run away. Quickly."

"I see. It is what you do, isn't it?"

Molly threw the bear back into the crib. "See? See? It *is* what I do. You know it, I know it. What's wrong with me? Why do I do that, Janie?"

Jane touched her arm. "Come on, sit down."

"I don't want to sit down. I want to run."

"Margaret Applegate, sit down," Jane said firmly, the born schoolteacher, the born disciplinarian. And the sane one; always the sane one.

Molly sat down.

"All right, at least now I'm not getting a crick in my neck, looking up at you."

Molly tried on a smile. "Little Miss Short-stuff."

"Molly Beanpole," Jane shot back, sitting down again. "Do you remember Darrin and Joe?"

"Joe wanted you. Darrin wanted me."

"No, Joe was the short one, the wrestler. He wanted you. Darrin played center on the basketball team. He wanted me."

Molly took a steadying breath, smiled again. "And we couldn't get them to realize that we were matched up wrong. I remember. Whatever happened to those two?"

"Joe's a doctor and Darrin moved to Alabama," Jane said, then changed the subject. "You know, I always disliked your parents, Molly, but now, now that I'm a grown-up, I'd really like to choke them both."

Molly inspected her manicure. Janie had always been so damn *honest.* "A person can't blame their every problem or shortcoming on their parents, Janie. I'm a grown-up now, too, remember?"

"Maybe I'm not the one who should be remembering that. Molly, I *saw* you grow up, remember? Your parents couldn't have cared less about you. That's a fact, lousy as it is. And you reacted to their indifference. I've taken a lot of child care courses, child psychology courses, and what you did was perfectly normal. You tried to get their attention."

Molly bit the insides of her cheeks, and nodded. She'd already figured that one out on her own.

"You overachieved. You underachieved. You acted out in a million and one ways. And not just to get their love and attention. That was when you were a child. As you grew you wanted something else. Not their love and attention, I think you'd given up on that one by then. Their approval maybe? You wanted them to at least approve of you—your brains, your looks, anything at all. Acknowledge, just in some small way, that you were there?"

"Maybe."

"And then *they* weren't there, were they? Just when you were becoming an adult, your own person, a person to reckon with, they went and died on you. They took away your last chance to force them to admit that you were a good person, a fine person, a loving, *worthy* person."

Molly sniffed. "I certainly hadn't done that yet, had I? Not with the terms of their will."

"Having to work ten months a year to keep your income, or marry to get it all. I know. They saw you as flighty, unstable, incapable of being any more than they had been. And you know what you did? You revolted."

"That was nothing new, Janie. I'd revolted, and been pretty revolting, since I was four."

"No, no, that's not what I meant. You wouldn't marry, because that's what they'd expect you to do. But you wouldn't settle down to one job, either, because then you'd be doing what they wanted you to do. How dare they tell you what to do? They'd never cared before, right?"

"I guess so . . . yes," Molly said, wiping at her eyes. "You and your mom and dad were the only ones who really cared. And Mrs. Clauser."

"We did love you, Molly. We *do* love you. On your terms. Because you'd never let us get too close. After all, you weren't worthy, were you? Your own parents didn't love you, so there had to be something wrong with you, some flaw we'd find and then kick you out. Sweetheart, you're textbook. Textbook with an unlimited pocketbook, and that's a pretty potent combination."

Molly attempted a laugh, but it was pitifully feeble. "Thanks. I can see one of us has given this a lot of thought. What else?"

"So you ran from the marriage idea, and I'm very glad you did, and found a way to live up to the wording in the will and still be in charge of yourself. You'd take jobs, but it wouldn't be one job. It wouldn't be a job even Gerry approved of—you'd do it your way. It was inspired, actually. A great revenge. But it was also ten years ago. Aren't you tired, Molly? Aren't you tired of punishing them? Of punishing yourself?"

Molly rubbed at her eyes. "I'm so tired."

"And now you're here. Tell me about this uncle."

Molly got to her feet, began pacing once more. "He's . . . he's . . . I told him about Mr. Hartzell's freezer."

"Oh." Jane sat back, folded her hands in her lap. "Then it is serious. You've been to bed with him?"

At last, Molly could summon a real smile. "Look who's asking that question. The last remaining virgin in three states."

"I haven't been a virgin since I was eighteen, and you know it."

"All right, then, *near* virgin. But, yes, I've been to bed with him. I've . . . I've made love with him."

"Yes. You mentioned that word earlier. *Love.* You know, I don't think I've ever heard you say that word, not about anything even remotely personal."

Molly walked over to the window, looked out at the rain. "I'm scared, Janie. I'm really scared." She turned to her cousin, a hand to her chest. "What if there's nothing in here? What if he thinks he sees something that's just not there?"

"What if you're your parents' child, you mean?"

"Yes!" Molly gestured wildly toward the door. "You saw those kids out there. Lizzie. Butch. I'm *crazy* about them. Now ask me if I want kids of my own. Go ahead, Janie, ask me."

"Do you want children of your own?"

"God, no," Molly said, turning back to the window, to the playground equipment sitting abandoned in the rain.

"Because you wouldn't trust yourself to be a good parent?"

Molly pressed her forehead against the window glass. "Would you?"

"Yes, I would. I think you have so much *love* in you, Molly. So much love that you're afraid to let it out. I think the man you allow yourself to love will be the luckiest man in the world, and your children truly blessed."

Molly turned around to see Jane standing just behind her, tears streaming down her face. They matched the tears on her own face.

"But first, Molly," Jane said quietly, "you have to learn to love yourself. Because you *are* worth being loved."

"I love you," Butch's small voice said from the doorway. "Is it okay if I love you?"

Janie grinned at her. "There you have it, Molly. An unbiased opinion. Of course, he's male, and they all love you. Now kiss that kid, find the other one, and go home. Home, Molly. I think you might know where that is now."

Chapter 26

It rained. And it rained. And as the afternoon ran on, it just flat-out poured.

Molly took the kids to lunch at a fast food restaurant, and then phoned Mrs. Jonnie to tell her they were going to a movie and wouldn't be home until dinnertime.

Not that she was avoiding anybody. . . .

She did see Dominic at dinner, but he was preoccupied, excusing himself from the table three times to take phone calls, and then disappearing again, to closet himself with Taylor in his office.

Lizzie agreed that a trip through the rain to the theater would be pretty soggy, so the two of them rehearsed a little in the living room, with Mrs. Jonnie and Butch as their audience. And, a little after nine, both children were washed, given a snack, and had gone to bed.

Leaving Molly free to think, which she really didn't want to do. So she called Gerry at home and instructed him to find out the names of the top three ear-nose-and-throat specialists in the Manhattan area. "For a friend, Gerry."

"I don't believe I inquired as to the reason behind your request, Margaret."

Molly wrinkled her nose. "I know, Gerry. You're the soul of discretion. Can you have it to me tomorrow morning? You can just call my cell phone."

"Or I could have one of my secretaries fax the information to you. Or are you on the move again?"

"No, Gerry, I didn't quit the job. I'm still here."

"That's not what I asked, Margaret, although I'm pleased to hear that you've found employment that satisfies you. And now, if you'll excuse me, I'm hosting a small dinner party."

"Stuffed chicken for the stuffed shirts?" Molly asked.

"No, Margaret. Shocking as this might be, I do have personal friends."

"Oops, sorry, Gerry. Did I drag you away from a hottie?"

Molly could have ice-skated on his response. "I beg your pardon?"

"Never mind, Gerry. I'll let you go now. But I really do need that information."

"Yes, so you said. Margaret?"

"Hmm?"

"You're being careful, aren't you? I know you're there for the Longstreet children, which is commendable in its own way, but these *are* theater people."

Molly smiled at the cell phone. "I haven't run off to join the circus, Gerry."

"Only because you haven't thought of it, I'm sure. Just remember, your money can be very attractive."

"So can I, Gerry," Molly said, losing her smile. "Be very attractive, that is."

"That goes without saying, my dear. You're quite the charismatic young woman," Gerry said, and Molly frowned at the tone of his voice. It was almost gentle.

"Thank you, Gerry. That was very nice. Unexpected, but very nice."

"Yes, well . . . I really must get back to my guest . . . guests. You'll stay in touch?"

Molly nodded at the cell phone, then realized she hadn't spoken. "Gerry?"

"Yes, Margaret," he said, and he was his businesslike self again.

"Do . . . Do you like me, Gerry?"

"Excuse me?"

"Do you like me, Gerry?" she asked again, more strongly this time. "Am I a job, or a friend?"

He was silent for so long that Molly thought he'd hung up on her, but that wasn't Gerry. He always liked having the last word.

"You are an endless source of worry to me, Margaret, the quixotic, always beautiful, often sad, complex product of two of the most egregiously selfish people I've ever met, and you've risen above that by dint of your own inimitable style. I'm proud of you, Margaret, extraordinarily proud of you. And now good night, you've kept me long enough."

"Good night, Gerry," Molly said, but the lawyer had already ended the connection. "Thank you."

She attached the cell phone to its overnight charger, changed into a black, thigh-skimming silk nightgown, and hit the Power button on the television remote controller as she climbed into bed.

She could catch up on the news, she supposed, but as she surfed the channels she stumbled over a program seemingly devoted to constructing workable go-carts out of material found in a junkyard. "Something from nothing. Okay, we'll try this one."

Next up was an hour devoted to life in a busy emergency room, and Molly became fascinated with the devotion shown by the nurses and doctors, and shed a tear when a three-year-old struck by an ice-cream truck was pronounced fine, suffering from only a few cuts and bruises.

With the television still on, she walked over to the windows, to look through the darkness and rain, toward the theater. There were lights on, both there and in Dominic's office.

What were they doing? Trying to find a way to ditch Cynara, as Derek said they would? Gerry had reminded her that Dominic was "theater folk," but that didn't mean he wasn't a businessman. Would he confront this as a businessman and cut his losses?

"None of your business," Molly told herself as she turned away from the window. "You've done enough."

She wandered around the room, picking up the same photographs Dominic had asked her about, and considered phoning her friend in California—the blonde in the green and blue paisley Ralph Lauren toga, because those were the only sheets she'd had. It was almost midnight here, but earlier in California.

But no. Suze would only ask her how she was doing, and she'd have no answer for her. Better to just brush her teeth and go to bed, try to sleep. Because she was tired. Tomorrow, when he was less frantic, she'd talk to Dominic, if he was still speaking to her.

"He was *so* angry," she told her reflection in the mirror above the sink, the toothbrush stuck in her mouth. "I hope he took his pills."

"I don't take pills, and you should give a little thought to talking to yourself when nobody else is around."

"Dominic?" she said, turning toward him, the toothbrush still in her mouth, her stomach somewhere in the region of her toes. "I thought you were—oh, wait, I have to spit."

"There's a turn-on I hadn't expected to be one," he said,

handing her a towel. "Here, you've still got some toothpaste on your chin." He wiped at her chin as he looked into her eyes. "I like you without makeup. And I like the way you smell. All minty. I thought you were gone."

"I told Mrs. Jonnie—"

"I know you did, but I didn't know that until I'd already seen that the Mercedes wasn't parked outside. I thought I'd scared you off."

Molly shook her head. Resisted the urge to fling herself into his arms. "I told you I wouldn't leave until your brother got home."

"Yes, and I told you that you could go. I'm glad you don't do what you're told."

She stepped past him, walked back into the bedroom. "I phoned Gerry and asked him to get me a short list of the best ENTs in Manhattan. I told Derek I'd do that. The fax should be here before eleven tomorrow."

"Derek told me. That's very nice of you, Molly."

"It was the least I could do, after dropping that bomb on everyone." Molly picked up the television controller and hit the Mute button. She kept her gaze on the screen, where a giddy-looking sweet young thing seemed to be planning a wedding with a lot of white doves in the decorating scheme. "And Cynara? How is she?"

"Hysterical. In denial. Weeping. Sleeping now. I gave her one of those pills I got at the Emergency Room."

"I would have thought she had her own supply," Molly said, holding onto the bedpost.

Dominic shrugged. "Probably. Come to think of it, she did seem to recognize what it was." He crossed the room, cupped her cheek in one large hand. "Let's not talk about Cynara anymore, all right? I've been talking about her all day."

"What are you going to do, Dominic? I know you and

Taylor have to have talked of nothing else. And there were all those phone calls. Is Derek right? Are you going to dump her?"

He kissed the corner of her mouth. "Tomorrow. We'll talk about it tomorrow."

Molly felt her knees going weak, and she closed her eyes. Part of her longed to talk about what had happened at Janie's today, but another part wanted more time to digest everything, try to separate rational thought from so much earth-shattering emotion. "Then . . . Then what will we talk about?"

He trailed kisses down her throat, turned his attention to her ear, nipped at the lobe with his teeth. "I don't want to talk right now. I'm all talked out."

"Me, too. Talked out, that is. Maybe we should just go to bed."

"Sounds like a plan," Dominic said, his hands on her breasts. "Especially since I have to go to New York tomorrow morning."

Molly covered his hands with her own. "You do? Why?"

"To yell at lawyers, convince investors, some of whom happen to be the damn lawyers."

"About Cynara? Things are moving fast, aren't they?"

"Not as fast as I want them to, at least not in this room," Dominic said, slipping his arms under her back and knees, and lifting her onto the bed. "No more talk. No questions, no answers, no threats, no promises. And no postmortems, not for us. Just come here, Molly. I really need you tonight."

She slipped her fingers into his hair as he leaned over her, looking so earnest, so weary. "Am I your medicine tonight, Dominic? Take one Molly and don't call her in the morning?"

"Oh, I'll call her in the morning. I think she's addictive, and I probably am already considerably more than halfway to being hooked." He frowned, rolling onto his back and pulling her against his shoulder. "That didn't sound right. Tony's the writer. I told you I didn't want to talk anymore tonight, and now I've gone and shoved my foot in my mouth."

"No, you didn't. I know what you meant, and I think it was cute. I think you're cute," she said, tickling her fingertips against his chest hair, because she'd already opened his shirt buttons. She was getting really good at opening his shirt buttons. "But if you wanted to shut up now, you silver-tongued devil, I wouldn't argue with you."

"Just shut up, big boy, and come here and kiss me?"

"That's good," she told him as he pushed her over onto her back. She felt his hand on her hip, strong and steady, and then closed her eyes as that hand slipped beneath the hem of her skimpy nightgown. "And that's even better . . ."

When she woke up, it was to the light of the television, the light in the bathroom, drapes opened wide on a gray, watery sky, and a note on the pillow beside her: *Back in three or four days. Don't go anywhere! Please?*

Molly smiled as she showered and dressed, her body still tingling from Dominic's inspired lovemaking, and went down to breakfast to be met by two very long faces. Three, if she counted Mrs. Jonnie.

"It's still raining," said Butch, again showing signs of being master of the obvious.

"It's going to rain for the rest of the week," Lizzie said. "I heard it on the news. And Uncle Dom and Uncle Taylor are gone. He forgot all about my audition."

Mrs. Jonnie slid a plate of bacon onto the table and looked at Molly, winking. "Are we having fun yet?"

Molly grinned at her. "Are we the only living cells left in this dead body, or is everyone else still in the guest house?"

"She's still here," Lizzie said, rolling her eyes.

"That she being Bethany?"

"Who else," Lizzie grumbled, picking up a piece of bacon

and biting it nearly in half. "And Mama Billie says they need the theater every afternoon. Like she owns it or something."

Molly gratefully accepted a glass of orange juice from Mrs. Jonnie. "We can rehearse in the morning, can't we? And in the evening, too, if you want."

Butch looked up at her, rather like a puppy. "I don't have anything to do. Can I rehearse with you?"

Lizzie opened her mouth, definitely to say *no,* but Molly shook her head, warning her to silence. "What do you want to do, Butch? Sing? Dance?" She had to shake her head again, because now Lizzie looked ready to burst.

"I can start the music," Butch said hopefully. "And then I can stop it, too."

"You could, couldn't you? Lizzie? Does that sound like a plan?" Molly kept smiling, but she was beginning to understand the job stress Solomon must have labored under all those centuries ago.

"Well, I've been thinking, Molly, and it would be cool if we could have someone throw us the canes while we're dancing. You know, have the hats on already, but instead of reaching down to pick up the canes, someone could throw them to us. Butch can throw them to us?"

"I can do that! I can do that!"

Molly smiled; crisis averted, victory declared. "Good. Now, let's finish our breakfast, help Mrs. Jonnie clean up, and then head down to the theater."

By the time she was limping back up to the house for lunch, a purple bruise throbbing on her shin, Molly wasn't quite as confident of her victory. But Butch had been getting better at throwing the canes after the first thousand times. If she took them back to the store this afternoon and bought herself some shin guards this could work out just fine.

"Oh, wait, kids," Molly said as she remembered something. "I've got to stop at the office. Someone is sending me a fax."

"I'll go with you. Uncle Dom locks the office when he goes away."

"You have a key?"

Lizzie giggled. "No, I don't have a key. Why would Uncle Dom give me a key? He doesn't want me in his office, re-member? He certainly wouldn't give me a key."

"You have a key," Molly said as beside her, beneath the huge umbrella, Butch giggled.

"I don't, really. But I do know where they hide it."

Molly gave her a one-armed hug. "A woman after my own heart. Tell me where it is. And it's only drizzling now, so you can take the umbrella, and I'll meet you guys back at the house. I have to give the fax to Cynara."

Five minutes later, Molly was knocking on the door to the guest house, and Mama Billie opened it, sneered, and tried to close it again. But Molly was too fast for her and stiff-armed the door, stepping inside and closing the door behind her. "I'm here to see Cynara. I'm not here to see you. And you know what, Bertha? You don't want me to be here to see you. You really, really don't. So go away."

Mama Billie, showing more sense than Molly would have supposed her possible of harboring, turned on her heels and headed for the kitchen.

"Molly?"

She turned to see Derek coming down the stairs. He looked exhausted, harried, and extremely happy to see her. "Hi, Derek. I've got that information I promised."

"Oh, God. Great. Can . . . Look, can you take it up to her? She just threw me out. Again. She's been throwing me out all night, all morning."

"Sure thing," Molly said, as her mind screamed, *No! This is going to be messy!*

"Second door on the right," Derek told her, stepping away from the stairs. "Thanks. I'm going to get a cup of coffee."

Molly squared her shoulders and climbed the stairs, then

knocked on Cynara's door. Knocked hard enough to be certain she could be heard.

"Damn you, Derek. I *told* you, I don't want you here."

"Oh, this is going to be fun," Molly grumbled, then opened the door, stepped inside.

Cynara was on the bed, lying there in a pink peignoir with swansdown trim, one hand to her forehead, a wadded tissue clutched in that hand. More tissues littered the bed, the floor. There were the remnants of a badly shattered lamp someone had tried to push into a corner. A broken vase spilled water and pink roses in the middle of the carpet.

Molly stepped over the vase and sat down at the end of the bed. "How are you doing, Cynara? It's me, Molly."

Cynara opened her eyes, lifted her head slightly. Then her beautiful face crumpled. *"Oh, Molly!"*

The next thing Molly knew she was being smothered in swansdown and scent as Cynara fell into her arms, sobbing. "I'm doomed! It's over. It's all over. All my dreams! I'm . . . I'm a *has-been!* An . . . an object of *pity!* I'm *defective!"*

And you're playing to the cheap seats, Molly thought, carefully disengaging herself from the woman's convulsive embrace. "Cynara, stop. It's not that bad. Lots of performers lose a little bit of their hearing over the years. Rock stars, people like that? I read about it. In *People,* I think. And they found a way to go on performing. Besides, I've got a list of names for you. Five of the top men in New York."

And they call me *mercurial,* was Molly's next thought, when Cynara let go so fast Molly nearly fell to the floor as the woman grabbed the paper from her hand.

"Dominic said he'd pay for tests," she said, scanning the list of names. "Well, the production would, but if they won't, then he will. Where's Derek? I need Derek. He has to call these people, impress on them that I must see one of them no later than tomorrow. *Derek! Derek!"*

She clambered off the bed and opened the door to the hallway, and Derek walked into the room. "I heard. I'll start packing. Thank you, Molly."

"Oh, yes, yes!" Cynara said, and Molly braced herself for another perfumed embrace. "You are my *savior*. First Angel, and now this. And Derek told me who you are, who you *really* are, that is. You're Margaret Applegate!"

"Word has a way of getting around, doesn't it?" Molly said, looking for the nearest exit, because Cynara had already stripped off her robe and was clearly going to strip to the buff in front of her in her hurry to be dressed and gone.

"Of course," Cynara said, starting to hitch her nightgown up her hips, "I didn't have the faintest idea who Margaret Applegate is. But Derek told me. You're an *heiress*. I knew it though, from the beginning. You had to be *somebody*. Nobody gets an immediate appointment with someone like Angel without being *somebody*. But I'll keep your secret, I promise."

Since Cynara and Derek were leaving, Molly didn't bother mentioning that the woman's promise had come a little late, so she just kissed them both goodbye, made them promise to call as soon as they knew something, and made her escape down the stairs . . . stopping short when she saw Mama Billie standing in front of the door. Blocking the door."

"You're Margaret Applegate?"

"You're in my way, Bertha."

"No. You're Margaret Applegate. I . . . I'm so sorry."

Molly's jaw tightened. "Sorry for what, Bertha?"

"For . . ." She stopped, shut her mouth for a moment. "For not recognizing you, my dear. Please, stay right here. I don't think you've really been introduced to my Bethany. Such a darling child. You could stay for lunch? Really. We should get to know each other."

"Too late, Bertha," Molly said, motioning for the woman to move away from the door. "I already know you."

Mama Billie didn't move. "Are you going to have Dom fire Bethany?"

"That's what you'd do if you were in my place, wouldn't you? No, Bertha. What Dominic does is his business, not mine. I'm the nanny here, remember?"

"But—"

"I said, Dominic does what he wants, and I do what I want. Right now, I want to go back up to the house and have some lunch. You stay out of my way, and I'll stay out of yours. And, in case you're wondering, that *is* a threat. Cross the line again and I'll take you down, and there won't be anything left for Dominic to keep or fire."

Molly grinned all the way back to the house, not caring that the drizzle had once more turned into a downpour. She deserved two Girl Scout badges for this one. Helping Hands, or whatever, for Cynara, and Kick Ass, for Bertha White.

And, in case Janie were to come jumping out from behind a tree to ask her, yes, she felt good about herself. Really, really *good* about herself.

Chapter 27

As Dominic drove home from the airport, the sun in his eyes, he marveled at the beauty of his surroundings. Lushly green, everywhere. Sky so blue, the few clouds as white as snow. Whitewashed split-rail fences thick with blood red rambling roses bordering sweeping pastures. Virginia was a beautiful state. His state. His home.

If he stopped the car, pulled over, he would be able to smell the flowers, hear the birds Molly could name from memory.

But, if he pulled over, he would delay his arrival at the compound, and that he was not going to do!

He'd been gone nearly four days, long enough to pick fights with about twenty people, then placate most of them with the report from Cynara's ENT specialist. She was fixable. Yes, she'd lost something in the higher registries of her hearing, or whatever the hell the specialist had said—a damn important loss to a performer—but the problem was definitely fixable, correctable.

Even if he'd ended up personally guaranteeing to make

good on the insurance payment if Cynara couldn't cut it during her run with the show on Broadway. Hey, what was life without a few gambles?

He was gambling now, with the two-carat engagement ring in his pocket. But if he wanted something, he had to go for it. Reach for it, damn it. And he couldn't be that wrong, that far off base. Molly loved him. She wanted him at least, and that was a start, better than just a start.

Which didn't mean he didn't automatically look for the Mercedes when he finally pulled into the circle in front of the main house, then let his breath out in relief when he saw it.

"The big bad producer brought to his knees by a long-legged bundle of nerves and heart," he said to himself as he climbed out of the car. "I'll say one thing for her; she sure can keep a person humble. I'd say two things, but now she's got me talking to myself the way she does, and a man has to have some limits."

Leaving his luggage in the SUV he'd driven to the airport with Taylor, who'd stayed behind in the city, Dominic bounded up the stairs to the house and banged open the screen door, calling Molly's name.

"Mr. Dom?"

"Mrs. Jonnie, hi," he said as the housekeeper walked into the foyer from the direction of the kitchen, wiping her hands on a towel. "I'm looking for Molly."

"Yes, I thought so. Welcome home, Mr. Dom. Everyone's down at the stables. It's been raining for days now, and Jonsey asked Molly if she'd help him exercise the horses. The children went with her, to watch."

Dominic was already heading for the door. "Thanks, Mrs. Jonnie."

"Mr. Dom? It's pretty muddy down there. Maybe you want to change out of that suit?"

"Good thought. I can help exercise Sylvester." Then he was off again, climbing the stairs two at a time. Ten minutes later, still stamping his feet into his boots, he was jogging toward the stables, not daring to leave the macadam path, as the grass looked too wet to not be damaged by his boots.

He passed the guest house, smiling to know that Cynara and Derek were gone, Taylor was gone, and all he had to do now was cut Bertha and Bethany loose. Production had to be delayed anyway, with the changes he and Taylor had talked about into the wee hours in the hotel bar, and Cynara couldn't be rushed, not when she was still feeling so delicate.

None of which mattered to Bertha and Bethany, because Bethany was now officially out. Lawyers were good for some things, and Dominic's were very good at a lot of things, including slipping in clauses to cover their client's ass. Left to his own devices, he wouldn't have thought to put a "creative differences" clause in a child actor's contract, but his lawyer had. Sure, it would cost him, but Dominic considered it money well spent. And maybe, just maybe, Bertha would wise up and step back from trying to manage her daughter's career.

Not that Dominic cared, not right now. Bethany would either fade away, or turn around one day and fire her mother. And, just to be sure Bethany wasn't getting screwed, Dominic had made a few calls, suggesting Bethany's financial records be audited by those in charge of watching out for the welfare of child actors.

So he felt good about that, all of that, all of that *business* that he would refuse to think about for at least until Tony got home. Plus a month, although he and Molly would probably have to honeymoon in Podunk Kansas if he wanted to take her somewhere she'd never been before.

Which seemed only fair. She'd already taken him places he'd never been before. . . .

Dominic squinted into the sunlight, trying to make out the various bodies standing around the fence.

There was Butch, hanging on to the top rail, his booted feet on the first rail. He was wearing Molly's immense black hat.

There were Rufus and Doofus, enjoying the sunshine.

There was Lizzie, standing beside Butch, holding Brownie's halter as if she'd soon mount the pony and exercise him in the ring.

There was Jonsey, astride Sylvester, whose flanks quivered, clearly already exercised.

There were Bertha and Bethany, dressed for a Noel Coward picnic, mincing their way across the muddy stable yard, doing God only knew what.

Not that Dominic spent more than a second wondering about it, because now, there was Molly. Astride Daisy, far in the distance, on the other side of the exercise yard, putting the mare through her paces in the meadow.

"Sits like a champ, don't she, Mr. Dom?" Jonsey asked, dismounting from Sylvester and leading him through the gate as Dominic approached. "I hope you don't mind me asking her for help, but I got my sister's anniversary party tonight and wanted to get everything done a little early."

"No problem, Jonsey. How long has your sister been married?"

"Thirty-seven years, Mr. Dom. I got her and Hank a real nice deep fryer."

"Longevity should be rewarded," Dominic said, remembering Molly's words about her aunt and uncle. "Give them my congratulations, will you?"

"Sure, Mr. Dom. Thanks. Uh-oh, here they come. Meanest woman I ever saw, Mr. Dom. She calls my horses broken-down nags, like they was something terrible. Just because I said the little girl would have to start out on Brownie or Rosie, just like Mr. Tony's two. She didn't like that."

"No, I imagine she wouldn't. Don't worry about it, Jonsey." With a last look toward the fields, and Molly, who either hadn't seen him or was determined to give Daisy her head for a while longer, he turned to watch Bertha and Bethany approach him. "Hello, ladies. Lovely day, isn't it?"

"Is it? You tell me, Dom," Bertha said, pushing her daughter behind her. "Who's replacing Cynara? I'll want approval, you know."

"Hi, Uncle Dom!" Lizzie and Butch said in unison, running over to hug him. That was nice. They didn't used to run to him for hugs.

"Molly's riding Daisy," Lizzie told him. "You should have seen her. They jumped the fence out of the yard. Just *whoosh,* up and over."

"Yeah, it was cool," Butch said, then tugged at Dominic's sleeve. "I've got a new nickname, Uncle Dom."

Lizzie rolled her eyes. "Here we go again. Except this is a good one."

"A.J.," Butch said proudly. "A for Anthony, and J for my middle name, Joseph. Molly says it's exactly right, and I took my time and tried things out, and that's how you get things to be exactly right."

"A.J. Longstreet," Dominic said, well aware that behind him, Bertha was fuming. "It's good, A.J. With a name like that, you could be a lawyer."

"No, Molly says I'm too honest to be a lawyer."

Dominic laughed. God, he felt so good. "All right, then, how about Senator A.J. Longstreet?"

"Molly said he's too honest for that, too," Lizzie told him. "Is Uncle Taylor back, too? You said you were going to let me audition, and I'm ready. I'm really ready."

"What? What did that little brat say?"

Dominic turned around to glare at Bertha. "Why don't we go up to my office, Bertha?"

"You're doing it. You're actually *doing* it. Well, you can't, do you understand? I won't let you. I'll sue you for every penny you have and every penny you ever hope to make. Do you hear me!"

He hadn't planned it this way, but the woman was asking for it. Begging for it. "I had my lawyers review Bethany's contract while I was in the city, Bertha, and damn if they didn't find a loophole. It's a shame, because Bethany's got some real talent, but I'm not going to deal with you for the next eighteen months. I won't, and I don't have to. You have until tonight to pack and leave. Bethany will receive a reasonable compensation, and I'll even pay your plane fare back to Connecticut."

"Oh, wow," Lizzie said, her eyes opened wide. "Does that mean I get to take her—"

"You little *beast,*" Bertha said, grabbing onto Lizzie's arm even as she raised her own, obviously to slap the child.

Dominic reacted, but Molly reacted faster. He hadn't noticed that she'd brought Daisy in, but even as he pulled on Lizzie's other arm, this *blur* went past him at about eye level as Molly launched herself from Daisy's back, over the fence, and landed one hell of a football block on Bertha White.

The two of them hit the ground an instant later, their fall broken as they landed in a huge mud puddle that instantly turned Bertha's white dress to reddish brown.

Over and over they rolled, Molly's long, boot-clad legs spinning as she tried to get a good grip on Bertha, both women so slick with mud that neither could do much more than try to defend herself.

Doofus, his bark ten times the size of his small, poodle body, circled the women, either protesting or barking encouragement, Dominic couldn't be sure, while Rufus, tongue lolling, just stood there as A.J. held his collar.

"Do something, Uncle Dom!" Lizzie pleaded.

"Shut up, you stupid girl. This is all your fault," Bethany said, glaring at Lizzie.

"Oh, why don't you just go home!" Lizzie bent down, picked up a clump of mud, and threw it at Bethany.

"Girls!" Dominic said, stepping between them, his arms out, just in time to get whacked in the side of the head by Bethany's muddy retaliation.

Everything became a bit of a blur after that. . . .

At some point Bethany, dripping muddy water, deserted the field, chased by Lizzie's triumphant cheer, and at one point A.J., whom no one had bothered to attack, sat down in the mud and piled some on himself. He'd probably felt left out.

Dominic was bending over, muddy water dripping off his forehead and nose, trying to figure out where to put his hands to separate the two women, when Molly finally got the upper hand. She straddled Bertha with those long legs, picked up her head by grabbing her hair, and tried to speak. Sputtered. Spit mud out of her mouth. Spoke again. "Uncle, Bertha. I warned you. Let me hear it, Bertha. Say *uncle.*"

"You bitch!"

"No, that's not it, sorry." Molly picked up some mud in her free hand and rubbed it in Bertha's face. "Try again?"

"Uncle!" Bertha spat, literally. *"Uncle,* damn you!"

Dominic stood back as Molly got to her feet, wiping at her face, which didn't do a whole lot of good. She was mud from head to foot. It dripped from her hair, plastered her clothing to her body. She blinked mud.

"Hi," she said, shaking her hands at her sides, which just sent more mud spraying. She smiled, and he saw that the only things white on her anymore were the whites of her eyes and those even white teeth. Everything else was mud. "Welcome home?"

Behind her, Bertha somehow got to her feet, and she put

her arms out, her fingers curled into claws, growled, and lunged at Molly's back . . . only to have the calm, incredibly intelligent—and never to be "snipped" if he, Dominic, had anything to say about it—Rufus move his bulk in between them and, with his massive head, *push* Bertha back down into the puddle.

"Hi, yourself," Dominic said with as much sangfroid as he could muster. "Anything interesting happen while I was gone?"

Molly grinned at him as she poked a finger in her ear, trying to get rid of some of the mud. "No. Nothing I can think of. It's been pretty quiet around here. How was your trip?"

"Good. Good. Will you marry me?"

She blinked. "What?"

"I said, would you please marry me?"

"Oh, wow! Lizzie, did you hear that? Uncle Dom just—"

"Shut up, A.J.," Lizzie said, clamping a hand over her brother's mouth. "Come on. We aren't supposed to hear this."

Dominic was still staring at Molly. He stared at her until a drop of muddy water slid off the end of her nose. "Well, will you?" He patted at his pockets. "I've got a ring here somewhere, unless it fell in the mud."

"Ooooooh, Dominic!" she exploded at last, pushing past him, running back to the house.

"What the hell?"

"Women, Mr. Dom," Jonsey said, handing him a towel. "Can't live with 'em, can't send them all to the moon. That's what my brother-in-law says. You going after her?"

"Oh, yeah, Jonsey. I'm going after her. Would you let her get away?"

"That one? Not me. Want a rope? I've got a lasso in the tack room."

"Thanks, but no," Dominic said, and started back toward the house.

He could have caught up with her before she reached the house, but he knew she couldn't run too far, so he decided to give her some time. But as he climbed the hill he saw a silver Lexus in the drive and a well-dressed older man standing there, looking at Molly as she stopped dead and looked back at him.

"Margaret?" he heard the man say.

"Gerry?" Molly answered.

"Obviously. What is not quite as obvious is your appearance."

"Oh, not now, Gerry," Molly said, and headed up the porch steps, into the house.

Attorney Gerard Hopkins of Hopkins, Goldblum, and Smythe, turned his attention to Dominic. "Mr. Dominic Longstreet, I presume? Please, we'll dispense with the formalities, no need to shake my hand. I'm—"

"I know who you are," Dominic said, eyeing the man warily. "What I don't know is why you're here."

"No, I wouldn't suppose you would. I spoke with Margaret the other evening, and she seemed troubled. I fear I was somewhat abrupt with her at the time, and it has been nagging at me ever since. So I decided to charter a flight down here to see her personally."

"And now you did," Dominic said, and then he grinned.

"Yes, I most certainly did, didn't I. And now I've also seen you."

Dominic swiped at his hair, came out with a clump of mud. "I was just asking Molly to marry me."

"Really? And is the rolling-in-mud portion of this proposal part of some native Virginia folklore?"

Dominic didn't know if he should laugh at this stuffed shirt, or just go with the flow. He decided to go with the flow, because the man did seem to genuinely have Molly's best interests at heart. "We like to start our own trends. Now, if you'll excuse me, I need to find Molly and hear her answer."

"I would think you already have your answer, Mr. Longstreet. Or am I so out-of-date that a woman running as quickly as possible in the opposite direction has some new, modern connotation?"

Dominic shook his head. "You know what, Gerry? It's been nice. But I gotta go."

"Mr. Dom!" Mrs. Jonnie scolded as he ran past her in the foyer as she knelt on the floor, wiping up mud with a kitchen towel. "Don't you dare go up those—oh! How am I ever going to clean all of this?"

"Sorry, Mrs. Jonnie. How about a ten percent raise?"

"Oh, go on, it's not as if the carpet isn't already ruined."

"Thanks, Mrs. Jonnie," Dominic said, and continued up the stairs, following increasingly faint mud tracks to Molly's door.

Which was locked.

"Molly?" he said, his hand on the doorknob. "Molly, open up. I know you're in there."

"I'm here to tell you, Mr. Longstreet, that if you break down that door, I shall find a way to press charges against you, even if this is your own house."

"Go away, Gerry!" Molly yelled from the other side of the door.

"Yeah, do that, Gerry. Go away. Molly! If you don't let me in, I'm going to make a fool of myself out here."

"That, young man, would be redundant," Attorney Hopkins said, folding his arms and leaning a shoulder against the wall.

"Gerry!" Molly yelled. "Don't help!"

Dominic ignored him, even ignored Molly. Because he had something to say. "Molly?" he said, going to his knees. "Molly, you can't see me, but I'm on my knees out here."

"I'm a witness, Margaret. He's on his knees out here," Gerry said, then sighed.

Dominic shot him a look. "Thanks."

"You're welcome. I'm beginning to believe you really do love Margaret."

"I do," Dominic said, damn near shouted. "I love her! I'm crazy about her. She makes me crazy, and I *want* to be crazy. I want to be with her, and love her, and have babies with her if she wants them, or dogs or hamsters or whatever she wants. I'll learn to sleep with the damn light on and eat my pizza without mushrooms, and, and—Molly? Let me in. Please let me in. Into your room, into your life. I love you, Good Golly Miss Molly. Please?"

"Well, that was marvelously muddled and dramatic. I told her. You theater folk can be quite volatile." Gerry stepped in front of Dominic and knocked on the door. "Margaret? I'm going downstairs now. Let the boy in."

Dominic stayed on his knees until the door opened, then got to his feet. "Molly?"

She'd wiped at her face, but she was still wearing her muddy clothes. "You'd keep the light on?"

"You know I would. Just as long as you need it on."

"Janie . . . Janie says that when they made me they threw away the mold, that I'm a one of a kind, and that much of the world is probably very happy about that."

She was crying. It was obvious, because dirt tracks were running down her cheeks.

"Then I'm the lucky one, aren't I, Molly. If I get to have you. Do I get to have you?"

"You really want me?"

He grinned. "More than I want a shower, and I'm starting to itch here."

"I ran away."

"You didn't run far."

"I know. You frightened me, surprising me like that, even before we had our talk. Because I was going to talk to you."

"We have years ahead of us to talk, Molly."

"Can I say just one thing?"

"After you say yes, sure."

"Yes."

He reached for her, but she put out her hands against his chest, holding him off.

"What I wanted to say, Dominic, is that I figured something out these past few days. I figured out that I'm much more afraid of not being with you than I am of being with you. I don't want to go back to a life you're not in, Dominic. I . . . I feel filled up here, with you here."

"I love you, Molly."

She smiled then, that beautiful smile that set her huge, witchy eyes to dancing as she grabbed his shirt in both hands and pulled him into the bedroom . . . and into her heart.

They didn't even hear the cheers and applause rising from the bottom of the stairs, or see Mrs. Jonnie smiling as she muttered, "I suppose now I'll have to add a new bedspread to the list. Come on, children, let's get you cleaned up. Would you care for a cup of coffee, sir?"

"Call me Gerry, please, as we must be past the formalities by now. And I think this calls for something a little stronger than coffee. Perhaps a nice dry sherry . . . ?"

Epilogue

Janie Romanowski stood at the window of her office in Preston Kiddie Kare, smiling as she watched the sunny playground, and her oldest, Johnny. He was King of the Playground, no question. At the ripe old age of five-and-three-quarters, he attended kindergarten five mornings a week, and then hopped off the bus and into his kingdom.

Not that she was an overly proud mama. But Johnny had been born with the sort of charisma that drew everyone to him: the nurses in the nursery, his besotted parents (that was a given), his doting grandparents (also a given), people passing by when she wheeled him in the supermarket aisles, dogs, cats, and the occasional grasshopper.

And now his sister, Amelia, only six months old, was busy captivating anyone Johnny had missed.

Janie laughed as Johnny, a receiving blanket pilfered from the nursery tied around his shoulders like a cape, began a march through the playground, leading a snaking parade of youngsters around the playground equipment as his little knees rose high with each step, as his smile lit the world.

"His father's son," Janie said as she headed for the front door, because she had seen the silver Mercedes pull into the parking lot.

She hesitated only a few moments to frown at Donald Furbish, who had been carrying on where his older brother Mason had left off, unfortunately. "Donald? Pull them back up, please. Some things are private, remember? That's a good boy, thank you."

Then she picked up speed, anxious to see Molly and Dom, who had been in New York for the past few months as Dom put the finishing touches on yet another new show.

Molly and Dom traveled a lot, but they also came home quite often, more and more this past year, and Janie still marveled at how happy her cousin was. No more shadows, thank God.

As Molly had told her about six months after the wedding, "I'm not ready to go spelunking in any dark cave, but I sleep without the TV on now. No more infomercials. Isn't it amazing? Sex is *so* much more interesting."

Good old Molly, making a joke of everything, even her traumatic youth.

"Molly!" Janie yelled as her cousin stood beside the trunk of the Mercedes, watching Dom unload gifts. FAO Schwartz must love seeing the Longstreets coming through the door.

"Janie!" Molly yelled back, then said something to Dom, who grinned at her and dropped the gaily wrapped boxes back into the trunk.

They held hands as they walked across the parking lot, bumping against each other, giggling (well, Molly was giggling; Dom was just looking his usual gloriously happy self).

"You two look like you've been up to no good," Janie said as Dom lifted his and Molly's joined arms and sent her into a spin, then pulled her against his side again, kissing her cheek.

"It's that obvious?" Molly asked, hugging Janie, but still

not letting go of Dom's hand, so they ended in a sort of group hug . . . Janie feeling very much like she'd just been swallowed up by giants.

"Okay, okay," Janie said once they'd disentangled. "What is it this time? Tell me you didn't buy Johnny another drum set, because John will have to murder you. And Amelia is not old enough for a two-wheeler. Come on, what's going on? You two are *way* too happy."

"She can tell," Molly said, looking up at her husband.

"You said she could," Dom said, tweaking his wife's nose with the tip of one finger.

"Ah, but she doesn't know *what.*"

"True. Maybe tomorrow. We'll tell her tomorrow. We've got the gifts for the kids, right? We'll wait until tomorrow."

Janie held up her hands, waved them to command silence. "Okay, you two. You're cute. We'll admit here that you're cute. But something's going on, and either you tell me or . . . or you'll have to go spend some quiet time until you do."

"Quiet time," Molly said, still grinning at her husband. "I think that was Rule twenty-six. Aren't you glad I kept her notes?"

Janie frowned. "Kept my notes? Why would you keep my notes? Do I look crazy? Because before I'd let you take over here again, Molly, I'd have myself committed. As it was, it took a good month before the kids stopped begging me to bring back Good Golly Miss Molly so she could finger-paint with them again."

"And another month to get all the finger-paint off the floors and walls. I know, I know. But I thought children should have free expression."

"Yeah, right. You'll change your tune if you ever have any of your own, believe me."

"Told you she'd guess," Molly said, batting her hip against Dom's, and he kissed her again.

"Told him I'd guess what? You know, I can get more sense out of a fifteen-month-old's baby talk than I can out of—Ohmigod! Molly?"

"Yup," Molly said and now her smile was a little moist, as tears stood in her beautiful eyes. "After a full year of trying, Dom here finally hit a home run. We're pregnant."

"The trying wasn't so terrible," Dom said as Janie launched herself at her cousin, hugging her, crying, hugging her some more. "Hey, don't I get a hug? It was a joint effort you know."

Janie hugged Dom as Molly wiped her eyes. "The big time producer sure did produce, didn't he?"

"He did, he did! When? How far along are you? Is everything okay?"

Molly patted her, Janie finally noticed, slightly rounded belly. "Four and one half months. He kicked me last night. Dom said it was probably my imagination, but I'm sure he kicked me."

Taking hold of her cousin's hands, Janie asked, "Scared?"

Molly blinked. "No, not at all. We both want this, so, so badly. I'm going to be a great mommy, and Dom's going to be a fantastic daddy. Aren't you, sweetheart?"

Dom looked at Molly, and Janie's eyes welled up at the pure love that shone from his face.

"We will, honey," he said softly. "Right up until each kid runs screaming off to college, just to get away from us. This kid, all our kids, are going to know who we are."

"Oh gosh, it's getting soppy here," Molly said, wiping at her eyes. "You know I don't do soppy really well. Dom? Go get the gifts now, okay?"

He kissed her again, then went to retrieve the gifts from the trunk.

Janie hugged Molly one more time, and then Molly frowned.

"What's wrong? You said everything was all right."

"Oh, it is, Janie, it is. You're looking at the happiest woman in the universe. It's just that . . . well, now that you're soon going to be giving gifts to *my* kid, maybe I should remember that revenge can be a terrible thing."

Janie smiled slowly, evilly, as she rubbed her hands together. "Oh, I hadn't thought of that one. There is a God. Let's see. We'll start with every toy that plays a song, over and over and over again. And then a dog that barks when you pet it . . . and the monkey that bangs cymbals together and plays the Macarena when you clap your hands . . . and then the drums . . . and then—"

"Dom? You want to put that big green and blue striped one back in the trunk?"

"Why?" Janie asked suspiciously. "What in there?"

"Oh, nothing," Molly said innocently. "Johnny and Amelia wouldn't have wanted a talking Tasmanian Devil doll that runs in circles, anyway."

"A talking—oh, I love you, Molly Longstreet."

"And I love you, Janie Romanowski," Molly said, watching as her husband made his way back to them, his arms piled high with gifts. "Isn't love just the most *wonderful* thing in the world?"

Welcome to the crazy world of best-selling New York City author Maggie Kelly . . . brought to you by *New York Times* best-selling author Kasey Michaels . . .

KELLY'S LAW #1: Just when things seem to be settling down, the other shoe drops . . . with a vengeance. In this case, it's more like a boot—a Regency-era riding boot belonging to Alexandre Blake, Viscount Saint Just, hero of the best-sellers I write. And the man who's been throwing gold-filigree monkey wrenches into my life for the past three months. When he defied all laws of time, space, and—let's face it—reality by walking out of my dreams and into my living room, I figured there must be a way to get him back home to the corner of my fevered imagination from which he'd escaped. Okay, so I was wrong. The thing is, I'm kind of getting used to having him around. Alex Blakely, as Saint Just now calls himself, isn't exactly hard on the eyes, and he's chock-full of editorial suggestions. Not that I need them. Much.

KELLY'S LAW #2: All's fair in love and WAR. WAR being We Are Romance, the country's largest romance writers' group. Despite the fact that the WAR-riors unofficially booted me from their little club a while back, I'm still technically a member, which is how I got the invitation to their Manhattan conference. How Alex convinced me to go—and take him along—is another story. I just *knew* it would be a bad thing. Bad for my blood pressure . . . and very bad for my budding flirtation with Lieutenant Steve Wendell—he of the shaggy hair and the NYPD—who's been suspicious of my relationship with Alex from the get-go. Of course, there's nothing to be suspicious *about* . . . yet. But my publisher and my agent are attending the conference. Plus, complimentary cocktails! When will I learn there's no such thing as a free drink?

KELLY'S LAW #3: That thing sticking in your back that looks like a knife? If you're at a writers' conference . . . it probably is. The best part of WAR thus far has been witnessing Alex play at being a cover model competition contestant. The worst part? Take your pick: Conniving colleagues. Overambitious wannabe writers. Homicidal maniacs. Then, one of the leading romance mavens is murdered. Now Alex is on the case. And so is Steve. And so am I. Killers to the left of me, hacks to the right, here I am . . . stuck in the middle without a clue. Looks like I picked the wrong week to quit smoking . . . again.

**Please turn the page for an exciting sneak peek of
MAGGIE BY THE BOOK
coming in paperback in June 2004!**

PROLOGUE

According to Saint Just, this is all perfectly logical, easily explainable, and all of that.

Let's give it a go, shall we?

Maggie Kelly—dear girl, really, if a bit muddled at times—created us. Granted, she did it within the pages of a series of rather prodigiously successful mystery novels, but as Saint Just says, she did it quite well. Well enough, in fact, that eventually we came to life, first inside Maggie's head, and then inside Maggie's Manhattan apartment.

Not that it happens every day, this sort of thing—but it is possible.

After all, we are here, aren't we?

To the world, Saint Just is no more than Maggie's very distantly related English cousin, and she took some of his name—and all of his physical attributes—to create her perfect storybook hero, Alexandre Blake, the Viscount Saint Just.

Along with Saint Just, Maggie created his good friend, Sterling Balder (that would be me. Hallo!), both of whom have now, according to Maggie, traveled across the pond to reside for a time with her.

Of course, that's all a hum, a shocking crammer as a matter of fact, because we're not real. We're characters; fictional characters.

Who at the moment just happen to be, as the current slang goes, "living large" in New York City.

In Manhattan, my good friend Saint Just is known as Alex Blakely, but as I have difficulty with such a banal name as Alex, I still call him Saint Just (you may have noticed that?). Maggie says this is easily explained away as being a "private joke," which makes no sense at all, as I refer to him as Saint Just in public as well as in private. As I said, Maggie can be a bit muddled.

All that to one side, this does seem to explain the names and physical appearances of Maggie's new housemates. At least to her friends. There is a police lieutenant, one Steve Wendell, who is still rather suspicious, but Saint Just says he's of no matter.

And that's that. Everything explained.

Well, not quite everything.

So far, nobody has explained why our dearest Maggie seems to attract . . . murder.

CHAPTER 1

I can't do this, I can't do this, I can't do this!

Maggie Kelly dropped her hands into her lap and let herself collapse forward, until her forehead hit the desktop, then she began rhythmically banging that forehead against the wood.

I can't do this, I can't do this, Icannotfreakingdothis!

Maggie was sitting at her nifty corner desk with the wings on either side of it—all that space meant to hold notes neatly and keep her life organized . . . and all of it cluttered with candy wrappers, ash trays and, most recently, a half-eaten tuna sub sandwich from Mario's Deli down the block.

Her desk lamp was faux brass with a plastic green shade that was supposed to look like glass. The whole lamp was supposed to look expensive. It looked . . . dusty. It also had a crack in the plastic, that had been there when Maggie first pulled the lamp from its box, but returning the thing would have been too much hassle for someone as busy as Maggie. It had nothing to do with fighting with some accusing salesperson about how the thing got broken in the first place. Nothing at all. Really.

Her computer, the one with the pink and blue flowers on it, was supposed to be overheating as Maggie typed verbal pearls onto the screen. It looked . . . blank. In fact, the only "writing" on the computer at all was a yellow Post-It note stuck to one side, scribbled with the words: "Yesterday, Mr. Hall wrote that the printer's proofreader was improving my punctuation for me, and I telegraphed orders to have him shot without giving him time to pray. Mark Twain."

Seated in a huge brown leather desk chair, perched rather on the edge of it, and with her head still resting on the desktop, Maggie Kelly was having a crisis.

A crisis of epic proportions.

Her goal for the day was to write Chapter Ten of her latest Saint Just mystery. The dreaded Chapter Ten. Sometimes, so reluctant was she to write Chapter Ten that Chapter Ten became, in fact, Chapter Twelve, because she kept writing around and about and trying never to get *to* Chapter Ten.

But here it was. Staring her in the face. Chapter Ten of *The Case of the Disappearing Dandy* . . . and the dreaded love scene.

"Whimper," Maggie said, lifting her head slightly and staring at the only two words on the screen: CHAPTER TEN.

She said "whimper" because she didn't know how to actually write anything that sounded like a whimper. Because she couldn't spell the sound that would normally come from her mouth at a time like this, she said "whimper." Just as, if she were a dog, she'd say "bark," because who could actually *spell* a bark? Sure, there was always *arf,* but that was so lame. Much better to say "bark." Or "whimper."

It made sense to Maggie . . . and she was digressing. She knew she was digressing, which was writer-speak for *stalling.*

Yes, Maggie Kelly is a writer. Being a rather punctilious sort, she would say *was* a writer, because she wasn't doing anything looking even remotely like writing this morning.

And it was all Saint Just's fault, damn him.

Once, Maggie had been Alicia Tate Evans, historical romance author. That had turned out to be pretty much a midlist bust (translation: lousy sales), so she'd reinvented herself, become Cleo Dooley, historical mystery writer. She'd tried the three-names ploy that worked so well for some romance authors, and then opted for Os, because, to Maggie, Os looked great on a book cover, and she had been looking for any edge she could find.

It's a cutthroat world, the world of romance writing. The world of writing, period.

She'd created Alexandre Blake, the Viscount Saint Just, and he'd been one hell of a creation. Her hero. Her perfect man.

Eyes: Paul Newman blue.

Winglike, expressive eyebrows: Jim Carrey.

Full, luscious, almost sneering lips: Val Kilmer in *Tombstone*.

Aristocratic nose: Peter O'Toole.

General all-over face and body: a young Clint Eastwood, he of the spaghetti westerns.

Give that man a cheroot and hear him say "Who's your huckleberry?" in—what else?—Sean Connery's *James Bond* voice.

Handsome as sin, witty, urbane, sarcastic and sensual.

Can we all say *New York Times Bestseller List?*

And this was good. This was very good . . . until the day just three short months ago, when Maggie had turned around to see her creation standing there, smack in the middle of her living room.

She'd made him real enough to materialize, he'd said. He'd come to help her with a plot problem in her last book, he'd said, and then stayed to help solve a murder . . . and he was still here, both Saint Just and his partner in crime-solving, Sterling Balder.

And now Maggie was facing the dreaded Chapter Ten . . . with her handsome, yummy, perfect hunk living in her guest room, leaving the cap off the toothpaste, running up her charge cards, and still playing the aristocratic, autocratic, to-die-for handsome Regency hero, for crying out loud.

Writing Tab A into Slot B scenes was bad enough, without the owner of Tab A not just visible in her mind, but running tame in her living room, 24-7.

Maggie sat up straighter, rubbed her palms together, and placed her fingers on the keyboard. She was a professional. She could do this. She had a deadline. She had to do this.

She moved her right hand to the mouse, checked back a few pages, to the lead-in that ended the last chapter.

"You know, Saint Just," Lady Sarah purred, sliding her hands down over his lapels as she stepped even closer. "I sometimes dream about you."

Maggie stifled a sigh. "Oh yeah. I hear you, Sarah baby, and I understand. Believe me, I *un-der-stand.*"

"Happy dreams, my lady, I most sincerely hope," Saint Just said, placing his hands over hers, then lifting them, one after the other, to place a kiss on each of her palms. "Your husband, ma'am?"

"Oh, Saint Just, forget him. Just hold me. I ache . . ."

"Now here's a thought. Perhaps you might wish to cast your dear husband in the role of physician? Where is he, by the way? I probably should have asked that before accepting your kind invitation this evening. I don't much fancy climbing down a drain pipe to escape the man. Perhaps I should go."

Lady Sarah winced at Saint Just's words.

He'd kissed Maggie's palm, that first day. She took hold of the collar of her T-shirt, and sort of fanned herself with it. "Oh, sweetie, I feel your pain."

"He's in Berkshire," Lady Sarah continued, then licked her

op lip with the tip of her tongue. *"Hunting, he says. Drinking, hat's more like it. Drinking, and wenching."*

"Leaving his adoring—no, adorable—wife here in London, o pine away, all by herself? The cad."

"The cad? And you said it with a straight face? Oh, you're njoying yourself, aren't you, Saint Just. You rotter," Maggie old the computer screen. "Always the man with two agen-las."

Cad indeed, Saint Just thought. The Earl wasn't in Berk-hire. He felt certain of that. Just as he was certain that the Earl, and the man's good chums, Levitt and Sir Gregory, were with him, the trio planning yet another murder. He had been pursuing the gang of murderers for months, and all roads had eventually led to the Earl.

Now all he needed was some proof. Because Sterling was the trio's logical next target, and they had to be stopped. Stopped, yes, but first they had to be found.

Saint Just looked past Lady Sarah's head, toward the open door to the Earl's private study. Ten minutes, that's all he'd need. Just ten minutes alone, in that study.

"Saint Just?" Lady Sarah said, rubbing herself against him, like a cat begging for attention. "I've dismissed the ser-vants for the night. We won't . . . we won't be disturbed."

"Oh, how sickeningly coy. The bitch," Maggie whispered. "Not that I'm jealous." She sat back, lifted her hair away from her nape. "Is it hot in here?"

"How . . . anticipatory of you, my dear," Saint Just drawled, with one last look toward the study, then glanced at the tall clock in the corner of the foyer. Two o'clock. With any luck, he'd be in the study by four. He smiled down at the blond-haired vixen, a woman in heat if he'd ever seen one. Yes, two hours. Perhaps three. No need to rush. "I say, are you by any chance trying to seduce me, ma'am?"

"Oh no. No, no, no. Where was my head when I wrote

that? Too *The Graduate*," Maggie said, striking out that last sentence. "Too here's-to-you-Mrs.-Robinson."

Her fingers flew over the keyboard. *"I say, my dear, would your bedchamber be on the left or the right of the stairs?"*

Maggie sat back, lit a cigarette. Better. That was better. That was also the last line of Chapter Nine, damn it. She couldn't stall anymore.

She scrolled down to the next page, placed the cursor on the line below the chapter heading. Took a deep breath, closed her eyes, and began:

She was no shy virgin. Saint Just wouldn't have been within ten miles of her, had she been a virgin.

Lady Sarah was a harlot with a title. A hot-blooded woman with appetites that had been whispered about in the clubs, hinted at, smiled over, and sworn to by at least one peer deep in his cups and too talkative for his own good.

Ask Evan Fleming, if you could find him. Except that Fleming, minus one of his ears, was now reportedly living on the continent, safely away from the Earl and his sword.

Had Fleming's sacrifice been worth it? Was an evening spent with the adventurous Lady Sarah worth the loss of an ear, or worse?

"Stalling, stalling," Maggie nagged at herself. "Get with it now." She sighed, plunged on. Well, someone was going to be plunging . . .

Saint Just, braced against the headboard of the large four-poster, watched Lady Sarah's long blond hair shimmering in the candlelight, shimmering against the skin of his bare belly as she bent over him, wrapped her mouth around his—

"Good gracious, woman. I see I'm having an interesting morning."

"Jesus H. Christ, Alex! Get away from me!" Maggie yelled, quickly covering the screen with both hands. Her heart was pounding hard in her throat. "Damn it! Wear shoes, will you, huh? Or *stomp*. Something?"

Saint Just remained where he was, which was directly behind Maggie. He was dressed in khaki slacks and a soft black
knit collarless shirt that clung to his every sleek muscle, and
he was grinning at her in a way that made her want to brain
him. "Am I being amorous today, Maggie? With the Lady
Sarah, I'll assume," he said, as she kept one hand on the screen
while she used the mouse to click the document shut.

"I thought you were still in bed," Maggie said, grabbing
another cigarette, because the one she'd lit earlier had burned
down to the filter, and gone out. She used her feet to push
herself around in the swiveling desk chair, to face Saint Just.
She breathed heavily through her nose as she watched her
hands shake, and was not at all grateful when he produced
his own Bic, and held the flame to the end of her cigarette.

"I agree that I do like the morning well-aired before joining it—my dear friend, Beau Brummell said that first, remember? But it's almost noon, my dear, and I promised
Sterling I'd walk with him in the park. He's never happy
without his daily ice, although he's promised not to indulge
in the blue one more than once a week. Stains the lips terri-
bly, you know. Man walks about the rest of the day, looking
like he's been sucking from the inkwell."

Bless and curse the man, he was rambling, deliberately
giving her time to compose herself. But, hey, it was working.
Maggie was beginning to get her breathing back under control. "Sterling's out already, with Socks. I guess he forgot
your date. Poor baby. You've been stood up, Alex. Now go
away, I'm working. I need to be able to support you in the
manner to which you've too easily become accustomed, remember?"

"Whatever," Saint Just said, pulling a cheroot from the
pack on the coffee table, then returning to the desk. "You
know what Sterling's about, don't you?"

Maggie shook her head. "About? No. He's outside with
Socks, that's all. Playing Junior Doorman again, I suppose.

He gets a kick out of carrying Mrs. Goldblum's groceries up for her. Why? What do you know?"

Saint Just inhaled deeply, blew out a stream of blue smoke, looking sexy as hell, sexy enough to make a lie out of the "and it's unattractive, too" message of any number of Stop Smoking public service announcements. "What I know, dear Maggie, is that Sterling has found himself a new . . . interest."

"Besides the Nick at Nite channel? Besides his scooter? Besides learning how to fetch cabs for Socks? What?"

"Rap," Saint Just said, shuddering slightly, as if the very word was distasteful on his tongue.

"Rap? Rap what? I don't—no." Maggie sat back in her chair. "Rap? As in Snoop Doggy whatever? *That* kind of rap?"

"Precisely. The poetry of the downtrodden, I believe he calls it. Sterling, for reasons unknown to me, associates himself with the downtrodden."

"Living with you, I'm surprised he doesn't feel just downtrodden, but damned oppressed. You can be a real pain in the—rap, you said? Is he singing it?"

"Writing it," Saint Just corrected. "The Prince Regent figures largely in his first composition. He plans recitations on several subjects. Luddites. Corn Laws. Starving peasants and cruel landlords. You know, the usual oppressions."

Maggie put a hand to her mouth, giggling. "You're kidding. He's doing a *Regency* rap? Oh, I've got to hear this."

"And I'm convinced you will, once Socks believes the man is ready. In the meantime, I do believe you have mail."

Maggie swiveled her chair around to the desk once more, to see the little mailbox blinking in the right top corner of her screen. She'd signed on to America Online earlier, and then forgotten about it. "Fan mail from some flounder?" she asked under her breath, doing her best Bullwinkle the Moose impersonation as she clicked the mouse, bringing AOL to the front of the screen.

"Enlarge your penis. . . . Hot Porn with Barnyard Chicks. . . . Viagra by mail. . . . Refinance your home, cheap. Delete, delete, delete, delete. MoveOn dot com. Okay, I'll keep that one. WAR. War? Oh, no. Not them. De—hey!"

"War?" Saint Just repeated, putting his hand over Maggie's, moving the mouse just as she was aiming toward Delete, and double-clicked it over the e-mail message from one 'YTORBUST:

> *Maggie! Long time no talk, huh? Can you believe WAR is coming back to NY? John says no, because I'm almost due, but I've just GOT to see you! You'll be there, right? I put a hotlink at the bottom. You can just click and sign up, right on line! Oh, I can't wait to SEE you, you big NYT person, you! It's been SO long! {{Hugs}} Virginia*

"Oh, God," Maggie said, sighing. "She's due? *Again?* The woman's trying to repopulate the entire state of Colorado. Yeah, well, I'll just tell her no. No, I'll tell her I'll come by and we can have lunch. But WAR? Ha! Not this lady. No damn way. Hey, cut that out!"

But Saint Just, leaning uncomfortably close to her (well, not completely uncomfortably), had already clicked on the blue hotlink, and the computer immediately connected to the homepage of We Are Romance, Incorporated, a "national association of romance writers."

"War? Didn't anybody notice that when they picked the name?" he asked, then clicked on the site's link to the conference.

"You'd think someone would have, wouldn't you?" Maggie groused, folding her arms across her chest as the page listing the highlights of this year's conference came up on the screen. "Are the dates listed? Oh, there they are. September eighteenth to the twenty-first. Damn, and here I made my GYN appointment for that week. I might even be able to fit in a root canal while I'm at it. Too bad, I'm going to have to miss the conference this year."

She gave Saint Just a push. "Would you back off? No, don't print it out. Alex, I could care less about this—oh, hell, print it out."

"Thank you," Saint Just said, watching the pages begin spitting from the printer. "I can't help myself, you know. Anything that so upsets you, dearest Maggie, will doubtless please me all hollow. Ah, here we go."

He took the pages, all five of them, and carried them over to the couch, where he sat down, neatly crossing one leg over the other. He held his chin high, a lock of his midnight black hair falling over his forehead, the cheroot neatly clamped between his lips. Maggie gritted her teeth. The man would look good if he was standing on his head in a Bozo the Clown outfit.

Picking up her cigarettes, Maggie followed after him, flouncing down on the facing couch, half burying herself in the cushions. "It's a romance writers association, okay? Published authors, still unpublished, psychopaths, you name it."

"Psychopaths?"

She shook her head. "Kidding, Alex. It's a great group. Ninety-eight percent fantastic, hardworking people. Me, I always seem to run into the other two percent. I mean, can we say Felicity Boothe Simmons? Yeech! Oh, and I'm a charter member, for my sins, although I'm surprised they haven't drummed me out of the corps."

Saint Just looked at her overtop the papers. "Why would they do that?"

Maggie sighed. "Why? They wouldn't, not really. But there's this annual contest, see, for published authors? There's one for the unpublished, too, but we're talking published authors. The Harriet, named after the founder. Big damn deal, if you're nto awards. Anyway, I won one, for my first book, before I signed with Bernie at Toland Books. It's over there," she said, pointing to the bookcase.

Saint Just followed her pointing finger. "That?" he said, nodding toward the statuette of a naked nymph, standing on tiptoe and holding an open book high in the air. He got up, walked over to the bookcase, and removed the statuette. "Best Historical Romance, Alicia Tate Evans, *This Flowering Passion.* How . . . how, well, nauseating."

"Hey, don't blame me, I didn't pick that title. I titled it *The Surrender of the Falcon.* Great damn title. Okay, not great, but at least it actually pertained to the story—which is a novel concept these days, let me tell you. But the publisher nixed it. I figured she didn't like the surrender part. Wrong. She didn't like falcons. Maybe she was scared by one before she got her witchly powers."

Maggie leaned over toward the coffee table, stubbed out the cigarette, and grabbed a handful of M&M's out of a crystal bowl. What was it about writing love scenes for Saint Just that had her reaching for all sorts of oral gratification . . . and did she really want to investigate that question in any depth? "Anyway, I have this theory. There's this big wheel in every publishing house, see. Like on *Wheel of Fortune?*"

She lay back against the cushions and popped two red M&M's into her mouth. "But this wheel, it has three wheels, one inside the other. There's words on each wheel, and they spin the wheels, and whatever three words come up, that's the title of your book. *Love's Fiery Passions. Desire's Sweetest Splendor. Barfing Almost Nightly.* You get the idea," she said, popping two plain brown M&M's into her mouth.

"Fascinated as I am by all of this," Saint Just said, returning the statuette to its place, and returning himself to the couch, "I still fail to see why this WAR association might drum you out of their corps."

"Okay, not drum out. But I entered my first Saint Just Mystery in the contest, and they disqualified it. It wasn't a romance, they said. Twelve romance novels, that's what I had as Alicia Tate Evans. Twelve of them, Alex, an even dozen. Put a mystery in the book, and suddenly I'm not eligible? I pay my dues, I'm still a member, I still list WAR as one of my associations, still say that I've won a Harriet in my press releases. I *support* War, damn it. And I'm disqualified. Hey, who cares? They can just kiss off, you know?"

"I'm not romantic?"

"Huh?" Maggie said, looking at Saint Just. He didn't look happy. He looked, in fact, decidedly unhappy. The sort of unhappy that, were she describing the look in one of her books, she'd call *dangerously alert.*

"I said, I'm not romantic? Is that what these Harriets are saying? That *I,* the Viscount Saint Just, am *not* romantic?"

Maggie grinned, beginning to enjoy herself. Everything had its up side. "You got it, Ace. You're not romantic. You're a stud, you're God's gift, but you're not romantic."

"Idiot females."

Three more M&M's hit her tonsils. "Yeah, that, too. But they're right, in a way. A romance novel, Alex, has a happy ending. Two people falling in love, happily ever after. You don't have a happily ever after, Alex. You don't fall in love with one woman, you love women—plural. You're a series."

"Uh-huh," he said, obviously no longer listening as he paged through the papers. "Interesting events, aren't they? Workshops on writing, on getting published, on staying published. Ah, and what's this? A Cover Model contest?" He looked at Maggie. "Explain, please."

Maggie sat up, held out her hand. "Gimme those," she said, grabbing the papers and shuffling them, her eyes growing wide. "They're kidding. They've invited Rose? God."

"And the mystery deepens," Saint Just said, examining the page he had reserved as his own. "Who, pray tell, is Rose?"

"Rose," Maggie said, still shuffling the papers. "From the online magazine, *Rose Knows Romance*. She's got this slogan. How does it go? Oh, yeah. Who knows romance? Rose knows! Gag me. I can't believe WAR has combined with her, just because the conference is in New York this year. They do that, add extra stuff, because it costs more to hold a conference here and they think they need an extra carrot or two. Stupid. Like, hello, this is New York. When you've got New York, what else do you need?"

"Yes, yes, Maggie, you love New York, I love New York, we all love New York. Now, back to the conference if you please? This Rose woman? She's not a nice person?" Saint Just spoke from the desk area, where he had sat down, picked up a pen.

Maggie shrugged. "I don't know. I guess she's *nice*. Pushy maybe, a little wacko with the way she dresses and these contests she thinks up, but nice enough. Like I said, she has this online magazine. She reviews romances, holds contests, has a pretty big base of readers who subscribe to her e–mail list, to hear her tell it. Once a year she holds an online contest for cover models, men and women, looking for new talent. She used to have her own conference, but that stopped a few years ago . . . oh, damn, she's not only going to be there, she's bringing along all the events she usually holds online."

"Such as?" Saint Just asked, still writing. He pulled out his wallet, extracted a credit card (made out to Margaret Kelly, but that was just something to quibble about, now wasn't it?).

"The cover model contest. A dress like your favorite character contest. A parade of local winners of the Most Favored Fan contest. A costume ball. And she's got corporate sponsors, for crying out loud. It's not just a costume ball. It's the Steelton Meats Costume Ball. What does the winner get? A side of beef? Jeez. Rose knows romance? Rose knows *marketing*."

Saint Just pushed at the keypad of the fax machine, saying, "This costume ball? What does everyone wear?"

Maggie threw the papers onto the coffee table and picked up another handful of M&M's. "You name it. Viking furs, Renaissance gowns, slave girl costumes."

"Regency dress?"

Maggie nodded. "Yeah, Regency dress. Why not." She looked at him as the fax machine began to hum. "What are you doing?"

"Why, registering all of us for the conference, of course. You as the member, Sterling and myself as your guests. You had to pay a small late fee, but I'm sure it's cheap at twice the price. Now, if you'll just ring up the Marriott in the theater district, and reserve us a suite of rooms?"

"God!" Maggie pressed her hands to her ears, grabbed two fists full of hair. "Tell me you didn't do that."

"Done and done, my dear," Saint Just said, handing her the large Manhattan telephone directory and the portable phone. "Here you go. Three bedrooms and a lovely parlor should be sufficient to our needs."

"Why?" she asked, glaring up at him. "Why do you want to do this?"

"Why?" he said, taking his quizzing glass from his pocket and dropping the riband over his head—he might dress like a modern man, but he was still very much attached to his quizzing glass. "I want to meet these women who don't think I'm romantic. That's one."

"Oy, jeez, can you believe this? The man's insulted."

"Too true, and I admit it. I'm insulted. Possibly crushed, if I were a lesser man. But I remain undaunted, and more than ready to prove that I, indeed, am above all things a romantic hero. And, of course, there is the Fragrances by Pierre Cover Model contest, which intrigues me more than a little bit."

Maggie spluttered, nearly choked on a mouthful of candy. "You're going to enter the contest? Be a piece of meat for all the women to scream over? You've got to be kidding."

"And you've got to have overlooked the ten thousand dollar prize for the winner, my dear Maggie, along with a guaranteed placement on a romance novel cover. Why, an entire new adventure awaits me, being handsomely recompensed just for being me. You do know how I detest any hint of insolvency. And it isn't as if I don't have a fine suit of clothes at the ready, as you've always written me as having the best of tailors. I believe Weston designed the rigout I traveled in to New York. My, but it will be wonderful to dress once more as a *real* gentleman should," Saint Just said, waggling a finger at her. "Dial, my dear, if you will. And most definitely a suite. We wouldn't want to feel cramped. Then you can finish Chapter Ten."

"Only if I can turn it into a death scene," Maggie groused, pulling the thick book onto her lap.